NOT DEAD YET

OTHER BOOKS AND AUDIOBOOKS

BY TRACI HUNTER ABRAMSON

UNDERCURRENTS SERIES

Undercurrents

Ripple Effect

The Deep End

SAINT SQUAD SERIES

Freefall

Lockdown

Crossfire

Backlash

Smoke Screen

Code Word

Lock and Key

Drop Zone

Spotlight

Tripwire

Redemption

ROYAL SERIES

Royal Target

Royal Secrets

Royal Brides

Royal Heir

GUARDIAN SERIES

Failsafe

Safe House

Sanctuary

On the Run

In Harm's Way

Not Dead Yet

DREAM'S EDGE SERIES

*Dancing to Freedom**

An Unlikely Pair

*Broken Dreams**

Dreams of Gold

FALCON POINT SERIES

Heirs of Falcon Point

The Danger with Diamonds

(coming October 2022)

STAND-ALONES

Obsession

Deep Cover

Chances Are

Chance for Home

Kept Secrets

*Twisted Fate**

Proximity

*Entangled**

Mistaken Reality

A Change of Fortune

*Sinister Secrets**

* Novella

NOT DEAD YET

A GUARDIAN NOVEL

TRACI HUNTER ABRAMSON

Covenant Communications, Inc.

Cover image *Women* © ultramarinfoto, istock.com. *Women's Shirt* © Ranta Images, istock.com. *Eiffel Tower at Sunset* © LUNAMARINA, istock.com. *Fire* © Art Konovalov, Shutter Stock.

Published by Covenant Communications, Inc.
American Fork, Utah

This is a work of fiction. The characters, names, incidents, places, and dialogue are either products of the author's imagination, and are not to be construed as real, or are used fictitiously.

Printed in the United States of America
First Printing: June 2022

31 30 29 28 27 26 25 24 23 22   10 9 8 7 6 5 4 3 2 1

ISBN 978-1-52441-987-5

PRAISE FOR TRACI HUNTER ABRAMSON

"I thoroughly enjoyed Not Dead Yet and several times found myself visualizing the events, people, and settings in a movie. It would make a good one. Adding to its appeal is the nicely developed romantic angle. That was handled more realistically than in so many action novels. The dialogue was plentiful, perfectly paced when Donovan and Cassidy were sharing food while getting to know each other, then sped up dramatically when all hell was breaking loose. Excellent writing and highly recommended reading."

—Readers' Favorite five-star review

"Complex, unexpected plots and an array of marvelous characters with the most incredible skill sets are the hallmark of Traci Abramson's books."

—Sian Ann Bessey, coauthor of *Heirs of Falcon Point*

"Abramson is excellent at engaging readers from the first pages, using multiple storylines to weave together an engaging plot."

—*Deseret News* Review

Praise for the Guardian Series

"From its gripping first chapter to the final page, *On the Run* is a riveting story that will keep the reader breathless through its twist and turns. I was pulling for Elle and Nolan all the way through. Highly recommended."

—Karen Tuft, author *An Accidental Romance*

"Abramson does it again! Buckle up and block out some time because you won't be able to put *On The Run* down--or catch your breath until the very last page."

—Paige Edwards, author *Deadly by Design*

"The nonstop action keeps the pages turning. Secret hideaways offer Nolan and Elle moments of respite to get better acquainted, though their budding feelings for each other are overshadowed by the constant danger Abramson puts them in. . . . Readers looking for excitement will find plenty to hold their attention."

—Publishers Weekly

"In *On the Run*, Traci Hunter Abramson creates a thrilling adventure that leaves the reader eager for more . . . . This book will keep readers on the edge of the seats, thirsty for more action and adventure from the guardians."

—*InD'Tale* Magazine Review

For Sian Bessey

Some friendships are meant to be. I'm grateful ours is one of them.

ACKNOWLEDGMENTS

Thank you to my wonderful friends and colleagues at Covenant Communications for your encouragement and support, especially Samantha Millburn and Amy Parker. Truly, thank you for all you do.

I also want to thank Lara Abramson for sharing your knowledge of Paris and the French language; Paige Edwards, Ellie Whitney, and Kyle Beecroft for your help in the early editing stage; and Mandy Biesinger and Lauryn Parker for sharing your beta reading skills.

Thanks to Coco Francois for helping me with the cultural side of things and for always being there when I need you. And thanks to Sarah Eden and Sian Bessey for introducing me to The Great British Bake Off. It came in handy when my characters needed it. Thank you to the CIA Publication Review Board for your efficiency and continued support.

Finally, thank you to my family who support me in doing what I love, and to the readers who are willing to share my fictional world.

CHAPTER 1

The tightness in her chest, the endless regrets. No matter how many years passed, the anniversary of her death always brought with it a sea of memories and an ache that penetrated her to the core.

Cas blamed herself for being in this situation. Her father had promised her the world, but Roshaun had offered her a happily ever after. Her goals had been so simple: finish her degree in linguistics, work at her father's broadcasting company, and support Roshaun in his dream of becoming a broadcast journalist. In the end, those dreams had imploded when Roshaun had taken her down the path that had led to her destruction. What had started as a mutual interest in lobbying for racial equality had dropped her into a rabbit hole of political corruption and hidden agendas. By the time she'd discovered the manipulation being used against the American public, she'd been in too deep, and her African-American heritage could no longer protect her.

She shoved aside the memories and crossed her narrow living room to the tall window that opened to a french balcony. She gripped the wrought-iron balustrade and breathed in the scents and sounds of Paris. As a dead woman and a member of the top-secret guardian program, she could live anywhere in western Europe, but Paris had always been her favorite city—the energy, the weather, the food, the fashion. Too bad she couldn't take advantage of the current runway trends more often. Living in the shadows meant blending in, not standing out.

The April breeze ruffled her long black hair that she had straightened into submission. She used her fingers to smooth it back from her face. On the street below, a horn blared, followed by the squeal of tires against pavement. Cas gasped as a truck cut across a lane of traffic and two other vehicles swerved.

She flashed back to her own car skidding out of control. A drive along the Florida coast, a dark SUV hitting her from behind. The cliff, the struggle with the door handle, her body hitting the ground, everything going dark. Had she remembered to buckle her seat belt after stopping for gas, she would have tumbled down the steep rock face with the car. Instead, she had been thrown free when her car had flipped.

Two weeks later, she'd woken up in the hospital, with Ace by her side. He'd offered her a way out of the Freedom Coalition—an organization that, despite its tens of thousands of supporters, didn't stand for creating political and racial equality, as they claimed, but rather was using its members' donations to unravel the political stability of the United States. Unfortunately, in order to escape the grasp of the coalition, Cas would have to lose her family in the process. She'd chosen his escape. Officially, she'd died that day.

Her body tensed now, and her heart raced as she fought the memories back again and focused on the scene playing out before her as though in slow motion. The black Audi on the street below couldn't stop in time. Its front fender clipped the back of the truck, and the car spun, the tires burning before coming to a jarring stop.

Cas drew an unsteady breath, and it shuddered out. That hadn't been her. She was in Paris, not the US. Even when the two drivers climbed out of their vehicles, apparently unharmed, she couldn't get her pulse to slow. *It's just a panic attack.* She repeated those words in her mind. She took a step back, then staggered to the couch and dropped onto the plush cushions. Another ragged breath brought with it the acrid scent of burnt rubber.

She lowered her head into her hands and fought for calm. It had been months since she had relived her accident that intensely. She straightened and shook out her hands. Even if the world thought she was dead, she was still breathing. She was still alive.

Determined to conquer her fears, she stood and crossed to the window. Despite the lingering smell of rubber in the air, the scene below revealed her earlier observation. Everyone had survived the accident. Just as she had survived hers. Only hers hadn't been an accident.

Her cell phone rang, jarring her more fully into the present. With a trembling hand, she pulled the phone from her pocket. The caller ID displayed a single letter: A. Code for Ace Samson, the man who typically ran the operational side of the guardian program. Since moving to Helsinki with his wife, he had turned over some of his responsibilities to one of the Stateside operatives.

Determined to hide her latest battle with the past from the man who was, in essence, her boss, she paced across the room to the window once more and hit the Talk button. "Don't tell me you already ate all the macarons I sent you."

"Cas, you need to get out of Paris. Now."

"Why?" Cas's heartbeat sped up again as she closed the windows and flipped the lock. "What's wrong?"

"Your parents are on the way there. They land within the hour."

Cas froze beside the single armchair in the room. Her family. Here? "How did I not know they were on the move? I didn't get any alerts on commercial flight reservations, and my dad's company jet is still in New Orleans."

"His old jet is in New Orleans. He upgraded last week. We just found out about it."

She should have known about such details in her father's life, but following her parents and her sister on social media or even in the news had proved too painful. Over the past four years, her family had become strangers, living in a universe she could no longer enter. "What airport are they flying into?"

"Le Bourget."

The airport closest to her. Adrenaline shot through her, not from fear but from anticipation. The desire to see her family, even from a distance, burst through her. Did her father still favor Burberry suits, or had her mother opened his wardrobe to new designers? Was her sister still working with animal charities, or had their mother pulled her into spending more time fundraising for schools and hospitals?

"Cas, don't even think about it," Ace said, clearly guessing at the cause of her silence. "You know better than anyone that we still don't know who put the hit out on you. If anyone realizes you're still alive, your family could be in as much danger as you are."

"I know." Cas fought back a sigh. "I'll take the next train to Brussels. I can catch a flight from there to wherever you want me to base myself while they're here."

"For now, go to the safe house in Bruges. I'll try to find out how long your family is staying in Paris."

"If Papa is using the company jet, there's no telling what his plans are."

"He'll have to go through passport control and declare his departure date and where he'll be while he's in town," Ace said. "For now, grab a bag, and get out of there without being seen. I'll monitor passport control and let you know when I have more information."

Cas grabbed the leather messenger bag she used as her go-bag and headed for the door. "I'm leaving now."

"Good." Ace paused before adding, "Don't forget what I said. You can't let anyone from your past know you're alive."

"I've been doing this for four years. I think you can stop reminding me."

"Safe travels."

Cas hung up and pocketed her phone. She left her apartment and descended the enclosed staircase leading from her third-floor apartment to the open entryway on the ground level. She was nearly to the exit when her phone rang again.

"*Oui?*"

"Change of plans. Stay in your apartment."

"Why? What changed?"

"Your family's flight arrived earlier than expected," Ace said. "It's too risky to have you on the road when we know they'll be on the move. You'll need to slip out of town after dark."

Cas reversed direction and climbed back up the stairs. "Any idea how long they're staying? I can stay in my apartment for a week without a problem."

"They're staying for over a month," Ace said. "Sorry, Cas, but you're going to have to relocate for a while."

"In that case, I'm going to pack an extra bag. You have until tonight to decide where you want me."

"We'll talk soon."

She reached her apartment and slipped back inside. She set her go-bag beside the door and dropped onto her chair. What were the odds of her family arriving in her favorite city on the anniversary of her death? This couldn't be a coincidence.

* * *

Donovan didn't like his odds. A tank, five armed guards, and a convoy of reinforcements on the way. How was he supposed to break the American spy out of the tent being used as a makeshift prison if he couldn't get past the front door? Or rather, the front flap.

The knife sheathed at his back would cut through the thick canvas of the tent if he could get close enough, but a guard was positioned at each corner, with the fifth stationed inside. Every half hour, the men rotated positions, leaving the prisoner alone for the two minutes it took to complete their rotation, but Donovan couldn't take out any of the guards without at least two others noticing.

Did these men know the American had been gathering intel on their organization for months and could potentially reveal their weaknesses? Or did they think he was simply a Westerner they could use to set an example of what happened to outside influences that weren't welcome?

Twenty meters. That was all that stood between Donovan and his objective. Well, that, the guards, an ancient jeep, and the two lanterns positioned on either side of the tent opening. The interior guard pushed his way outside. As soon as he straightened, he scanned the area, not as though searching for something out of place but, rather, as though making sure he was alone with his comrades. Donovan remained motionless, trusting the cloak of night and the darkness of his clothes and skin to hide him.

The guard's gaze passed by him without seeing. A spark of hope ignited when the man reached back into the tent and reemerged with a loaf of bread and a water pouch. Were the guards not supposed to be eating on duty, or was the guard's caution due to what was inside the waterskin? Intoxicated guards would be so much easier to overcome, but Donovan rarely experienced that kind of luck. Muslims didn't drink alcohol, and from what Donovan had observed of this group, the Alnaazir, the only aspect of Islam they seemed confused about was the principle of not harming others. The guard ripped off a piece of bread and took a bite before he moved to the man he was supposed to relieve. He passed him a drink and spoke a few words.

For a brief moment, both guards looked in the opposite direction. Donovan quickly traversed the five yards between his former hiding place and two water drums and ducked behind them, adrenaline pumping. If he could get a little closer . . .

The interior guard relieved his comrade and shook his head sharply as though trying to stay alert. Donovan didn't know how long these men had been on duty, but he suspected they were nearing the end of their shift. He checked his cell phone, which revealed the path of the guards' reinforcements. Forty-five more minutes until they arrived.

Donovan doubted he would get an opening better than this. With fatigued guards, one distraction might give him exactly what he needed. Of course, he would have preferred to have a team of Navy SEALs at his disposal right about now, but the US couldn't cross the border into Sudan without starting a potential war. Instead, he was the last line of defense. He didn't exist; therefore, if caught, he couldn't be used against the United States. Such was the life of a guardian.

* * *

Another dead end. FBI Special Agent Doug Valdez pushed back from his desk and let out a sigh.

"I know that look," Hector said from the cubicle across from Doug's. "Which case has you beat?"

"The same one that's been beating me for the past ten months." Doug didn't explain further. He didn't need to. Hector was the only other agent in the office who knew of Doug's continuing investigation into a possible leak in the bureau. Well, Hector and their boss, Max.

"The conference room is open. Want to talk it out?"

"I don't think talking is going to help."

"Then come blow off some steam." Hector stood.

"Fine." Doug grabbed the latest chapter in his paper file and followed Hector to the conference room.

Hector closed the door. "What have you got?"

"Proof that Marsha Parham couldn't have been involved in Cassidy Edgemont's death." Doug dropped the file on the conference table with a thud.

"She was a long shot, at best. We had the recording of the call, and Edgemont never said what she was coming in for."

"I know, but Marsha was the dispatcher for the first two witnesses," Doug said. "If she was already involved with the coalition, she could have recognized Cassidy's voice."

"What got you off that possibility?" Hector pulled out a chair and sat.

Doug dropped into the seat beside him and flipped open the file. "This." He pulled out photos from the FBI security cameras for the Florida office along with a security log. "The only gap of time Marsha wasn't accounted for when she could have contacted the coalition was during her lunch break."

"That's right. The call from Edgemont came in at nine forty-seven that morning, and security footage showed her leaving the dispatch office a few minutes later," Hector said. "The accident was at two fourteen the same day."

"Yes, but our lunch theory doesn't work. Marsha checked her personal cell phone in at security when she came into work that day."

"So?" Hector slid the exit log closer. His eyes narrowed. "This doesn't have Marsha leaving the building."

"That's right. I thought she slipped out without the guards logging her out, but it turns out she had a polygraph at ten o'clock."

"Which is why she left right after taking that call." Hector shook his head. "Why didn't we have this info earlier? This happened four years ago."

"I know, but when Marsha was questioned about Edgemont's call, everything she said was consistent with what was on the recording of the call. Security didn't need to ask her where she was during the time between taking the call and when the accident occurred, because they already knew the answer."

"It would have been nice if we'd known the answer sooner."

"No joke."

"How did you find this anyway?"

"I was taking a shot in the dark. I pulled the poly records for everyone on our suspect list to see if anyone had had any trouble passing. When I was looking over Marsha's, I noticed the date and called security to nail down when it had been administered."

"And since polys are in the confidential part of our personnel files, they aren't recorded where the rest of us would be able to find the information."

"Yep."

"What now? Who else do you have on your suspect list?"

"I don't know. Everyone has an alibi for at least one of the cases, and no one from Florida could have had any knowledge of Derrick Massey's coming into the New Orleans office."

"Which brings us back to someone tracking these people from outside the bureau," Hector said.

Doug let out a sigh. "I'll have cyber take another look at the victims' cell phones and other electronic signatures to see if there's anything they might have missed on tracking devices."

"I hate to say it, Doug, but this case may be one that won't be solved."

"Every case can be solved," Doug said. "I can't let this one go until I identify Cassidy's killer. Her family deserves that much."

"They deserve to know the truth, but that doesn't mean you'll be able to find it. The evidence in this case is flimsy, at best."

"Then, I guess it's time for me to go back to the beginning and look at everything fresh."

"Good luck."

"Thanks." Doug closed the file. "I'm going to need it."

CHAPTER 2

Of all the days to have nothing to do, it had to be today. Cas had scrolled through intelligence reports for hours, hoping for a distraction, but her assistance wasn't needed at the moment. Not that most intelligence operatives would know to ask for her help. The guardian database gave her and her counterparts a unique look at all intelligence operations for the United States, but few in the government knew of their access, much less their existence.

It was better that way. The fewer people who knew about the operatives serving from the shadows, the better.

With the United States' national security stable for the moment, she spent another hour researching her pet project: searching for a man she had nicknamed "the Newsmaker." For months, stories had appeared in various publications around the world, particularly in Europe and the United States, and all of them held grains of truth as well as underlying attacks on public confidence in their respective governments. The purpose behind the fake news was not yet known, but Cas suspected someone planned to profit from the consistent ripples of discontent. How, she wasn't sure.

After wasting another hour scouring information she had read many times before, she turned to other pursuits to fill the rest of her daytime hours. She baked cookies. She cleaned her bathroom. She organized her closet. She rearranged the living room furniture. She watched the sun go down. All the while, she struggled against the fact that her family was staying a few short miles away and she couldn't see them. Even worse was the idea that they might be here in Paris to remember her, to mourn a death that hadn't happened.

As soon as darkness fell, she left her apartment and walked the two blocks to the nearest metro station.

With her go-bag over her shoulder, cross-body style, and her leather duffel bag in her hand, she stepped onto the train and grabbed the bar closest to the door. The train pulled away from the station and followed the elevated track that gave her a view of the surrounding neighborhood. Streetlamps illuminated the sidewalks, as did the wash of light spilling out of local restaurant and shop windows. To avoid eye contact with the other passengers, she gazed into the night beyond the glass. When the metro emerged from a tunnel, she watched the pedestrians below—locals sitting at a sidewalk café, some people lined up at a crepe stand.

As the train approached the second stop, one of the few above ground within the city limits, Cas focused on the handful of people walking on the sidewalk. A boy in his early teens followed a woman who appeared to be an American tourist. In a split second, the outer pocket of the woman's backpack was hanging open and her wallet was in the boy's hand. The woman continued forward, oblivious to her loss.

Though Cas's instinct was to alert the authorities, she didn't. She pushed aside the prick of guilt that surfaced. Getting involved, even in the form of a phone call, was a sure way to bring attention to herself. Her survival depended on remaining anonymous.

The train pulled into the station, the street no longer in view. Several passengers disembarked, and others boarded. When the train moved again and the station no longer blocked her view of the surrounding area, Cas spotted the pickpocket again. He had moved farther down the street and now skulked behind a couple who appeared to be around her age. The woman's long braided hair was pulled into a ponytail high on her head, and her arm was tucked into the crook of the man's arm. Their clothes screamed of the wealth Cas had once enjoyed, back when her clothes had been custom tailored instead of purchased off the rack. A sense of familiarity rose within Cas. The man's gait, the tilt of the woman's head.

The pickpocket brushed past the man, leaving an open backpack behind him. The train pulled past the couple, and Cas shifted so she could see their faces.

Her stomach clenched, and the scab holding together her wounded heart broke open. Roshaun was here in Paris. Clinging to his arm was none other than her younger sister.

What was Roshaun doing here? Was he dating Makayla? Her heart squeezed as anger rushed through her. How could the two people she cared so much about betray her this way? The anger faded to a low simmer as a more important question pushed to the forefront: Was Roshaun the man who had caused her fictional death, and was he a risk to her family?

Cas's cell phone rang. She checked the caller ID before she hit the automatic reply to Ace: *I can't talk now*. An instant later, her phone buzzed with an incoming text message. Cas kept her eyes on the couple. Not until they faded from sight did she finally force herself to read her latest message. *Warning: Roshaun is in Paris.*

Another pain sliced through her heart, and she texted him back. *I know.*

* * *

The lantern hanging at the north corner of the tent flickered, the flame low, its fuel supply probably nearly out. The man to Donovan's right shifted his weight from one foot to the other, most likely to keep himself from falling asleep. Five more minutes until the next guard change. Eighteen minutes until the convoy would arrive. This was going to be tight. Only thirteen minutes to get past the guards, retrieve the prisoner, and escape the rebel camp.

Donovan had managed to creep forward another ten meters while the men ate their meager dinner and drank from their shared waterskin. Slowly, he reached into his pack and retrieved a small explosive device. Keeping his eyes on the two guards in view, he waited until they both glanced away, then he pressed the explosive to the underside of the jeep and pocketed the detonator. Three minutes later, the tent flap opened. The inside guard staggered outside and rubbed at his eyes. Had he been sleeping while out of sight of the others? Hope leapt inside Donovan. The guard turned to the left. Donovan edged to the right.

Donovan drew his tranquilizer gun, and his hand flexed on the grip.

The first guard to be relieved moved out of sight toward the back corner of the tent. Donovan took aim at the guard closest to him and squeezed the trigger. Immediately, he swung toward the other guard and shot another tranquilizer dart.

Both guards crumpled to the ground.

Donovan sprinted the last few meters to the tent entrance and burst inside.

In the center, a man lay on the ground, tethered to the center pole. The man's back immediately straightened, and his eyes darted up.

Donovan studied the man's face, quickly identifying him as Tucker Baldwin, the operative he was sent to retrieve. "I'm here to help," Donovan whispered in English. "Can you walk?"

Tucker nodded. Donovan unsheathed his knife and cut through the thick rope binding Tucker's hands and feet. Tucker pushed to a stand but stumbled a step as he tried to gain his balance.

Donovan caught him. "You sure you can walk?" If Donovan needed to carry the man out of here, he'd rather know now.

"I can walk." Tucker straightened. "What's the plan?"

With his knife still in one hand, Donovan waited for Tucker to steady himself before he released him. Then he retrieved the detonator and handed it to Tucker. "When I tell you, push this button and follow me."

"Ready when you are."

Donovan took a step toward the back of the tent.

A shout sounded from the front corner.

"Now."

Tucker pushed the detonator. An explosion rocked the ground.

Unable to hear footsteps over the roar of the fire the explosion had created, Donovan waited two seconds for the rear guards to abandon their post. Then he lifted his knife and sliced through the back wall of the tent. He sheathed his knife, traded it for his pistol, and grabbed Tucker's arm. Together they slipped out of the tent and ran as fast as Tucker was able. Shouts sounded over the crackling of the fire, but Donovan didn't look back. Transportation was a half mile away. It was time to get Tucker out of Sudan and back to safety.

* * *

Cas debated her options all the way to Gare du Nord, Paris's busiest train station, and then got in the queue to buy a ticket at the kiosk. A short distance away, two girls, about six and eight years old, stood by their mother near the escalator. A man texting on his cell phone hurried forward, his path taking him toward the younger child. The older girl grabbed her sister by the arm and pulled her safely out of the man's way.

Cas had watched after her sister that way before, always making sure nothing happened to her. Yet now, when her sister could be in more danger than ever, she was supposed to leave? She couldn't do it. She wanted to know what Roshaun was doing with Makayla, but she *needed* to know if he was still working with the coalition.

Cas returned to the metro and took several trains on a circuitous route back to her apartment to avoid the arrondissement where she had seen Roshaun and Makayla as well as the neighborhood where her family always stayed when visiting Paris. Her phone rang when she reached her stop, but she ignored it. She couldn't afford being overheard by the people around her.

As soon as she reached her apartment, she flipped the lock behind her and checked her caller ID. Ace. She dialed his number.

"Thank goodness," Ace said in lieu of a greeting, his anxiety overshadowed by relief. "I didn't know if you made it."

"What do you mean?"

"There was a bombing at Gare du Nord station."

"When? I was just there."

"Six minutes ago. Where are you now?"

"Back at my apartment." She picked up her remote and turned the TV on to the news.

"As much as I want to have a guardian in Paris right now, you can't stay there," Ace said.

"If we have terrorist activity in Paris, I can't leave, especially not with my family here."

"Is it your family you're worried about, or is it Roshaun?" Suspicion filled Ace's voice. "And how did you know he was in Paris anyway?"

Cas swallowed the lump in her throat. "I saw him."

"What?" Ace's voice rose in volume. "When? Where? Did he see you?"

"He didn't see me. I was on the metro on my way to the train station. He was on the street below."

"You're sure you weren't compromised?"

"I'm sure, but don't you find it odd that Roshaun shows up in Paris on the anniversary of my death, and with my sister, no less?"

"With your sister? Define *with*."

"They were walking together. It looked like they were a couple."

"Ouch."

The suspicions Cas had harbored for the past four years grew. She hesitated a moment before she forced herself to repeat those suspicions to the man who had mentored her when she'd first joined the guardians. "I've always wondered why he didn't go with me when I went to meet with the FBI. What if Roshaun was using me to gain favor with my father? Papa runs one of the biggest news networks in the world. If Roshaun is still working with the coalition, maybe he's trying to gain influence with my father now by dating my sister."

"You still think he got you into the coalition to get your father to help spread their message?"

"It would make sense. Edge Broadcasting is a worldwide company," Cas said. "What better way to spread propaganda than by infiltrating my family?"

"It's possible, but we never found anything that linked Roshaun to the car that ran you off that cliff."

Cas shuddered at the memory. "Roshaun was the only person who knew where I was that day." Cas had trusted him. She'd shared her concerns and had thought he supported her decision to report the corruption within the coalition to the authorities. Now she wasn't so sure. "He's the only person I told about my meeting with the FBI."

"I know, and I understand that you need to get to the bottom of this, but I can't have you following your family and your ex-boyfriend around Paris when you're supposed to be dead, especially when we have a terrorist on the loose."

"Then, you do it. I can work support from my apartment."

"I can't. I have some operations running in eastern Europe right now. I need to stay in Helsinki."

"What about another guardian? You could have Troy or Kade come over here."

"I'm sorry, but your family showing up in Paris is not a matter of national security."

"And the terrorist attack?"

"The local authorities are equipped to deal with it. Besides, you know they'll share information with the CIA. You can work support by tapping into their reports."

A headline flashed across the television screen. *Bomb threat received hours ago. Ignored by local authorities.*

"Oh, this isn't good," Cas said.

"What?"

"The local news is reporting a bomb threat was received before the incident at Gare du Nord hours before the bomb went off."

"Did the authorities know the target?"

"According to the news, they did."

"That doesn't make sense. The French don't sit on tips like that without acting."

"You're right, but the story looks credible. People are going to believe it."

"You think it's a fake report," Ace said.

"Yeah, I do. The bomb went off less than ten minutes ago, and they already have sources giving that kind of information? A credible news station wouldn't have had time to fact-check that, much less put it on the air."

"You're the expert when it comes to that kind of thing."

"Someone is trying to disrupt the stability here in France. We need to find out who's behind this, and I can't do that if I'm locked in my apartment."

Ace's sigh carried over the phone. "I'll see if I can free someone up."

"Thank you." Cas crossed to her go-bag and took out one of the alfajores she had made earlier. The specialty cookie always reminded her of home and the days she had spent in the kitchen with the family's chef, Antoine Peters.

"Stay on top of the investigation into the bombing," Ace said.

"And my family?"

He sighed again. "Go ahead and get a local address on Roshaun. Since you're stuck inside anyway, you might as well satisfy your curiosity about your family and your ex."

Relief bloomed. "Let me know when I can expect some support. I don't want to be locked in my apartment any longer than necessary."

"I'll put the info on the message board as soon as I get the details sorted out."

"Thanks." She bit into the cookie and put the rest of the batch into the freezer.

"And, Cas?"

"Yeah?"

"Stay out of sight."

* * *

Donovan stood in the darkness on the deserted Cairo street and waited for Tucker to disappear into the CIA station. Donovan had gotten him this far. The CIA would take over from here and make sure the former prisoner was debriefed and given any necessary medical attention.

Donovan remained motionless for a minute longer. As expected, the exterior door to the station opened, and someone peeked outside. No matter how many times Donovan played the role of liberator, the drop-off always included someone trying to figure out who he was. The guardians had long ago earned the nickname "Ghost" largely because of how they could vanish into thin air. More often than not, their disappearing acts were little more than knowing when to move and when to stay still.

For years, whispered rumors of the guardians had circulated through the different intelligence organizations in the US. He had heard a few himself in the halls at Langley before Ace had pulled him out of a firefight in Abolstan. Donovan had intended to return to his intelligence work until he and Ace had uncovered a terrifying truth: an Abolstani-based terrorist group, Yuearid, knew who he was, and they wanted him dead. Ace had helped Yuearid accomplish their objective while still allowing Donovan to keep breathing.

What would have happened had his identity not been leaked? He didn't know. As much as he loved the desk work that went with intelligence, he hated the politics. Had it not been for the need to walk away from his family to save his life, and possibly theirs, working as a guardian would have been the perfect job.

The door to the CIA station closed again, and Donovan slipped around the corner to where he had left his vehicle. As soon as he was safely in his car, he pulled his cell phone from his pocket. An unread message from Ace flashed on the screen.

Temporary reassignment: Paris.

Donovan's eyebrows drew together, and he texted back. *Details?*

C will explain when you arrive.

His heart thudded twice before returning to its normal rhythm. C. Short for Cas, one of only two female guardians. Most of the guardians were former military or intelligence. Cas was neither, but he knew from firsthand experience how adaptable she was. The woman could step into character faster than anyone he'd ever worked with. Even though her file didn't reveal a lot of details about how she had come to Ace's attention, from what Donovan could tell, she came from money and had somehow ended up in the wrong place at the wrong time. He didn't know exactly why she'd been invited into the guardians' inner circle, but she had proved herself to be a valuable asset on more than one occasion.

Another text interrupted his thoughts. *ETA?*

Tomorrow. Donovan started the car. He needed a hot shower and a hot meal because in a matter of hours, he was going to Paris.

CHAPTER 3

It was worse than Cas had thought. The bombing at Gare du Nord had left sixteen dead and twenty-two injured. Had she continued with her original plan to go to Belgium, she might have been one of them. She tried not to think about that. For now, all she could do was to help support intel and track down the people responsible. She had hoped the report on the bomb threat had been a mistake, but so far, everything she had seen online as well as through her back-channel sources confirmed that a call had been made. The identity of the caller remained a mystery, but Cas had narrowed down where the call had originated from. She hoped local security cameras would provide more insight.

Hiding behind the firewalls of the guardian computer systems, she had searched through video feed all night and half the morning while also waiting for passport control to update their system so she could retrieve Roshaun's complete information. She still had no clues on the tipster, and now that she had the location of Roshaun's temporary home, she wished she hadn't let her curiosity drive her forward. Not only was Roshaun staying in the same hotel her parents and sister always frequented when they were in Paris, but it was also only a block away from the café where the bomb threat had originated.

Could Roshaun have been involved? She couldn't fathom it, but part of her was still afraid to find out.

Grip your courage with two hands. Her grandmother used to say that any time Cas faced a tough decision. According to her father, that was also the advice Grandma had given him when he'd gambled on the purchase of an independent television station in New Orleans when he was not yet thirty. That gamble had paid off, but Cas didn't anticipate her father's luck would extend to her.

Needing a break from the bombing investigation, she logged into the fake social media account she used to monitor her family. The most recent post on Makayla's feed was a plea for donations for one of her favorite charities. The girl really was predictable. At least, in some areas of her life. Never would Cas have pictured her dating Roshaun.

The next thing that popped up on Makayla's feed was an article from their father's news network, followed by a photo of Makayla on the red carpet with several celebrities on their way to the Grammys. She always had enjoyed the spotlight.

Cas scrolled down to the next post. An image popped up of Makayla and Roshaun, arm in arm, Makayla's hand displaying an oversized diamond on her left ring finger. Cas's blood ran cold. Once upon a time, she had dreamed of a similar moment with Roshaun. Never had she expected the nightmare that appeared before her.

She flipped through several more photos of the happy couple at the moment of their engagement. She didn't have to read the caption to identify the location. The Amalfi Coast, one of her sister's favorite spots in Italy. Despair seeped through Cas and left a heaviness at her core.

How had she missed this? She shook that question away. She knew exactly how. Watching her family experience life while she was stuck in an alternate existence had been too much for her to handle. It was too easy to remember what it had been like to have family and friends to travel with, parties to attend, a driver always ready and waiting to take her wherever she needed to go. And she couldn't deny the convenience of carrying a no-limit credit card.

For the first few months after her fictional death, she had obsessed over everything her family had done, as much to make sure they remained safe as to remind herself of the future that had so abruptly been ripped from her. Ultimately, the pain of seeing them move on while she stood still had proved too difficult to bear. She had stepped away from her constant monitoring, leaving her family to live their lives as though she truly had died.

A knock sounded at her door. Her eyebrows drew together. She wasn't expecting backup until tomorrow morning. Cautiously, she crossed the room and peeked through the peephole. A tall, broad-shouldered man stood on the other side. Dark skin, expressive eyes, a scar on the left side of his forehead.

Donovan? She blew out a breath. The man was good-looking and self-assured, and more often than not, he drove her crazy. Every time he asked for her help, it was so she could don a hijab and abaya. And was there a reason he only needed her help in the summer? Did he have any idea how hot the traditional Muslim clothing was when the heat was already stifling?

Cas unlocked the door and pulled it open. "What are you doing here?"

Both eyebrows arched over dark eyes. "I was hoping you could tell me." He motioned toward her apartment. "Maybe we should take this conversation inside."

"Sorry." Flustered from being caught off guard, she stepped back. As soon as Donovan entered, she secured the door behind her. "I was expecting Troy or Kade to be my backup."

"Ace sent me." Donovan reached the living room and turned to face her. "Want to tell me why?"

"I assume you heard about the bombing here in Paris."

"Yeah, but you've never asked for help with this sort of thing before. What's different this time?"

Cas wasn't sure where to begin. Rather than try, she fell back on the Southern hospitality that had been drilled into her since birth. "Are you hungry?"

"Starving."

"Me too." Cas moved to the kitchen and pulled out ham and cheese from the refrigerator. "Is croque monsieur okay? Or croque madame."

Donovan set his backpack on the floor and slid onto one of the kitchen stools. "What's the difference?"

"Madame is with an egg; monsieur is without."

"Without."

Cas retrieved a loaf of bread and buttered four slices.

"What's going on, Cas?"

Cas lifted her gaze to meet his. Forcing the truth out, she said, "My family is here in Paris."

His eyebrows drew together. "Then, why are you still here?"

"I saw my sister." Her grip tightened on the butter knife. "She was with my old boyfriend."

"That's tough, but it doesn't explain why you haven't left the area."

"I can't leave while my family might be in danger."

"Danger from what?"

"Not from what. From whom." Cas drew in a deep breath. "I think my ex may have been the man who tried to kill me."

* * *

Donovan couldn't have heard her right. "You became a guardian because of your old boyfriend? I thought someone from the coalition tried to have you killed."

"They did, but Roshaun is the one who got me involved with them in the first place." Cas piled bread, ham, and cheese on a baking sheet and put it in the oven. "He was supposed to be with me the day I was run off the road, but he canceled last minute."

Suspicion rose within Donovan. "You think he set you up."

"Ace and I both looked, but we never found any proof. But yeah, the thought crossed my mind."

"And now you want me to spy on him." Donovan wasn't sure what else he could do. If Ace hadn't found anything, there probably wasn't anything to find.

"You are experienced in this sort of thing." Cas set a skillet and a saucepan on the stove before her dark eyes met his. "His hotel is only a block away from where the bomb threat originated yesterday."

"Whoa. You think he could be involved in a terrorist attack too?"

"I don't know, but I want to rule out the possibility," Cas said. "I also need to know for sure that he isn't using my sister the same way he used me."

"Care to be more specific?"

"Roshaun had his heart set on making it big as a news anchor for one of the major networks in New York. After he started dating me, my father gave him his first real break."

"Roshaun." The image of a newscaster with World News Extra popped into Donovan's mind. Sharply dressed, charismatic, with a deep, no-nonsense voice. "Are you talking about Roshaun Davis?"

"Yes." She poured milk into the saucepan and turned on the burner.

"How did your father play into this?"

Cas added flour and butter to the mixture on the stove before she glanced up. "My father is Josiah Edgemont."

Donovan's jaw dropped. He had done a report on Edgemont in college. The man was brilliant. He was also one of the most admired and accomplished men in the country. Starting out as the owner of a small television station, he had risen above numerous challenges to gain success and had ultimately expanded into radio, newspapers, and online news sources. "I can't imagine what it would be like to have so much and then let it all go."

She tilted her head to the side. "You had family when you faked your death, right?"

Regret stabbed at him. "Yeah."

"Then you know what it's like to lose what's most important."

She was right. It wasn't the things he had left behind that he still regretted but the people. Focusing on the current issue, he asked, "If Roshaun already has the job he wants, what makes you think he's using your sister?"

"I don't know, but I have a bad feeling about him being here."

"Are you sure you aren't jealous?"

Fury lit her eyes. Whether she was angry at Donovan for the suggestion or just angry at Roshaun, he wasn't sure, but her reaction left no doubt that he'd hit a sore spot. He automatically leaned back to put extra distance between them and held his hands up. "Hey, you can't blame me for asking. This isn't exactly a help-someone-in-need kind of situation."

"No, it isn't." She took a deep breath and seemed to rein in her emotions. "The point is, if Roshaun is still sympathetic to the coalition and their agenda, his position with World News Extra could compromise the integrity of the news my father puts out into the world and could influence public opinion in a very dangerous way."

"It sounds like he's had that ability for years. What's changed now?"

"I don't know, but I need you to help me find out." She pulled the baking tray out of the oven, added sauce to the sandwiches, and set one on a plate in front of him. "Bon appétit."

He took a bite and rolled his eyes toward heaven. "This is amazing."

"Glad you like it, because I'm going to need you to pick up some groceries on your way back from the Four Seasons if we're going to eat anything beyond the meat and cheese I have in the fridge. You'll want some basics for your apartment anyway. I thought you could stay in the safe house down the block."

"I hate grocery shopping," he grumbled.

"Did I mention I baked cookies yesterday?"

If her cookies were anything like the sandwiches she made, he was going to eat well on this assignment. "What kind of cookies? Chocolate chip?"

"Better than chocolate chip. They're a specialty cookie from Argentina."

Better than chocolate chip. He was definitely going to eat well. "Fine. If you cook, I'll do the shopping."

"And the spying."

"Yes. That too."

CHAPTER 4

Cas settled at the kitchen table with her laptop and scrolled through the latest newsfeed. Over the past hour, stories of the upcoming protests had flooded the local news and internet feed. Worry gnawed at her. Would her family leave Paris until the culprits behind the bombing were captured? If they did try to relocate, would they be in danger of getting caught in another terrorist attack? Knowing her father, he'd choose to stay in Paris, if for no other reason than to be close to the best sources of real-time news.

She glanced up when Donovan retrieved his backpack and sat opposite her, struck by the novelty of having someone working in the same room with her.

"Where do you want me to start?" he asked.

The river of tumultuous emotions coursing through her settled as she tapped into logic. "First thing I want to know is who called in that bomb threat."

"Nothing from the local authorities on that yet?"

"Nothing that they're sharing with our intelligence services anyway."

"We can hack into their security cameras though, right?"

"I already did." Cas clicked on her mouse to bring up the next surveillance video. Who knew that hanging out in her father's television studios would serve her so well now that she was a dead woman. "I only have two more cameras to check."

"Give me the link for one of them."

Cas shared the information and pulled up the other camera on her screen, the image of the sidewalk in front of the café giving her a similar view to several others she had already watched. She pinpointed the time starting a few minutes before the bomb threat was called in. When she didn't see anyone on the phone in her view, she started over from an hour before the call.

"I don't see anyone suspicious on any of this," Donovan said. "At the time of the call, there isn't a single person in view who is talking on the phone."

"Same here." Cas grabbed her phone and dialed. No way she was giving up without exhausting every available resource.

"Who are you calling?"

"Kade," she said, referring to the guardian who had the most expertise in all things electronic. "It doesn't make sense to me that the authorities didn't act if they got a tip."

Kade answered in his typical gruff fashion. "Yeah?"

"I need a favor."

"No one ever calls me unless they need a favor," Kade grumbled.

"It's a good thing I always need a favor, or you would get lonely."

"I am married, remember?"

"Yeah." A spark of humor lit inside her. "How did you get Renee to say yes? She's way too good for you."

"I can't disagree with you there." Kade's tone warmed. "What do you need anyway?"

"I need you to research whether or not the Paris police actually received a bomb threat before the attack at Gare du Nord."

"How soon do you need it?"

"An hour ago."

"I'm fast, but not that fast," Kade said. "I'll look into it."

Relieved to have Kade on board, she asked, "Anything I can do to help?"

"Yeah. Pinpoint when the news broke on the tip."

"I'll start working on that right now."

As soon as Cas hung up, Donovan asked, "What did he say?"

"He wants us to pinpoint when the news broke about the bomb threat."

"Us? Kade doesn't even know I'm here."

"So maybe he didn't mention you specifically." Eager to find answers, Cas said, "Let's get to work. The sooner we get to the bottom of this bombing, the sooner you can help me find out what my ex is really up to."

"I think you're more worried about your ex than the person who just killed sixteen people."

"What if my ex is the person who killed sixteen people?"

"He's a public figure. Millions of people know who he is. You don't really think he's involved with terrorists, do you?"

"I don't know what to think." She glanced down at her hands. She really needed a manicure. Too bad she had to take care of her nails herself these days.

"The coalition is primarily a US organization. Their goals are political. It doesn't make sense that they would plan something here in Paris."

Donovan was right, but that didn't chase away Cas's unease. "Maybe not, but we can't ignore the coincidence that he's here and a bomb went off."

"Man, you really don't trust this guy."

She let out an exasperated sigh. "Just help me search for the news sources that reported the bomb threat and when their stories first hit."

"You got it."

Cas hadn't expected Donovan to agree so easily. The arrogance he often displayed when they worked together in Africa wasn't present at all. Had he adopted that superior attitude because it was expected in the local area, or had he figured out she wouldn't put up with it here? It didn't matter. For now, they had information to find.

She opened a new window on her screen. "While you're making your list, I'll verify where each story originated from."

Donovan tapped a few keys before he looked around. "Do you have some paper and a pen or pencil?"

"Why? You can use your laptop to make notes."

"I work better with paper."

"Fine." Cas retrieved a notepad and a pen from a kitchen drawer and fought to settle her emotions. Donovan wasn't Roshaun. It wasn't his fault that her whole world had imploded, nor did he deserve to end up on the brunt end of her frustration. She set the legal pad in front of him.

"Thanks." Donovan promptly tore the top page off, slipped the pad aside, and jotted down notes on the single sheet.

Cas started her trace on the original story from the TV. It led straight back to the television station's website. After confirming that the story appeared to be sourced through the station, she opened a spreadsheet and logged her findings. "Do you have anything that hit before nine o'clock last night?"

"Two so far." Donovan slid his notes across the table to her.

"Thanks."

He ripped another page off the pad and scribbled down another note.

Cas identified the earliest news story, one from a small internet news organization in Spain. "Why would news about the bomb threat in France hit in Spain first? How would someone there get a lead on this before the local networks?"

"I have no idea."

Cas read Donovan's notes for the Spain article. "Do you have anything that came before eight fifty-five local time?"

"Let me narrow my search." He'd barely finished typing before his eyebrows rose.

"What?"

"I have two dozen hits for that same time."

"That's odd. Is it possible they're all from subsidiaries of the same organization?" Cas asked.

He shook his head. "I don't think so."

"What about anything that hit right beforehand?"

"Nothing." Donovan set his pen aside. "If they all hit at the same time, they had to get their information from the same source."

"Or they're mirroring a story from the same place. We need to find out which one was the original." Cas opened the internet. "Help me verify the IP addresses for these news stories. I want to see if they're all legit."

"I'll try, but I'm more of a field guy."

Cas didn't doubt that. The last time she'd worked with Donovan, she'd been tasked with scouting out a medical clinic in search of a female intelligence asset who had disappeared. Cas had barely given Donovan the information of where the woman had been hiding before he'd slipped in and liberated her without anyone even knowing he'd been there until after he'd been long gone.

She focused back on the present. She scanned through the headlines and the networks they belonged to. Her chest tightened as she identified three as Edge Broadcasting subsidiaries. Searching for the truth was one thing. Targeting her father's empire was another.

* * *

Donovan and Cas had verified that all of the various news stories had come from legitimate websites and networks. Once they'd finished, they had continued with the search for the golden nugget that had sourced the information to all of them.

Donovan pushed back from the table and rolled his shoulders. "I need a break."

"I'm not finding anything." Cas leaned back in her chair. "The story of the police ignoring the bomb threat must have been sent as a press release with a sample article already prepared. That's the only thing that would explain so many stories hitting in such a short period of time."

"The first story popped only ten minutes after the bomb went off. How would anyone get that information and write a press release that quickly?"

"Someone in the department would have had to leak it right away," Cas said. "Either that or it originated from the bomber or someone working with him."

Donovan moved to the tall window across the room. In the distance, lights illuminated the Eiffel Tower. Despite the chaos in the city, the iconic landmark was such an impressive sight, and it gave him an odd sense of peace and reassurance that life would eventually return to normal. At least, for most people. He hadn't known normal for longer than he cared to admit. Sympathy flowed through him as he thought of the victims of today's attack.

Curiosity combined with logic. "What's the bomber's motivation? Why leak a story like that?"

"There's no reason to, unless it isn't true." Cas stood and crossed into the kitchen. She poured a glass of water. "Do you want some?"

"Sure." He walked into the kitchen and accepted the glass she held out. "You think the terrorists bombed a train station *and* made up the story that the police ignored a bomb threat? Why?"

"To discredit the police, to create bad information." She leaned back against the kitchen counter and glanced at the clock on the stove. "I've been tracking someone I call the Newsmaker for the past year or so. He uses the same methods. Bad information hidden behind a grain of truth."

"I saw some of your notes on the message board about that. You think this Newsmaker guy is trying to undermine the stability of first-world countries."

"Something along those lines."

"We've been at this for hours. Let's do something else for a bit." Donovan waved toward the living room. "Want to watch a movie?"

"It would be nice to get my mind off of all this for a couple hours." Mischief glinted in her eyes. "I have the whole Jane Austen collection in my private library."

Donovan cocked both eyebrows. "Do I look like someone who watches chick flicks?"

"We're in Europe. You should embrace the culture."

"Jane Austen lived, like, a thousand years ago."

"It was barely over two hundred years ago."

"Same difference." Donovan led the way to the living room. "Where's the remote?"

Cas opened a decorative box on the coffee table and held it up but out of Donovan's reach. "If we're going to take a break, we should at least pretend like we aren't living in the real world for it."

"You'd rather watch life about people living hundreds of years ago?"

"Yeah." Cas let out a little sigh. "Life was simpler back then. No terrorist attacks. People generally were who they said they were."

"I get that, but sorry, I'm not watching Jane Austen." Donovan debated briefly. "I know. If you want European culture, how about *The Great British Bake Off*?"

"You watch *Bake Off*?"

"When I get the chance. It reminds me that there's real food somewhere in the world, even when I spend most of my time camping out in a desert with no access to a kitchen."

"The new season for *Bake Off* won't start for months, but we can watch a rerun if you want." Cas turned on the TV that hung on the wall.

"Sounds good to me." Donovan sat on the couch.

"I'll be right back." Cas handed him the remote and disappeared into her bedroom. She reemerged a moment later holding some sort of makeup bag and sat on the chair beside him. She laid out an emery board, a bottle of red nail polish, and an assortment of other items he couldn't name.

"You're doing your nails?" he asked. "Now?"

"Yes." She tore open an individual wipe to clean the polish off her fingernails. "Unless manicurist is one of your hidden talents."

"No." Donovan settled against the plush cushions and selected an episode. Biscuit week.

"Oh, this is a good one," Cas said.

"Don't tell me who gets kicked off." He held up a hand. "Or who gets star baker."

Cas grinned. "I won't spoil it for you."

The scent of nail polish carried to him, a reminder of what life had been like growing up. His mom had polished her nails every Friday, just in time for her date night with his dad. Next month, his parents would celebrate their anniversary. Thirty-seven years together. Donovan had been dead for the last six of them.

Cas applied a coat of polish to her left hand and then blew on her nails.

"Why are you doing your nails when you know you won't see anyone for at least a few days?"

"Because the polish was starting to chip." She shrugged. "I hate it when that happens."

"Yeah," Donovan said, feigning empathy. "Me too."

Cas laughed. Her gaze lowered to his hands. "Want me to do your nails too?"

"I'll pass." He held his hands up and spread out his fingers. "I'll stick with the rugged look."

"If you're sure." Cas proceeded to finish her nails while they watched the show together. Both commentated on the contestants' various creations throughout the episode. When it ended, Cas glanced at the time on her cell phone. "I thought we would have heard from Kade by now."

"Call him. Push to see if he has any information for you yet."

"Push Kade? I don't think so." Cas had tried that tactic with the Virginia-based guardian in the past. Her impatience had only made the man crankier and slowed him down. "He'll call as soon as he has anything."

"If we have to wait on him to know if the story was faked, are you going to make us dinner?"

Irritation flashed in her eyes. "You never went grocery shopping. Remember?"

"Yeah, but you said you had some meat and cheese in the fridge. We can make do with whatever you have here."

She folded her arms and glared. "So you think because I'm a woman, I should be cooking for you?"

"No." Donovan suspected Cas's volatile emotions had more to do with the events of the past few days than their dinner options. He kept his voice deliberately calm when he added, "Watching a cooking show all the time doesn't equal knowing how to cook. And this is your kitchen."

"Until you go shopping, I don't have much I can cook."

"Want me to run out and pick up some dinner for us?" Donovan asked. "I saw a crepe stand down the street."

Apparently mollified, Cas nodded. "Do you need euros?"

"I have some. What do you want?"

Cas gave him her order.

He was already to the door when her phone rang. He stopped. "Is it Kade?"

"Yes."

"Put him on speaker."

Cas answered and hit the Speaker button. "What did you find?"

"A call came in when the newspaper said it did, but the signal bounced all over the city. It didn't originate from the café like we thought."

"So it was a real bomb threat?" Cas asked.

"No. All of the calls into the police department are recorded. The one I tried tracing was a man reporting a pickpocketing at the metro station by the Eiffel Tower," Kade said. "I went through everything else that came in around that time, and nothing was even close to being a threat or a warning of any kind."

"Kade, it's Donovan. Any idea who was behind this?"

"What are you doing in Paris?"

"Long story," Donovan said. "What else do you know about the caller?"

"Male, probably not a native French speaker. I loaded a recording of the audio file into the database."

"If we find who it was, we'll be one step closer to finding who was behind the attack," Donovan said.

"Good luck."

"Thanks." Cas hung up and pulled up the audio file of the questionable call. She hit play, and a man's voice carried into the room. "He's not French," Cas said, confirming Kade's assessment. "Late twenties or early thirties."

"Sounds about right." Donovan's stomach grumbled. "We may be at this a while. I'm going to get us dinner."

"Thanks." Cas shut off the recording and started it again. "I'll try to pin down where this guy is from."

"Not sure you'll be able to get much from a twenty-second recording."

Cas's only response was to start the audio file a third time. Leaving her to her task, Donovan headed for the door. Time to take advantage of having a second real meal in one day. With any luck, he might even get to sleep on a bed tonight. Or at least on a couch. Both scenarios were a huge step up from hiding out in an African desert.

CHAPTER 5

Cas played the audio file a dozen times. When she had studied linguistics in college, she had never anticipated she would use those skills in an intelligence capacity. Yet, here she was, profiling a voice to identify the origin of the speaker.

If only the man had stayed on longer or, more specifically, had spoken more words.

Donovan returned with their dinner. The scent of crepes, melted cheese, sauteed vegetables, and some kind of cooked meat filled the air. Ham maybe? Judging from the size of the bag Donovan carried, he hadn't limited himself to one crepe.

Cas closed and locked the door behind him. "How much food did you get?"

"One for you, two for me, and a couple of dessert crepes." Donovan set the bag on the table and pulled out two crepes filled with Nutella and strawberries.

"Let me get some plates." Cas retrieved three—one for her, one for him, and one for the desserts. "You really didn't need to buy so much."

"Sure I did. This way I won't have to go grocery shopping tonight." He set the two dessert crepes on the plate.

"You're just delaying the inevitable."

"I know, but there's a bakery down the street I can hit for breakfast in the morning." He took his crepes before passing the bag to Cas.

"When do you plan to look into Roshaun?"

"As soon as this terrorist issue is resolved or, at least, dies down," Donovan said. "The last thing I need is to spy on someone when everyone is looking for suspicious characters."

Impatience shimmered through her, but she fought to tamp it down. Donovan was right.

He took a bite of his crepe. "Mmm. This is good."

His obvious appreciation for French cuisine chased away the worst of her frustration. "You're acting like you've never eaten a meal before. We just had lunch four hours ago."

"Yeah, but it's been a few days since I've had real food."

"Don't you eat in Africa?"

"Sure, but my options are limited when I'm in the field. The last four days, I was living on MREs."

Cas had a few military meals in her go-bag, but she avoided consuming them whenever possible.

Donovan swallowed another bite. "Any luck with our mystery caller?"

"Best guess is he's from Algeria."

Donovan set his food down and stared. "You can tell what country the guy is from with less than a minute of conversation?"

"He could be from another African country where French and Arabic are both widely used, but Algeria has struggled with terrorist cells hiding out there lately, so that's my guess."

"Could he be from Sudan?"

"It's not as likely. His French is too fluent. He probably started studying it when he was a child."

"What about Chad? There are a decent number of French speakers in that country."

"Linguistically, someone from that part of Africa would fit the profile. Why?"

Donovan slid his plate aside and pulled Cas's laptop closer. He retrieved a file off the database and turned the screen toward her. "I liberated a CIA operative from a rebel camp in Sudan yesterday, not far from the Chad border."

"You think your rescue and this terrorist attack could be related?"

"I don't know. The CIA should have debriefed their agent by now." Donovan accessed the CIA's portal and started a search for cable traffic from the Cairo station. "I don't see anything yet."

"Kade's wife still has ties with the CIA. Put a message in to see if Renee can shake something loose."

"Good idea." Donovan typed in the message before he took another bite.

"Slide my laptop over here. I need to put in our suspicions about the caller so intel can share it with the French authorities."

He pushed the computer in front of her, and they ate in silence for a moment. After Donovan bit into his second crepe, he rolled his eyes toward the ceiling. He swallowed and leaned back in his chair. "Do you eat like this every day?"

"Pretty much."

"Man, I should have fought for a European post."

"You're the only guardian who speaks Arabic. I'm afraid you're stuck in Africa."

Donovan wrinkled his nose. "And the Middle East."

"That's an area I prefer to avoid."

"I don't blame you. It's a hard place to be for a Western woman." Donovan's eyes met hers. "Of course, you already know that."

"Yes, I do."

* * *

Donovan made it until nine o'clock Paris time before his full stomach and lack of sleep caught up with him. "I don't think we can do much more until we hear back from Kade. I'm going to grab some sleep, and we can start fresh tomorrow." He stood and reached for his bags. "What time do you want me here in the morning?"

"Seven?"

"Make it eight and I'll grab breakfast at the bakery," Donovan said. "Where's the place I'm staying anyway?"

Cas opened a glass box on her bookshelf and retrieved a set of keys. "From the front of my building, go left. It's the first building past the bakery. I'll text you the address."

"One more thing. Do you have a spare weapon? I had to leave my sidearm in Cairo."

"I'll be right back." She disappeared into the bedroom and returned a moment later with a box. "Here you go."

"Thanks." Donovan flipped open the lid. Inside lay a semiautomatic pistol, three clips, and a waistband holster. He removed the weapon and ensured the safety was engaged before loading and holstering the gun. Once it was secure, he adjusted his jacket to cover the slight bulge and added the extra ammo to his go-bag.

He moved to the door, and Cas followed. "See you tomorrow."

As soon as he stepped into the hall, the locks clicked behind him. A moment later, his cell phone buzzed with her text. He opened the address in his GPS and made his way outside. The wail of an emergency vehicle carried along the otherwise quiet street. Donovan skirted past the swath of light coming from a streetlamp. He strolled toward his destination as though Paris were his home rather than someplace he'd visited only a handful of times. Three minutes later, he reached the apartment building and climbed the five flights of stairs to his temporary housing.

He unlocked the door and quickly searched the one-bedroom apartment. As soon as he was satisfied it was secure, he circled back to the living area and soaked up his surroundings. The furnishings didn't extend beyond the basics—a couple bar stools at the kitchen counter, a couch in the living room, and a small desk with a straight-backed chair by the window—but even in its simplicity, the place had class.

Flashing lights filtered through the curtains, which Donovan drew aside. In the distance, the Eiffel Tower glimmered in all its nighttime glory. He didn't know how the guardians had been fortunate enough to purchase property that accentuated that particular amenity, but he couldn't have asked for a better backdrop.

He kicked off his shoes and dropped onto the couch, where he could enjoy the view. His body relaxed, and his eyes drooped closed. The thought flitted through his mind that he should take advantage of the bed in the next room, but he didn't have the energy. Even the couch was a huge improvement over his sleeping options of the past week.

He tucked a throw pillow under his head and settled more firmly into the soft cushions.

His phone rang.

He groaned and rolled over, then pulled the phone from his pocket. Ace. "Yeah?"

"Are you still with Cas?"

"No. Why?"

"The bomber was picked up outside of Paris fifteen minutes ago."

"Are they sure they have the right guy?"

"They're sure. He was caught on camera leaving the train station a few minutes before the bomb went off. His phone log also shows he was the one who called the police."

"Where's he from?"

"Chad."

"If the guy is in custody, how long do you want me to stay here and indulge Cas's curiosity about her ex?"

"As long as it takes."

"As long as it takes to what? To show Cas that her sister is dating her ex? Or that the guy really tried to kill her four years ago?"

"Long enough for Cas to find what she needs. Who knows, maybe in your digging, you two can find the link to the Freedom Coalition and whatever group is controlling them," Ace said. "I also need you to confirm if our bomber is connected to the Alnaazir in Sudan."

"What evidence do you have that he is?"

"He had Sudanese pounds on him when he was taken into custody. If he is with the Alnaazir, this could be an indication that whatever these guys are up to, it's escalating."

"Has anyone been able to access the debriefing report for Tucker?"

"Not yet, but we should have it tomorrow," Ace said. "Get some sleep. You're going to need it."

"Story of my life."

"Hey, at least you have a bed tonight."

"For that, I'm grateful." Donovan ended the call, set his phone on the coffee table, and rolled over again on the couch. Maybe he'd try out the bed tomorrow night.

* * *

Cas fought against the urge to take the metro to the Four Seasons hotel. Donovan was right. Researching her family could wait until tomorrow, but no amount of common sense could reduce the impatience boiling inside her. The desire to catch a glimpse of her parents was nearly as strong as her need to know what Roshaun was really up to.

In an effort to distract herself from the flood of questions, Cas washed the dishes and wiped down the counters. Once those tasks were complete, she headed to her room with the intent of going to bed early. If she was right, tomorrow was going to be a busy day.

She stopped when she reached the living room and studied the layout of the furniture. With no control over what was going on outside her apartment, the desire to put her life in order tugged at her. She leaned over and shoved at the couch until it was once again against the wall. Then she moved her favorite chair next to the window. It really did look better there.

Satisfied with the new arrangement, she got ready for bed. By nine thirty, her face was washed, her teeth were brushed, and her mind was spinning. It took her only fifteen minutes to give up on sleep and return to her kitchen table, her computer in front of her and the surveillance feed from the Four Seasons' lobby cameras displayed on her screen.

Two security guards stood at the entrance, a nod to the potential danger from the terrorist activity in the city as well as the possibility of protests against the authorities' inability to stop it. Cas watched for an hour before she carried her laptop with her to her bedroom. Keeping her screen in front of her, she climbed into bed, then grabbed the remote on her bedside table and turned on the TV for background noise.

A newscaster on her father's French affiliate recapped the investigation into the terrorist attack, including the capture of the suspected bomber. Following that piece of good news came the announcement of a planned demonstration on Saturday to protest the lack of response by the police to the bomb threat.

Only two days to identify the person behind the fake news story. Otherwise, the police would have to divert significant resources to keeping the protests peaceful. No one wanted a repeat of the weeks of civil unrest that had occurred the last time Parisians took to the streets. There had been looting, burning cars, and minor injuries for both civilians and law enforcement. Knowing her family, they would line up for a front-row seat. At least they would be able to watch from the penthouse balcony where they would be safe.

Cas straightened when the camera showed her sister exiting the hotel elevator. Roshaun stepped off right behind her and slipped his arm around her shoulders. They crossed into the main lobby camera view. Makayla looked up and laughed at something Roshaun said.

Something sharp and jagged ripped through Cas's heart.

CHAPTER 6

Birds chirped. A truck engine roared to life. The scent of fresh bread lingered in the air. Donovan stretched his arms over his head, the movement nearly toppling him off the couch. He regained his balance and sat up. Bleary-eyed, he stared at the tall window across the room, the Eiffel Tower perfectly framed in the center, a cloudless blue sky creating the perfect scene. Was he really here for work, or had Ace sent him here for a much-needed vacation? Spending time searching on the computer with Cas and trailing an ex-boyfriend would be a piece of cake compared to his usual.

Donovan headed for the shower and dressed for the day. After he threw his clothes in the washing machine, he gathered his computer bag and left the apartment.

He was in line at the bakery, debating what to buy, when Ace called.

"Where are you?" Ace asked.

"At the bakery, on my way to a friend's," Donovan said, deliberately not mentioning Cas's name in public. "Can I call you back?"

"Just answer yes or no. Did you do a search on Cas's background this morning?"

"No. Why?"

"Someone did, and the search originated in Paris."

Donovan's heartbeat picked up. "Did you already tell her?"

"She isn't answering."

Donovan stepped out of line. "I'm supposed to be there in fifteen minutes. Maybe she's in the shower."

"Or maybe she's been compromised."

"I'm on my way to her apartment now." Donovan rushed out the door. "ETA four minutes."

"I'll call her again."

"Let me know if you reach her." Donovan hung up and picked up his pace. The moment he entered Cas's building, he pushed past three men waiting near the elevators in the spacious lobby and made his way into the stairwell. As soon as he was out of their line of sight, he broke into a run and sprinted up the stairs. He forced himself to slow when he reached the third floor, taking a moment to verify the hall was clear. He reached Cas's door, listened for a brief moment, and knocked with a heavy hand.

No answer. He knocked again.

"Coming." Cas yanked the door open. "You're early."

Donovan pushed his way inside and glanced around. The living room furniture had been rearranged, but other than that, nothing appeared to be out of place.

Cas closed the door and looked at his empty hands. "What happened to you bringing breakfast?"

Donovan ignored her question and asked one of his own. "Did you talk to Ace?"

"No. Why?"

"He's been trying to call you."

Cas pulled her phone out of her pocket and unlocked her screen. "My phone is right here, and it doesn't show any missed calls."

"Let me see it." Donovan snatched it out of her hand.

Cas crossed her arms. "Want to tell me what's going on?"

Donovan opened Cas's favorites and hit the button to call Ace. Nothing. He tried again, using his own phone. Again, the call didn't go through.

"Our phones aren't working. We have to get out of here."

Cas opened the coat closet door and grabbed her leather go-bag. "A cell tower could be down."

"Or someone is using a dampening field," Donovan said. "Ace called me. Someone here in Paris did a search on your real name this morning."

Cas whirled to face him. "Who?"

"I don't know."

Cas rushed into the kitchen, opened the freezer, and grabbed a Ziploc bag full of . . . cookies.

"You might be compromised and you grabbed dessert?"

"Long story." She dropped them into her messenger bag. "Let's go." She paused at the door long enough to look through the peephole.

"Clear?" Donovan asked.

"So far." Cas led the way into the hall. She turned away from the nearest stairwell and opted for the one farther away.

"Does your building have surveillance?" Donovan asked.

"Yes, but if there's a dampening field, we won't be able to tap into it."

Donovan contemplated their limited options. "Maybe instead of going down, we should go up."

"Good idea." Cas climbed the stairs to the fourth floor. Donovan glanced at his phone and tried calling Ace again. "Still nothing."

"Do we risk the elevator? Or should we take the stairs?"

"Any idea who might have compromised you?" Donovan asked, his voice low. "Could your sister or Roshaun have seen you?"

"No. I'm sure they didn't notice me."

"Someone did."

"Or this is a false alarm. The anniversary of my death was this week. It could be someone was looking me up because of my family being here in Paris."

"Maybe, but that doesn't explain why our phones aren't working."

"I usually take the stairs. Maybe the elevator is the smarter choice."

Donovan followed her to the small glass-encased elevator. He pressed the button, and a moment later, the doors slid open to reveal an empty elevator.

They stepped inside the cramped space, and Cas hit the button for the first floor. "We'll be able to see the ground-level lobby from the first-floor hallway."

"Good." They reached their stop and peeked over the railing. Three men stood on the ground floor, one beside the elevator and the other two next to the staircase entrances.

So much for a quiet week in Paris.

* * *

Cas studied the familiar figures, and panic streaked through her. It couldn't be. How did they find her?

"Looks like you have a welcome party," Donovan whispered. "Do you know them?"

"Yes, and they know me." Cas took a step back, and her heart jolted. "The man in the center is Jamal Williams, a member of the coalition's board of directors."

"And the other two?"

"Ezra Jackson is on the left. He's a protest organizer for the coalition." Cas took another step back. "I don't know the other one."

"But you can guess he'll know you," Donovan said. "Is there another exit?"

Cas fought for calm. She was no longer the naive girl who didn't understand the evil in the world. She was a trained intelligence operative. Various exit strategies raced through her mind. "The fire escape, if we can get to it."

"What are the chances they'll have someone watching for you outside?"

"I don't know. It's possible." Cas leaned forward. "They aren't trying to find me at my apartment."

"Which means they either don't know which one you live in . . ."

"Or they have more men with them." Cas took another quick look at the men below. "None of these guys is carrying anything large enough to suppress cell signals for a whole building."

"They must have someone outside."

"And going down the fire escape will leave us vulnerable."

"Are any of the apartments on this floor vacant?"

"No, but a cop lives in 107." Cas started down the hall.

"Looking for backup?"

"Either that or a way to the fire escape," Cas said. "With all the chaos going on in the city right now, I doubt anyone's home."

"Only one way to find out." Donovan strode beside her and knocked on the door. No answer. He knocked again. Still no response. Donovan retrieved a lockpick from his bag. "I really hope this guy isn't in the shower." He turned the lock.

"Woman, actually. A female cop lives here."

Donovan stepped back. "You go first."

Cas slipped inside, and Donovan followed, closing the door behind him. The lamp on the end table cast a soft glow in the otherwise dark apartment. The shutters on the windows were closed, and no sound indicated anyone was home.

"Wait here," Cas whispered. She crept through the living area of the apartment that was nearly identical to her own and made her way down the hall. The bedroom door hung open. Cas peeked inside. Empty. After checking the closet and bathroom, Cas called out, "Clear." She moved to the window where a traditional metal fire escape filled her view.

Donovan approached behind her. "Move over. I'll look out and see if anyone is at the bottom." He opened the window and leaned out to get a better look. He didn't speak until he leaned back inside. "Looks like your friends are covering all of the exits."

Fear merged with determination. "Now what?"

"We need a distraction." Donovan glanced around the room. "Too bad the cop who lives here doesn't have an alarm system."

"There's a fire alarm in the main hall," Cas said. "If we pull it, I might be able to slip outside in the crowd."

"That may be our best bet." He snapped his fingers and opened the closet. After a brief search, he plucked out a police uniform and held it in front of him. "Put this on. It will help you blend in."

Cas took it from him. Would the uniform allow her to hide in plain sight, or would it draw attention to her when she needed to be invisible? She blew out a breath. Whether she liked it or not, this was her best option. She carried the uniform into the bathroom to change. Time for a new kind of undercover work.

CHAPTER 7

Donovan checked his phone again while he waited for Cas to change. Still no service. Ace had to be going crazy right about now, not knowing what was going on.

Cas opened the bathroom door and stepped into the bedroom. Donovan clenched his jaw to keep his mouth from dropping open. How the woman could make a police uniform look good was beyond him. She held up the brown ankle boots she had been wearing. "I hope her feet are the same size as mine because no one is going to believe I'm a cop wearing these."

Donovan opened the closet door and pulled out a pair of practical loafers in black. "Try these."

Cas checked the size. "Close enough." She opened her bag and retrieved her pistol with its waistband holster before she packed her boots inside. She sat on the bed and pushed her feet into the shoes. "I didn't see a belt. Is there one in the closet?"

"No, sorry."

"Is our guy still by the fire escape?"

Donovan glanced out the window. "Yeah."

"I don't know which is safer, trying to exit through the lobby or going down the fire escape." She tucked her weapon into the front of her waistband. "If we get lucky, the alarm system is hardwired and emergency personnel will respond. If not, we go wherever the crowd is."

Donovan led the way back into the living room. "You ready?"

She moved to the window where she could see the fire escape. "Ready."

Donovan opened the door and crossed to the fire alarm on the wall between the cop's apartment and the next one. After a quick check to make sure the hall was clear, he elbowed the glass that covered the alarm and pulled the lever.

Instantly, an alarm shrieked through the air. Donovan darted back into the apartment and closed the door. The last thing he needed was to be noticed by one of the policewoman's neighbors.

Doors and windows opened. Footsteps clanged on the metal fire escape. More echoed in the hallway.

"How's it looking out there?" Donovan asked.

"Only five people on the fire escape. How about the hall?"

Donovan peeked through the peep hole. "One couple heading for the stairs. We need to wait for the upper floors to empty so we have more of a crowd."

"Half the tenants have probably already left for work." She pressed against the wall beside the window. "No sign of emergency vehicles either."

"Give it another thirty seconds. After that, we pick our escape route." Donovan debated their options. Two against one on the fire escape, but the guy would have plenty of time to identify Cas on their way down. The two against three in the lobby might make more sense. If Cas kept her hat on, maybe she wouldn't be recognized.

As though reading his mind, Cas said, "I'll be too exposed on the fire escape. Let's go through the lobby."

"All right." Donovan checked the hall, but the crowd he had hoped for had yet to materialize. A woman in her thirties opened the stairwell door and disappeared inside. "Come on. See if you can slip out between that lady and me."

Cas sprinted to the stairs, Donovan following behind her. They had barely entered the stairwell when a woman with gray hair and a wide berth called out in French, "Officer! Help. Please."

Donovan had to give Cas credit. She turned as though she were used to responding to the title of officer.

"What's wrong?"

"It's my husband. I need help getting him down the stairs. He has a bad knee."

Whatever internal debate Cas entertained, it lasted for less than three seconds. She spoke to Donovan instead of the woman. "The phones aren't working here. See if you can get outside and call for help."

Leave her? Not the wisest option. They could tell the woman the fire wasn't real, but to do so would be to announce that truth to the others filing down the stairs. A woman carrying a toddler pushed past them.

"You're needed outside," Donovan told Cas, trying for another option. "I'll come back and help her husband."

"Don't leave me. Please," the woman pleaded.

Cas cast an apologetic glance at Donovan and asked the woman, "What floor?"

"Two."

Resigned to helping the older couple exit the building that wasn't really on fire, Donovan followed the two women up the stairs as a steady stream of residents continued toward safety. If only Cas would join them, assuming she could slip out unnoticed. They reached the second floor, where a man leaned heavily on a cane beside the stairwell. Donovan moved to his side and spoke in French. "Lean on me. I'll help you down."

The relief on the man's face was immediate. "*Merci.*"

Cas stepped to his other side and took him by the arm to give him extra support. She spoke to the wife. "You go down first. We've got him."

Though concern still illuminated the woman's face, she nodded. They entered the nearly empty stairwell. With no one walking behind them, they moved slowly, one step at a time.

By the time they reached the first-floor landing, they were alone on the stairs. One more flight and they would reach the lobby. The question was, Would it be empty, or were the men looking for Cas still waiting there?

* * *

Cas's heartbeat thudded in her chest, and her anxiety rose as she neared the stairwell door. The man's wife reached the bottom and stopped by the door leading to the lobby. In the distance, a siren wailed. Finally. The rest of them reached the ground floor, and the man planted his cane. "I think I can make it from here."

"We'll help you all the way outside," Cas said, praying they would all be able to make it there safely.

Donovan caught Cas's eye and tilted his head to signal for her to shift positions. Though she hated that her presence might put these two civilians in danger, she released the man's arm and stepped back so she was behind him with Donovan at her side. With her human screen in place, Cas spoke to the woman. "Can you get the door?"

The woman nodded and grabbed the handle. An instant later, she pulled the door open, and Cas caught a glimpse of Jamal looming on the other side of the threshold.

"Is anyone else up there?" he asked in English.

The woman answered in French. "Move back. My husband needs to get through."

"Back up," Donovan added in English, with a French accent.

The sirens grew louder, and Cas prayed a flood of emergency personnel would burst through the door any second. Another man came into view, but he wasn't in uniform. Ezra. Great.

Cas's hand went to her weapon, but she hesitated. If she drew her gun, she would abandon all hope of escaping without notice. Donovan pushed into the lobby, forcing Jamal back.

The man with the cane followed Donovan. Cas stepped forward with the intent of keeping the older gentleman between her and the men from the coalition, but the wife moved toward her husband and released the door, leaving Cas no choice but to grab it.

Donovan's reaction was instant. He dropped his backpack, and his elbow came up and connected with Jamal's jaw. Jamal stumbled back as Ezra rushed forward.

"Go." Donovan delivered the order in a low but firm voice.

Though she hated leaving Donovan on his own, Cas scooped up Donovan's backpack and rushed to the exit. The older couple blocked the right side of the double doors leading outside, so Cas pushed open the left. She glanced over her shoulder. Two men now lay on the floor, and another was rushing toward Donovan with a knife in his hand.

"Watch out!" Cas shouted.

Rather than engage the third man, Donovan sprinted after Cas. "Go!"

Cas hurried outside but held the door until Donovan burst through it. She took a quick look in both directions.

"This way." Donovan grabbed her arm and pulled her away from the crowd of displaced residents.

They made it to the corner as a fire engine roared toward them. "Now they show up," Donovan muttered. He tugged on Cas's arm before sprinting down a side street. "What's your escape plan?"

"Keep going. Take a left at the light." Cas glanced behind her. No one was following them, but she could never go back. If the coalition knew she was alive, her life in Paris was over. Could she find safety somewhere else, or would the coalition keep hunting her until she died a more permanent death?

CHAPTER 8

They were half a kilometer from Cas's apartment when Donovan's phone rang. Donovan winced when he reached for it. One of his opponents had landed an elbow in his ribs, and it was going to leave a nasty bruise. He checked the caller ID. "It's Ace." Donovan hit the Talk button. "I've got her."

"That's a relief. Sitrep?" Ace asked, using the shorthand term for situation report.

Where to begin? "She's been compromised. We're leaving the city."

"You'll have to take the bus. There's too much security at the train station right now for you to slip out unnoticed."

"Not my first choice of transportation."

"It can't be helped."

"Someone needs to scrub Cas's apartment here. She didn't have time to pack out."

"I'll turn that over to Renee. She can have the CIA sanitize it and secure any weapons Cas left behind," Ace said. "For now, get to the bus station. I'll text you your tickets."

"Got it. Thanks." Donovan hung up. "Looks like we're taking the bus."

"I figured as much, but I have to find somewhere to change first."

"I need to pick up some extra clothes anyway. Is there a store on our way?" Donovan's phone buzzed, and he read the incoming text. "We have three hours before our bus leaves."

"Okay, then, follow me." Cas turned at the next corner. They strolled down the street, passing buildings that appeared to have been built centuries ago. Pale yellow exteriors appeared to be popular in the area, each structure rising to the height of five or six floors. Car exhaust mixed with the scent of fresh crepes as they passed a crepe stand. What Donovan wouldn't give to have one of those in the rural regions of Africa. When they turned the next corner, an enormous Gothic building sprawled across an open space, a wide lawn surrounding it.

"Is that a church?" Donovan asked.

"Yes. Eglise Saint-Eustache," she said. "This is the part of town where old architecture meets new."

When the mall came into view a moment later, Donovan couldn't miss the contrast between the Gothic building behind him and the modern structure of the expansive mall. A steady stream of shoppers flowed through the main entrance.

Donovan lowered his voice. "You sure you want to go somewhere this crowded?"

"We can get everything we need in one place," Cas said, her voice low as well. "I doubt anyone is watching their security feed, and we won't be here long enough for anyone to find us anyway."

"I hope not."

Cas slowed her pace when she reached the base of the stairs. "It'll take me a few minutes to change. Can you grab some food for us?"

Though sending Cas in on her own left him uneasy, Donovan couldn't deny that splitting up made sense. He nodded. "I'll meet you back here in twenty minutes."

Donovan leaned down, taking his time to untie his laces and tie them again. He gave Cas a thirty-second head start before he followed her into the mall. He identified the location of the security cameras and turned his face away from the one aimed at the entrance when he walked through. When he reemerged twenty-two minutes later, Cas wasn't anywhere in sight. He continued to their planned meeting spot, deliberately not looking around.

A woman headed toward him from one of the outside tables of a nearby café. A wide-brimmed hat shielded her face, and her purse hung across her body at her hip, the flap turned inward. A beige duffel hung from one shoulder, and she gripped several shopping bags in her gloved hand.

Without revealing her face, she stepped beside Donovan. "Ready?"

"Yeah." Donovan had to give it to Cas. She really did know how to hide in plain sight. "Where to next?"

"This way." Cas led him to the street. A few minutes later, she turned down a sidewalk behind a bakery. She set her purchases on the ground. "I want to pack everything into my duffel before we get to the bus station."

After they consolidated their purchases into the new bags they had purchased, she headed toward a modern-looking building on the opposite side of the mall from where they had arrived. She spoke in a low voice. "We can cross to the other side of the street and catch a city bus to the station. It'll take a while to get there, but I'd rather avoid the metro."

"Lead the way."

* * *

Cas slid into the seat beside the window as passengers filed onto the bus headed for Bruges, Belgium. She pressed her lips together and fought back the emotions welling inside her. She had lost everything once before and survived. Why was the thought of leaving Paris so hard? It didn't compare to losing her family, yet the sensation was much the same as when she had agreed to let Ace fake her death.

She'd managed to stay focused on her task of creating a new wardrobe on a budget—never an easy task—but now that she and Donovan were entering the final stage of her exit plan, the flood of loss penetrated her to the core. For the first time in four years, the coalition had somehow managed to not only discover she was alive but also succeed in tracking her down. Now, here she was, leaving her home and abandoning her life all over again.

After Donovan stored his bag in the overhead rack, he slid into the spot beside her and tucked his backpack under the seat in front of him. He winced as he straightened.

His obvious discomfort pulled her out of her spiraling emotions. "Are you okay?"

He sat straighter in his seat and winced again. "Took a hit to the ribs earlier. I'll be fine."

"Are you sure nothing is broken?"

"It's just bruised."

"I'm sorry."

"You don't have anything to be sorry about."

"Don't I?" She lowered her voice. "They knew where I was. That's never happened to one of us before."

"Don't stress over what you can't control."

Her lips curved slightly. "My mother used to say that."

"Smart lady."

"Yes, she is." Cas looked around the bus, the seats nearly full.

The driver closed the doors, then spoke into the intercom, first in French and then in English, announcing the direct route to Bruges and the estimated travel time of four hours and forty minutes.

Four hours and forty minutes of sitting on a bus, helpless. She couldn't access the guardian database without secure internet, and she and Donovan couldn't discuss anything classified in public.

The bus engine roared to life. Cas used her foot to pull down her footrest, and she settled back in her seat. "I guess I should have grabbed a book to read while we were at the mall."

"Afraid I won't be good company?" Donovan asked as the bus pulled out of the station.

"I'm afraid there isn't much we can talk about here."

"Sure there is. We have the whole drive to get to know each other," Donovan said. "What kind of books do you like?"

"I'm not telling you that."

"Why not?"

A flush of embarrassment warmed her skin. "Because you'll laugh."

"I already know you like Jane Austen."

"All women like Jane Austen."

"No, they don't." Donovan shifted in his seat so he was facing her more fully. "Are you one of those poetry girls?"

"I'm not sure what a poetry girl is, but I will admit, Emily Dickenson is pretty amazing."

"I bet you read those sappy romances too, don't you?"

"Not exactly."

"Then, what?" Donovan lifted his eyebrows and stared, waiting patiently.

She should say she liked suspense or fantasy. He wouldn't know that she was skipping over her favorite genre, yet something compelled her to share the truth. "I love historical romance, the ones that are so good they transport me back in time."

"So, like I said, sappy romances."

And this was why she'd hesitated in sharing the truth. "They aren't sappy." She folded her arms. "Have you ever read Sian Ann Bessey? Or Sarah M. Eden?"

"Nope. Never."

"You're missing out." She relaxed her arms. "Every time I read one of their books, I learn something."

"They're your escape."

Her escape from the real world, the world that had caught up with her today in a way she had never expected.

The Eiffel Tower came into view in the distance, and Cas couldn't help but wonder if she would ever see it again. An ache originated in her chest and spread outward. "I'm not really in the mood for twenty questions."

"We can eat first. Are you hungry?"

"Now that you mention it, I'm starving. We missed breakfast."

"Yeah. Sorry about that." Donovan stood and retrieved the bag of food. He pulled out two half baguettes wrapped in butcher's paper. "I hope you like whatever this is. I ordered the first thing on the menu."

Grateful for the distraction, Cas took the offering. "This is great. Thanks."

Donovan bit into his sandwich. He nodded his approval. "This is pretty good."

"The food here is incredible. The little cafés, the bakeries, the hole-in-the-wall restaurants that only the locals go to."

"You're going to miss it."

"I will. Paris is my favorite city."

"So far." He wiped at a smear of butter on the side of his lips.

Cas frowned. "What?"

"Paris is your favorite city so far. You never know if there's someplace else you'll love just as much."

"That's hard to imagine."

CHAPTER 9

The longer Donovan talked to Cas, the more he wanted to know. Even though their conversation couldn't wander into personal territory, he enjoyed learning more about his fellow guardian. Simply identifying her expressions was entertaining in itself. The little lift of the eyebrows when she was surprised, the lowering of her gaze when someone got up to use the restroom, her instinctive greeting to the bus driver when they had boarded. She was acting so much like a French person that had he not known better, he would have sworn she was a native.

How would she adapt to her new surroundings, and where would that be?

The bus rolled to a stop with a whoosh of the brakes. Donovan stood, wincing slightly from the pain in his side when he gathered his belongings and Cas's overnight bag.

Cas settled her hat on her head and reached out her hand. "I can take that."

"It's okay. I've got it."

"You're hurt. I'm not."

She was right. Donovan passed the bag to her and leaned back to let her exit before him. He was halfway to the door before he recognized his mistake. She was the one with people after her. Should he really let her step out into the open before he checked out the area? The likelihood of someone tracking them was slim at best, but then the probability of someone locating Cas in the first place fell into the astronomical range.

Donovan put his hand on her shoulder to stop her forward progress. He leaned forward and whispered in her ear. "Hey, slide into the next seat so I can go out first to check the area."

Her jaw clenched, but she complied. As soon as he passed her, she fell in behind him again. Donovan stepped off the bus and did a quick scan. Several fellow passengers stood beside the bus where the driver was unloading luggage. Others had already dispersed toward the pickup zone and the parking lot.

Once satisfied there weren't any perceivable threats, Donovan glanced back at Cas and gave a brief nod of approval before continuing forward.

She put her hand on his back and leaned close. "The house is this way."

The simple touch brought with it a sense of connection. He missed being around people.

They made their way through the stream of passengers, left the station, and headed down the street. Ten minutes later, Cas turned onto a narrow road and led the way to a two-story row house. She punched a code into the electronic lock and opened the door. Donovan followed her inside. An open staircase was situated to his left. Directly in front of him, a glass door led to a living room on the main level.

Cas dropped her overnight bag on the oak flooring in the entryway. "The bedrooms are upstairs."

Donovan locked the front door behind him, dropped his bag beside Cas's, and followed her into the main section of the house. Light spilled in from the glass-encased courtyard situated between the living room and kitchen. The back wall of the courtyard afforded privacy from any backyard neighbors, and the enclosed area included a round table and two chairs covered in a clear plastic tarp. It was like having a walled patio plopped right into the middle of the house. White cabinets and slate-colored countertops stretched the length of the kitchen.

Cas set her purse on the round kitchen table. "I usually work in here."

"Do you come to Belgium often?"

"I visit every month or so to check on supplies, but I typically only stay here when I need a safe house to get someone out of Paris." She dropped into a chair. "This is the first time I've had to use it for me."

Donovan pulled out his cell phone. "We'd better check in with Ace." He hit Speaker and set the phone on the table between them. Ace answered a moment later. "Are you at the safe house?"

"Yes." Donovan leaned closer. "You're on speaker with both of us. What do you know so far?"

"We traced the internet search on Cas back to a sidewalk café in Paris. We've been watching security feed from an ATM across the street, but the view is limited."

"Cas recognized a couple of the men at her apartment," Donovan said.

"Who were they?" Ace asked.

"Ezra Jackson and Jamal Williams. They were both in the inner circle of the coalition." Cas linked her fingers together. "I heard a few comments when I was still working with them that made me think Ezra was some sort of enforcer. He always seemed to take care of problems, but no one ever asked how."

"Those guys looked like they knew what they were doing," Donovan said. "If we're dealing with pros, you're not going to find them on camera."

"How did they know to look for me in the first place?" Cas asked. "Everyone thinks I'm dead."

"Could your sister have seen you the other day?" Ace asked. "Or Roshaun?"

"No. I was on the train above them. They never looked up."

"You're sure?" Ace asked.

"Positive. They were so clueless to their surroundings, neither one of them even noticed when Roshaun got pickpocketed."

"You didn't tell me about that," Ace said.

"I was still trying to absorb the idea of my ex dating my sister when I talked to you," Cas said.

"If his wallet was stolen, there might be a police report." Donovan drummed his fingers on the table. "If we find when it was filed, we can check the police station's surveillance feed."

"What would that do for us?" Cas asked.

"It would let us see if anyone else was with him," Donovan said.

"That's true," Ace said. "Cas, you were focused on Roshaun and Makayla. It's possible they weren't alone."

"I doubt it. Like I said, Roshaun was pickpocketed. If someone was behind them or they had any kind of security, they would have alerted them to the problem when it happened."

"She has a point." Donovan leaned back in his chair. "If you weren't seen by your sister or your ex and they didn't have anyone else with them who would recognize you, where else could you have been spotted?"

"I have no idea." Cas blew out a breath. "Even if someone did see me, how would they have found my apartment? I check constantly to make sure I'm not being followed."

"Could someone from your family have seen you at a grocery store or a bakery in the last couple of days?" Donovan asked.

"It would have had to be someone else who knew me, but if that was the case, I don't know why they would have waited so long to act," Cas said. "Other than when I tried to leave the city, the only time I went out was to get bread two days before. My family wasn't even in town yet."

"Maybe someone else who knows you was already there. Where did you go?"

"A bakery half a kilometer away from my apartment," Cas said. "And I used evasion tactics. No one was following me."

"Someone had to have seen you when you were trying to leave town," Ace said. "Donovan, follow up on the police report and their surveillance feed. Cas, hack into the public transportation system and see if anyone looks familiar or suspicious."

"We'll let you know what we find." Donovan picked up his phone.

"And, Cas? Stay out of sight," Ace said.

Donovan ended the call. "Looks like I really am going to have to do some grocery shopping."

"I'll make you a list."

* * *

Cas put the finishing touches on the salad and carried it to the table.

Donovan walked in from the living room. "I took our bags upstairs. Yours is in the room on the right. Is that okay?"

"That's fine." She stirred the garlic chicken and poked a fork into one of the thighs. Deciding it needed to cook a little longer, she put a lid on the pan and reset the timer. "The chicken still needs a few more minutes, but we can start on the salad."

"Fresh vegetables. This is a novelty for me."

"Don't tell me they don't have fresh produce in Africa."

"They do, but I'm not often in a place where it's easy to find." Donovan pushed their laptops to the other side of the table and waited until Cas sat before he lowered himself into a chair.

Manners. She hadn't expected that from someone who had been living alone for years.

"Did you find anything while I was gone?" he asked.

She added salad to her plate and passed the bowl to Donovan. "I watched all the video around the time when Roshaun filed his police report. As far as I could tell, he went in alone and he left alone."

"What about the subway feed?"

"I'm still writing out my timeline and what path I took." Cas motioned to where her phone lay beside her laptop. "I have the time stamp on the text from Ace telling me to leave Paris, so I'm working with that as my starting point."

"Smart," Donovan said. "How much information was in the police report your ex filed?"

"I don't know. I only pulled the time off the report. I didn't go through it."

"We should check it. Depending on the amount of detail he provided, the report might mention anyone else he might have been with that day and what time he was by the metro where you saw him."

Her stomach clenched. She wasn't sure she wanted to know who else he had been with. "I guess I can pull that up after dinner."

"I can do it for you," Donovan said. "Your time will be better served looking for familiar faces on the metro security feed."

"Maybe." The timer buzzed. Cas pushed back from the table and retrieved a hot pad. "I hope you like what I made, because we'll be eating leftovers for lunch tomorrow."

"It smells amazing."

Cas transferred the chicken and side dishes to the table. She served herself a portion and handed Donovan the serving spoon.

Donovan sampled the chicken. "Mmm." His eyes lifted to meet hers. "Where did you learn to cook like this?"

Oddly pleased by his reaction, she said, "Growing up with a French chef didn't hurt."

"This kind of cooking isn't learned by watching."

"Antoine may have let me act as his sous chef as often as not," Cas admitted. "The cooking shows in France are pretty good entertainment too."

"I approve of how you spend your free time, although from what I see on the message board, it doesn't seem like you have much of that."

"If my cover was really blown, I'll have a lot of free time from now on."

"Paris may not be part of your future, but I'm sure Ace will want you to keep working with the guardians."

"It's hard to wrap my brain around what comes next."

"We'll have plenty of time to talk about that tonight." He took another bite. "After dinner."

* * *

Donovan couldn't move. He was pretty sure if someone walked into the house and pointed a gun at him, he would take the bullet and die a happy man. Cas was seriously an amazing cook. He had managed to help Cas put away the leftovers and clean the kitchen, but once he'd sat back down at the table, the rich food and his full stomach had caught up with him and left him in a state of contentment he wasn't eager to leave.

Cas glanced at him. "You aren't going to fall asleep over there, are you?"

"If I was sitting on the couch instead of at the table, I'd already be asleep." He stretched his arms over his head to get the blood moving again. "If things don't work out for you to stay in Europe, you can always go undercover as my personal chef."

"Nice try." Cas shook her head. "I'm not about to become anyone's servant, especially not where I'd have to veil my face."

"It was worth a shot." With some effort, he reached across the table and slid his laptop toward him.

Cas sat across from him. "I put the link to the police report in the guardian database."

"I'm accessing it now." Donovan pulled it up and scrolled to the bottom, where he read Roshaun's account of where he'd been from the time he'd last seen his wallet to when he'd noticed it missing. A restaurant, a jeweler, two clothing stores, and the Arc de Triomphe, but other than when he'd left the hotel, the timing of when he'd visited each spot was vague, at best. "There isn't anything here that's going to help us."

"No mention of who he was with?" Cas asked.

"No. The stores and restaurant he went to are listed, but he didn't know what time he left each one."

"Run his credit card. His charges will be time stamped," Cas said. "If you look up the addresses of where he went, you should be able to narrow down when he was by the metro where I saw him."

"Good idea."

"Better run my sister's credit cards too. Makayla isn't one to expect someone else to buy stuff for her."

Donovan retrieved the information. After fifteen minutes of plugging in addresses and credit card charges, a timeline emerged. "Good call on running your sister's cards. I have a charge at a clothing store a block from the metro station."

"What time?"

"Four fifty-nine. There was another charge on Roshaun's card at a restaurant down the street three hours later." Donovan gestured toward her computer. "That must have been a long dinner."

"That's not uncommon in Paris. The waiters don't bring you the bill until you ask for it, and if they had hors d'oeuvres and dessert, their dinner could have easily lasted that long."

"Sorry I missed that experience," Donovan said. "How's it going for you?"

"I'm watching the video feed at the metro station now," Cas said. "I was focused on looking for Makayla and Roshaun. I want to see if there are any familiar faces in the crowd that I might have missed."

"Give me the link for when you first got on the train. I can watch for other passengers who took a special interest in you."

"Sounds good."

Donovan shifted on the cushioned seat. "Let's move into the living room though. I'm not used to sitting in a chair for so long."

"I'm not sure a couch will be much better." Cas stood and rolled her shoulders. She picked up her laptop and carried it into the living room.

Donovan followed. "I can't believe I'm saying this after that dinner you made, but we still have a couple of tortes left from lunch. Do you want to split one?"

"I don't want something that heavy. I have a better idea. I'll be right back." Cas set her laptop on the couch and disappeared up the stairs. A moment later, she returned holding a plastic bag of cookies. "Try one of these."

"These are the cookies you grabbed when we were leaving your apartment."

"Yeah. I baked them the day my family arrived in Paris." She unzipped the bag that contained several dozen cookies and held it out.

He took one of the layered cookies coated in coconut. "These must be pretty amazing if you weren't willing to leave them behind."

"They are amazing, but that wasn't why I grabbed them."

"Why did you?"

"We aren't supposed to leave anything behind that can identify us."

Donovan's eyebrows went up. "These cookies can identify you?"

"They're an adaptation of alfajores that I created with Antoine."

"Your old chef?"

"That's right. I made them all the time when I lived at home, and I brought them into the office at the coalition every few weeks."

"Do you really think anyone would know these were your handiwork? France is known for its cuisine."

"Yes, but these aren't French. They have alfajores in Spain, but this recipe is actually based on a version that's more common in Argentina," Cas said. "Antoine lived there for a couple years before he came to work for my family."

"So they are unique enough to possibly identify you to someone who knows you well." Donovan took a bite. Honey, almond, caramel, coconut. The confection melted in his mouth, leaving his taste buds craving more. "Wow." He took two more cookies. "If I'd known these tasted this good, I would have grabbed them for you on our way out."

Cas's face lit up with the beginnings of a smile. "I'm glad you like them."

"*Like* is an understatement." He stepped toward the kitchen. "Want some milk?"

"Sure." Cas set the cookies on a round wooden table beside the couch. "Can you grab some napkins too?"

Donovan took another bite of cookie. He retreated to the kitchen and returned a moment later with two glasses of milk and a stack of napkins. He handed one glass to Cas and set the napkins beside the cookies.

"Ready to get back to work?" Cas asked.

He took a drink of milk and sat beside her. "I have milk, cookies, and a computer. Sounds like a formula for success to me."

CHAPTER 10

Cas awoke to the sound of running water. Her hand shot out for her gun on her bedside table but found only air. Coming more fully awake, she focused on her surroundings. The angled ceiling, the simple furnishings, the wide-plank oak floor. This wasn't her Paris apartment. She sat up as the events of the past few days flooded her mind. Roshaun, Makayla, Ezra, Jamal. The steady stream of water shut off in the bathroom downstairs. Donovan.

Cas flopped back onto her bed. For nearly five hours last night, she and Donovan had scoured video feed of the subway system, but nowhere had she seen anyone paying any particular attention to her, nor had she seen any familiar faces. Though she wasn't eager to continue her quest, she grabbed fresh clothes. She briefly considered changing out of her pajamas before going downstairs, but the practical flannels she kept in her go-bag were modest enough. Besides, it was silly to change right before showering. Oddly self-conscious of being without makeup, she headed downstairs.

The bathroom door swung open as she reached the landing, and Donovan emerged, the white of his T-shirt contrasting with his dark skin.

"Looks like we have good timing." He carried his rolled-up dirty clothes in one hand and a shaving kit in the other. He moved out of the doorway and shifted to the side to give her access. "I was going to do a quick perimeter check. Anything I need to know about the area?"

"Yeah, our address. Don't forget it."

"Very funny. I think I can figure out that much." Donovan headed for the stairs. "I'll be back in a few minutes."

Cas expected Donovan to be back by the time she finished showering, but the house was quiet when she returned to the foyer. Restless, she opened the storage closet under the stairs and retrieved the tennis racket and ball she kept there. She carried them outside to the enclosed atrium and shivered against the morning chill.

Moving to the center of the walled-in space, she set the tennis ball on top of the strings of her racket and bounced it into the air, repeating the process over and over again. What would it be like to have access to the private tennis court in her parents' backyard? Or have ready access to a partner?

She was still lost in memories of her past life when the atrium door opened and Donovan walked outside.

"What are you doing?" he asked.

Cas let the ball drop onto the concrete patio floor so she could bounce it against the ground instead of into the air. "Thinking."

"This is how you think?" Donovan gave her a skeptical look.

"It was either this or go for a run, but I didn't think you would be thrilled if you came back and I wasn't here."

"Getting cabin fever already?"

"A little bit." She grabbed the tennis ball and lowered her racket. "Any issues out there?"

"No. The streets are pretty quiet for a Saturday."

"It's early yet. The tourists will be out in full force by midday."

"How has that been for you?"

"What?"

"Working where there are always tourists. That can't be easy trying to stay invisible when you never know who from your old life might show up." Donovan pulled out one of the chairs at the patio table and held it for her. "As evidenced by your current situation."

Cas sat in the offered chair. "Usually, I'm alerted if anyone close to me is on the move."

"What happened with your family this time?" Donovan took the seat beside her.

"They didn't take their usual transportation. Ace told me they were on their way when they were almost to Paris." She tapped her fingers on the table. "I'm still not sure how Roshaun and my sister got here without my knowing it."

"They must have flown private, or they would have flagged on the reservation system," Donovan said. "Do you want me to track down how they got to Paris? It might show if Roshaun was traveling with any of his old coalition buddies."

"Maybe Ace can run that search for us." Cas rubbed her hands together to warm them. "Do you ever feel like we're adding more work every time we talk instead of getting closer to answers?"

"Half the battle in intelligence work is asking the right questions."

"My biggest one is pretty straightforward. How did the coalition find out where I was living?"

"I think the first one we should be asking is, How did they find out you *are* living?"

Cas pushed back from the table. "I guess it's back to watching video feed."

"I'm afraid so." Donovan stood. "Come on. We got through most of it last night. I'm sure we'll find something soon."

* * *

Donovan blinked against the stinging sensation in his eyes. He and Cas had yet to find anything useful on the subway security feed, and they were running out of footage. True to her nickname of Ghost, the name all guardians used when dealing with clients, Cas did a remarkable job of avoiding cameras. Only rarely did she pop into view, but when she did, she always looked away so her face wouldn't be caught on camera. Her actions were so automatic Donovan suspected she had memorized the location of the security cameras rather than scanning for them when taking public transportation.

Cas leaned back on the couch and let out a sigh. "I don't see anything."

"Me neither." He picked up his phone. "It's only eleven. Let's look at the spot where you saw your sister and ex again."

"You can look, but I'm telling you there's nothing there." Cas pulled the images onto her screen.

Twenty minutes later, Donovan conceded the truth. Roshaun Davis and Makayla Edgemont hadn't ever looked up, and Cas didn't recognize anyone else on the metro or on the street below.

"Okay. I give up. Back to square one."

"I have no idea where square one is."

Donovan opened the message board. The debriefing from Tucker Baldwin, the CIA operative he had pulled out of Sudan, topped the feed. "Finally."

"What?"

"It's a CIA report I've been looking for." Donovan opened the document and scanned. "Looks like Alnaazir had some dealings with Wayne Aguilar."

"The bombmaker?"

"The very same."

"Then the terrorist arrested in Paris was probably working for them."

Donovan glanced at her. "You sound disappointed."

"No, but I had the crazy idea that the coalition might have been involved."

Donovan closed the document and continued through the rest of the new messages. "Here's something. Ace found the flight that your sister and Roshaun came in on. They flew in from Geneva on a private charter."

"When did they get to Paris?"

"Six days ago."

Cas's face paled. "So they could have seen me, just not when I thought."

Donovan could see her mind racing, and he grabbed a piece of paper and a pen. "We need to reconstruct where you were after they arrived."

"Thankfully, I only had to help one client this past week, so I wasn't out in public much."

"What is your usual routine? Where did you go besides helping your client?"

"I go to the bakery every day or two to get fresh bread, but I change the time I go, and I rarely visit the same bakery twice in the same month."

"You have enough bakeries near you that you can change it up that often?"

"Pretty much. I usually have to go to other parts of the city every week or two, so that's another way for me to avoid routines."

"Let's trace your steps for the days your sister was in Paris."

Cas set her laptop aside and stood. "I need to stretch my legs before I start another round." She cast a longing look at the door. "I really wish I could go for a walk."

Sympathy stirred inside Donovan. "Starting to empathize with our clients when we put them in safe houses?"

"Very much so."

"You could always walk into the kitchen and get us some milk and cookies."

One eyebrow winged up, and Cas's hand fisted on her hip. "Do I look like a waitress to you?"

"No, but since you wanted to stretch your legs anyway . . ." Donovan shot her a hopeful look.

The defiance in her eyes melted into humor. "Oh, okay."

Wisely, Donovan fought against his smile until she turned her back on him. Once she was out of the room, it broke free, and he caught himself watching her instead of starting a new search. He pulled the round wooden table from beside the couch and positioned it in front of him in preparation for his snack, and then he opened a new search and pulled up the manifest for Makayla's flight. When Cas returned, he already had the passenger list on his screen.

"Do you know Tyrell Fenmore or Isaac Castille?" he asked.

"Tyrell is one of the security guys who has been with my family for years. I don't know the other one." She set both glasses of milk on the table and settled back into her spot.

"Antoine was also on the flight. Why would he be traveling with your sister?"

"Could be that he came over early to prepare for my parents. It's not uncommon for them to bring some of their staff with them." Cas took a cookie for herself and held out the bag.

"Thanks." Donovan took one. "With Tyrell and Antoine arriving early, we add to the list of people who might have seen you."

"Unfortunately, yes. Who else was on the flight?"

"Only the pilot." Donovan took a bite and looked heavenward. "This is so good."

"You are the epitome of the saying 'The way to a man's heart is through his stomach.'"

He grinned. "Trying to get to my heart, huh?"

Cas rolled her eyes. "Let's start our search at Du Pain. It's the bakery I went to the day before my parents arrived in Paris. It's not too far from my apartment."

"Got an address?"

Cas pulled up a map on her screen and showed him. "It's right there."

"Time to search for cameras that might have caught something."

"I'm so sick of searching online."

"I know, but once we find out who saw you and how they found your apartment, we'll be one step closer to knowing who sent those guys after you."

"Even if we find them, I'll never get my life back."

"We've both been through this before." Donovan's sympathy stirred again. "I'm sorry you have to go through it twice."

"Who did you leave behind when you died?"

Though his mind went to his parents and sister, the sympathy and concern in Cas's voice prompted Donovan to share his deepest regret. "My daughter."

CHAPTER 11

Cas's jaw dropped. "Your daughter? I didn't think the guardians would take anyone who was married." As soon as the words were out of her mouth, the truth caught up with her. Maybe he hadn't been married.

"I *was* married. My ex didn't like being married to an intelligence officer. She couldn't stand the secrets or the separation." His jaw clenched, but his voice remained calm and even. "I got home from an op in Abolstan right before our daughter was born. Three months later, Tayandra handed me divorce papers."

"I'm so sorry. I can't imagine how difficult that must have been."

"It wasn't easy, but that divorce probably saved my ex-wife's and my daughter's life. Had they been home when the Yuearid came after me, I'm not sure any of us would have made it out alive."

Donovan shrugged, but Cas suspected he was fighting his emotions. "How old is your daughter?"

"Almost seven."

Cas did the math. Donovan had entered the guardian program at least a year before her.

As though he'd heard her unspoken question, he said, "Siara was ten months old when I died."

Cas opened her mouth to offer words of comfort, but what could she say?

"She doesn't remember me, but maybe that's better for her," Donovan said, his voice wistful. "My ex remarried when my daughter was two. They seem to have made a good life."

"Wow. You are amazing to find that kind of perspective."

"We all want the people we love to be happy and to have good lives. It's not their fault we can't have the future we wanted." Donovan reached for his laptop. "I guess we should get started on this."

"You're right." Though Cas's curiosity was still humming, she slid her computer onto her lap.

"Let's start with the bakery's security system," Donovan said.

"Doesn't it seem odd that a bakery would even need a security system?" Cas asked.

"Yes, but in today's world, just about everyone has one."

"It does make our jobs easier." Cas didn't want to think about how many hours she spent watching security footage for her job. What she wouldn't give to watch a movie that had nothing to do with reality.

Donovan showed her his screen. "What time were you there on Tuesday?"

"I was up late with a client the night before and slept in, so it was probably around nine thirty."

Donovan opened the feed for the correct day and started at nine fifteen. He set it for two times the normal speed. "Is the camera going to show you entering?"

"Yeah." She shifted on the couch to get more comfortable. "You won't see my face, but I was wearing a red overcoat."

"Red? That's a bold color for a guardian."

"In Paris, unless I want to wear black all the time, dressing in drab colors is more likely to get me noticed." On the video, the door opened. "There I am."

"You got there at nine twenty-one." Donovan froze the image and pointed at a man with blond hair. "I only see one other customer."

"There were two. A woman was sitting at a little table out of the camera's view. Thin, medium-brown hair, maybe early fifties."

Donovan hit play and ran the feed until after Cas left with her order. No one else came in.

"There's a bank across the street. Let's check the feed from the ATM," Cas suggested. Donovan reached for another cookie. Amused by his endless appetite, she said, "You eat your snack. I'll access it."

"Thanks." He chased the cookie down with a long swallow of milk. Two cookies later, he moved her laptop so they could both watch it. A few pedestrians passed by, but Cas didn't recognize anyone. "Anything?" Donovan asked.

"No." She let out a frustrated sigh.

"Run it again from five minutes before you got there until five minutes after."

"Okay." She watched again. "I don't see—"

Donovan straightened. "Freeze it."

Cas hit the pause button. "That car. I saw one just like it at the metro where Roshaun was pickpocketed."

"It's a black BMW. Those are everywhere around Paris."

"I can only get a partial on the license plate. See if you can catch the rest when it leaves."

Cas hit fast-forward. A couple of minutes went by, and she increased the speed. Over an hour passed before a man approached the car and slid into the driver's seat, his back to the camera.

"Recognize him?" Donovan asked.

"I can't tell. He's Black, and I'd guess him to be about six feet tall, but I don't see anything that makes him stand out."

He climbed into the car, and a moment later, the vehicle pulled onto the street. When it passed the bank, Cas gasped. "That's Tyrell."

"He's your sister's bodyguard?"

"Well, he works for my father, but basically, yes." Cas rewound the video again. "I didn't see my sister or Roshaun with him."

"He doesn't need your sister or your ex with him to be able to recognize you."

Cas's heart sank. "The car was there for almost an hour. That's plenty of time for him to have followed me to my apartment on foot and then circle back to his car."

"If anyone was able to successfully follow a guardian without being spotted, it makes sense that it was a security type."

"I can't believe I didn't see him."

"He must have been in one of the other buildings and saw you through a window. Otherwise, I'm sure you would have spotted him," Donovan said. "Did you take the elevator or the stairs when you got back to your apartment?"

"I always take the stairs. It's easier to evade if someone does follow me."

"That explains why those guys were waiting in the lobby. They must have been trying to figure out which apartment you were in."

"I'm surprised they didn't pull the fire alarm on us."

"Maybe they were going to, but I'm sure that was their last resort. Drawing attention to themselves couldn't have been their first choice. I hate to ask this, but is there any chance your parents or your sister could be involved in the coalition?" Donovan asked. "Roshaun, Tyrell. It seems like all of our suspects are connected to your family."

Cas shook her head. "There's no way my family is involved. Besides, Ace did a deep background check on them when I entered the guardian program, and all of them tried to talk me out of joining the coalition."

"Even your sister?"

"Especially my sister. She and my mom are all about creating equality through their charities. They're big believers that the good you put out into the world will come back to you."

"What about your dad? A self-made billionaire? Could he owe people who helped him rise to the top? People who could be pulling his strings?"

Cas hated that she had asked herself the same questions when she'd first joined the guardians. "I looked into that possibility myself, but every story my dad told about his rise to success, every business transaction he ever made was consistent with what I've always known to be true."

"You researched your own father?"

"Ace had me help. I think he wanted to let me prove to myself that my family is as amazing as I've always believed them to be." Cas pushed her hair behind her shoulders. "Trusting that my family isn't involved and Tyrell is, where do we go from here?"

"Well, we have the who. Let's see if we can connect him to Roshaun or the coalition."

"More online searching." Cas sighed. "Great."

* * *

Donovan couldn't believe he'd told Cas about Siara. And why had he opened up about his ex? Not exactly the kind of conversation a guy should have with an attractive woman, especially one he would be spending the foreseeable future with, one who smelled like flowers and sunshine.

He glanced at her sitting on the couch beside him, her fingers flying over her keyboard. Maybe it was the informal setting of the living room contributing to this odd rapport between them.

He scrolled through the latest messages on the guardian message board and struggled to focus. Cas was a coworker. Nothing more. Sure, she looked amazing with or without makeup, and he admired the way her back stiffened every time she thought he was being chauvinistic. Not to mention her culinary skills were a dream come true. He didn't know how he was going to adapt to living off MREs again after being so spoiled.

Cas glanced at him, a little crease on her brow. "What are you thinking?"

Surprised she'd caught him daydreaming, he shrugged. "I was thinking how hard it's going to be when I'm back in Africa. I've missed having someone to work with."

"Me too." Cas motioned to the television on the wall. "Watching TV isn't the same as having someone to talk to who will actually talk back."

"Isn't that the truth." Donovan propped a foot up on the coffee table. "Of course, watching you cook is way better than watching *The Great British Bake Off*."

"Why is that?"

"Because with you, I get to sample what you're making."

Cas laughed. "You're enjoying this, aren't you?"

"Are you kidding? Of course I am. Gourmet cuisine every day. I could get used to this." The reason for his current situation caught up with him, and his playfulness faded. "I'm sorry. I know this is hard for you."

"I keep rolling the events of the past few days over and over in my head," Cas said, a somberness chasing away her smile from a moment ago. "I don't know which is worse: seeing my sister and Roshaun together, finding out I was almost the victim of a bombing, or learning that the coalition knows I'm alive."

"What do you mean you were almost the victim of a bombing? You didn't tell me you were there."

"I left Gare du Nord twenty minutes before the bomb went off, but the explosion was right next to the train I should have been boarding."

"I didn't put that timing together." The coincidence was too glaring to ignore. "How long were you at the station?"

"Long enough to buy my ticket."

"Then where did you go?"

"I decided to go back to my apartment, so I caught the metro and made a few transfers on my way back."

"Specifics. Did you buy your ticket and go straight to the subway, or did you go somewhere first?"

"I'm a guardian. I know better than to go from point A to point B without making a few detours first to make sure I'm not being followed."

"Fair enough, but your trip from your apartment to the train station was a direct shot?"

"Yes. I had planned to change trains, but after seeing Roshaun and Makayla, I decided it was less risky to go straight there." Her eyes narrowed. "You aren't thinking someone followed me there and planted the bomb to try to get me, are you?"

"It would be a pretty ingenious way to get rid of you."

"Sorry, but I can't see it. No way someone was sitting outside my apartment building with a bomb so they could follow me to a train station to stage a terrorist attack."

"When you put it that way, it sounds pretty far-fetched, but doesn't it strike you as odd that you would have been in the kill zone?" Donovan asked.

"Of course it does. That's not the kind of coincidence most people live to tell about."

"I'm glad you did."

"Me too." Cas glanced back at her screen and leaned forward. "Did you see this? Six people were injured in the protests yesterday, including two police officers."

"That's not good."

"Especially since they're protesting the police not responding to a tip they never even received."

"Maybe one of us should go back to researching the source," Donovan suggested. "Tell me what to look for, and I can do it."

She hesitated before she shook her head. "No, I'll do it. I'm more familiar with how the news industry works."

"You sure?"

"Yeah. You can run the matrix on Roshaun's and Tyrell's communications as easily as I can. One of them had to have reached out to someone in the coalition."

"I'll check them along with the men you identified at your apartment," Donovan said. "It shouldn't take me more than a couple hours."

"Good, because if I'm cooking dinner, you get to help."

"What are we making?"

"Do you mind eating crepes again?" Cas asked, making his mouth water. "We can use the leftovers from lunch for our filling."

"You know how to make crepes?"

"Before we're done tonight, you'll know how to make them too."

CHAPTER 12

Cas dug into the early news sources of the bomb threat in Paris, her frustration rising steadily. She needed answers, and her impatience pushed her to consider an option she hadn't used since joining the guardians. She opened the portal into her father's network, her heart pounding. Did she dare use the access he had granted her while she was still actively working for him?

They knew she was alive, she reminded herself. If she couldn't hide that fact from her family anymore, there was no reason not to use all the resources available to her, especially if it would help her expose the threats to her family and anyone else who might be victimized by the coalition's activities. Besides, thousands of employees worked for Edge Broadcasting. The chances that they would think to flag her username at this point was miniscule, at best.

She drew a deep breath and logged in. Using her corporate access, she retrieved the first posting on the bomb threat and clicked on the link that would reveal who had uploaded the file. In the spot where the username should have been listed, the field was blank. She scanned to the next line, the IP address for the upload. It, too, was missing.

"Donovan, look at this." She turned her laptop toward him. "The story on the bomb threat showed up on my dad's news website, but all of the tracking information that identifies the reporter is missing."

"Could someone have deliberately left those fields blank?"

"No. They're generated automatically based on the user and location."

"Looks like your father's company got hacked."

"That would be one way to get misleading information out into the world." She leaned closer so she could see his computer. "Have you found anything?"

"No. I've looked through known associations twice, but Tyrell doesn't connect anywhere with members of the coalition."

Disappointment swept through her. "What about Roshaun?"

"The only contact that pops is Jamal," Donovan said, "but it doesn't show any contact between them for almost four years."

"If that's correct, they broke off contact right after I died," Cas said. "Or they found a new method to communicate."

"That was my thought, but from what I can tell, Ace and Kade did a pretty good job of trying to tie Roshaun to the coalition after your car went over the cliff, but neither found anything."

"In that case, want to help me with the other news sites?" Cas asked. "If whoever planted this story had the ability to hack this system, maybe all the other sites were hacked too."

"Sure."

They worked in companionable silence for the next several minutes. "This one doesn't have an originator listed either," Donovan said.

"It was the same with my father's other network that broke the story." Cas punched the last few keys to break through the firewalls with yet another news station. "It's the same with this one."

"Someone went to a lot of trouble to push this story out into the world."

"Whoever it was also had some serious computer skills. They not only hacked into all of these sites, but they also erased their electronic footprint when they planted the article."

"I say we turn this over to Kade and Renee," Donovan said. "They're the computer experts."

"Probably should tag Hannah too," Cas said, referring to the lead programmer for the guardian database.

"Good idea."

Cas set her laptop aside. "I think we're at a good stopping point. Ready to learn to make crepes?"

"I'm ready to try."

"I'll start on the batter while you finish up." Cas left Donovan in the living room and collected the ingredients she needed for the crepe batter. She was adding the flour when Donovan walked in.

"Renee already responded and said they would work on tracing the signals to the different stations for the day of the bombing."

"Great." She retrieved a whisk from the drawer and mixed the flour with the milk and eggs. "Can you grab the leftover chicken? I need you to pull the meat off the bones."

"That's easy enough." Donovan washed his hands, then retrieved the chicken, a bowl, and a fork. Working side by side, they finished the filling.

Cas retrieved a crepe pan from the cabinet and a wooden crepe turner from the drawer. "I'll make the first one. Then it's your turn." After she heated the pan, she demonstrated how to tilt the pan so the batter would coat the bottom.

"You make that look so easy."

"It is easy." After a minute or two, she loosened the sides and flipped the crepe over. "That's all there is to it. You ready to try?"

He made an exaggerated movement of his shoulders, as though preparing for a marathon. "Okay. Let's do this."

Cas laughed and transferred the first crepe onto a plate. "This isn't an Olympic sport."

"Maybe not, but this is my dinner at stake." He picked up the bowl of batter and started to pour.

Cas grabbed his wrist so he wouldn't use too much. "That's good. Now pick up the pan and roll your wrist."

He tried to follow her directions, but the motion was jerky.

Cas placed her hand over his and guided the movement. "Like this."

He looked down at her, their faces close. Time froze. Her pulse quickened; their breath mingled. Donovan's eyes lowered to her lips, and she could imagine too easily closing the distance between them. What was she thinking? Cas released his hand and edged back. "You've got it. Now put it on the burner for a minute."

She turned and added filling to the first crepe.

"Are you going to help me flip it?" Donovan held out the crepe turner.

The request was a simple one, so why had her palms gone damp? She rubbed her hands on her pants and closed the distance between them. "Start by loosening the edges."

Donovan moved the turner along the side and promptly ripped the crepe. "I don't think that was supposed to happen."

"It's okay. We'll try again." She took the turner from him, flipped the crepe over, and let it cook the rest of the way. As soon as she removed the ripped crepe from the pan and set it aside, she handed him the batter. "Remember, pour the batter in nice and easy."

Donovan poured in some batter and then a little more. "How's that?"

"Good. Now spread it around."

They repeated the process, Cas keeping a safe distance. This time when he went to flip it, Cas guided his hand so the delicate crepe would remain whole.

When he flipped it, his face lit up. "I did it."

Delighted with his success, she asked, "Ready to eat your creation?"

"I'm going to want more than one."

"Okay." Cas couldn't help but smile. "Let's do another one."

Donovan poured batter into the pan, his movements a little more confident than moments before. Cas added the filling to his crepe and rolled it up.

"Can we use this recipe for dessert crepes too?" he asked.

"Sure, but I didn't make any filling."

"That's okay. I saw some Nutella in the pantry."

"You're starting to think like a Frenchman already."

Donovan flipped the crepe. "I don't care about thinking like a Frenchman, but I'm ready to eat like one."

"Add some filling to that one, then." Cas turned off the stove and put the remaining batter in the refrigerator. "I'm hungry."

Donovan did so and carried his plate to the table. As soon as they sat down, he reached across the table and laid his hand on hers. "Thanks for teaching me."

A shiver worked up her spine. "You're welcome."

CHAPTER 13

Donovan slipped outside in the predawn light. Despite the absurdity of the bombing being meant for Cas, the timing continued to plague him. Could the two incidents be connected? It didn't make sense, but neither did the coalition coming after Cas four years after their failed attempt to kill her. As far as he knew, she hadn't done anything to upset their organization since her initial debriefing before entering into the guardian ranks.

Donovan locked the door behind him and zipped his jacket against the morning chill. After a quick glance down the quiet street, he circled the house. All quiet. Satisfied that no one had tracked them to Bruges, he started down the cobbled sidewalk. Gaining a better feel of the land wouldn't hurt. Besides, he needed to clear his head to get Cas out of his thoughts.

Cooking dinner together had awakened dreams in him best left buried—family, future. Those dreams had died with his divorce. His fictional death added an exclamation point to his certainty that relationships would never expand beyond the loose camaraderie between him and his fellow guardians and the brief connections he shared with the men and women he helped in the course of his missions.

Donovan turned the corner, remaining in the shadows in case anyone happened by. An engine sounded, and he pressed himself against the brick building beside him. A man walking the streets this time of morning was bound to gain unwanted attention.

A car emerged from a nearby street and turned in the opposite direction. Resigned that it would be best to wait until the bakeries and coffee shops opened for the morning to continue familiarizing himself with the area, Donovan reversed direction.

Thoughts of Cas invaded his mind. No longer was she the cool, business-like operative who did her job and then moved on to her next assignment.

Sure, she still went about her work with a determination he couldn't help but admire, but those pockets of personality and fun added to a fascinating whole. The fact that she could relax enough to teach him basic cooking skills while knowing people wanted her dead was a feat in itself.

What did Cas know about the coalition that made her such a threat? Or was it pure revenge that drove the leadership of the popular movement?

He turned the corner and approached the safe house. Lights glowed from the front window as though beckoning him forward. Had he left them on?

He reached the door and slid the key into the lock. Silently, he slipped inside. He was alone in the brightly lit entryway, so he flipped the lock and continued into the dark living room, where he turned on the light and caught a glimpse of movement. He whirled toward it. Cas, clad in her flannel pajamas, stood in the doorway, a butcher's knife in her hand.

His heart jumped in his chest, and he threw his hands up. "It's just me."

Cas lowered the knife and pressed her free hand to her own chest. "You about gave me a heart attack. What are you doing up so early?"

"I couldn't sleep. I went out to check the area." He shrugged out of his jacket. "What are you doing up? What time is it anyway?"

"It's a little after five." Cas led the way into the kitchen. Milk, butter, and eggs lined the counter.

"Do you normally get up this early?"

"I couldn't stop thinking about the timing of everything. My family and Roshaun coming to Paris, the bombing, Tyrell finding me, Ezra and Jamal showing up at my apartment with their friends."

"You've had a pretty eventful week."

"Not even a week. All of that was within a few days." Cas opened the cabinet and pulled out canisters of flour and sugar.

"What are you doing?"

She retrieved a jar of yeast from the refrigerator. "I'm making bread."

"At five in the morning."

"It won't be ready for a few hours." She measured water into a measuring cup and dumped it into a large bowl. "I bake when I need to clear my head."

Donovan leaned against the counter while she added sugar and yeast to the water. A quiet yearning pierced through him, and he took a picture in his mind of this moment. The quiet kitchen, Cas combining ingredients without the aid of a recipe, the glow of her skin beneath the overhead lights.

"I keep wondering why the coalition is going to such trouble to find me," Cas said, interrupting his thoughts.

"I was asking myself the same question," Donovan admitted. "I assume you shared everything you knew when you first entered the guardian program."

"I did." Cas added butter and salt. "Two members of their leadership were arrested for terrorism."

"Only two?"

"They were the only ones the FBI had enough evidence on to make the charges stick."

"I'm surprised the negative press didn't take the whole coalition down."

"That was our hope, but the rest of the organization did a good job of distancing themselves from the men arrested." Cas scooped some flour into the bowl. "They even had an article about how shocked everyone was to find out people had used the coalition's reputation to harm others."

"They do have a way with spinning a story, don't they?"

"Yeah. People want to believe in the basic premise of social reform and making life better for all Americans, regardless of race or gender. Unfortunately, most don't dig deep enough to find that the coalition's version of reform is to create chaos, mistrust, and contention."

"To what end?"

"I've asked myself that question more times than I can count," Cas said. "At first, I thought it was to generate more donations, but now I'm not so sure. The leadership isn't just soliciting money. It seems to be going after the very foundation of American freedoms."

"Maybe we've been going at our research all wrong."

"What do you mean?"

"We keep trying to connect people from your past to the coalition. Let's reverse that," Donovan said. "We should research the members of the coalition and track their movements and contacts. Maybe if we know what they're doing, we can find the connection to you."

"It's worth a try." Cas abandoned her spoon and used her hands to knead the ball of dough. "After I finish here, I'm going to take a shower, but then I'll be ready to get started."

"Is the bread for breakfast?"

"Part of it anyway." Cas finished her task. After she washed her hands, she covered the bowl with a thin cloth. "I can make eggs and bacon to go with it, or we can have crepes instead."

"I'll be happy with either. You're an amazing cook."

"Glad you think so, because I'll need you to go to the store again tomorrow."

"More groceries? I just went two days ago."

"Yes, but I don't have everything I need to make beef bourguignon."

"You're using my stomach to manipulate me."

Cas grinned. "And to think it took us so little time to get to know each other."

* * *

Cas was going in circles. Every time she traced a contact for one coalition member, it connected right back to another one. She and Donovan had spent all day on their laptops, first in the living room and now at the kitchen table. The scent of dinner still hung in the air and mingled with the undertones of Donovan's musky aftershave.

Trying not to think of the man across from her or the way his thermal shirt showed off his lean muscles, she started another search. After fifteen minutes, she reached another dead end.

"This is useless," she said. "I'm not finding anything."

"Give it time."

She leaned back in her chair and struggled against the unwelcome frustration. She hated feeling out of control, and being locked inside was only aggravating her sense of helplessness.

As though sensing her inner turmoil, Donovan pushed back from the table. "Come on. We need to get some fresh air."

Part of her wanted to rush straight to the door. Another part battled fear. "I don't know . . ."

"It's twilight, the best time to be invisible." Donovan left the kitchen and led the way to the entryway. He opened the closet under the stairs where extra clothing was kept for unexpected guests. A tennis racket fell out. He replaced it and dug through an assortment of outerwear. When he turned, he held out a simple trench coat and knit cap. "Here. Put these on."

She took them but hesitated.

"I won't let anything happen to you."

Her eyebrows rose, and some of the fear dropped away. "I feel like your client right now instead of your coworker."

"Maybe it's time to stop thinking of yourself as either of those things. Let me be your friend. You can trust me."

The sincerity in his voice swayed her. Her gaze met his, and something undefinable passed between them. Maybe it wasn't the coalition she should be worried about; maybe it should be spending so much time with Donovan and how it was going to impact her life once he returned to Africa.

Donovan grabbed his jacket and slipped it on, then reached for the doorknob. "Come on. We'll go for a nice walk and work up an appetite for dessert."

"Are you expecting me to make something for you?"

"No. I'm going to make us crepes."

His announcement and the confidence in his voice gave her an unexplained sense of comfort. Or perhaps it was trust. She followed him outside and did a quick check of the deserted street.

Donovan turned toward the quiet part of the neighborhood, positioning himself between her and the street. When another couple approached on the opposite sidewalk, Donovan slipped his arm around her shoulders. The now familiar spurt of attraction flared, and Cas fought against it. Her connection to him was normal, considering how much time they had spent together. Once they went back to their normal lives, all of this would become a sweet memory to look back on. Well, it would be a good memory except for the people chasing her.

Her throat closed, but she wasn't sure if it was from the warmth of Donovan beside her or the fear of someone trying to kill her again.

She didn't speak until the couple passed by and were out of earshot. Struggling to regain her footing, she asked, "Getting a little friendly, aren't you?"

Donovan gave her shoulder a squeeze but kept his arm in place. "No one looking for you would expect you to be half of a couple."

She couldn't fault his thought process. They walked in silence for another minute.

"Turn left up here." She pointed at an upcoming intersection.

Donovan complied. A few minutes later, they reached one of the canals that flowed through the city.

Cas laid her hand on the brick wall that ran the length of it. The last fingers of sunlight shimmered off the water along with the lights of the houses opposite them. "I love how so many European cities have waterways as part of their transportation systems."

"It's peaceful here." Donovan's arm dropped away, and he leaned on the wall beside her. "You can almost forget there are people in the world trying to cause others pain."

"That's why I like it here. It's like the outside world doesn't exist."

"It's quite the change from where you lived in Paris. You were in the middle of everything."

It was true. "I love the energy of the city, but everyone needs time to get away and reflect on what's really important."

"What's important to you, Cas?"

"My family," she answered without hesitation. "What about you? What memories keep you going when you're alone for days on end?"

"That's an interesting question, one I'm not sure how to answer." He pushed away from the wall. "We should get back."

As much as she hated to leave the serenity in front of her, she fell into step beside him. Donovan took her hand in his, and her throat went dry.

They were halfway back to the house when he broke the silence. "I saw a deck of cards in the living room. Want to play some gin rummy when we get back?"

"Loser does the dishes?"

"We already did the dishes."

"No, the ones you're going to dirty from making dessert," Cas said.

"Okay. You're on." He linked his fingers through hers, and her stomach somersaulted. "I should probably warn you that I rarely lose."

The challenge in his voice settled her insides, leaving her with a comfortable warm glow. She fought back a smile. "That's good to know."

CHAPTER 14

The woman was a card shark. Not only did he have to do the dishes, but Cas had manipulated him into walking an extra six blocks to her favorite local bakery to pick up quiche for breakfast.

With a paper bag in one hand, Donovan walked two blocks out of the way to make sure he wasn't being followed before returning to the safe house. So far, he hadn't seen anything to indicate their location had been compromised, but until they could trace Tyrell back to the coalition, Cas was a prisoner to fear and the isolation forced upon her.

He almost felt guilty that he was benefiting from her misfortune. Spending time with her, discovering the pockets of dry humor mixed with her fierce determination, reminded him of what life had been like once. Someone to talk to, a colleague to share ideas with. His role as a guardian fulfilled him in many ways, but he missed the in-person connection he'd experienced with the agency.

Donovan approached the safe house, and a sense of home washed over him. He was letting himself get too comfortable. His walk with Cas last night was a clear example that he wasn't thinking straight. Even though he hadn't detected any sign of danger since their arrival in Bruges, he never would have taken a client out in the open like that when it wasn't necessary. Yet, he sensed her need and couldn't stand not finding a solution.

He walked inside to the low, weeping notes of a saxophone accompanied by a piano. Jazz in the morning. He hadn't expected that.

He followed the music into the kitchen, where Cas sat at the table, her fingers tapping on her keyboard.

She glanced up and turned down the music. "Did you find it okay?"

"Yeah." He retrieved two plates and dished out the large wedges of quiche. "I didn't peg you for a Coltrane fan."

"Music helps me think."

"What are you working on?"

"I'm tracking my family's cell phones to see where they're at." Her eyes lifted to meet his again. "Another protest is scheduled in Paris on Saturday."

Donovan grabbed two forks and carried their breakfast to the table. "You're worried it'll turn violent?"

"Yeah, especially after this morning's news."

"What news?" He sat in the chair beside her.

"Take a look at this." She turned off the music and angled her laptop toward him. She pulled up a video file and clicked play.

Roshaun Davis's face filled the screen, his no-nonsense tone a jarring intrusion into Donovan's time with Cas. "Another protest has been scheduled in Paris for this Saturday amid the fallout of alleged new evidence that police buried evidence and deleted call logs about a bomb threat called in hours before the explosion at Gare du Nord train station, one of the transportation hubs for Paris."

Cas stopped the video. "He doesn't have confirmation of the information, but he's putting it out there anyway."

"How do you know he didn't find something we missed?"

"He said *a* bomb threat, not *the* bomb threat."

"So?"

"That's a typical news tactic legal departments have reporters use to keep from getting sued." Cas turned the music back on. "That tells me no one has been able to provide proof of this new evidence."

"Any idea where the story came from?"

"Looks like another hack, this one at a station in Lyon, France." She picked up her fork and took a bite. "This is good. Thanks for picking it up."

"I always honor my bets." He motioned to her screen. "Is the station in Lyon one of the networks that broke the news about the bomb threat?"

"It is." Cas pushed her laptop into the center of the table and took another bite.

"Sounds like whoever is behind this has incredible computer skills, or they have a back door into the security software the different networks are using."

"I had that same thought," Cas said. "That's what I was working on before I saw Roshaun's newscast."

"Any chance the companies that broke the story use the same security software?"

"As a matter of fact, all of them do, except for three, which brings us right back to my family."

"How so?" Donovan asked.

"The three stations that use a different cybersecurity software are all owned by Edge Broadcasting."

"It's possible that one of your dad's stations picked up the story and shared it with the other two."

"I would have thought so too, except for one thing. Everyone besides Edge uses Magellan for protection. Edge used the same software until a few months ago," Cas said. "They've been upgrading their stations around the world for the past two years."

"Which means either someone figured out a hack or back door into two security systems . . ."

"Or they work for Edge and knew about the back door in Magellan."

"If you're right, maybe we can trace who was on the system when the articles were planted on the Edge websites."

"I already looked. Whoever is behind the hack is skilled enough to erase their electronic footprint. The posting of the stories was scheduled ahead of time, making it nearly impossible to pinpoint when the code was uploaded."

"Sounds like we're back to searching for connections between the coalition and your family or their employees."

"Yes, but there is one other thing we can do."

"What's that?"

"I say we create some news of our own." Her face lit with determination. "Have you met Nolan and Elle?"

"I've worked a couple ops with Nolan," Donovan said of the guardian who had transferred from Europe to South America last year. "I've never met his fiancée."

"Actually, Elle is his wife now. They got married a few weeks ago."

"I must have missed that."

"Anyway, Elle is an investigative reporter. She could craft a story to undermine the protests in Paris and expose the disinformation being sent out there."

"Do you think people will listen?"

"If it's timed right, I think so, but there is one thing we have to do."

"What's that?"

"We have to find the back door to Magellan's security software so we can post the story on everyone's website."

"That sounds like a job for Kade. Do you want to call him, or should I?"

"It's your turn. He's already complained to me this week, and he's grumpy because he and Renee weren't able to trace the signals for the last planted stories. He needs a new victim."

"He isn't going to yell at me, is he?"

"I don't know, but it'll be fun to find out."

* * *

Following her family's movements was pure torture. Cas had input their cell phone information into a program to map and record their whereabouts, but every time she looked at the two dots that represented Roshaun and Makayla, her stomach turned sour. Except for when Roshaun was at the Paris television station, the two had been inseparable all day.

Even when she and Roshaun had gone on a vacation to Bora Bora, they hadn't spent that much time together. Inevitably, Roshaun had wanted time to go for a solitary run in the mornings, and he had often retired to his room early while Cas had enjoyed the various social events the resort had offered. She had spent nearly three years dating the man, and never once had he spoken of marriage, yet here he was, engaged to her sister after less than a year.

Donovan walked into the kitchen. Welcoming the distraction, Cas looked up. "How did it go with Kade?"

"Good talk." Donovan grinned. "I told him you were scared to call him."

"What?" Indignation spurted through her. "I wasn't scared."

"I know, but it got Kade going for a minute before he figured out I was messing with him."

Amused, Cas shook her head. "Did he have any useful information for us?"

"He said he agrees with you that someone must have had direct access to the broadcasting companies' systems. He didn't find anything that showed all of them were simultaneously hacked."

"Tyrell works security for the family. I doubt he has access, and Roshaun wouldn't work with the computer systems."

"Kade made the same assessment. Have you talked to Elle?" Donovan asked.

"I sent her a note on the message board."

Donovan sat in the chair beside her. "How's it going with you? Anything new?"

"My family is still in Paris."

"All of them?"

"Yes." She pointed at her screen. "My father is spending his time in his Paris office. Mom has spent most of her day shopping."

Donovan pointed at her screen. "I gather these are Makayla and Roshaun."

"Yeah. They spent the morning in Montmartre. Now they're at Luxembourg Gardens." One of Cas's favorite places.

"Let's expand your search and see if anyone else is consistently in close proximity to your family," Donovan suggested.

"I already did, but nothing is popping except for Tyrell with Roshaun and Makayla and Antoine with my mom."

"Are you tracking them too?"

"Yeah."

"Then let's expand the parameters." Donovan motioned to Cas's laptop. "May I?"

"Go ahead." She nudged it toward him.

Donovan opened the control settings on the tracking program and added a string of code to search for overlaying signals with the six people she was tracking.

"I didn't realize you were that good with programming."

"Kade taught me a few things when he came to Africa."

"When did Kade go to Africa? He usually avoids international travel."

"About five years ago. I needed his expertise on a corporate espionage case that was beyond my technical abilities."

"I've never been able to get him to come help me." Her brows furrowed. "Maybe he likes you better than me."

"Nah. You just don't have any elephants here."

"Kade wanted to see elephants?"

"He wanted to ride an elephant. He was like a kid opening a present from Santa on Christmas morning."

"Kade rode an elephant? I would have loved to see that."

"I took a picture." Donovan waited a beat before adding, "He deleted it."

"Of course he did."

Cas's phone rang. "If Kade already found our culprit, he's even better than I thought," Donovan said.

"It's not Kade. It's Ace." Cas hit the Talk button.

"What were you thinking?" Ace demanded in lieu of a greeting. "You used your personal access to log into Edge Broadcasting's computer system?"

Cas's eyes flashed. "You're acting like my cover wasn't already blown. The people who matter already know I'm alive."

"No, they don't. Your father just contacted the police and is demanding they conduct a search for you."

"The police in Paris?"

He drew a breath and diverted back to his original rant. "What does that matter? You completely broke protocol."

Her back stiffened. "As far as I know, there isn't a protocol for what happens when a guardian's death is proven to be a lie."

"I guarantee that announcing to your family you're alive wouldn't be a first choice no matter what the situation is."

"My father's security system is top of the line. I'm not sure even Kade would be able to hack his way in. Even if one of us did succeed, the information is all compartmentalized. It would have taken us days to get the information that instead only took me minutes."

"Tell me you did your search while you were still in Paris."

"I could tell you that, but I'd be lying."

"What's going on?" Donovan asked.

"Ace is mad because I logged into Edge Broadcasting."

"Is that Donovan?" Ace asked as though she would have another man sitting beside her. "Put me on speaker."

Cas hit the Speaker button and set her phone down. "Look, I know it was a risk, and I'm sorry, but I couldn't sit by and do nothing when my sister could be dating a killer." She sucked in a breath and willed her heartbeat to steady.

"No one has ever been able to break through the guardian firewalls and trace any of us," Donovan added. "At least we have that going for us."

"I didn't stay logged in for long," Cas continued, "and like I said, people already knew I was alive."

"The coalition knew it, but your family didn't. Otherwise, why didn't your father reach out to the police before now?"

Ace was right. Her father wasn't someone to sit idly by and wait for information. He had always actively pursued the truth. "That means Tyrell didn't tell my family I was alive. Why?"

"That's an excellent question," Ace said, his frustration still humming through his voice.

"I would have thought he would have gone to your parents as soon as he saw you," Donovan said. "We've been operating under the assumption that Roshaun and the Edgemonts learned Cas was alive because Tyrell told him and the family."

"One of them must have gone directly to the coalition," Cas said, "but we haven't been able to figure out who they passed the information to."

"Do a deep dive into Tyrell," Ace said. "See what he's been up to since he got to Paris."

"We've been following his movement for the past day. We haven't found any connections between him and the coalition."

"You need to find a new rock to look under, then, because if we're right, he's at the heart of this."

CHAPTER 15

All the data in front of Donovan indicated Tyrell was a longtime, loyal employee of the Edgemont family. No questionable relationships in the past, no excessive debt or gambling problems. His social media presence was nonexistent, and the man rarely went anywhere on his own. Donovan stretched his legs out in front of him, the couch cushion giving beneath the motion. "I'm not finding anything on Tyrell."

"It's hard to look into him from here when the man barely has an electronic presence." Cas set her laptop aside. "We need to follow him."

Donovan's protective streak surged. "*We* aren't doing anything." He wasn't about to take Cas anywhere near Paris. "And I'm not leaving you here alone. We can pawn that task off on the CIA."

Her eyebrows went up. "Believe it or not, I did manage to survive on my own before you came along."

"I'm not questioning your abilities. I'm using common sense," Donovan countered. Did Cas have any idea how gorgeous she was when she had that hint of temper in her eyes? "People are looking for you. I'm not sure our training is enough to keep us invisible in Paris right now."

Acceptance and frustration merged. "I'll put the request in to the CIA."

"Better add Roshaun to that request too," Donovan said. "It wouldn't hurt to have eyes on him."

"You're right, but I hate that by doing that, it puts my sister under surveillance too."

"Think of it as an extra protection for her."

"I guess." Cas typed on her laptop for a moment and then pushed to her feet. She studied the living space as though in deep thought. Then she gripped the chair she had been sitting in and moved it across the room.

"What are you doing?

"Rearranging the furniture. The couch would work better over there." She pointed at the atrium wall.

"But then I would have my back to the natural light coming through those windows."

"That's a good thing."

"Not when it will create a glare on my screen." Donovan stood and stepped closer. "Why the sudden need to move everything around?"

"I just need a change."

"A change or a new sense of order?" Donovan asked.

"Both."

Donovan could relate to that. He debated the options for where the couch could be positioned and not impede the natural flow in the room. He motioned to where Cas's chair had been a moment ago. "What about putting the couch over here?"

"And the chairs over there?" Cas waved at the space by the far wall. "I guess that could work."

Together they pushed the couch into its new position and rearranged the chairs. As soon as everything was in place, Cas settled back into her chair.

"Better?" Donovan asked.

"Yeah. Thanks." Cas's phone rang. "*Allo*?" She stiffened and grabbed her laptop, typing something urgently. Donovan leaned closer so he could read her notes, but before he could, she ended the call and jumped up. "We have to go." Cas slid her laptop into her oversized purse. "We have an agent who needs support."

"Where?"

"Lille."

"France or Belgium?" Donovan asked.

"France."

"What ops do we have going on there?"

"I'm not entirely sure. The operative who called isn't the one involved. Jasmine said our guy has been tracking a bombmaker who may have been responsible for building the one that went off in Paris." Cas zipped her purse. "Her agent missed his check-in, but the electronic signature on his phone has him near the area they suspect the bombmaker was hiding out."

"Why didn't she call the Brussels or Paris office for support?"

"She tried, but both of those offices are stretched thin because of the bombing. The higher-ups told her they would put someone on it if he missed the next check-in."

"By then, the guy could be dead, if he isn't already." Donovan had worked intel long enough to know how hard it was to prioritize equally important goals, but when it came to a comrade in trouble, that always came first. "I can't believe the Paris office is leaving one of their own hanging out to dry."

"The guy we're looking for is based out of the Vienna office. Jasmine was running support out of Germany."

"This Paris bombing is stretching the CIA's resources more than I thought." As much as he hated to leave Cas alone, he stood. "I'll go."

"You can't. It has to be me," Cas insisted.

"You're supposed to stay out of sight, remember?"

"Yes, but the agent doesn't know you. I've run support for him before."

Donovan couldn't fault her point. CIA agents didn't trust easily. Resigned, he asked, "Who is this guy anyway?"

"Cole Bridger."

Donovan knew the name. Not only had his name been a constant on the CIA's overseas postings for the past few years, but the Bridger family was a legend in the agency. Both Cole's father and grandfather had served in intelligence before him. Donovan had probably even talked to Cole's grandfather on the phone a time or two.

"We need to protect you from being seen on any security feed," Donovan said. "Any chance you have a headscarf or an abaya?"

"Not with me, but we're not taking the train. We have a car garaged at the car park down the street."

"I've been walking six blocks to get groceries when I could have been driving?"

"Locals don't drive to the store. Tourists do." She headed for the stairs. "Better grab all your stuff in case we don't come straight back here."

"Okay, but just so you know, I'm highly motivated to complete this mission and get back here as soon as possible."

"Why's that?"

"I already bought all the ingredients for you to make beef bourguignon."

Cas shook her head, but the corners of her mouth twitched up. "Get your stuff. The sooner we find Bridger, the sooner we can come home."

Come home. The words repeated in Donovan's mind. Years ago, *home* had invoked an image of the little townhouse he and his wife had shared, but since joining the guardians, his various apartments around Africa were little more than places to lay his head for a night and find sustenance to last him through the day. What would it be like to have the word *home* mean something again?

Cas reached the top of the stairs and glanced down at him. "You coming?"

"Yeah, I'm coming."

* * *

Doug couldn't believe it. He read the email from billionaire Josiah Edgemont twice. Was it really possible that Cassidy Edgemont was still alive? An unexpected use of her login information was hardly proof, but the fact that this had never happened before sent up a host of red flags.

Hector approached carrying a folder. He handed it to Doug. "This is the court schedule for the Hawthorne case. We're scheduled to testify next month."

"Thanks."

"No problem." Hector motioned to the open file on Doug's desk. "Are you still working on the Edgemont case?"

Doug nodded. While four potential witnesses had been killed or gone missing, Cassidy Edgemont was the most prominent of the victims.

Doug trusted Hector implicitly, but Josiah Edgemont's request that he keep his suspicions private caused Doug to sidestep his reason for opening the file today. "I know there's something here. It's like I can see the last puzzle piece, but I can't quite figure out where it fits."

"You also have fifty other cases that are a lot more likely to get solved."

"Fifty-two," Doug corrected.

"Close enough." Hector sat at his desk. "You're wasting your time with that one."

"Maybe." Doug scanned through the accident report when Cassidy Edgemont's car went over the cliff. Her body was never found. Was it possible the woman had survived? And if so, why hadn't she ever come forward? And how had she been providing for herself over the past four years? She hadn't ever accessed her personal accounts or used her credit cards. According to the family, she'd had only a few hundred dollars on her at the time of her supposed death. Not much to get out of town on, much less to live off of.

Doug skimmed over several other files related to the coalition, including the arrest and subsequent conviction of two members for terrorism. That case had been a bombing that had thankfully been thwarted before the attack occurred.

The date of a witness statement caught his eye, and he set the file beside Cassidy Edgemont's. His eyes narrowed. The key witness who provided the evidence that led to the two men's convictions had been interviewed two and a half weeks after Edgemont's accident. Was it possible Cassidy had been the witness? And if so, why hadn't he been informed she'd been placed in witness protection?

With more questions than answers, Doug started reading the file from the beginning. The answers had to be in here somewhere. And someone had to know if Cassidy Edgemont was really still alive.

CHAPTER 16

Cas didn't like it. The last known location for Cole Bridger was a sidewalk café in the heart of the city.

Donovan slowed the car as they drove by. "See anything?"

"No, but I doubt we're going to. Even though the GPS on Bridger's car indicates he's here, I can't get a signal on his phone."

"When was the last time it was active?"

"Three hours ago." Anticipating Donovan's next question, she added, "The car has been here since eighteen hundred hours."

"So he was here for a half hour, and then he probably put a scrambler on his phone so he could follow someone."

Worry surfaced. "Or someone disabled his phone," Cas said.

"I like my version better."

"Me too."

"Let me find a place to park. We'll see if Kade can tap into the restaurant's security cameras."

Cas read the license plates in the glow of the headlights as they passed. "Slow down. That's his car."

Donovan eased off the gas pedal. "I don't see anyone near it."

"We can walk by after you park." The brake lights on a nearby parked car illuminated. Donovan stopped and waited for the vehicle to pull out so he could take the parking spot. He turned off the engine.

"I'll check out the car if you'll call Kade," Donovan said.

Though Cas would have preferred to check out the area herself, it made sense for her to stay out of sight. "I suppose it's my turn to call him."

"I'll be right back." Donovan handed her the car keys before he opened the door.

Cas made her call.

"What do you need now?" Kade asked.

"Surveillance footage." Cas described the restaurant where Cole Bridger's phone had last been active as well as the location the CIA agent had parked his car and the time window.

"Are you on site?" Kade asked.

"Yes. Donovan's checking out Bridger's car now."

"Then you want me to look through the security feed."

"Yes, please." Cas offered the nicety to soften the blow that she was adding to his workload. Not that Kade ever said no to a real need.

"I should be getting paid overtime for this."

"Good luck with that. You haven't been alive to get a paycheck for a decade."

"I should still get a raise," he grumbled. "I'm looking at the surveillance now. Bridger didn't leave his car until right after the GPS on his phone went dark."

"So he's the one masking his signal."

"Looks that way to me."

"Can you tell which way he went?" Cas asked. If Bridger was on foot, he had to be close.

"Yeah. He went to the corner and got into a car. Looks like it was an Uber or something like that."

"Can you tap into his user account? That could give us his location."

"Checking now."

Donovan approached the car and slid behind the wheel. "No sign of our guy. Did Kade find anything?"

"Bridger took an Uber. Kade's trying to find out where he went." Cas put her phone on speaker.

A moment later, Kade's voice rang out. "Bridger changed his destination once he got in the car. Looks like he may have been following someone."

"Can you tap into traffic cameras to see who?"

"I'll work on that, but for now, I'm texting you the coordinates of where he was dropped off."

"Thanks, Kade."

"If you really want to say thanks, send chocolate."

Despite her concern for the missing agent, Cas couldn't help but laugh. "I'll see what I can do."

* * *

Donovan didn't know which was worse, taking Cas into a populated area or searching through the deserted warehouse district for their missing agent. What was it about rows of dark buildings that always made him feel like he was about to become victim number three in a horror film?

He approached the intersection where the Uber driver had dropped off Bridger. A single lightbulb burned outside a building constructed of corrugated metal. A box truck rumbled toward them from the other direction—whether picking up a load or dropping one off, Donovan couldn't tell.

"He could be anywhere in here," Cas said.

Donovan turned right and drove slowly. "See any security cameras Kade can tap into?"

"Nothing." Cas retrieved her phone from her purse. "I'll try messaging Bridger again."

Up ahead, lights shone from a loading area where several men used loading dollies to move boxes into the back of a tractor trailer. Donovan did a quick analysis, but nothing about the scene appeared to be anything beyond a night crew loading product to be shipped.

"Still no response." Cas held up her phone. "Maybe the driver can tell us which way he went."

"If Bridger was following someone, he would have hid first or deliberately gone the other way to avoid suspicion."

"You're right."

Donovan reached a crossroad and turned. "All we can do is drive around to see if anything looks off."

"We could question those guys we passed back there, but if Bridger came here on his own, you can bet he didn't let anyone see him," Cas said.

"I agree. We may not be able to do much until Bridger gives us some clue of where he's at."

"I've messaged him, and so has Jasmine." Cas's eyes remained focused on the warehouses. "If Bridger wants to be found, it's up to him to send us a signal."

Methodically, Donovan drove down one street and then another, one warehouse looking much like the next. They passed a cargo van parked outside a dark building.

"Can you catch the license plate on that van?" Donovan asked.

"No. There's not enough light."

"I'll circle back around. That's the only vehicle I've seen besides that semi." Donovan turned at the next corner. He was halfway down the next block when the screen on Cas's phone lit up.

"The GPS on Bridger's cell just went live."

"Where is he?"

"Looks like he's on the next street over. It might be the same building where that van was parked."

Donovan sped up. When he turned the corner, the street was empty and the van was gone.

"Keep going." Cas pointed to the left. "The signal is coming from right up there."

Donovan hit the brakes and threw the gearshift into park. "Wait here."

Cas ignored him and climbed out of the car. Before he could protest, she circled the front and held out her hand. She lowered her voice to a whisper. "Give me the keys in case we need to make a fast break."

Donovan handed them over and drew the gun holstered at his waist. He glanced back to ensure Cas was safely in the car before he approached the single entrance, a garage-style corrugated door with a thick padlock ensuring no one could enter. Seeing no easy alternative, he holstered his weapon again and withdrew his lockpick kit. He made several unsuccessful attempts, the lack of light rendering his task nearly impossible. He whirled when a footstep crunched on gravel.

Cas stood behind him, a beam of light shining from her phone. "Try now."

Donovan inserted the two narrow tools. This time, the lock popped open on the first try. Rather than utter his thanks, he nodded and pocketed his tools.

Silently, Donovan removed the padlock and set it aside. He moved to the center of the door where the handle would allow him to open it. Of course, the minute he rolled the metal door up, he would be exposed to whoever was inside. He prayed Bridger was alone and that he wasn't trigger-happy.

Cas put her hand on his arm. "Let me open the door. Bridger is expecting his support to be a woman. You can cover me from the side."

"Try messaging him first."

Cas typed a message into her phone and hit Send. A moment later, a response popped.

"He said he was locked in a warehouse," Cas said. "I'll tell him he can open the door now from the inside."

"Good." Donovan stepped to the side.

Cas moved back to the car and opened the driver's-side door, but she didn't move to get inside. The warehouse door jangled and opened. Donovan's hand went to his gun.

A man emerged slowly, both hands visible. Blond, average build, in his late twenties. His eyes swept down to Donovan's weapon, but after a quick analysis, he focused on Cas. Even if Donovan had not recognized Cole Bridger from his service photo, the man's lack of concern facing an armed man would have given him away as an intelligence operative.

"Did you see a van out here?" Urgency vibrated through Bridger's words. "Black Mercedes?"

"Yeah," Cas said. "It was here when we drove by a minute ago."

"We need to find it." Bridger took another step forward. "I assume Jazz sent you."

"She did," Cas said.

"Thanks for helping me out. I was afraid I was going to be locked in there all night."

"This is my friend Ghost."

Bridger's eyebrows drew together. "I thought you were Ghost."

"We both are."

"This is going to get confusing." Bridger closed the door behind him. "You'd better lock that back up in case they come back."

"What's the situation?" Donovan asked.

"There's a bomb in the back of that van. We need to stop it."

CHAPTER 17

ANOTHER BOMB. CAS HAD KNOWN she might face that possibility after the one in Paris had gone off, but finding Cole Bridger was supposed to be a simple locate-and-liberate operation.

"I don't see it anywhere," Cas said.

"What do you know about the target?" Donovan asked from the passenger seat. "Maybe we can intercept them."

Bridger leaned forward and rested his arm on the back of the front seat. "When I sneaked into the warehouse, I heard someone mention Brussels. Best guess is it will be the train station."

"Which one? There are three," Cas said.

"Whichever one is the busiest."

"That would be the north station." Cas debated her options and turned onto the road that would give her the most direct route to Brussels.

"How many people are we chasing?" Donovan asked.

"Two. Wayne Aguilar and a guy I don't know. He was the buyer."

"I'm aware of Aguilar's reputation," Donovan said. "Do you have a picture of the other guy?"

"Yeah." Bridger retrieved an image on his phone and stretched his hand over the back seat to show it to Donovan.

Donovan's body tensed. "It's Jamal."

"Who is he?" Bridger asked in a clipped tone. "And how do you know him?"

Donovan motioned toward Cas. "He came looking for Ghost here a few days ago in Paris."

Cas's hands tightened on the steering wheel. "He's a member of the Freedom Coalition."

"That's a US-based organization," Bridger said. "What are they doing bombing train stations over here?"

Beside her, Donovan shook his head. "I have no idea."

"How did you track the bombmaker to the warehouse here in Lille?" Cas asked.

"And why didn't you share your intel with the agency?" Donovan added.

"I was about to when I intercepted a call between our guy and his buyer. They set up a meeting at a café not too far from here."

"Where you left your car?"

"Yeah. I had already found the warehouse, but I didn't have anything on our guy other than suspicions. When I saw him with Jamal, I was afraid Aguilar would spook if he saw my car behind him, so I killed the GPS on my phone and called an Uber."

"You should check in with Jasmine. She's been worried about you," Cas said.

"She's a mother hen sometimes." For a man who had been trapped a minute ago, Bridger didn't seem the least bit fazed.

"Maybe so." Cas glanced at Bridger. "But that mother hen saved you from being locked in a warehouse for who knows how long."

"True." Bridger leaned back in the seat behind Cas and dialed his phone. "Hey, Jazz. I'm good." He proceeded to give her an update along with a license plate number to track. After he hung up, he said, "She's going to run the registration for the van and search for it using its GPS."

"I hope she can track it down," Cas said.

"Yeah. I'd much rather head these guys off than clean up the aftermath," Bridger said.

"That makes three of us."

* * *

Donovan grabbed the door to hold himself steady as Cas made a quick turn, the back of the car fishtailing briefly before she controlled it. No doubt about it: the woman had a lead foot and the driving skills to rival a race car driver.

"Take the next left." Bridger gripped the back of Cas's seat with one hand and pointed at the upcoming intersection with the other. "The van should be right in front of us."

Donovan braced as Cas whipped around the corner. The black van came into view six cars up on the right.

"There it is," Donovan said.

"What's the plan?" Cas asked. "I can cut them off."

"Not my first choice since they have a bomb in there," Donovan said.

"It's not my first choice either. I'm open to other suggestions." Cas glanced at him, her demeanor surprisingly calm. "The train station is only a kilometer away. We need to act now."

"Let her cut him off," Bridger said. "The two of us can take care of the threat."

"Does either of you know how to defuse a bomb?" Cas asked.

"Depends on how much time I have," Donovan said.

"Same here."

Cas weaved between two cars and cut off a third. Someone honked. She settled behind a Mercedes for a second before snaking past it. Donovan gripped his seat when she accelerated past two more vehicles and approached the van. "Hold on," she said.

"Already am," Donovan muttered.

Cas stomped on the gas pedal, cut in front of the van, and hit the brakes.

Tires squealed against pavement. Donovan's hand flew to the dashboard, and his seat belt jerked him against his seat. The van screeched to a stop.

Moving as one, Donovan and Bridger pushed out of the car and drew their weapons.

Donovan keyed in on the driver, the man he had seen only a few days ago in Cas's apartment building. "Hold it right there," Donovan called out in English.

Jamal flung the van door open, ducked behind it, and sprinted to the back of the vehicle. Donovan raced after him. When he rounded the back, Jamal had his hand on the rear door. He pulled it open, slamming the door into Donovan. His gun dropped to the ground and skidded under the van.

Donovan gripped the door to keep it from being used against him a second time and skirted past it. When Jamal grabbed for a backpack in the van, Donovan dove at him and knocked him to the pavement.

Both men grunted as they impacted the unforgiving surface. Donovan blocked an elbow aimed at his head, but he wasn't as successful in avoiding the heel that kicked against his shin. Donovan's grip faltered, and Jamal broke free. He scrambled up and ran onto the sidewalk. Donovan followed, ignoring the throbbing in his shin. No way he was letting this guy get away, especially when he could provide answers about who was after Cas.

Jamal made the mistake of looking behind him. That brief hesitation gave Donovan the second he needed to catch up to him. He grabbed him around the waist and tackled him, but this time, Donovan secured the man's arms and rolled him onto his stomach. He pressed a knee into the man's back, preventing him from slithering away a second time.

Cole approached, hauling the passenger from the van with him, the man's hands secured behind his back.

"Got any handcuffs?" Donovan asked.

"No, but here's a zip tie." Cole passed one to him, his other hand securely gripping his prisoner's arm.

Donovan secured Jamal's hands and pulled him to his feet. "Where's the bomb?"

Jamal didn't respond. Donovan pulled the man toward the back of the van. The door still hung open, and a pair of slender legs clad in fitted jeans were visible beneath it. Cas?

Donovan rounded the van. Cas stood at the back of the van, a pocketknife in her hand and a bomb in front of her.

"You might want to back up," Cas said without turning her head. "We only have twenty-nine seconds left."

Donovan's heartbeat quickened. "What?" The bombers wouldn't have even been inside the station by now.

"The timer jumped forward as soon as I opened the casing." She separated the tangle of wires with her free hand.

"Come on. We need to get out of here."

"Just another second . . ." Cas separated the white wire from a group of colored ones. She slipped the knife beneath it.

"Wait. Not that—" Before Donovan could protest further, Cas cut through the wire and the timer froze.

CHAPTER 18

Cas's breath shuddered out. Twelve seconds to spare. Not exactly the cushion she had planned for, but at least this bomb wasn't going to leave any casualties. The thought of how close she had come to dying crashed over her. Twelve seconds. Her throat clogged, and she struggled for composure. She couldn't show weakness, especially not in public. She fisted her hands to hide how much they were trembling and turned to face the men behind her. Donovan and Bridger both held prisoners beside them.

She identified the man beside Donovan. Jamal Williams.

Jamal's eyes widened. "You are alive."

"I died a long time ago," Cas said, relieved her voice was steady.

Bridger motioned to the now-disarmed explosive device. "You know about bombs? I thought you needed one of us to disarm it."

"You both said you'd need some time to be able to do it. We didn't have time."

"Obviously, she went through explosives training too," Donovan added.

Cas turned her attention to Jamal. "Who's behind this? Is the coalition involved?"

Jamal's lips pressed together.

Donovan jerked his arm. "The lady asked you a question." No response. Sirens sounded in the distance. Donovan turned to Cas. "I hate to say it, but we should get out of here."

"I can handle the authorities," Bridger said.

"Keep an eye on this one." Donovan nudged Jamal toward him. Bridger used his free hand to grab Jamal's arm. As soon as Donovan had both hands free, he dropped onto his stomach and scooted underneath the van.

"What are you doing?" Cas asked.

"I dropped my gun." A moment later, Donovan slid free of the vehicle and stood. He turned to Bridger. "Text us when you're done with the police, and we'll pick you up and take you back to get your car."

"Don't worry about it. I'll stay the night here and then catch a bus or train back to Lille tomorrow."

"I'll be right back." Cas hurried to the car and retrieved a spare cell phone from her purse, then returned to where Donovan and Bridger still stood by the van. She handed Bridger the phone. "If you have any trouble, call one of us on this phone. Our numbers are programmed in. I'm C. He's D."

"Thanks." Bridger pocketed the phone. "And thanks for getting me out of that warehouse."

"Anytime." Cas pointed at Jamal. "When you turn these guys over to the authorities, make sure they know he's associated with the Freedom Coalition. We need to know why they're operating in Europe."

"I'll call you with an update as soon as I know anything," Bridger said.

A police car rounded the corner, the lights flashing.

Donovan touched Cas's elbow, a reminder that they needed to steer clear of the authorities. Together they slipped around the side of the van and made their way to their car.

"Do you want me to drive?" Donovan asked.

"No. It'll be easier if I do." Cas slid behind the wheel and started the car.

As soon as Donovan got in and closed his door, he asked, "Why is it easier if you drive? Because you know your way around here better?"

"That." Cas put the car in gear and started down the road. "And I know where I can get away with speeding without getting caught."

"I noticed."

Cas glanced sideways. "Which means we'll get home faster. I'm ready for bed."

"Just promise me one thing."

"What's that?"

"Remember to brake when you turn the corner."

"I'll consider it."

* * *

Fingers wrapped tightly around the steering wheel, eyes hyperfocused on the road. Cas might look like she had everything under control, but Donovan knew better. She was shaken and trying hard to hide it.

They had already cleared the main part of the city, and residential homes were now on either side of them. Despite her pledge to get them home faster,

Cas had kept her speed right at the limit and had signaled at every turn, more signs that something wasn't quite right.

"Pull over." Donovan pointed at the side of the road.

"Why?"

"Just do it."

Cas checked her mirrors before slowing the car and parking between two houses where the porch lights didn't reach. Donovan climbed out of the car and circled to the driver's side. He opened her door. Not sure how to approach the situation, he adopted a no-nonsense tone. "Come on. My turn to drive."

"I'm perfectly capable of driving."

"I never said you weren't." Donovan offered his hand. She ignored it. "You're upset. That bomb rattled all of us."

"I'm fine." Cas bit off the words.

Though Donovan's inclination was to demand, he lowered his voice. "Please, let me drive."

"Fine." Cas climbed out. The moment she stood, her body trembled.

"Hey." Donovan put his hand on her shoulder, preventing her from moving past him. "Everyone is okay."

Cas blinked rapidly against the tears forming in her eyes. Her gaze lowered to the pavement. Donovan's insides churned, his own emotions still heightened after the near-death experience. But he hadn't been on the frontline watching the seconds tick off. The crisis had already been averted by the time he'd learned how close they had come to getting blown up.

Unable to resist, Donovan slid his finger under Cas's chin, gently applying pressure so she would look at him. Tears swam in her eyes, and embarrassment flashed.

"Thank you. You saved my life tonight," he said.

"Barely," she managed, her voice hoarse.

"You saved my life. You saved Bridger's." Donovan wasn't sure who moved first, but in an instant, Cas was in his arms. Hot tears spilled onto his shirt, her face pressed against his shoulder. A jolt worked through him, shooting from his very core all the way to his fingertips and toes. Cas's hands pressed against his back as though their combined strength could chase away the storm brewing inside her. Her body kept trembling, and a desire to protect her twisted inside him.

His hand trailed over her back as he held her close. How long they stood there on the side of the road, he wasn't sure, but Cas's body finally stilled, and then she pulled away.

She swiped at the tears on her cheeks and let out a frustrated sigh. "I'm sorry. I hate to cry."

"Sometimes you have to let it all out." The cool breeze whipped over him, and Donovan already missed the warmth of having Cas in his arms. Her eyebrows lifted. How she could look confident and teary at the same time was a mystery.

"Somehow, I don't see you having a good cry with Ace or Kade. It just doesn't seem like it would be much fun."

"It wouldn't be as much fun. That's for sure."

"Fun? I doubt any guy having a woman cry all over him would consider it fun."

"I guess it depends on the woman." Donovan nearly reached for her hand, but he stopped himself. Cas was his colleague. They would never live in the same place. Best not to forget that. "You okay?"

"Yeah. The bomb just rattled me." She moved to the passenger side and climbed into the car.

Donovan adjusted the driver's seat and took his place behind the wheel.

When he put the car in gear, Cas reached over and put her hand on his. "Thanks for not making me feel like an idiot."

"No big deal. I owed you."

"For what?"

"Like I said, you saved my life tonight."

"That was a side benefit of saving my own."

"Either way, you did good." Donovan pulled onto the street. "How did you learn about bombs anyway? Cutting the white wire? That wasn't out of some textbook or online tutorial."

"Maybe not, but I've seen a bomb like that before."

"When?"

"The night before the coalition tried to have me killed."

* * *

Cas's lips trembled. She was already embarrassed because Donovan had seen her at her weakest, and her body still tingled every time she so much as thought of the sensation of being in his arms. It hadn't been the strength of his embrace that had gotten to her as much as the quiet understanding the gesture had provided.

Tonight had been such a contrast to the first time she had seen an explosive device up close. The bomb from four years ago had been the Freedom Coalition's way of making a point. At least that was what Kadeem and Lincoln had told her. Cas's part in their plan had been simple. She had just needed to comb through the upcoming stories on Edge Broadcasting's news desk to help the coalition find an event that would be big enough for their purposes.

Donovan's voice cut through the memory. "You can't leave me hanging." He glanced at her before training his gaze on the road once more. "Tell me what happened."

Cas let the memory form. "Kadeem took notice of me because of my father's business." She cringed at how naive she had been only four years ago. "He and the others running things at the coalition wanted help writing press releases and creating content they could use on social media and different news sites."

"Where did the bomb come in?"

"The coalition had started making their own news. They'd take some minor incident and flood social media with exaggerated facts to get the public involved." Cas's stomach dropped at the thought of the coldhearted methods the coalition used. "They'd even hire professional protesters to provoke the cops."

"I heard they were behind the riots a few years ago, after that accidental shooting in Tampa."

Cas nodded. "They were. A truth advocacy group caught on to what they were doing, and Kadeem decided it was time to take things up a notch."

"A bombing."

"Yeah. They told me they were using the bomb to get the local authorities to pay attention and to prove that they were covering real news with real sources. They even said the bomb was just a prop."

"How did you find out it wasn't?" Donovan asked.

"Something didn't feel right." Cas gestured with her hand before letting it rest in her lap again. "I had just left the house they were using as their home base when I realized I left my jacket inside."

Why was she doing this to herself? Why was she forcing herself to relive the moment that had changed everything for her? Could it be the need to expand on the connection she had experienced in Donovan's arms?

She studied him, his strong features, his complete acceptance of her past decisions. "Kadeem was talking to another man. After tonight, I now know it was Wayne Aguilar."

"You saw Aguilar the night you were killed?"

"It wasn't until the next day when I was on my way to meet with the FBI that they ran me off the road, but yeah, I saw him." Cas gripped her hands together. "I hid while Wayne explained to Lincoln how the bomb worked. After I joined the guardians, I made a point to learn more about explosives."

"Your training was as good as anything a CIA agent would have received, if not better."

"I did go through the CIA training when I first became a guardian," Cas said. "Then I trained with the people who teach Navy SEALs."

"You took the civilian *and* the navy route?"

"Something like that."

"I have to ask, How in the world did you get involved with the Freedom Coalition in the first place?"

"I wanted change." She sighed. "I was too blind to see that the change the coalition wanted had nothing to do with creating a better life. In reality, they wanted to hurt and alarm Americans."

"What's their end goal?"

"I've asked myself that a million times. When I originally went through my debriefing when I joined the guardians, we thought it was to create political unrest going into the election."

"And now?" Donovan asked.

"It's been four years. We're coming up on another election. It could be the same thing."

"You don't sound convinced."

"I'm not anymore. Terrorist attacks in Europe don't necessarily have a huge impact on the polls in the US," Cas said. "Besides, if our bomber really was working with Alnaazir, it's possible there's a connection between it and the coalition."

"We've all had suspicions that the coalition is involved with a terrorist group, but no one has ever proven it."

"We may have taken a step in the right direction tonight," Cas said. "I wish we knew more about their motives though."

"Some of these groups create chaos simply for the sake of creating chaos."

Though Cas would never understand such a motive, her years as a guardian proved it was valid. And yet . . . "I think there's more to it than that. Kadeem didn't just advocate for change. He wanted power and wealth. If he hadn't been arrested after I tipped off the FBI, he likely would have run for office."

"As in run for president?"

"I'm not sure. Maybe he would have gone for the senate first, but he had big plans."

"And you messed them up," Donovan said.

"Yes. The question is, What plans did we mess up tonight? And who would have gained from a bomb going off in Brussels?"

"Sounds like we have more research to do tomorrow."

"I'm afraid so."

CHAPTER 19

Rain pattering against his bedroom windows, the give of the mattress beneath him, the scent of bacon in the air. Donovan stretched out a hand and ran it over the empty space beside him. The lack of warmth there struck him for a brief moment. Then he remembered. He didn't have a wife anymore or an infant daughter to cuddle with. He was alone. That stark fact was the main reason he preferred to avoid sleeping in a bed. Even after six years, it was still too easy for his semiconscious mind to jump back in time to when he'd thought his life was perfect.

Metal clanged in the kitchen. Donovan came more fully awake, a flutter stirring inside him. The memory of holding Cas last night flooded his mind, pushing away the regrets of the past. Even though his time with her might very well create a new set of regrets, he was ready to make new mistakes if for no other reason than to chase the old memories away.

He climbed out of bed and tugged on a pair of jeans and a fresh T-shirt. A minute later, he entered the kitchen, and his insides warmed. Cas stood at the stove, her feet clad in thick cotton socks, an oversized dish towel tied around her waist like an apron. A light dusting of makeup enhanced her expressive eyes, her full lips darkened with lipstick. The woman was even more gorgeous this morning than she had been yesterday. How was that possible?

Cas picked up a fork and transferred bacon onto the plate beside her. Another plate was already stacked high with pancakes. His favorite.

"Morning." Donovan retrieved a glass and poured some milk.

Cas glanced over her shoulder. "Are you hungry? Breakfast is ready." She turned off the burner.

"I should check the perimeter before I sit down to eat."

"I already checked it."

"What?" His fingers tightened on his glass. What little sense of security he had gained after their clean escape from Paris had disappeared after last night. "You should stay inside."

"I woke up early." She carried the food to the table. "Besides, with the rain, our street was deserted."

"I'd still prefer you to stay out of sight."

"After last night, I needed to make sure we hadn't been followed."

"I'm sorry. I should have gotten up early to check things out."

"You don't need to babysit me." Cas sat at the table and transferred two pancakes onto her plate. "I hope you like pancakes. I was in the mood for an American breakfast."

Donovan sat beside her. "This looks great."

Cas poured some maple syrup onto her stack.

"I didn't expect you to have syrup here. I thought it was more of an American thing."

"It is, but Ace brought some when he and Kristi moved here from Maine." She passed him the bottle. "They put some in several of our European safe houses."

"How is Kristi doing anyway?" Donovan asked. "Isn't she pretty close to having her baby?"

"She's due in a couple weeks. Yet another reason why my cover getting blown is awful timing," Cas said. "We can't afford to be without an active guardian in Europe."

Donovan took a bite of his pancakes and tasted home. He enjoyed his breakfast in silence while the logistics of moving personnel simmered in his thoughts. "Ace could always have Nolan or Troy come back for a while."

"Maybe, but no matter who comes here, we'll have a part of the world more vulnerable than usual," Cas said. "With the elections coming up this fall, I doubt Ace will want to pull anyone from the States, not with as many attempts as they've had on Senator Whitmore's life." Senator James Whitmore, the top candidate for president and the member of the Senate Intelligence Committee who kept the funds flowing to the guardians.

"If the Freedom Coalition is working toward upsetting the political balance in the US, I have to think Whitmore would be the last person they'd want in office."

"You've got that right. They'll support whichever candidate comes out against him, provided it's someone of color."

"Think they care if it's a man or a woman?"

"As long as it's someone who can win," Cas said. "I've already seen a few articles floating around that were likely planted by the coalition."

"Such as?"

"The usual. Examples of the government trying to take away our rights of anything from free speech to the right to bear arms. Throw those basics in with some unfair labor practices and discrimination and they take real issues and twist them to suit their purposes."

"Maybe Bridger's interrogation of Jamal will give us some insight into their endgame." Donovan took another bite of his pancakes.

"I'd hoped to hear from him by now."

Donovan chewed and swallowed. "Me too. I'll give him a call." He pulled out his phone and dialed the secure phone Cas had given Bridger. It rang six times before going to voice mail. "No answer."

"Maybe he'd rather talk to me."

"Probably, but I think he'd answer my call if he were able to." Donovan barely spoke the words before his phone rang. "This is him." He answered his cell. "Any update on our prisoners?"

"Yes, but you aren't going to like it," Bridger said.

"Let me guess. They lawyered up."

"Yes, but that isn't the problem." Bridger's voice tensed. "Both men are dead. Poisoned."

"What?" Donovan straightened. "You can't be serious. How?"

"The lawyer asked for water for him and his clients. The police think the lawyer brought cyanide with him."

"Was the cyanide self-inflicted?"

"The police aren't sure, but I don't think so. Neither one of those guys looked like they were afraid for their lives when I handed them over to the authorities," Bridger said. "I don't think they had a clue what was coming."

"What do you have on the lawyer?"

"I'm working with the police to get a photo now. I'll text it to you as soon as I get it."

"Thanks," Donovan said.

"No problem."

Donovan debated his current circumstances and took a step toward gathering the information he and Cas needed on Roshaun and Tyrell. "What are the chances you'd be able to spend a couple days in Paris?"

"I'm game. What do you need?"

"Surveillance."

"If you can get me the travel order, I can be there today," Bridger said.

"Where are you now? Brussels or Lille?"

"Brussels," Bridger said. "If I need a car in Paris, I can go to Lille and drive from there. Otherwise, I'll take a train into Paris."

"Take the train. It'll be faster. You can pick up your car after this mission."

"And the travel order?"

"I'll take care of it." Donovan hung up the phone.

"Want to fill me in?" Cas asked.

Donovan replayed the conversation.

"I can't believe this." Cas pushed back from the table and carried her dishes to the sink. "Every time we get a lead, something happens."

"Yes, but I'm going to put Bridger on Roshaun and Tyrell. Maybe he can help us connect the dots."

"It's a good idea to put someone on surveillance, but I'm not sure Bridger will be able to get close enough to get any real intel."

"At this point, I'll take whatever we can get."

* * *

All day, Cas worked beside Donovan and tried not to notice the scent of his aftershave or the way his T-shirt stretched over his athletic physique. She certainly didn't want to remember the sensation of him holding her or the way his voice had soothed away the worst of her memories last night.

They had eaten dinner over an hour before—beef bourguignon, as promised—and now their kitchen resembled a command center. She supposed, in essence, that was exactly what it was.

"You ready for this?" Donovan asked. He adjusted his laptop on the kitchen table so he and Cas would both be able to view the security feed from the hotel elevators.

"I'm all set." Cas studied her screen, which revealed the camera views of the hotel lobby and the valet area.

For the entire two hours Bridger was on the train from Brussels to Paris, the three of them used their secure phones to formulate their plan. Cas still wasn't thrilled that they were focusing on Tyrell instead of Roshaun, but with their limited access, it was the best they could do. Besides, Tyrell drove Roshaun around the city as often as not. They could only hope their bugs and hidden cameras would go undetected and give them much-needed information on both men.

Bridger passed into view, his wireless earphones providing them the ability to communicate.

"You're all clear," Donovan said. "No sign of movement from our targets."

The targets, meaning Tyrell, Roshaun, her parents, and her sister. Cas couldn't believe she was spying on her own family.

Bridger passed out of the hotel camera's view and disappeared into a stairwell. The communication cut out for a moment, but after fifteen seconds, Bridger's voice came over the phone. "Entering the garage. Am I clear?"

"Affirmative," Donovan said.

"I wish we had a view of the car," Cas said.

Bridger's voice sounded again. "It's better for me that you don't have one."

He was right. While Cas and Donovan couldn't monitor Bridger's progress on camera, no one from the hotel staff would see him either.

A click carried over the phone. "I'm in."

Nerves fluttered in Cas's stomach. "I hate being on the surveillance end."

"Me too."

"I've got the first camera installed," Bridger said. "Check the feed."

Cas quickly activated the camera, and an image of the interior of a car popped onto her screen. "You're good."

Donovan straightened. "I've got activity coming from the penthouse elevator."

Cas trained her gaze on the elevator doors as they slid open. Makayla walked in, followed by Roshaun. He put his hand on Makayla's back as though he wanted to maintain a connection to her. "Be advised, we have two targets coming down the elevator," Cas said.

"I've almost got the second camera installed," Bridger said. "How much time do I have?"

"If they come to the garage, forty-five seconds. A minute tops."

Another elevator stopped on the fifth floor. Tyrell stepped inside.

"Get out of there," Donovan said. "You've got another one headed your way."

"Thirty more seconds," Bridger said.

Cas calculated the time it would take Tyrell to reach the underground garage, plus the few seconds to walk to the car. "You've only got fifteen seconds."

"Almost done." Victory sounded in his voice a moment later when he said, "Got it."

A second later another camera view popped up.

The elevator carrying Tyrell reached the garage level.

"Get out of there," Donovan said.

Bridger went silent.

The second elevator reached the garage. "We're blind," Donovan said. "They're in the garage but out of our view."

Cas muted the phone and adjusted the sound from the hidden cameras. Footsteps clicked against concrete. "That has to be them."

A beep followed and then locks clicking open. Makayla slid into the back seat of the car, and Cas got her first good look at her sister in four years. Thick mascara lengthened her already long lashes, her lips were painted a dark berry color, and her tight black curls had been teased back from her face. The natural bond Cas had always shared with Makayla snaked around her heart and squeezed.

"Wow. My sister is even prettier than I remembered."

"She looks a lot like you." Donovan's compliment may have been subtle, but it also brought with it a flood of memories from her teenage and college years. Everyone had always compared Cas to her sister, from the paparazzi to their friends. Only their parents had avoided pitting one sister against another. Perhaps that was how she and Makayla had managed to stay close despite others trying to cause problems between them.

On camera, Roshaun took the seat beside Makayla, who now sat in the center. As soon as their driver took his place behind the wheel and they had both buckled their seat belts, Roshaun slid his arm around Makayla's shoulders, his fingers teasing the ends of her hair.

A sick sensation squeezed at Cas and sank into the pit of her stomach. She looked away.

Donovan put his hand on hers. He gave it a squeeze as though he understood the turmoil swirling inside her, but his voice was businesslike when he spoke. "I haven't seen or heard any sign of Bridger."

The engine started, and Cas unmuted the phone. As soon as the car pulled away, Donovan asked, "Bridger, you there?"

"Yeah, I'm here." A frustrated sigh carried over the line. "Does either of you know how to get oil out of your clothes?"

Donovan shook his head. "Did you hide under their car?"

"No. Are you crazy? They might have run me over." Bridger paused. "I hid under the car next to theirs."

"Sounds like you need to do some shopping before you leave Paris."

"I hate shopping."

Sympathy stirred inside Cas. Her father had often made the same comment. Shaking the image of Makayla and Roshaun aside, she said, "Text me your sizes, and I'll have some fresh clothes delivered to your hotel tonight."

"You can do that?" Bridger asked.

"Yeah. Shopping happens to be one of my superpowers." One she didn't get to indulge in nearly often enough.

"I'll owe you big-time if you can keep me away from the mall."

"After your work tonight, I think we can call it even," Cas said. After she ended the call, she forced herself to look at the images of Roshaun and Makayla on her screen.

Donovan turned the laptop around so she could no longer see it. "I'll keep an eye on their movements. I don't want you to have to watch your sister with your ex."

"I'm fine."

"Cas, you don't have anything to prove." Donovan squeezed her hand again. "Let me do this for you."

"Fine." She stood and left the kitchen, crossing through the living room to reach the entryway. The front door beckoned her outside, but she resisted the temptation. Even if her concern for her safety hadn't trapped her inside, the steady rain would have. She glanced up the stairs. Nothing up there for her besides a place to sleep and a change of clothes.

Footsteps approached, and a hand came down on her shoulder. "Hey, I didn't mean to chase you off. I just know how hard it is to see someone you loved with someone else."

Cas turned to face him. The compassion in his eyes diluted her frustration. "You're talking about your ex-wife and your daughter."

"Yes." His hand slid down her arm to her elbow. "Come on. Let's go sit on the couch and find a movie to watch or something."

"I thought you were going to watch Roshaun and Makayla."

"We've worked hard enough today. I texted Kade and asked him and Renee to take over for tonight."

Oddly relieved to have someone beside her, Cas lifted her gaze to his. Her heart fluttered, and a yearning she hadn't experienced in years rose within her. "This almost feels like you're asking me out on a date."

"I think I'm asking you to stay in for a date." Donovan kept his gaze on her. "Do you mind?"

"No. I think I'd like that."

"Great." He released her arm and took her hand in his. "You pick a movie. I'll grab the cookies and milk."

"No popcorn?"

"Sorry. You didn't tell me to buy any."

"I'll have you pick some up tomorrow."

"More shopping?" Donovan groaned.

"Unless you'd rather not have a second date."

He stared at her for a brief moment before humor flashed in his eyes. "I'll go to the store first thing tomorrow."

CHAPTER 20

For two days, Donovan watched surveillance video on Tyrell and Roshaun. He'd moved back into the living room so Cas wouldn't constantly have the images nearby when she was cooking and baking. One thing he had learned during his time living in the same house as her: the more stressed the woman was, the more time she spent in the kitchen. The freezer now had an ample supply of cookies, muffins, dinner rolls, and homemade strawberry jam.

At the moment, the scent of her fancy grilled cheese sandwiches hung heavy in the air. The woman was amazing, and not only in the kitchen. Her sense of humor when she'd let herself relax for more than thirty seconds at a time, her sharp mind, and her stunning looks. Even the way she could go from blend-in beautiful to runway-model gorgeous fascinated him.

Ironically, while his ex-wife had never dressed up unless there was a special occasion, Cas seemed to enjoy spending time on her clothes and makeup even when she wasn't going anywhere. How Roshaun had managed to get over her, even after four years, was beyond Donovan, but the man had clearly moved on. On the surveillance video, Roshaun and Makayla were frequent passengers in the car Tyrell drove. That fact had pushed Donovan to keep this task solely to himself.

It hadn't been hard to convince Cas that her time was better spent searching for questionable news stories that might have been created by the Alnaazir or the coalition or the person she called the Newsmaker. With each day, she became more convinced the stories might be a coordinated effort by all three.

On Donovan's screen, Roshaun opened the car door and Makayla slid out behind him.

Cas walked into the living room. "Any luck with the surveillance?"

"Nothing suspicious yet."

Frustration flashed on Cas's face but was quickly gone. "Want to take a break? Lunch is ready."

"That sounds great." Donovan hit the button to pause the live feed so he'd know where to start up again after lunch.

Cas headed into the kitchen and waved at her laptop on the counter beside the stove. "I found a bunch of planted articles, but the topics are so scattered, I can't be sure they're even by the same group."

"You were searching news sites while cooking?"

"What can I say? I'm a multitasker."

"And you're good at it." Donovan glanced at the kitchen table, which had been set like something out of *Better Homes & Gardens*. At least, he was pretty sure that was what the magazine was called that his mom used to read when she was looking for decorating ideas. White dishes, bright-yellow place mats, a cluster of delicate red and purple flowers. "Wow. You went all out."

Cas opened a drawer and retrieved a hot pad. "If I can't go outside, I can at least change things up in here."

"As long as we don't have to move the couch again."

"No guarantees on that." She pulled a cookie sheet from the oven and transferred a croque monsieur onto each of their plates.

"Where did the flowers come from?"

"The cabinet above the refrigerator." She touched a bloom. "They're plastic."

"Could have fooled me." He waited for Cas to sit before he took the seat beside her. "This is great. Thank you."

"You're welcome. Making lunch was a nice distraction. No one has come up with anything useful over the past couple days, and I'm worried the bomb we stopped in Brussels might not be the only other one out there."

"I've had the same thought." Donovan picked up his sandwich and took a bite. He pondered the results of Cas's search for a moment. "Maybe your Newsmaker, Alnaazir, and the coalition are all using the same tactics."

"It's possible. All of these planted articles are using the same back door." Cas took a sip of her water. "It's either the same organization behind all of these, or they're all hiring the same guy to get their stories out there."

"Your first option is the most likely."

"I think so too."

"Can I ask you a personal question?" Donovan asked.

"You can ask."

Which meant she might not answer. Though he knew he was pushing the lines between professional and personal, he asked, "Were you and Roshaun engaged when you had your accident?"

"No."

"But you dated for a long time."

"Yes. Almost three years." Cas took a bite of her sandwich. She brushed a crumb from her beautifully full lips. "I think that's one of the things that threw me off about Roshaun and Makayla. From what I could tell on social media, they've been together less than a year."

"But she already has a ring on her finger."

Cas nodded. "Kind of fast, don't you think?"

"Maybe for some people, but every situation is different," Donovan said gently. "Could be that losing you has made them afraid of not grabbing life while they can."

A little crease formed between her eyebrows. "Maybe."

"How did the two of you meet?"

"At college. I was a cheerleader. He was on the basketball team. Everyone thought we were the perfect couple." She shrugged. "Obviously not."

Guilt pricked at Donovan for bringing up a painful subject. As much to distract her as to gain more information, he said, "Tell me about the articles. You said they were on a lot of different topics?"

"Yeah. One is on term limits in congress; another is about research grants for pharmaceutical companies. I even found one on grazing rights in Montana."

"Those are all over the board."

"Yeah, and none of them have anything to do with our relationships with any European countries."

"The more we dig, the less we know."

"I hate research projects that work this way."

"Me too."

* * *

Cas read through the article Elle had written for her. The woman really did have a way with words. If successful, the few hours Elle had spent crafting this news piece would result in the protests getting canceled this weekend. Now to plant it in the right spots to garner public attention.

She glanced over her shoulder. Through the glass walls of the atrium, she could see Donovan on the couch in the living room, his eyes on his computer screen. He rolled his head to one side and then to the other as though trying to work out the kinks from sitting too long. She understood that feeling all too well.

Without looking, Donovan retrieved a cookie off the plate beside his laptop and took a bite. He hummed in appreciation. The man really did love his food.

Reining in her thoughts, she turned back to her screen. Hadn't she deliberately moved her workstation to this side of the table so Donovan wouldn't constantly be in her line of sight? He was too attractive, too understanding, and far too appreciative to be ignored without some effort. In truth, the man was a distraction she wanted but couldn't afford.

She had barely regained her focus when he walked into the kitchen. "This last batch of cookies may have been your best yet."

"Thanks." Cas swiveled in her seat. She had made alfajores this morning when she'd needed to settle her thoughts. To make them last longer this time, she had hidden some of them in the freezer. There was no way Donovan would go searching through frozen vegetables to find a snack.

Donovan set his empty plate on the counter and opened the plastic bag of cookies to grab three. "Do you want any?"

"I'll take one." Cas stood and reached into the bag he held out.

"I don't know how you can eat just one."

"Discipline." Cas held it up. "That and I know I can always make more."

"I know you said your family chef taught you how to cook. Did you ever consider pursuing a career in culinary arts? Maybe open your own restaurant?"

"No. Cooking has always been an escape for me, something to do when I need to clear my head. I don't think I could handle it if it ever started feeling like a job."

"Maybe it wouldn't ever get that way. You've heard the saying that if you choose a job you love, you'll never work a day in your life."

"I've heard that. My dad is a great example of it, but after watching Antoine's love of cooking fade over the years, I decided not to go down that road."

"Your family chef doesn't like to cook?"

"I wouldn't say he doesn't like it. I think it's more that he wanted to have more time to explore other interests too." Cas took a bite of her cookie. "What about you? I doubt being a guardian was the job you aspired to."

"Actually, it's pretty close. I like helping people, and I enjoy the research."

"I can't imagine you enjoy nearly getting blown up."

"No, but I want to make a difference in the world. Sometimes, to do that, it means facing some danger along the way." He leaned back against the counter and crossed his ankles. "You handle yourself well enough in those situations."

"I guess, but it isn't something I would have chosen for myself."

"What would you have chosen?"

"I don't know. I enjoyed working at the TV studio, but I always assumed I'd follow in my mom's footsteps."

"Which are?"

"Being a wife, a mother. Spending my time and money trying to make the world a better place."

"You're already making the world a better place." Donovan's eyes connected with hers and held. "It's not too late for you to have everything else you want. I mean, look at Ace and Kristi. They never thought they'd have the chance to be together, much less have a family."

"Yes, but all of the guardians who are in relationships are men."

"I hate to break it to you, but until the new girl came on, you were the only female guardian. Besides, what does being a woman have to do with you having a family?"

"Kristi isn't in hiding. Neither is Renee, or Elle. They can go to a hospital and have a baby without complicating anything beyond naming the father. That isn't the case for me."

"I guess, but anything is possible."

"Even now, when people know I'm alive? I don't think so."

Donovan took her hand. The familiar ripple of attraction shot up her arm and speared right to her heart.

"Don't close yourself off to the possibilities. If you can't see your future the way you want it, maybe it's time to invent a new way to get to where you want to be."

"That's sweet but overly simplistic."

"Most solutions are simple. People make them complicated."

Donovan's words rushed through her. "Solutions are simple." Her mind raced. "I need some paper or some index cards."

Donovan's forehead creased in confusion, but he opened the junk drawer and held up a square of yellow sticky notes. "How about some Post-it Notes?"

"That'll work." Cas leaned over and grabbed a pen. "I'll need your help."

"To do what?"

"To find our real list of suspects."

* * *

Yellow notes covered the glass wall between the kitchen and the atrium. Cas wrote another headline on her pad and added yet another note to the glass.

"All of these stories are random. Unconnected," Donovan said.

"Exactly. Why would someone go to all the trouble of hacking into news stations to post an article on health care reform and then, two days later, upload something on retirement cuts for federal employees?"

"I have no idea."

Cas's face came alive. "Even though these topics are random, the political motivation behind them isn't."

"I'm not following."

Cas plucked one note off the wall and aligned it with another. She moved several more before she stepped back. "See any correlations now?"

Environmental concerns. Known toxins allowed in food. In another column, articles on advances in health care in various parts of the world were listed beside others about rising medical costs in the United States and the lobbying power of the pharmaceutical companies.

"These all cluster into political ideals."

"Exactly."

"This is great, but how do we narrow it down to one group? Some of these articles cross party lines."

"I know. And all of these views aren't consistent with the coalition."

"Are you sure?"

"The leadership never worried about things like grazing rights or the cost of a heart transplant in India," Cas said. "Their entire focus was creating unrest to advance minorities, eliminate racial inequality, and reduce the poverty levels in inner cities."

"Other than the creating-unrest part, all of those goals are worthy."

"They are, but the bombing attempt that ultimately led to my death is proof that they had taken things too far."

"How do we narrow this down?" Donovan moved a couple more notes, clustering together three about US military presence in the Middle East. "Do you think it's possible a group splintered off after you left them?"

"That, or maybe they've changed their goals." Cas took a step back. Excitement filled her voice when she added, "One of the things Jamal always talked about was utilizing others' beliefs to get them to align with our own. I think this is the big picture of that plan."

"So they plant articles to get people worked up about different political issues as a way to create change within our governmental structure."

"That's what they were trying to do when I was with them, but they never could get much done, especially under the two-party system. Both political parties have the power to make it very difficult for a candidate to succeed if it's someone they don't support."

"This looks like they're escalating their efforts."

"Yes, but why? What's different now? Or what are they planning that will make things different?"

"We have to find a way to narrow this down," Donovan said. "I think our best bet is to focus on the known coalition members. Let's see who falls in line with the political views in these articles."

"If you work on that, I'll try to break down the linguistic patterns of the writing. I should be able to at least determine what part of the country the writer is from."

"Do you think these are all written by the same person?"

"I haven't analyzed them all, but the cadence and word usage are consistent," Cas said.

"That's impressive."

"It'll be more impressive if between the two of us, we can figure out who our writer is."

"The articles you've shown me are pretty well written," Donovan said.

"Yeah. I thought so too."

"Maybe whoever this is has also published elsewhere."

"It wouldn't surprise me, but searching for similar writing styles with all that's out there will be like searching for peanut butter in Hong Kong."

A sticky note fell from the glass. Both Cas and Donovan leaned over to pick it up. Cas got there first. When she straightened, her body was close to his, the scent of her raspberry soap mixing with the lingering smell of freshly baked bread from breakfast this morning. Donovan's mouth went dry, and he struggled to pull his thoughts from the gorgeous eyes staring up at him.

He swallowed and grasped at the last tendrils of their conversation. "I've never searched for peanut butter in Hong Kong."

"I have." Her voice had gone husky. She cleared her throat and stepped back. "Trust me. It's not an experience worth repeating."

"Maybe not." Against his better judgment, Donovan edged closer. "But if you want something bad enough, you have to try, right?"

Her eyes lifted to his. "Yeah. I suppose you do."

CHAPTER 21

Donovan was driving her crazy. Those long, intense stares, the subtle brushes of his arm against hers when they worked together, the unique musky scent of aftershave and soap. Cas had never considered this safe house to be small, but with the undertones of attraction simmering between them, it wasn't nearly large enough for her to keep a safe distance. If only Donovan would demonstrate some annoying qualities that would undermine her growing fascination with him, but so far, that wasn't happening. The man even did the dishes.

Cas analyzed yet another article and debated what to fix for dinner. Too bad they couldn't go out to eat for a change. Then again, maybe she should appreciate her current situation. The rhythm of their time together created a comfort and a combined sense of purpose she hadn't shared with anyone in years. In truth, even Roshaun hadn't been this easy to be around. Donovan didn't seem to care whether she dressed up, dressed down, cooked, or relied on leftovers. The man was entirely too easygoing, and he was making her yearn for dreams best left buried.

How Donovan had accepted the loss of his daughter in his life, Cas didn't know, but she couldn't help but admire the way he accepted his current situation and made the best of it.

The front door opened, and Donovan walked in from his latest perimeter sweep, a plastic shopping bag dangling from one hand. He continued through the living room to the kitchen. "Did you already start on dinner?"

"Not yet. I'm not really in the mood to cook."

"Good. While I was out, I picked up some banh mi from the Vietnamese place down the street." Donovan set the bag of sandwiches on the table in front of her. "Not that these are anything like your cooking, but I thought you might need a break."

How had he known? He picked up her empty water glass beside her computer. "Do you want more water or something else to drink?"

"Water's fine. Thanks."

"No problem." He filled her glass and poured milk into another for himself. As soon as he sat across from her, he pulled four sub-shaped sandwiches out of the bag.

She selected one and unwrapped it. "What all is in this?"

"Meat, carrots, cucumber, cilantro."

All foods she liked. She took a bite. Instantly, her tongue caught on fire, and her eyes burned. She hastily swallowed and grabbed her water.

"And jalapeños."

Cas gulped more water and blinked against the tears in her eyes. When the sensation of spiciness faded, she glared at Donovan.

He gave her a sheepish grin. "Sorry. Really." He opened his sandwich and plucked out three slices of jalapeño. "I usually tell them not to put those on, but I couldn't remember how to say *peppers* in French."

"You could have said *jalapeño*."

"Yeah. I guess that would have worked." He motioned to her sandwich. "There should be two more in there."

Cas opened her sandwich and fished them out. "Let's try this again." She bit into the soft bread, this time appreciating the contrast of crunch along with the delicately flavored chicken. "Much better without the peppers."

"Glad you like it." He wiped at a bit of sauce on his lip. "How's the analysis going?"

"It's a lot harder than I expected," Cas admitted. "On the plus side, I put Elle's article up, and already, it's hitting the news that the protests for tomorrow have been canceled."

"I can't imagine whoever was behind those planted stories is going to be happy about that."

"I'm sure they're not. Kade is monitoring the different websites for the news services so he can delete any new planted articles that might counteract our efforts."

"That ought to keep him busy for a while."

"Yeah. He roped Renee into helping him too."

"What do you know so far about our mystery writer?"

"Best guess is our writer is multilingual. The articles span French, Spanish, and English, but they don't feel like they're being translated so much as rewritten into a new version."

"What else?"

"Our guy is educated, but there are odd gaps every once in a while."

"What do you mean 'gaps'?" Donovan took a bite.

"It's hard to explain. It's almost like someone who is writing a college paper, but they missed a key source, so part of the information is missing."

"Any idea what this guy's primary language is?"

"My guess is French."

"Then maybe we aren't dealing with an American after all."

"I didn't say that. I learned to speak French before I learned English. At least, that's what my parents said."

"You were raised in Louisiana." Donovan's eyes lit up. "Could our writer be from there too? Tyrell grew up in Shreveport, and Roshaun is from St. Martin's Parish."

"Tyrell isn't a native French speaker. He can communicate if he has to, but it isn't pretty."

"So he's not our writer."

"No."

"And Roshaun?"

Cas's heart sank. "Roshaun speaks French."

"And Spanish?"

"Yes, Spanish too."

* * *

The glorious scent of bacon sizzling filled the kitchen. Donovan tried to ignore the grumbling in his stomach so he could focus on the latest development, a development that would change Cas's life completely. Using headphones, he played the interview on his screen. Roshaun was conducting it, and his interviewee was none other than Cas's father.

Donovan didn't know much about Josiah Edgemont, but one thing was certain: he loved his daughter, and he would stop at nothing to find her. Today, that included a hefty reward for information leading to locating Cas. Donovan glanced over his shoulder to where Cas stood at the counter with a knife in her hand.

She chopped some kind of herb, probably the parsley or thyme she'd had him buy at the store. Or maybe it was both. Without measuring, she added the herbs to the cast-iron pan in front of her. Donovan studied the photo on the screen. Cas's hair had been much shorter before she'd joined the guardians, her features enhanced by makeup and a designer dress. She carried herself as though she knew someone would take her picture, her confidence evident.

Despite her efforts to blend into her surroundings since becoming a guardian, the resemblance to her former self couldn't be missed. Donovan fisted his hand and gathered his courage. She deserved to know the truth. "Cas, as much as I hate to interrupt you while you're cooking, you're going to want to see this."

"What?" She gave the contents of the pan another stir before turning the burner down and setting the spoon aside.

"Your father has taken his search public."

Cas's face paled. "He didn't."

"I'm afraid so." He clicked on the newscast, and her father's voice filled the room.

"Four years ago, my family and I were informed of a tragic accident that claimed my daughter's life. Cassidy's body was never found. We now have new information that she may still be alive. I'm pleading for anyone with information about her whereabouts to contact the authorities as soon as possible."

Donovan stopped the recording. "He waited a week before going public. You have to give him that."

"Please don't tell me there's a reward."

Donovan couldn't imagine what turmoil Cas was going through, but he couldn't withhold the truth. "To use your words, I wish I could, but I'd be lying."

Her jaw clenched, and she blinked rapidly, as though something were in her eye. "How much?"

"A quarter of a million euros."

She turned back toward the stove. "At least he's starting small."

"A quarter of a million is small?"

"It is for him." She picked up her spoon.

"I hate to break it to you, but that's still enough to get most people's attention," Donovan said. "How many people do you think will remember you well enough to offer information?"

"I don't know. The only people I've had any real contact with are the operatives I've helped over the years."

"None of them are going to blow your cover."

"At this point, my cover is nonexistent." Her breath shuddered out. "I'll never be able to work in Europe again, at least not western Europe, and I don't have the language skills to live in eastern Europe."

"Or the wardrobe. It's cold in those countries." His attempt to distract her from the gravity of her situation didn't work, so he tried again. "You could always come to Africa. There are plenty of countries that speak English and French."

"Sorry, but I'm not interested in living in some desert country where women have to cover their faces even when it's over a hundred degrees outside."

"There are plenty of countries that don't follow Islam." Donovan held up his arm and pointed at his dark skin. "We have the advantage of being able to blend in."

"The color of my skin might help me look like I belong, but my attitude wouldn't." Cas added sliced carrots to the pot and stirred. "Not to mention, I prefer indoor plumbing. Hiding out in some rural village in Burundi isn't in my plans."

"I was thinking the Democratic Republic of the Congo, but if you want a more developed home base, I think Kenya would be more to your taste."

"Are you trying to distract me with elephants?"

"Maybe. Is it working?"

"Not really, but it was a good try." Cas continued to add ingredients to the pot. When she didn't speak for several minutes, he retrieved his playlist off his computer. A moment later, the sweet music of Miles Davis filled the silence.

Cas glanced at him. "You like jazz too?"

"What's not to like?" Donovan stood and moved to her side. "It must have been great growing up in New Orleans with all of the fantastic musicians down there."

"Believe it or not, I got to listen to more jazz when I lived in New York. Papa didn't like me hanging around the French Quarter, especially at night."

"Rough neighborhood?"

"Lots of tourists, lots of drinking. Not exactly the kind of area my father wanted me hanging out in, especially by myself."

A flash of regret shot through him as he thought of his own daughter. "All fathers are protective of their little girls."

"I suppose that's true." Cas stirred the last ingredients into the others and used two hot pads to transfer the pot into the oven. She leaned back against the counter so she was facing him. "What am I going to do? I can't contact my family, or they could be in danger, but if my father keeps broadcasting my picture all over the place, he could end up on the coalition's radar anyway."

"Maybe we should use our contacts with the CIA to get a message to your dad."

"We can't send anyone in who is intelligence, especially someone who might be undercover. News is my father's business. He won't be satisfied unless he knows the whole truth."

"Then maybe we give him the truth, at least as much as we can." Donovan tapped a finger on the counter. "Your father is well known. What if we arrange for the US ambassador to France to have him over for dinner? We could then pass a message to your father through the ambassador to explain why you went into hiding."

"It's not a bad idea, but I'm not sure that will appease him."

"He's going to want proof that you're alive."

"Yes."

"We could try a secure conference call after their dinner," Donovan suggested.

"Assuming I can convince him not to tell anyone else I'm really alive," Cas said. "I'm sure he'll have Tyrell with him, and I can't imagine the ambassador would be able to invite my father without including the rest of my family."

"He could invite just your parents."

Cas leaned her head back and looked toward the ceiling. "This is such a mess, and all because I went to the wrong bakery."

"We all run the risk of a chance meeting with someone from our past. As hard as we try to avoid places we might be recognized, the world is a small place."

"And getting smaller."

"We have a while before dinner is ready. Let's see what else we can find on your family's movements and if anyone intersects with the coalition."

"I need a change of scenery. Want to work outside for a while?"

"Sure. Do you want me to bring the music?"

"Yes." Cas picked up her laptop and headed for the atrium. "We both need to think."

CHAPTER 22

Cas could only imagine the anguish her family was going through all because of her. Her insides twisted at the knowledge that her family and friends had already grieved her death. For them to now find hope amid so much uncertainty only proved that fate could be cruel.

Sitting across the table from Donovan in the atrium, she searched yet again for anything that would connect Tyrell or Roshaun to the men who had shown up at her apartment or anyone else known to associate with the coalition or the bomber who had been arrested. Even though several guardians had helped in the search, no one had found anything definitive that tied them to either of the bombings or the coalition.

The invitation for dinner at the embassy this coming Tuesday had gone out to her family. Cas prayed they would accept. If they did, in three days' time, her family would finally know she was really alive.

"You've been watching surveillance on Tyrell and Roshaun for days. Are you sure there isn't anything suspicious?" she asked Donovan.

"Nothing."

"Obviously, whoever was working with Ezra and Jamal must be using burner phones. Otherwise we would have found something by now."

"I agree. We need to find a new angle."

"Whoever is running the coalition is good. The guardians couldn't crack the hierarchy four years ago, and we aren't any closer now to identifying the people in charge, even after throwing half our resources at searching for them."

"We're more motivated now," Donovan said.

Motivated to keep her alive. His unspoken words rang out over Billie Holiday's sultry voice. Cas's thoughts drifted to the possibility of seeing her parents, even if it was just on a screen. Revealing her role with the guardians, or even that the guardian program existed, would never be approved, but barring government secrets, at least her parents would know that she was indeed alive.

If she and the other guardians could identify the people leading the coalition, she might even be able to go back to her old life. She shook that thought away. She couldn't give in to dreams when she was in as much danger now as she had been four years ago. "This has to be killing my parents. I hate knowing I'm putting them through so much."

"We'll find a way to get word to them." Donovan put a reassuring hand on her arm. "I already outlined our plan to involve the ambassador and put it on the message board. If Ace approves it, you could talk to your parents as early as Tuesday night."

"I can't even imagine." For so many years, she had lived with the truth that if she tried to communicate with her family, the likelihood of her surviving the day was less than one percent. She prayed Donovan's idea would work. Her parents needed to call off the search for her, or she really would end up dead. No parents should ever have to bury their child. To do so twice was unthinkable.

Cas's phone rang, and she checked the caller ID. "It's Bridger." She clicked on the Talk button. "This is Ghost."

"Shouldn't you let me call you Cassidy now that your photo is all over the news?" Bridger asked.

Cas sucked in a breath. "What do you want? I hope you're above trying to collect a reward."

The moment the words left her mouth, Donovan straightened, his eyes searching hers.

"As it turns out, I actually don't need the money," Bridger said.

"That's a relief." And it was.

"I'm calling to let you know we intercepted another bomb."

"How? Where?"

"Jasmine tracked the movements of Wayne Aguilar when he was in Barcelona. A couple of local agents found a bomb locked in a warehouse not far from the docks."

"Any idea what the target was?"

"Looks like it was another train station."

"What about the people responsible?"

"I'm afraid they didn't survive to meet with their lawyer." The flat tone in Bridger's voice spoke louder than his words. The man clearly didn't like killing in self-defense any more than she did. "I'll text you their photos. We're still working on their IDs. Their fingerprints weren't in our system."

"Anything else?"

"We're still processing the warehouse for fingerprints, but we didn't find anything that pointed at any future targets or what group they're associated with."

"We need to know if there are other bombs out there."

"The agency is trying to follow the money, but Aguilar was notorious for operating with cash."

"Let me know if you find anything else," Cas said.

"Will do, Cassidy." The oddity of hearing her real name struck her. He wasn't a threat, she reminded herself. Bridger was intel. He understood enough to keep her secret. She hoped.

A touch of humor seeped into Bridger's voice when he added, "I'll give you a call if I decide to collect on that reward."

Her tension eased. "Thanks."

"Least I can do," Bridger said. "Let me know if you find any leads on the photos I send you."

"I will," Cas said. "And, Bridger?"

"Yeah?"

"My friends call me Cas."

As soon as she hung up, Donovan said, "Bridger saw the news?"

"He promised to warn me before he collects a reward." The concern on Donovan's face caused Cas to put her hand on his arm. "He was kidding."

"He'd better be."

The flare of protectiveness caught Cas off guard. Or was that jealousy? Her phone chimed. "Bridger is sending me photos. The CIA found another bomb in Barcelona." She pulled up the images, and Donovan leaned closer.

A photo of a Caucasian man in his forties popped up first. "Do you recognize him?" Donovan asked.

"No." She scrolled to the next image. Ezra. "But I know him."

"He was at your apartment."

"We've got to find more information on who is running the coalition. I don't know why they're operating in Europe, but this proves they're the ones behind these bombings."

"Text what you know about Ezra to Bridger. Let's get the CIA's help on this," Donovan said. "I'm calling Ace. It's time we see if the FBI or any other intelligence agencies have information they aren't sharing."

"We have access to everyone's databases."

"Yes, but someone has to know something. We just have to find out who."

* * *

Donovan waited until Cas went to bed before he called Kade. "Let me guess," Kade answered in his typical sarcastic tone. "You need another favor."

"It's like you're a mind reader." Donovan stepped into the atrium to ensure Cas wouldn't overhear his conversation. "I need more information on the coalition than what we're finding in the FBI and CIA databases."

"You think someone has a closed file on them?"

"I do. There hasn't been any new information for almost a year." Donovan paced across the glass-encased space. "Someone has to have an open investigation going."

"If they aren't updating information in the database, either someone is undercover or they suspect someone is leaking information."

Awareness dawned. "Cas has always assumed her ex-boyfriend told the coalition that she was meeting with the FBI. What if someone in the FBI was behind the leak?"

"I looked into that possibility back when she first joined the guardians."

"Any suspects?"

"Hold on a sec. Let me pull up the file." Kade fell silent for a moment. "Here we go. The only person I could identify who knew Cas was coming in was Doug Valdez. I also looked into Marsha Parham, the person who took her initial call."

"And nothing flagged?"

"No. Marsha has been with the bureau for twenty years, and from what Cas told me, the woman didn't know what she was coming in for anyway."

"And Valdez?"

"I checked his call log from the time Cas made her appointment until she was run off the road. Nothing flagged that was out of the ordinary. Calls to family and other agents."

"Wait. Valdez. Why does that name sound familiar?" Donovan asked.

"You probably saw it on the message board when we brought Nolan into the program. Valdez was the FBI agent who helped stage Nolan's death."

Suspicion rose. "So he knows about the guardians."

"Yeah, but the guy is as squeaky clean as they get. He's even tight with the Whitmore family."

"Maybe Valdez is where we should start," Donovan said. "If he was the one who was supposed to take Cas's statement, he might also know who is actively investigating the coalition within the FBI."

"I'll track him down. If he can't help, I'll reach out to Charlie Whitmore and my other contacts within the bureau."

"Let me know if you're able to shake something loose. With Cas's family blasting her picture all over the news, she isn't safe here in Europe."

"Maybe it's time for her to move to Africa," Kade suggested. "If she were living in an Islamic country, she could wear a niqab, and no one would see her face."

A burst of hope bubbled inside Donovan before reality popped it. "You really think Cas could live like that? Even if she weren't hindered by language and cultural barriers, as a woman she would be too limited to be very effective in the Islamic countries."

"You're right. That would be tough on her if she had to live that way for more than a week or two at a time."

Even as Kade agreed with him, regret overwhelmed him. Whatever connection Donovan had experienced with Cas during their time together, eventually they would go their separate ways. His focus now needed to be on making sure Cas was still living and breathing when he had to leave.

"I'll put whatever I find on the message board," Kade said.

"I'd rather you call me."

"It's already late in Europe. You want me to wake you up in the middle of the night?"

"If you have answers for me, then yeah."

"Okay. Suit yourself, but if your phone wakes Cas up, you get to deal with her."

Deal with Cas? Anticipation fluttered in his stomach. "Not a problem."

CHAPTER 23

Doug didn't believe in ghosts, but when one popped up right in front of him, he could hardly ignore its existence. His plan to beat the evening rush hour home from the office disintegrated into a knot of uncertainty. If a ghost were here, what world-changing event was about to happen?

The dark-haired man emerged from the shadows of the parking garage and walked to the other side of Doug's car. "I need a favor."

"What kind of favor?" Doug asked.

"Information." Ghost motioned to his car. "Maybe we should take the conversation inside."

Doug unlocked his car and slid behind the wheel. Ghost took the seat beside him.

"What's all this about? In my experience with the guardians, you had a pretty good finger on the pulse of the intelligence community."

"Yes, but someone in the FBI is keeping information out of your database. I'm hoping it's you," Ghost said. "I need the latest information about the coalition."

Doug tensed. How did this man know to come to him?

"I know you were the one who was supposed to meet with Cassidy Edgemont the day she was killed."

"According to her father, she's still alive."

"I can't confirm that, but if it were true, you can imagine her safety would be greatly jeopardized if the coalition isn't stopped before it's too late."

"Look, I appreciate your interest in this case, but I can't just hand over classified information without authorization."

"I had a feeling you might say that." Ghost pulled out his phone and dialed.

"Who are you calling?"

"Senator Whitmore."

"I know he's on the Senate Intelligence Committee, but he can't authorize the release of classified material."

Ghost ignored him. "Senator, can you have an authorization emailed to Doug Valdez? I need everything he has on the Freedom Coalition." He paused. "Better make it a blanket release. We don't want the wrong keyword to pop up if someone is monitoring his communication." Another pause. "Yes. He's right here." Ghost held the phone out. "It's for you."

Doug took the phone. "Hello?"

"Doug, I'll call your director and have that authorization emailed to you right now, but I'm giving you the verbal okay to give Ghost whatever he needs."

"I appreciate that, Senator, but you know I can't do that without the proper documentation."

"You'll have it any minute," the senator said. "And give my love to your family."

"I will. Thank you, sir." Doug ended the call and handed the phone back to Ghost. "I didn't realize you were friends with the senator."

"He's a good man. He'll make a good president."

"I agree." Doug retrieved his cell phone from his pocket and pulled up his emails. Three unread messages, all from coworkers. A fourth one popped up, this one not from his director but from the director of the FBI. He scanned it. Sure enough, it was authorization to share information with the individual code-named Ghost.

"You good now?" Ghost asked.

"Yeah." Doug glanced around the parking garage. "I don't know how much you already have on the coalition, but Cassidy Edgemont wasn't the first prospective witness to go missing. Two others before her called in and offered information. One died of a heart attack the night before his scheduled interview. The other simply disappeared."

"You suspect a mole within the bureau."

"I've been investigating the possibility for years, first in the Florida office and then in the DC office. I've yet to find a common link between all the witnesses."

"What do you know so far about the coalition's leadership? Who's running it?"

"I'm not sure. I have a pretty good list of their board of directors and the inner circle of management, but I'm convinced I'm missing someone."

"Any idea why they would be setting off bombs in Europe?"

"Are you talking about the bombing in Paris?" Doug asked.

"Yeah."

"That's news to me, but a lot of the top leadership have been on the move for the past few weeks."

"I need names and anything else that will help us track these guys down."

"The majority of my files are locked up at my house."

"Your house? How did you get permission to keep classified information off site?"

"My boss wants this case solved as badly as I do. If we do have a mole, we can't risk having details on soft copy where someone can hack my computer or download files."

"I'll follow you home, and I'll scan everything there."

"No offense, but I'd rather not explain who you are to my wife and daughter."

"Fair enough. Scan or copy whatever you've got. I'll meet you tonight."

"I'm not crazy about carrying this stuff around outside."

"You won't have to go far."

* * *

Cas tried to sleep, but every time she closed her eyes, the image of her father pleading for information about her surfaced full force. She had imagined seeing her family a million times, but would it really be possible? If Donovan's plan worked for her to call them at the embassy, what would she say? How much would Ace let her tell them? And what would happen next?

She couldn't hide in the United States. She couldn't stay in Europe. Even east Asia would be risky with the number of Edge Broadcasting ventures in that part of the world.

China? Africa? South America maybe? None held much appeal. Well, maybe Africa, but not because of the home she could build there but rather because of the possibility of seeing Donovan after she moved past the worst of this ordeal.

How strange to think that she had been annoyed when Donovan had shown up on her doorstep to help her. Now, she couldn't deny she would miss him when he was gone.

Cas rolled over in bed and grabbed her cell phone off her nightstand. Two fifteen in the morning. So much for getting a good night's sleep.

She swung her legs over the side of the bed, her body instantly chilled when her covers fell from her. She tugged on the socks she had left on the floor beside her bed and fished an oversized sweatshirt out of the closet. After she pulled it on, she opened her bedroom door. Donovan's room was dark and quiet. At least he would be rested when the sun came up.

She padded downstairs, debating whether she should try to occupy herself with baking something or watch a movie on her computer. Maybe both. Then again, if she couldn't sleep anyway, she could watch some of the surveillance video of Tyrell and Roshaun. Maybe she would notice something that Donovan had missed. After all, she had personal knowledge of the men and their habits.

She flipped on the entryway light as she passed through. When she stepped into the living room, she stopped abruptly. There stretched out on the couch lay Donovan, one of his arms hooked behind his head as a makeshift pillow.

Her heart did a slow roll in her chest, and she couldn't deny the magnetic pull that seemed to increase between them with each passing day. The respect he'd shown her over the past two weeks had erased her previous resentment of him, and his classic good looks certainly were easy on the eyes, but more than that, she enjoyed his company. His appreciation for everything she did, his taste in music, even his willingness to indulge her when she couldn't go outside herself to run simple errands.

She should do something for him. With baking in mind, she took a step forward. In an instant, Donovan's eyes flew open, he rolled off the couch, and his hand disappeared beneath the couch cushion.

Cas took a defensive step back. "It's just me," she said as his hand resurfaced with a gun.

Donovan focused on her for a fraction of a second before he let out a heavy sigh and lowered his weapon.

"Sorry." Cas let out a pent-up breath of her own. "I didn't expect you to be down here."

"What time is it?" Donovan set his pistol on the table and stood.

"Quarter after two."

"What are you doing up?"

"I couldn't sleep."

"Thinking about your family?"

"That and thinking about the coalition and the bombs and the articles. I hate not having all the answers."

"You know as well as anyone that these things take time."

Cas's eyebrows drew together. "Why are you sleeping down here?"

"I'm waiting on a call from Kade. I didn't want my phone to wake you."

"That's sweet." She waved toward the kitchen. "I was thinking about making some cookies. Do you have a preference for what kind?"

"As much as I love your baking, I have a better idea," Donovan said. "Come sit with me. We can watch a movie together."

"If we watch a movie, we won't have anything to eat at the end of it."

"Maybe not, but it might help take your mind off of things." He reached out and took her hand.

The naturalness of the gesture struck her, as did the zing of the chemistry bubbling between them. Her eyes lifted to his, and her mind went blank.

He stepped into the wash of light from the entryway, leaving only a foot of space between them. Interest flickered on his face along with a flash of uncertainty. His gaze lowered to her lips.

Her heartbeat quickened, but this time the cause was from a new kind of danger.

Donovan's fingers linked with hers, and his head lowered until their lips were mere inches apart. Their breath mingled.

Her stomach somersaulted. Sweet attraction rose within her and built until her body ached from the tension shimmering between them. She should step back. She was sure there was a reason she shouldn't kiss him, but her reasons had deserted her.

The distance between them disappeared, and Donovan's lips met hers. Her heart bounced into her throat, and her stomach leapt inside her as though she were racing down the freefall of a roller coaster. His free hand lifted to her waist and pulled her closer. The connection sparked between them, and she let herself pretend she had a future to give. Long-buried needs rose inside her: the joy of having someone to talk to, someone to dream with, someone to walk beside.

Her hand lifted to his shoulder. Muscles bunched beneath her touch.

The kiss deepened, and the ground dropped away. Cas indulged herself and rode the storm of sensations a minute longer.

When she pulled away, Donovan's eyes locked on hers. "You are so beautiful."

The sincerity of his statement washed over her, but with it came doubts. Someone wanted her dead, and anyone near her was at risk. Though it pained her to do so, she took a step back and pulled her hand free of his.

"What's wrong?" Donovan closed the distance between them again. He put his hand on her arm as though afraid she might disappear if he didn't maintain contact.

She blew out a breath. "Obviously, I have feelings for you, or I never would have kissed you, but this is a bad idea." Cas took another step back. "With my dad blasting my name and picture all over the place, who knows if I'll even survive the week."

"I'm not going to let anything happen to you."

"How many times have we both said those words to clients?" Cas asked. "The truth is, we do the best we can, but there aren't any guarantees."

"Nothing in life has guarantees." Donovan caressed her arm. "Come on. Let's sit and watch a movie together. We can call this another date."

Her mind said no, but the boyish expression on his face was too irresistible. "Okay, but I get to pick the movie."

"Oh, no. I'm not giving you a free pass on that. With my luck, you'll want to bore me to sleep with *Dense and Densibility* or something like that."

"You mean *Sense and Sensibility*?"

"Same thing."

"Okay, fine. We'll decide together."

"See. We're learning to live together already."

The casual mention of living together struck her, and she instantly shook her head. "I'm not living with you. We're simply residing at the same safe house."

"Right." Donovan took her hand and tugged her toward the couch. "But you're still not picking the movie."

CHAPTER 24

Doug gripped the old backpack that held a copy of his research from the past ten months. Ghost hadn't been kidding about not needing to go far to meet him. Rather than drive to some public place to hand off the information, Doug only had to take the dog for a walk. He turned the corner on the street where Ghost waited beside a motorcycle, a phone in his hand as though he had stopped to take a call.

As Doug and his dog approached, Ghost set a black leather backpack on the ground beside his motorcycle and ended his call, or pretended to. Doug couldn't be sure.

Unconcerned about Ghost's presence, the dog sniffed a nearby tree, stretching to the end of his leash.

"Hey, can you give me directions to the freeway?" Ghost asked.

"Yeah, sure." Doug set his backpack down and proceeded to give directions even though Ghost didn't really need them.

"Thanks." Ghost reached down and picked up Doug's backpack and motioned to his. "Don't forget that."

"Thanks. I won't." Doug picked up Ghost's bag.

Ghost got back onto his motorcycle, started it, and drove off without a backward glance.

Eager to examine the contents of his new backpack, Doug tugged on Buster's leash and turned back toward home. Buster fell into step beside him for a few yards, but when they reached the stop sign, the dog sniffed at the post.

"Come on." Doug tugged on the leash to urge the dog forward. Buster trotted around the corner until they reached the next tree. Then he wandered into the grass to relieve himself. Doug fought for patience. When the dog finished, he pulled on the leash again. This time, they made it only a few steps before Buster stopped to examine a patch of grass.

"Seriously? You've gone to the bathroom, like, six times already."

The dog looked up as though questioning why Doug wouldn't want him to examine every single blade of grass between here and their house.

"Come on." Doug shortened the leash and urged the dog forward until they arrived home.

He was barely in the door when his daughter rushed into the living room. "There you are. I need the keys to your car."

Buster barked, and Doug released him from his leash. Though he itched to know what Ghost had given him, Doug focused on Reagan. "If you think I'm handing my keys over to a fifteen-year-old, you've got another thing coming." How had she gotten old enough to have her driver's permit in the first place?

"Don't worry. We're taking mom's car, but she wanted to move your car to the curb before she lets me back out of the driveway."

"In that case . . ." Doug fished out his keys before the oddity of Jill not having her key to his car struck him. "Wait. Where are Mom's keys?" His eyes narrowed. "Did she lose them again?"

"Maybe." Jill walked in, and Reagan turned to her. "I tried."

"You really lost your keys again?"

Jill gave him a sheepish grin. "I'm sure they're in my teaching bag, but they're hiding, and we only have a half hour to practice driving before Reagan's soccer practice."

Doug held out the keys to Reagan. "Don't let Mom lose these."

"I won't." She grabbed her soccer ball and opened the door. "Thanks, Dad."

"We'll see you later." Jill stopped and gave him a kiss before she followed their daughter outside.

Doug watched them leave, his heart warming. He gave himself a moment to appreciate the positive things in his life before sitting at his desk in the corner and opening the backpack. He drew out a manila envelope, the words *Top Secret* stamped across the outside in red. He opened it and dumped the contents out. Along with several sheets of paper, a cell phone dropped onto his desk.

Curious, he picked it up, but the screen was locked. Doug scanned through the top sheet that accompanied the phone until he found a passcode to access the phone and the note, *I'm on speed dial. Call me with any updates.*

Doug opened the phone with the passcode and promptly changed it to one he would remember. He then read the other information Ghost had given him. His eyes widened. Jamal Williams and Ezra Jackson, both active players in the coalition's inner circle, were listed as deceased. Details of the bombing in Paris and the man from Chad arrested for the attack. Two other thwarted bombing attempts in Europe, the bombs identical to the one in Paris. The other two incidents included evidence that tied them to the coalition.

What in the world was the coalition trying to accomplish? Bombings in Europe went beyond political influence. They were up to something bigger. The question was, Did this change in focus have to do with influencing the upcoming election, or had the group decided to explore terrorism as a way to create chaos that went beyond the US borders? Whichever was the case, he needed to find out, even if that meant relying on a ghost to gain answers.

* * *

Need, belonging, and something less identifiable swelled in Donovan as he slipped his arm around Cas and pulled her closer. She didn't resist but, rather, tucked her legs up on the couch and leaned into him. Satisfaction joined the other emotions coursing through him. For all Cas's talk about this being a bad idea, she didn't seem any more interested in destroying the connection between them than he was.

The movie started, though he wasn't sure if this one was any better than one of those Jane Austen flicks. Had Cas suggested they watch *Roman Holiday* because she wanted to remind him that a lasting relationship was a long shot at best? Donovan hadn't admitted that he'd already seen the movie. And he certainly wasn't about to tell her he'd seen it eleven times. Or was it twelve? He couldn't remember.

His ex-wife had never liked classic movies, always preferring the latest chick flick where the happily ever after was spelled out in the end. Donovan rather liked movies that left him wanting more, stories where he had to use his imagination to find the solution of how the characters could reach a place of contentment. The image of a princess in an ornate hotel room brought new questions to the surface.

"Did you ever stay in places like that?" Donovan asked.

"What? A presidential suite?"

"Yeah. I mean, your dad is Josiah Edgemont."

"Sometimes, but I think it was more because the upper floors of hotels are easier to secure." Cas's voice thickened. "Papa overcame a lot of opposition to get to where he is today. He worried someone might try to use our family as a way to rattle him."

"What kind of opposition?" Donovan asked.

"Broadcasting was a white-male-dominated industry when my father started. Some didn't like the way his company crashed through barriers."

"So the old boys' network wasn't very welcoming of your dad, huh?"

"Some weren't. Others helped him tremendously. When Lyle Powell retired, he had multiple offers for his TV network. If he hadn't wanted to see a Black man succeed, he could have thrown up a huge brick wall. Instead, he accepted my father's offer and stayed on for a year to help my dad smooth the transition."

"That was the deal that propelled him into the big-time?"

"Yeah. Lyle could have easily handed the company down to his children or sold it to someone else, but he believed in helping people get ahead in life, especially when those people were willing to work for their success."

"I heard Lyle Powell was an amazing man. That must have been hard on your dad when he passed away a few years ago."

"It was. Even harder was being told by Lyle's son that he wasn't welcome at the funeral."

"But I saw a photo of your dad at the funeral. There was a big article about it."

"Only because Lyle's wife reached out to my dad. Steven wasn't happy."

"Losing someone is never easy."

"No, it's not."

Donovan squeezed her shoulder and pulled her closer. "Don't think about your family right now. Just watch the movie."

Cas leaned her head against his shoulder, her hair brushing against his jaw. A sweet yearning started in his chest and radiated outward. This was what he wanted. Quiet moments with an amazing woman beside him, companionship, conversation that went beyond how to survive the day.

Donovan's phone rang, and he straightened. "Sorry. That's probably Kade." He hit the Talk button. "Any luck?"

"Yeah. It'll take an hour or so to scan these documents into the guardian database, but I've got the highlights for you."

Donovan hit the Speaker button. "Cas is here too."

"Don't you two sleep?"

"We'll sleep once my family is safe from the coalition," Cas said.

Her family. Not her. Donovan appreciated Cas's sentiment, but it sent a ripple of unease through him. How far would she go to protect her loved ones?

"What did you find out?" she asked.

"Doug Valdez has been investigating a possible leak within the bureau since your brush with death," Kade said. "You were the third witness who disappeared after offering to turn over evidence against the coalition."

"It's been four years. If he hasn't found anything by now, there may not be anything to find."

"Actually, I think there is. For a few years, Valdez thought you were the last informant to go missing or die. But then he found a fourth. That's why he took his investigation off-line."

"Who was it?" Cas asked.

"Derrick Massey. Did you know him?"

"No, but the coalition has a lot of members. I didn't know everyone."

"Maybe not, but this guy worked for Edge Broadcasting."

"What?" Cas asked.

"When?" Donovan asked at the same time.

"He worked in their cybersecurity division for three years. He was killed in a car accident almost a year ago."

"Then it's possible he was the one helping the coalition figure out how to hack the different news sites," Cas said.

"I thought your father changed his security programming only a few months ago."

"He did, but he phased it in. If this guy was working in cybersecurity at the corporate level, he would have had access to all the information he needed well over a year ago."

"If he was helping them, why did they kill him?" Kade asked.

"Maybe he didn't know the coalition was going to be involved in creating the news related to what they were reporting," Cas said.

"Whatever the reason, he didn't survive to make his appointment with the FBI in New Orleans."

"New Orleans?" Cas asked. "I was in Florida when I tried to meet with the FBI. There can't be too many agents who were working in both places at the times the tips came in."

"Valdez already looked for commonalities. Only two agents transferred from the Florida office to the one in New Orleans during that period of time, but neither of them had any access to the call logs or the files on the coalition."

"Someone had to be in both places," Cas said.

"Or two different people were passing information to the coalition," Donovan said.

"That's a scary thought."

"If you have time tomorrow, you can help look through Valdez's research. Cas, maybe you'll recognize a name we don't."

"Thanks, Kade. We'll talk to you tomorrow." Donovan ended the call. "At least we have another starting place."

"I keep dreaming about what it would be like if we could identify the person who wanted me dead, but then, in the next minute, I can't imagine I'll ever be free to live my life again."

"We've all been through that." Donovan put his hand on hers. "There's nothing we can do tonight. I think it's time to get back to our distraction. That is, if you want to watch the rest of the movie."

"Sorry, but I'm not sure I'm in the mood right now to watch one that doesn't have a happily ever after."

"I always like to imagine they found a way to be together, even with all of the obstacles between them."

"Wait." Cas pulled back so she could see him more clearly. "You've seen this before?"

"Don't look so surprised. The movie has been around since 1953."

"Yeah, but a lot of people don't ever bother to watch anything that came out in black-and-white."

"I guess I'm not a lot of people." Donovan glanced at the time on his phone. "It's after three. We should probably get some sleep while we can. Sounds like we're going to be busy tomorrow."

"You mean today."

"Yeah, I guess so." Not quite ready to let their time together end, Donovan ran his finger over the back of her hand. "I know you said this thing between us is a bad idea . . ."

Regret flashed on her face. Donovan took it as a sign to finish his thought. "Our lives are unpredictable. Don't you think we should enjoy what we have while we can?" Donovan asked. "Neither of us knows what tomorrow will look like."

Cas stood, and Donovan followed suit. The regret in her expression melted into uncertainty. Unable to resist, Donovan leaned forward and captured her mouth with his. Fire shot through him, sparks bouncing from his fingers to his toes. The woman was potent. She also intrigued him on every possible level. Smart and sassy, warm and genuine. Throw in her determination and those flashes of uncertainty and he doubted any man would be able to resist her.

Cas broke the kiss. Breathless, she took a step back. "I'll see you in a few hours."

"Good night." Donovan watched her disappear up the stairs, his heart lighter than it had been moments ago. He stretched out on the couch, and a smile flitted over his face. Time to let sleep bridge the darkness with the light. The sooner he fell asleep, the sooner he'd wake up, and he was rather looking forward to a good-morning kiss.

CHAPTER 25

Cas woke thinking about him. She'd told Donovan she couldn't afford any distractions right now, but there he was, slipping under her guard and invading her thoughts.

Birds chirped outside her window, and she burrowed beneath her blankets against the chill in the air. If she closed her eyes and imagined the scent of fresh beignets, she could almost pretend she was in her home in New Orleans, Antoine rattling around in the kitchen while her dad prepared to leave for work.

She sniffed the air. Something was cooking, but it wasn't donuts.

She pushed out of bed and put on her sweatshirt. After a quick stop in the bathroom to brush her teeth, she continued into the kitchen.

Donovan stood by the stove, his sleeves pushed up to his elbows and a spatula in his hand.

"What are you making?" she asked.

"Omelets." He leaned toward her and gave her a quick kiss.

A familiar attraction punched through her along with a contentment she hadn't experienced since this whole ordeal had started. How odd to think that her routine with Donovan had eased the pain of leaving the city she loved and the turmoil that stemmed from her changing family dynamics.

"Are you hungry?" he asked.

"Starving." She stepped closer to the stove and looked in the pan. Cooked egg, cheese, and ham, but the mixture had separated into a mess that resembled chunks of scrambled eggs. "I hate to say it, but that is the saddest looking omelet I've ever seen."

"It doesn't matter what it looks like as long as it tastes good." He scooped some up with a fork and held it out. Bracing herself, Cas leaned forward and let him feed her a bite. The cheesy egg mixture didn't taste anything like how it looked. "Well? What do you think?"

"It's actually good. I didn't know you could cook like that."

"I'm not Cassidy Edgemont, but I can manage the basics." He motioned to the table, where his laptop was pushed to the side and two plates had already been laid out. "Let's eat."

Cas sat down and served herself some eggs. She debated whether to fix toast to go with it, but with how proud Donovan was about making her breakfast, she decided against it.

She ate several bites before she asked, "Have you already started looking through the stuff Kade uploaded?"

"Yeah." He nudged his plate aside and turned the laptop toward her. "The list of agents Valdez has looked into are on there. I didn't see anything on those, so I went to the more extensive list of agents who were working in Florida at the time of your accident and New Orleans at the time of Massey's death. One name stood out."

"Which one?"

"Germain Peters. Any chance he's related to your chef?"

Her stomach clenched. "He's Antoine's son."

"Is there any way he could have known you were meeting with the FBI?"

A flash of memory bolted through her mind. "He stayed at our house for a couple weeks right before my accident. He was buying a house, but the closing got pushed back, and he had to move out of his apartment. My parents let him stay with us."

"Did you talk to Roshaun about meeting with the FBI while he was there?"

"We talked when we were at the house. It was late, after the staff usually went to bed, so I didn't think to look around to see if anyone else was nearby."

"If Germain was staying at your house, why didn't you talk to him about your concerns about the coalition?" Donovan asked.

"One of the people who was planning the bombing was Lincoln Jones. He and Germain went to college together," Cas said. "I didn't want to put him in the position of questioning a friend. I had no idea he might have been sympathetic to the coalition the whole time."

"He may have been more than sympathetic." Donovan cleared their breakfast dishes.

"All this time, I thought it was Roshaun who told the coalition I was meeting with the FBI."

"We don't know if it was or not," Donovan said. "If Roshaun and Germain were both involved, that could explain why we couldn't find any phone records between Roshaun and the coalition."

"Short of a confession, there's no way to know for sure."

"Maybe it's time to have a chat with Roshaun."

"Excuse me?" Cas's eyebrows shot up. "Even if we could talk to him, he's not going to admit to being involved in my accident, even if he was behind it."

"First of all, *we* aren't going to talk to him. *I* am. Secondly, I wasn't planning on taking a direct approach. I'm just going to get a feel for what this guy is all about."

"We were together for almost three years. I have a pretty good sense of what he's all about."

"It's been four years since you dated. Let's find out how much he's changed since you saw him last." Donovan scooted back in his chair and reached for his cell phone on the counter behind him. "Time to expand the guest list for the ambassador's dinner party."

* * *

Donovan settled back on the couch and read Germain's personnel file on his computer. Another dead end. "So much for finding the connection to the coalition. Germain took a disability retirement before Massey was killed."

"It would have been too easy to find a connection that quickly." Cas set her laptop on the cushion beside her and leaned forward to read Donovan's screen. "Why did he end up on disability?"

Donovan clicked on the incident file. "The guy was shot by a fellow agent during a raid."

"Friendly fire? You don't hear about that happening often in the bureau."

"No, you don't." Donovan's eyes narrowed. "In fact, I didn't hear about this, and it was only three years ago. This is the kind of thing the media usually makes a big deal out of."

"The bureau's public affairs office must have managed to keep it out of the news," Cas said. "How badly was he injured?"

"It was a leg wound. Looks like it left him with some nerve damage, but I don't know why they didn't reassign him to a desk job," Donovan said. "He might have a bit of a limp, but as far as I can tell, he's still mobile."

"He's lucky the injury wasn't worse."

"Let's see what he's been up to since he left the government."

Cas picked up her laptop again. "While you look into him, I'm going to see if my dad has RSVP'd yet for dinner with the ambassador."

"Good luck." Donovan did an internet search for Germain, but nothing popped up. Taking a more direct route, Donovan accessed the IRS database and pulled up Germain's taxes. He only had to go as far as the man's W2 to find the piece of the puzzle that tied all their research together.

"You aren't going to believe this. Guess where Germain has been working since leaving the bureau."

"Where?" Cas asked.

"Edge Broadcasting."

"You can't be serious."

"I'm afraid so." Donovan read the screen, his mind working through the new development. "If he was working for Edge when Massey was killed and he was with the FBI at the time of your accident . . ."

"He could be the mole the FBI was looking for," Cas finished for him.

"Can you access his personnel file for Edge?"

"Only if I log into their system with my user ID."

"Which is how your dad found out you might still be alive."

"He already suspects something. What can it hurt now?" Cas asked.

Donovan let the question roll through his mind. They needed answers, but was it worth the risk?

Cas didn't wait for him to answer. She opened her internet browser. "Here goes nothing."

Donovan set his laptop aside and stretched his arm across the back of the couch behind Cas. A protectiveness and pride simultaneously swelled inside him as Cas set up a series of firewalls to hide their location. She logged into the Edge Broadcasting computer network, and after a few clicks, Germain's personnel file filled the screen.

"It looks like he came to work for my dad's company a couple months after his early retirement," Cas said. "I guess that shouldn't surprise me since his father has worked for my family since Papa bought Powell Broadcasting."

"I'm surprised your family could afford a personal chef when your dad's company was so new."

"We couldn't. From what Antoine told me, he started out running the restaurant located in the studio's building."

"Powell owned a restaurant and a broadcasting studio?"

"Yeah. It was his way of diversifying his assets and making sure his employees had somewhere close by to eat when world events demanded long hours from everyone," Cas said. "My father kept the restaurant going for a few years, but when one of the chain restaurants offered to lease the space from him, he decided it was more feasible to get out of the food industry."

"How did Antoine feel about that?"

"I think he was happy to have normal hours after so many nights away from his family."

"Did he have other kids besides Germain?"

"No, and his wife died not long before my dad closed the restaurant," Cas said. "I think that was the other reason Antoine didn't mind leaving the high stress of being a head chef for a restaurant."

"It sounds like your family has been good to the Peterses."

"Yeah, but if we're right and Germain is behind my accident, the Peterses didn't do a very good job returning the favor." She scrolled down on the personnel file to the summary of his employment. "Looks like we found our man. He works in computer security."

"He's our guy." An alert popped up on the screen. Donovan straightened. "And he's tracking you."

Cas immediately severed her internet access. "I can't tell if he located us."

Donovan grabbed his cell phone and called Kade. Cas jumped up and rushed to the kitchen and started pulling sticky notes off the glass wall.

Kade answered on the third ring, and Donovan got right to the point. "We may have a security breach. I need you to see if Edge Broadcasting was able to track our location. Cas was logged on to their system when the alert popped."

"How long was she on?"

"Three minutes. Maybe four."

"Your location has been compromised. Get out of there," Kade said. "I'll tap into the local security cameras and keep a lookout for you."

"Thanks." Donovan hung up and called out to Cas. "We've been made. Come on. We need to clear out."

Cas collected the last few notes and hurried back to the living room. She quickly packed up her electronics and stuffed the notes into her backpack. Donovan grabbed his laptop and raced up the stairs. Cas followed. Two minutes later, they both reemerged from their rooms with their go-bags and collected their coats. Donovan had half expected Cas to try to bring her suitcase with her and had to remind himself that she too had been trained. If they had to hide, their go-bags would be all they'd be able to manage.

"You have the car keys?" Donovan asked.

Cas held them up.

"Let me check the road before you come out." Donovan opened the door and peered outside at the empty street. He reached back and took Cas's hand to draw her outside with him.

"Oh, wait. The alfajores."

"They're all gone. I ate the last of them this morning."

"Except for the ones I hid in the freezer." Cas started to return inside, but when Donovan's phone rang, he held her hand firm.

The moment Donovan answered, Kade's voice came over the line. "You've got two guys heading your way. They don't look friendly. ETA less than a minute."

Cas tried to tug her hand free. Donovan hung up his phone and shook his head. "There's no time."

They turned toward the parking garage, and Donovan glanced over his shoulder as two Black men rounded the corner from the main street. Though he'd hoped the newcomers would assume they were still inside the house, one of them pointed at them and reached into his waistband in a practiced move.

Donovan drew his own weapon and fired a warning shot. "Run!" he shouted.

CHAPTER 26

Cas darted into a narrow alley as a bullet hit the wall directly behind her. She gasped but didn't slow. They'd found her. Again. This could be it. This could be the day she died for real. And Donovan could get caught in the crossfire.

These men had to be locals to have found them so quickly. Was it just the two of them? Or did they have reinforcements waiting at the various transportation hubs in the city? Would they anticipate where Cas and Donovan had their car parked? And could she and Donovan reach it before they were intercepted—or worse, shot?

Rather than continue toward the garage, Cas grabbed Donovan's sleeve and tugged before pushing through an unlocked gate. She led the way into a narrow courtyard as footsteps pounded toward them.

Her gaze swept the area and zeroed in on the work ladder in the corner of the courtyard and on the balcony above her.

"Cover me," she whispered. She grabbed the ladder and moved it below the balcony. If she could climb that far, the railing would give her enough height to get onto the roof. The ladder squeaked when she opened it.

Footsteps slowed, then shots fired. Cas checked to make sure Donovan was still standing before she scrambled up the ladder. As soon as she reached the balcony, she drew her weapon, spotted the two men on either side of the gate, and fired off a shot of her own. "Come on!"

Donovan climbed upward. A hand holding a gun appeared by the gate, and Cas squeezed off another shot. The man's gun sparked and dropped from his hand.

"Up to the roof," Donovan said. "You go first."

Cas grabbed the side of the house and climbed onto the balcony railing. Her heartbeat quickened at the thought that one misstep could send her plummeting to the ground. She stretched her arm above her, but her fingertips barely grazed the rooftop. "I can't reach."

Donovan fired another shot, expelled his clip, and reloaded. After shooting again, he moved beside her. "Climb onto my shoulders." A new fear bubbled inside her, but Cas lifted her foot to his shoulder. Donovan shot again and then grabbed her foot to steady her. "Hurry."

Pretending this was simply a cheerleading stunt being conducted a few feet from the ground, she pushed straight up. The weight of her go-bag threw off her balance, and she wavered. Her palms clutched the roof, and she held on. Donovan must have adjusted his position because her free foot found his other shoulder, his hand still gripping her first leg to hold her steady.

With a quick count to three, she bent her legs, and launched herself upward. She pulled herself onto the roof. Two more shots fired.

Cas scrambled to the edge of the roof, drew her weapon, and fired two more shots, one at each side of the gate. Relief swept through her when she looked down where Donovan still stood. "Come on. I'll cover you."

Donovan shot another round and holstered his weapon, then climbed onto the railing and used his long arms to reach the edge of the roof. He pushed himself up, his torso landing on the roof, his legs hanging in the air.

Cas fired again. So did one of their pursuers. Donovan used his hands and legs to crawl farther from the line of fire. He grunted as though in pain.

"You okay?" Cas asked.

"Yeah, but where are we going now?"

"These roofs all connect until we get to the main roads. We can either use our elevated position to try to pick off our pursuers, or we can keep going to the garage."

"They're too well protected behind that wall. I say we move forward."

"Okay, but stay down and watch your step. We may be just as easy to spot as they are."

Another bullet ripped into the edge of the roof between them.

Donovan scooted back another foot. "You don't have to tell me twice."

* * *

Sirens rang out, and traffic stopped on the road below. Donovan didn't have to see the police cars to know what the local authorities were up to. Someone had called the cops, and they had locked down the local roads to find the shooters. All of the shooters.

Donovan and Cas had been too busy traversing a particularly steep roof when the police had arrived to see where their pursuers had gone. Donovan suspected they had fled the scene, which left him and Cas as the potential fall guys for the incident the two men had started.

Getting arrested wasn't in his plans, and he certainly wasn't about to give up his sidearm when someone was trying to kill Cas.

He reached out and touched Cas's arm. When she glanced at him, he signaled for her to stay still. She complied, and he shifted closer. He lowered his voice to a whisper. "We should wait here until the police clear the area. I doubt they'll think to check the rooftops."

A rumble sounded in the distance. "Maybe not, but if that's a helicopter heading our way . . ."

Donovan's heart sank. "We have to find somewhere to hide."

"Where? We can't stay up here."

She was right. They were too exposed on the rooftop, and they were on the wrong side of the street to get back to the safe house. He turned to survey their limited options. To keep his balance, he instinctively grabbed on to the smokestack. The heat from the metal seared his hand, and he snatched it away. Steam puffed out the top of the vent. He looked down the row of rooftops and at the exhaust from each of the corresponding vents in front of them. When he looked in the other direction, he identified a new option.

The helicopter flew closer.

"This way." With one hand on the roof to steady himself, he made his way to the roof two houses over. He put his hand on the smokestack and confirmed it was cool. "Looks like this one is vacant."

Carefully, he climbed down the backside of the roof until he could peer over the edge. He sent up a silent prayer of gratitude when a solid wood balcony came into view beneath him.

"This way."

A siren approached and cut off a short distance away.

Donovan slid his body off the edge of the roof and used his feet to find the balcony rail. Once he had his bearings, he dropped down onto the balcony. Cas followed him, and Donovan reached up to grab her waist so he could help her down. As soon as she dropped beside him, he retrieved his lockpick from his bag. Ten seconds later, the lock clicked open, and he led the way inside. Cas closed the door behind them.

Finding himself in an empty bedroom, Donovan slipped past the full-sized bed and paused by the open door. Light streamed through the windows and illuminated the stairway and the two other doorways that opened off the hall.

Cas tapped his shoulder and signaled which room she would take. Together they cleared the other two rooms and cautiously made their way downstairs. The chill in the air confirmed the heat wasn't on. A minute later, they finished clearing the house, proving they were alone.

"Now what?" Cas asked. "I didn't see where those guys went. I have to think they'll stay nearby until the police clear out."

The possibility was far too likely. "We can stay here until it gets dark. Then I can sneak out and pick up the car. If I drive here to pick you up, we should be able to get out without them seeing us."

Though concern flashed on her face, she nodded. "I can't think of a better idea." She crossed to the thermostat on the wall. "Let's get some heat going in here."

Donovan took a better look around. The streamlined furnishings, the lack of clutter, the decor. "Think this could be a rental home?"

"One way to find out." Cas walked into the kitchen and opened the refrigerator. Donovan looked over her shoulder. Empty.

"Yep," Cas said. "It's a rental home."

Donovan's stomach grumbled. "I should have let you go back for the cookies."

CHAPTER 27

Cas paced the length of the beautifully decorated living room while Donovan sat on the plush couch, his feet up on the coffee table. How could he be so calm while the police walked up and down the street, knocking on doors? Training. She should be calm too, but even after nearly two weeks, she still wasn't used to filling the role of protectee instead of protector.

A knock sounded at the door. Cas froze.

Donovan signaled for her to move out of sight. She stepped beside the chair where she and Donovan had set their coats and backpacks. Donovan removed his holster and slipped it, gun and all, under the chair cushion. He then toed off his shoes and left them lying haphazardly by the couch.

He was making the house look lived in. Cas nodded her approval and opened her backpack. She set her laptop on the couch and turned it on so it would look like Donovan had been using it.

He moved to the door and opened it. A policeman introduced himself, and Donovan responded in his language. "What is the trouble, officer?" Donovan asked, his French fluent but with an accent that wasn't easily identifiable.

"Did you not hear the gunfire?"

"Gunfire?" Donovan asked. "I thought the Laurents had their television up too loud again."

"No. We are conducting a search of all houses in the area. May we come in?"

"Of course, but my girlfriend and I haven't seen anyone since we arrived home from the airport," Donovan said. "We had hoped you were the deliveryman bringing our luggage."

"You've been traveling?"

"Yes. I had business in Prague," Donovan said. "I'm sorry. Please come in out of the cold."

Cas froze for a second. Should she sit down and pretend she had been lounging in the living room? She backtracked to the kitchen. Assuming the officer wanted to search the entire house, she and Donovan had to make it believable that they had just arrived, thus explaining why the closets were bare. After a brief moment, she took a steadying breath and forced herself forward. Before she reached the living room, she called out, "Honey, I'm going out to the store. We need groceries." Cas pulled up short when she reached the two men. "Hello. Is everything okay?"

"There was a shooting on our street," Donovan said with the appropriate amount of surprise and disbelief.

"Really?"

"*Oui*, madame. May I search the rest of the house?"

"Of course." Cas stepped beside Donovan and slipped her arm around his waist.

The policeman did a cursory search of the main level and headed up the stairs.

Cas lowered her voice. "How do we explain the empty closets?"

"We say we were renting our place out while we were gone."

"And the missing luggage explains why we don't have any clothes with us. Smooth."

"I try." He moved to the couch and slipped his shoes on. Footsteps approached down the stairs before he spoke again. "I don't want you going out to the store today. Make me a list, and I'll go."

"What if it isn't safe for you either?"

The officer joined them. "Thank you for your time. Please stay inside until our search is complete."

"How much longer until the street opens back up?" Donovan asked. "We really would like to get our luggage."

"And some food," Cas added.

"Another hour or so."

"Thank you, officer." Donovan escorted him to the door. As soon as he closed it, Donovan leaned back against it and blew out a breath. "That was close."

"Do you think he believed us?"

"He didn't ask for our proof of travel or search us for weapons." Donovan retrieved his pistol and slid the holster into his waistband again.

"He may have bought our story for now, but if anyone saw who was shooting, they may be back. There aren't a lot of people around here with our skin color."

"Maybe, but both of the shooters were men. Hopefully witnesses will report that rather than giving our descriptions."

"I hope so." Cas dropped onto the couch. "I'll check in with Kade and give him the name of our suspected mole."

"I'll call Ace and let him know what's happening here."

She shook her head. "He isn't going to be happy to know we've blown another safe house."

"We only lost yours in Paris. The one I was staying at is still clean."

"Maybe that's where we should go next," Cas suggested.

"Take you back to Paris? Not a good idea."

"Maybe not, but it's the last place anyone would expect me to be."

"Good luck selling that argument to Ace."

"Thanks." Cas dialed his number. "I'm going to need it."

* * *

Doug awoke Sunday morning to the chime of a text message on his cell phone. He rolled over and grabbed it. Probably someone from church looking for a substitute Sunday School teacher. He checked his messages, but there weren't any. He set the phone back on his bedside table. He must be hearing things.

He closed his eyes and drifted back into a contented semiconscious state. The sound repeated. He checked his phone a second time. Then he remembered. He had another phone. Forcing his eyes open, he reached for the phone on the other side of his bedside lamp. Sure enough, an alert filled the screen. He opened it, the words pushing the sleep from his brain.

Mole: Germain Peters. Doug read the text message from Ghost several times, but this new information still didn't make sense. Doug and Hector had investigated the man at the time Cassidy Edgemont had died, but a shooting incident had ended his career with the bureau by the time Massey was killed. Germain couldn't have been the leak for all four compromised witnesses. As though reading his thoughts, Ghost sent a second text message. *Check your email.*

Donovan grabbed his work cell phone and opened his email. He clicked on the most recent unread message and scanned the information. His eyes widened. Doug and Hector had eliminated Germain from their suspect list because he couldn't have had access to information about Derrick Massey, but according to Ghost, he had close contact with the most recent victim.

This could be it, the development in this case he had been searching for. He lay back in bed, his mind sorting through the information Ghost had provided. First thing tomorrow, he would arrange to fly down to New Orleans to question Germain. With any luck, he'd have the man behind bars by tomorrow afternoon.

A niggling sense of doubt poked at him, an urgency he couldn't explain. He tried to push it away. Sunday was his day of rest. This case had been on his desk for years, and this was the first development in ten months. Surely, questioning Germain could wait until Monday.

Doug rolled over and tried to go back to sleep, but his mind wouldn't quit. Details of the case swirled in his thoughts, pieces connecting like a jigsaw puzzle finally revealing its true identity.

Ten minutes was all it took for Doug to give up on sleep. If his mind wouldn't quiet down until he sorted this picture out, he'd organize the information so it would all be ready for tomorrow.

Careful not to wake Jill, he slid out of bed and grabbed his work laptop. He went into the living room and settled at the desk in the corner. He read through Ghost's email again, this time adding notes to his case file.

Even though Germain had worked in the Miami office at the time of the first three leaks, he had been directly involved with questioning only the first witness, the only witness who had made it to the FBI before disappearing or turning up dead.

Doug opened the witness statement and scanned through it. His eyes narrowed. The first victim's name was at the top, and the time and date of the interview was listed, but the transcription of the man's report wasn't included. Doug searched the case file for the audio recording of the interview session but couldn't find one.

Jill padded into the living room, her hair tumbled from sleep and her face free of makeup. She put her hand on his shoulder and leaned down to kiss him. "What are you doing up so early?"

"I got a text this morning, and my mind wouldn't stop thinking about it." He shot her an apologetic look. "Sorry. You know I don't like to work on Sundays, but this one isn't letting me rest."

"If you're being prompted to look into it now, there's probably a reason."

"Maybe."

"I'm going to make some breakfast. Are you hungry?"

"A little, but it may be a while before I'm ready to take a break."

"I'll bring you a plate."

"Thanks."

Doug turned back to the information on his screen. One witness statement missing, the witness unaccounted for since leaving the FBI Miami office, and three other witnesses killed before they could speak with an agent. And Germain was in the position to know about each victim.

From everything in front of him, Doug had to agree with Ghost. Germain Peters was the mole. If they could understand the man's motives, maybe they would finally be able to crack through the invisible shield the coalition had constructed around their leadership and bring the destructive organization down.

CHAPTER 28

Donovan still wasn't sure what powers of persuasion Cas had used to get Ace to allow them to go back to Paris, but Donovan was far from comfortable with the prospect of keeping her safe there. If they were right, not only was Germain the man responsible for identifying Cas as a threat to the coalition, but his father also still had direct access to her family. Was it possible that the father's beliefs mirrored the son's?

Donovan hoped to answer many of their questions once they returned to Paris, but first, he had to get Cas safely out of Bruges. Reservations flowed through him as he walked to the door. As much as he hated leaving Cas alone in their temporary shelter, he didn't have a choice.

It was now dark, but the likelihood of her being noticed was still too high for her to be outside again. In truth, he didn't know if their earlier pursuers had gotten a good look at him, but he wasn't the one they were after. His death served no purpose to the coalition. Cas's did.

Cas followed Donovan to the door and put a hand on his arm. "Be careful."

"I will." He covered her hand with his own. "Stay safe. I'll be back as soon as I can."

She didn't speak, but her gaze remained on him. Concern flashed in her eyes, but he suspected it was for him rather than for herself.

Unable to resist, he leaned down and pressed his lips to hers. His heart swelled. "I'll be back soon."

Cas nodded. She moved so she wouldn't be visible when he opened the door. He stepped outside, and a cold breeze whipped over him. He flipped the collar of his coat up to fight the wind and strolled down the street as though he didn't have a care in the world.

Following standard evasive protocol, he walked two blocks out of the way before he turned toward his objective. Winding his way through the streets, he made his way past tourists and locals alike. One restaurant after another tempted him to stop and ease his hunger, but he resisted even though it had been far too many hours since breakfast.

He rounded the last turn and slowed when he spotted one of the men who had been chasing them earlier. The familiar figure sat on a bench outside the library where the car park was located. Using a trio of tourists to shield him from view, Donovan continued forward and scanned for the man's partner. Had the two known Cas had a car parked here, or were they guessing it was one of her possible means of transportation?

With only one of the men visible, Donovan detoured into a bistro and got in line. If it were him looking for someone here in Bruges, how would he narrow his search? The airport was too far away to reach without a train, bus, or car. That left the other three options. He pulled out his phone and texted Cas.

Problem at the car park. Check surveillance cameras at the bus and train stations.

On it.

The line moved forward slowly, but not slowly enough for Cas to accomplish her task and respond. Donovan ordered two sandwiches for takeaway. After he received his food, he selected a table in the back of the narrow restaurant. He set the food down and sent another text to Cas. *Any luck?*

Still looking.

Resigned to waiting a few minutes longer, Donovan dug a sandwich from the bag and unwrapped it. A little tinge of guilt pricked at him that he was able to eat and Cas still didn't have access to food, but when his stomach growled, he pushed the guilt aside. He wouldn't do either one of them any good if he didn't have the energy to outwit the man waiting down the street.

He finished his sandwich and waited another five minutes until Cas finally texted him again.

Found him. One of our gunmen is at the train station entrance. There's also a car parked near where the buses drop people off, and it hasn't moved since I've been watching.

Thanks.

Two men plus possible reinforcements. These men were determined. Donovan pulled the remaining sandwich from the bag and stuffed it in his coat pocket. He then pulled his cell phone out and sent the request for an Uber with the library as the pickup spot. After he threw out his trash, he headed for the rear exit.

Slowly, he weaved his way through a narrow alley to the street that ran parallel to the one he had been on. He reached the last building and peeked around the corner. The shooter was still on the bench, and all that separated Donovan and the parking garage was a street and the man with a gun.

Donovan checked his app to see how close the Uber was from arriving. Less than one minute. He wrapped his scarf around his neck and adjusted it so it would cover the lower part of his face.

A red BMW pulled up to the curb, a placard in the window identifying the vehicle as a car hire. When no one approached, the driver rolled down his passenger side window and called out to the man on the bench.

Quickly, Donovan crossed the street and headed for the car park entrance. The Uber driver continued to talk to the man on the bench, who tried to shoo him away. Donovan made it all the way to the entrance before the gunman saw him. The man jumped up and started after him.

Donovan sprinted down the ramp into the parking garage, turned the corner, and ducked behind the first car on his left. Footsteps pounded after him.

Crouching, Donovan used the row of cars to shield him. Silently, he moved past the first several cars. The footsteps slowed, the man clearly searching for a sign of where Donovan was. Donovan lowered to the concrete floor.

Shoes of brown leather appeared on the opposite side of the car Donovan currently hid behind. Relying on his training, Donovan slowed his breathing and held his position. The shoes and the legs attached to them stepped forward, stopped, and then began walking again.

Donovan waited two full minutes before he started forward again and made his way toward the car. When he reached it, he listened for footsteps but heard none. Quietly, he used the key rather than the fob to unlock the door. Keeping his head down, he pulled the door open, slipped behind the wheel, and put the key in the ignition. Once in position, he straightened and scanned the garage for any movement. Not seeing any, he clicked his seat belt in place, closed his door, and started the engine.

Instantly, the man searching for him raced into view. Donovan put the car in gear and hit the gas. Tires squealed. A gunshot fired. Glass shattered.

Donovan ducked and glanced back at what remained of the rear window. He swerved around a concrete pillar and made the turn to the exit. He fumbled for the remote to raise the barrier at the exit. The boom raised steadily, Donovan increased speed, and another shot fired.

The car whipped past the barrier, barely avoiding impact, and Donovan made a quick turn toward the safe house. If he and Cas were going to get out of Bruges tonight, he couldn't afford to take the long way back. He pulled out his phone and dialed her number.

"I'm coming in hot. Be ready when I get there."

"ETA?"

"Two minutes."

* * *

Cas slipped her arms through the straps of Donovan's backpack and grabbed her bag. Thirty seconds. Tires skidded against pavement. An engine revved as a car approached. Cas prayed it was the car she expected. She'd had enough surprises for one day.

Fifteen seconds. She turned the doorknob, counted down to five. Then she pulled the door open and hurried down the front steps as the car skidded to a stop.

Donovan reached over from the driver's side and pushed open the passenger-side door. "Get in!"

With the backpack still encumbering her, she climbed in and slammed the car door closed. Once she was inside, Donovan punched the gas.

"What happened?" Cas asked. She dropped her bag on the floor and bent her arm to take off the backpack.

"One of the gunmen was waiting for me by the car park."

Wind whistled through the car, and Cas took in the broken rear window. "Did he do that?"

"Yeah."

"Are you okay?"

"I'm fine, but we need to dump this car and find a new ride."

"We don't have a lot of options. Eight o'clock on a Sunday night? All the car hire places are already closed, except at the airport." What she wouldn't give to be able to call a limo service right now.

"What about the local car rental places?" Donovan said. "Is there one nearby?"

"The only one I can think of is at the train station. Obviously, we wouldn't want to go there, even if it was open."

"I'm not worried about finding one that's open," Donovan said.

Cas read between the lines. They were going to "rent" a car without filling out the proper paperwork first. Though risky, it was better than getting pulled over by the police because of the shattered back window.

She shifted Donovan's backpack so she could use her phone to search for other rental locations. "Take a left at the light. There's another one a couple kilometers away that isn't too close to public transit."

Donovan made the turn. A couple minutes later, he parked down the street from a car hire office located in a strip of shops. The fleet of cars consisted of a half dozen vehicles in the same parking lot that served their customers.

"The cars will be easy to access. Their keys may be more of a challenge." Cas pointed at the office front. "Looks like they have a security system. We can't afford to have the police looking for us in a stolen car."

"Borrowed car. I'll take care of the alarm if you'll wipe down this car," Donovan said. "Monitor the police channel too, just in case."

"I will, but do me a favor and don't get caught."

Donovan leaned closer and gave her a quick kiss. "Don't worry. I've got this."

Cas tried not to think about the naturalness of the gesture or the concern that hummed through her. She opened the glove compartment and pulled out a package of disinfecting wipes and a pair of nitrate gloves.

"Let me have a pair of those too," Donovan said.

Cas handed him a pair. As soon as he put his on, he climbed out of the car. Cas opened the app on her phone to listen to the police channel and set about wiping down the car. She was still working on the interior when a car engine started. Cas quickly cleaned the back of the rearview mirror and the gearshift. Headlights flashed in the windshield, and she looked up. The car parked behind hers, and Donovan climbed out. He retrieved their bags and transferred them to the rental.

"You about finished?"

"Almost." She held out the pack of wipes. "Can you do the exterior door handles?"

"Yeah."

She proceeded to finish the inside. Seat belts, the adjustment bar beneath the seats, the steering wheel. Once satisfied, she grabbed the used wipes and the rest of the package of new ones and climbed out of the car. She used her hip to close the door. "All done."

"Me too." Donovan led the way to their new ride and used a wipe to open his door, even though he was still wearing gloves. Cas climbed in, stuffed the package of wipes into her bag, and dropped the used ones in a pile on the floor.

Donovan clicked his seat belt in place. "Where to now? I don't want to drive to Paris, or this car will lead those guys right to you."

"You're right. Let's go the other direction. Antwerp is about an hour and a half away. We can drive there, dump this car, and find a hotel for the night. Tomorrow we can take the train to Paris."

"I'm not thrilled with the idea of taking public transportation," Donovan said. "I say we pick up another car once the rental places open."

"I have a better idea." Cas retrieved her phone from her pocket and called Ace.

"I was just about to call you," Ace said. "Was that the two of you involved in the latest shooting in Bruges?"

Cas switched the phone from one ear to the other. "That's what I'm calling about. Someone shot out the rear window of our car. We need a replacement."

"And Senator Whitmore wondered why I wanted to increase our budget," Ace muttered. "Where are you?"

"Heading to Antwerp," Cas said. "Can you and Kristi arrange for a new car for us there in the morning?"

"If you're still going back to Paris, I'd rather have you pick up a car there. It'll be easier to have local license plates."

"That's true."

"I'll reserve a rental for you near your hotel," Ace said.

"You're taking care of our hotel too?"

"Yes. I'll text you the address and room numbers."

"Thanks, Ace."

"No problem, but do me a favor. Stop getting shot at."

"I'll do my best."

Cas hung up and replayed the conversation. Her stomach protested its lack of food, and she started a new search, this time for restaurants that were still open.

"What are you doing?"

"Looking for a place we can get something to eat. This time of night, we may have to settle for whatever we can find at a gas station."

Donovan reached into his coat pocket and pulled out a paper-wrapped something. "Here. I bought you a sandwich on my way to get the car."

"Bless you. I'm starving."

"Do you think Ace will give us a hotel that includes breakfast?"

"I hope so."

CHAPTER 29

Doug still couldn't explain why he'd felt prompted to spend most of his Sunday reviewing case files and plugging in the new information from Ghost. Max had denied his request to travel to Louisiana to question Germain personally, but his fellow agents in the New Orleans office should be on their way to pick him up this morning.

Though Doug had more than fifty other cases competing for his attention, he drew out the hardcopy file on the coalition. Grabbing a bunch of magnets from his desk drawer, he arranged photos of the known coalition leadership on the whiteboard attached to the side of his cubicle. Five known members of the board of directors, one of whom was now deceased, along with the lead protest organizer. Of the remaining leadership, all were US citizens, all from Southern states.

Despite the coalition receiving a steady stream of funding through their bank accounts in the Caymans, the suspicion that a foreign entity was involved in creating havoc within the US had never been substantiated, nor was there any obvious connection between the known board members and Alnaazir or any other organization overseas.

Hector crossed to his cubicle. "Back to looking for the missing pieces?"

Doug leaned back in his chair. "The intel I received over the weekend showed two higher-ups in the coalition died in Europe last week. There's also evidence that indicates the coalition may have been connected to the Paris bombing and two other attempts."

"Any word yet on Germain?" Hector asked.

"Last I heard, the agents were on their way to pick him up." Doug checked his watch. "I'm surprised I haven't heard anything."

"Unless they can get him to talk, we still don't have anything that links the coalition to anyone overseas."

"My money is on either Yuearid or Alnaazir," Doug said.

"You don't bet," Hector pointed out. "Let's say you're right though. You're assuming that some foreign entity is trying to influence the United States, but what are they trying to accomplish?"

"The more civil unrest we have here, the harder it is for our government to handle issues abroad. If one of these groups is trying to undermine our society, it could be to keep the US out of their business."

"Yuearid's main focus is gaining power, especially in the Middle East."

"While Alnaazir has always been about limiting Western influence."

Hector grabbed his desk chair and rolled it into Doug's cubicle. "According to an intel report that came through on Friday, Alnaazir is angling for control too. The group has taken over a region in Sudan that's rich in gold and silver deposits. They've also claimed ownership of several mines."

"This is all about money?" Doug shook his head. "That doesn't make sense. The coalition is always more active here in the US during our presidential elections. Why would they care about that if their primary motive is money?"

"I don't know. Maybe the two organizations aren't related," Hector said. "The foreign funding for the coalition could be coming from another group we haven't identified yet."

"Maybe." Doug motioned to the whiteboard. "If we could identify who is in charge of the local chapter of the coalition, I'm convinced it would link us to whoever is really pulling the strings."

Doug's cell phone rang. He snatched it up, but the screen remained dark. He retrieved the phone Ghost had given him and answered. "Valdez."

"Germain Peters is in the wind. He wasn't there when your agents showed up to bring him in."

"How do you know that? I'm still waiting for an update."

"I have my ways," Ghost said. "I flagged Peters's passport. So far no hits."

A fragment of memory pushed forward in Doug's thoughts. "Did you flag both passports?"

"What do you mean, 'both passports'?"

"Germain has dual citizenship. The US and Argentina."

"That's not in his file."

"Maybe not, but I remember him being sent on assignment before because he could travel on his personal passport from Argentina and not be identified as a US federal agent."

"I'll look it up. Thanks."

"We'll start a search too, but let me know if you find him first."

"Yeah. You too."

As soon as Doug hung up the phone, Hector asked, "What was that all about?"

"A source said that Germain is on the run."

"What source? And how does he know about Germain?"

"I have no idea."

Doug's work phone rang, and he answered. An agent from New Orleans repeated the information Ghost had given him a moment before.

"It's official. Our best suspect is missing."

* * *

Breakfast at the hotel, a new rental car, buying a new car, returning the rental car. All Donovan wanted was a hot meal and a soft bed. Or a soft couch. Cas could take the bed.

He drove through the free parking zone closest to their intended destination. "See any sign of trouble?"

"No, but I don't see any parking spaces either. It may be easier to park closer to the apartment. We won't have to pay for the overnight hours anyway."

Cas was right, and he was hungry. He circled back to the street where the guardian apartment was located and found a spot a few buildings away. "I say we pick up food on our way."

"There's a crepe vendor over there."

"Perfect. Want to wait here while I get our food?"

"Yeah. It's probably best if I stay out of sight as much as possible."

"Be right back." Donovan did a quick scan of their surroundings before he climbed out of the car and walked down the cobbled sidewalk to the crepe truck parked a short distance away. As soon as he had their food, he took another quick glance around before he nodded at Cas.

She climbed out of the car and joined him on the sidewalk. He took his backpack from her, slipped it over his shoulder, and took her hand. They made their way to the apartment building without incident.

As soon as they reached the apartment door, Donovan retrieved his weapon and held out the bag of food. "Can you hold this while I clear the apartment?"

Cas's eyebrows went up, and she drew her weapon.

"Right. You aren't a client."

"No, I'm not."

"Fine. We'll both clear the apartment." Donovan unlocked the door, stepped inside, and lowered the bag of food and his backpack to the floor. Using hand signals, he indicated he would check the bedroom. Cas lowered her bag beside Donovan's and moved toward the kitchen. He made it only as far as the bathroom doorway when he paused. Why was the door closed?

A toilet flushed, and the water in the sink turned on. Donovan lifted his weapon and aimed. The door swung open, and the man inside froze.

"Whoa!" Troy's hands went up. "It's just me."

Cas rushed into the hall to see their fellow guardian. "Troy, what are you doing here? I thought you were in Maine."

"I was. Ace thought you might need some backup." He nodded at Donovan's gun. "Do you mind?" Donovan lowered his weapon and holstered it. "Jocelyn is right," Troy said. "It is unnerving having someone point a gun at you when you walk out of the bathroom."

"Who?" Donovan asked.

"Kristi's sister."

"Ah, that's right," Donovan said. "The girlfriend."

"How's that going?" Cas asked.

"Good. She's already looking into apartments in Helsinki for when I transfer back to Europe." Troy stepped past Donovan and walked into the living room. "What are you two doing here anyway? Ace said you were in Bruges."

"We were." Donovan returned to the door, secured it, and picked up his food. "Ace knew we were coming. I'm surprised he didn't give you an update."

"That was probably Kristi's fault."

"How so?" Cas asked.

"I had a message from Jocelyn when I landed. Kristi went into labor sometime late last night. Ace is going to be a father anytime now."

"That's great." Donovan pulled a crepe out and handed one to Cas. "Are you ready to eat? You have to be starving."

"Did you bring me any?" Troy asked.

"I didn't know you were here." At Troy's crestfallen look, Donovan grabbed the extra crepe he had planned to eat himself. "Here. You can have one of mine, but only if you promise to go out and get us breakfast in the morning."

"Deal."

They all sat at the table, and Cas unwrapped her crepe. "Do you ever feel like your life is centered around where your next meal is coming from?"

"I've been living in Africa for the past six years, half of that camping out in unpopulated areas, searching for terrorists," Donovan reminded her. "My life is always about where my next meal is coming from."

"Man, you should get hardship pay," Troy said.

"I'd need to be alive to cash a paycheck."

"True."

"While you're feeling sorry for me, though, I'm calling the couch to sleep on tonight."

"That's fine. I'll take the bed," Troy said.

Cas shook her head. "Not a chance."

"I just flew across the Atlantic to help you. You can't seriously want me to sleep on the floor."

"There's a futon in the closet," Cas offered. "You can sleep on that."

"Fine, but if this thing with the coalition stretches out more than a few days, I'm getting a hotel."

"Cas's family is scheduled to have dinner with the ambassador tomorrow night. I think you can rough it for a day or two."

"Assuming they accepted the invitation," Cas said.

"We'll check on the RSVP." Donovan used the pad of his thumb to wipe some cheese off his lip. "After dinner."

* * *

Doug conducted another search for Germain, but either he was still in the country or whatever airport he had flown out of had yet to sync with the database. No matches. Again.

Doug revised his search, this time only looking for the last name Peters. Two dozen hits popped up. He scrolled through the results. Still nothing that could have been Germain.

"Any luck with tracking down Germain?" Hector asked from where he sat at his desk.

"No. No hits on either of his passports." Doug raked his fingers through his hair. "He must still be in the country."

"I don't think so." Hector motioned to his computer screen. "His cell phone hasn't had any activity since yesterday morning, and his car is parked at his house."

"The New Orleans office already searched his house. He isn't there."

"No, but if his phone and car are, he must be trying to make it look like he is."

"If he didn't leave in his car, someone must have picked him up."

"I've already checked the taxi and rideshare companies. No hits at his address in the window since he last used his phone."

"Pull traffic cam footage for the area."

"I already did. Germain's neighborhood only has two entrances, and both have traffic cameras at the stoplights. I just sent you the link for one."

Doug opened the link Hector sent him. "Were you able to narrow down when Germain left his house?"

"He last used his phone at nine sixteen on Sunday morning, and he was gone by the time our agents showed up this morning"

"A twenty-four-hour window. Let's see if we can narrow it down." Doug rolled back the video feed from the traffic camera to the time of the last phone call. He checked each license plate, verifying if the owners lived in the neighborhood. He made it only a half hour into the video feed when a silver Lexus registered to a security company entered the neighborhood. Eight minutes later, it reappeared, and this time, a passenger was visible in the back seat.

"I think I've got something." Doug jotted down the license plate number, the make, and the model, then crossed to Hector's desk and handed it to him. "Looks like a security company picked someone up only half an hour after the last time Germain used his phone."

"Which way did he go?"

"He turned north out of the main entrance." Doug sat back at his desk. "Let's see if we can track where he went."

Together they used various traffic cameras to follow the movement of the vehicle. Less than two miles from Germain's house, the car disappeared from sight.

"They must have turned off into one of these neighborhoods." Doug studied the map on his computer screen.

"You jump to the main street on the west side. I'll take the east," Hector suggested.

Doug calculated the amount of time it should have taken the car to travel through the neighborhoods and reach the parallel main road. He watched the feed for one of the traffic cameras for several minutes before switching to another. When he didn't find anything, he opened the feed for yet another traffic cam farther down the road.

"I got him." Hector's eyes remained on his screen. "He's heading away from the city."

"Once he gets too far down the freeway, we're going to lose our ability to track him."

Hector looked up. "He didn't get on the freeway."

"Then where's he going?"

"To the regional airport."

"See if you can figure out what time he got there. I'll request a list of flights for everything that flew out of there yesterday." Doug put in his request to the airport for surveillance video and for the flight manifests.

"Best I can tell, they arrived around ten thirty," Hector said.

"I requested the surveillance files from the airport. We should be able to ID our guy if he's really in that car."

"Maybe we should grab some lunch while we're waiting."

"You can if you want, but I'm going to wait for the files," Doug said. "I have a bad feeling about this guy."

"With good reason. If we're right, he killed at least three people."

A new message popped up on Doug's screen. "I got the files."

"That was fast." Hector sat back at his desk. "Send me the surveillance files, and I'll start on those."

Doug forwarded the email and opened the flight listing. "Four flights left in the hour after the Lexus arrived. Three more flights departed during the hour after that."

"Is Germain on any of the passenger lists?"

"I'm checking." Doug scanned through each one. "Two have unidentified passengers on them."

"Where were they headed?"

"One went to Houston. The other went to Charlotte." Doug picked up his phone and called the two airports where the planes had landed. The regional airport in Houston confirmed the arrival of the flight and that the plane was currently parked at their airport. When Doug called Charlotte International, he was transferred from one office to another, the second of which immediately put him on hold. "I hate dealing with the international airports."

"Hey, you're going to want to see this." Hector turned his screen to face Doug. "That's our guy."

"Can you tell which flight he was on?"

"He was in the terminal for about ten minutes before he went outside."

"The flight for Houston left almost two hours later."

"And the one for Charlotte?" Hector asked.

"It took off thirty minutes after they arrived."

The airport authority finally came on the line. "May I help you?"

"Yes. This is Special Agent Valdez with the FBI. I need information on an inbound flight from New Orleans." Doug relayed the flight number and estimated time of arrival.

"Yes. The flight arrived on time. It then refueled and departed two hours later."

"Do you have a passenger list?"

"Yes. I have a pilot, copilot, and one passenger."

"There should have been two passengers."

"That's not what my paperwork says."

"We're quite certain an unnamed passenger on that flight is a person of interest in a case I'm working," Doug said. "Can you send me your security footage for the gate this flight was assigned?"

"It isn't possible anyone deplaned. The plane never came to the terminal."

"Did the transit authority check the passengers before they departed?"

"Yes. They collected the passport information on Mr. Norton and the pilots."

"What are the chances they did a search of the plane before departure?"

"Our agent would have checked the cockpit and passenger area."

"But not necessarily the bathroom or cargo hold."

"I'm sorry, sir. I can't confirm if an in-depth search was conducted based on the information in front of me."

"Just one more thing. What was the plane's destination?"

"Paris."

CHAPTER 30

Cas stood by the window and stared at the street below. In the distance, the Eiffel Tower lit up the night, a shining beacon of the life Cas would soon have to leave behind yet again. Footsteps approached, but she didn't turn. Even though she and Donovan were no longer alone, she sensed his presence behind her.

"You doing okay?" Donovan asked.

Cas lifted her shoulders. Coalition members wanted her dead, her family wanted proof she was alive, and the life she had built for herself as a guardian was in shambles. She wasn't sure how the word *okay* could begin to describe the turmoil swirling inside her.

"Hey." Donovan put his hand on her arm and stepped beside her. "Talk to me."

"What do you want me to say? That it hurts to be back in Paris? That I'm scared to tell my parents I'm still alive, especially since that information could put them in danger?"

"And you'll be watching me talk to your ex-boyfriend and your sister," Donovan added.

"I can't even think about that right now."

Troy walked in from the kitchen, holding his laptop. "I just looked over the file on Germain. Did you know about the injury that caused Germain to leave the bureau?"

"Yeah. A friendly fire accident."

"It wasn't just friendly fire." Troy nodded at his screen. "Germain came out of an alley, and a white agent shot him."

"The coalition uses race as a tool for hatred," Cas said. "If Germain was sympathetic to their cause, a career-ending injury would certainly add fuel to the fire. Black law enforcement officer shot by white fed. I'm surprised the press didn't jump all over that when it happened."

"They probably would have, but the case was classified." Troy set his laptop on the coffee table. "The incident was covered up."

"Even more reason for Germain to be bitter."

Donovan gave her arm a squeeze before letting his hand drop to his side. "Now that we know he had access to Massey, I don't think anyone has any doubt that Germain is our guy."

"Yes, but will he give up the rest of the coalition leadership?" Cas asked. "Unless he does, my family is in danger as long as they believe I'm still alive."

"They?" Troy asked. "As in the coalition or your family?"

"Both."

Troy's cell phone rang. He answered it and put it on speaker. "Hey, Kade. You have all of us here."

"Another party and no one invited me."

"You don't want to come," Troy said without missing a beat. "Cas and Donovan are making me sleep on the floor."

"Stop whining," Donovan countered. "Kade, what do you have for us? Any news on Germain?"

"Yeah. He slipped out of the country on an Argentinian passport."

"Any idea where he went?" Cas asked.

"He flew into Paris, but we haven't been able to locate where he's staying."

"He's here?" Concern vibrated in Donovan's voice.

"Yeah. We don't know what he's doing there. Could be he's coming to help find Cas, or it could be something completely unrelated."

"When did he arrive?"

"Eight o'clock this morning."

"That was hours ago." Cas glanced out the window. "He could be just about anywhere by now."

"Yeah, which is why I need all of you to help us track him," Kade said. "Oh, and one more thing."

"Every time you say that, you give us more bad news," Cas said.

"Not this time. Kristi had the baby. It's a girl."

A guardian with a family. This was a first. Maybe miracles could happen, miracles like staying alive long enough to see her own family again.

* * *

Germain might as well be a ghost. With his FBI training, he would qualify if it weren't for his twisted loyalties and his involvement in the death of at least two witnesses.

Donovan sat beside Cas on the couch while Troy worked at the kitchen table. The three of them had searched through airport surveillance footage for Charles de Gaulle Airport for the past six hours, and so far, the only possible glimpse they'd had of Germain was when they'd caught sight of a man with a noticeable limp coming out of a restroom, his face hidden by a ball cap.

Cas stifled a yawn.

Donovan put his hand on her knee. "You should get some sleep."

"What about you? You have to be as tired as I am."

"We can turn this over to Kade and Renee for now. It's still only six o'clock in the States," Donovan said. "We can start up again first thing tomorrow."

"Yeah. That's probably a good idea." Cas pushed to a stand. "I'll see you in the morning."

Though Donovan itched to give her a kiss good night, Troy's presence caused him to remain seated. "Good night."

The bedroom door closed, and Donovan plugged his laptop in to charge before opening the hall closet where extra blankets and pillows were stored. He pulled out one of each and set the pillow at one end of the couch before he spread out the blanket.

Troy's phone rang, and Donovan straightened. "Is it Kade?"

"No, it's Jocelyn." Troy answered his phone. "Hey there. How's everything going?" He settled back in his chair and chatted with his girlfriend. Judging from the ease of conversation and the look on Troy's face, Donovan suspected another guardian engagement was imminent. When Troy expressed his love to Jocelyn, those suspicions only heightened.

"I'm going to crash for a few hours," Donovan said as soon as Troy hung up.

"Yeah, me too." Troy fetched the futon mattress and a pillow and blanket from the closet, then moved the coffee table aside and made up his bed on the floor near the couch. As soon as he lay down, he asked, "Are you going to tell me what's going on with you and Cas?"

"You know what's happening. The coalition knows she's alive, and I've been trying to keep her that way."

"That's not what I'm talking about." Troy propped himself up on one elbow. "You two were looking pretty cozy tonight."

How had Troy noticed anything? Donovan had made a point of keeping things professional since they'd arrived and found Troy in the apartment. "We sat together on the couch. That's not exactly getting cozy."

"It's not a big deal," Troy said. "You two make a good couple."

"Except that I live in Africa, and Cas lives in Europe."

"You know she's going to have to be reassigned."

"Yeah, but can you imagine her living in Africa? She doesn't even speak the language in half the places I cover," Donovan said. "She'd hate that."

"Yeah, you're right."

Donovan's disappointment crawled through him. It was one thing to suspect a relationship with Cas couldn't go anywhere, but it was disheartening to hear someone agree with his assessment.

"It's too bad though," Troy said. "You do make a good couple."

Donovan agreed, but he changed the subject. "What's the deal with you and Kristi's sister?"

"She's flying into Helsinki to visit Kristi and Ace tomorrow. I'll meet up with her after we secure Cas's safety and neutralize the situation with the coalition."

"That's not what I meant."

"I stopped and bought this earlier today." Troy produced a small jewelry box from his bag. He flipped it open to reveal a tear-shaped diamond.

"Wow. Getting engaged. That's huge."

"I know. I've never been so scared before in my life."

"It's a big step, especially with someone who isn't part of the guardian program."

"Ace is going to let me use my Coast Guard alias with Jocelyn's family so we won't have to hide our marriage from the people closest to her." Troy snapped the ring box closed. "Assuming she says yes."

"Good luck."

"Thanks." Troy settled down on the futon. "I think Kade and Renee should find Germain for us so we can close this case down. I'd rather not be carrying a diamond ring around with me for long."

"I don't blame you."

CHAPTER 31

IMPATIENCE AND NERVES SKITTERED THROUGH Cas as she showered and dressed for the day. She studied herself in the mirror. Clothes off the rack, minimal makeup, and long hair. Cas barely resembled the woman she had been the day of her accident. What would her parents think of who she was now? How would they react when their suspicions were confirmed that she was indeed alive, that she had deliberately hidden the truth from them? What would Makayla think? And Roshaun?

With all the new evidence that Germain was the person behind her accident, did that mean Roshaun was innocent? Or had they been working together all along?

The water in the shower turned on. Cas finished putting on her makeup and padded down the hall. She peeked into the living room, expecting either Donovan or Troy to still be in bed at this early hour, but the room was empty, the bedding already stored away.

She continued into the kitchen to find it also empty. She opened the narrow pantry. The herbal tea Troy favored and the basic emergency canned food sat on a shelf. So much for cooking as a way to relieve her nerves.

The front door opened, and Donovan walked in carrying a bag from the bakery downstairs. "Good morning." He set the bag down and leaned in for a kiss. The gesture soothed and chased away the worst of her nerves. "I thought Troy was getting breakfast this morning," Cas said.

"I woke up first and didn't want to wait. Besides, this way Troy will owe me, and he'll have to go get us lunch . . . or groceries."

"Anything to avoid the grocery store."

"Yep." Donovan set the bag on the counter.

"How long have you been up?"

"A couple hours."

"Any luck on the surveillance?"

"We caught a visual of Germain at the Paris airport, but we lost him once he got into the city."

Cas tensed. "Where in the city?"

"The first arrondissement."

Her heartbeat quickened, and she grabbed his hand. "My parents' hotel is in the first arrondissement."

"He hasn't popped up on any hotel registries, so it's possible he's staying with his father."

"We should be able to check the feed from the hotel's security cameras. All of the entrances are monitored."

"That was my next task." He opened the bag and retrieved two croissants. "Do you want almond or chocolate?"

"I'll eat later." She took a step toward the living room, but Donovan moved into her path.

"Hey, you aren't going to do anyone any good if you starve yourself, and today is going to be a long day." He waited until her eyes lifted to his before he continued. "Besides, we can eat while we watch the video feed."

"Fine." Cas took the croissant in the hand closest to her. She slipped past him and set her breakfast aside while she retrieved her laptop.

Donovan followed a moment later, carrying a half-eaten croissant and a glass of milk. "Here. You can eat while your laptop boots up."

"Thanks." Cas took a sip without taking her eyes off the screen. Donovan moved back to the kitchen and returned a moment later with his own drink. He settled on the couch beside her. "If you take the lobby, I'll check the other entrances."

"Sounds good." Cas accessed the security portal and pulled up the feed. "What time did Germain's train arrive?"

"Nine o'clock last night."

Troy walked into the room and held up his phone. "Did you see the latest?"

"I'm afraid to ask, but what now?" Donovan asked.

Troy held out his phone so Donovan and Cas could both read the screen. *Reward doubled. One million euros. News mogul Josiah Edgemont has increased the reward for information leading to the whereabouts of his daughter . . .*

"You've got to be kidding me." Cas snatched the phone from Troy. "I thought the reward was still at a quarter million."

"No. He increased it a couple days ago to half a million."

Cas read the rest of the article, scrolling down until she reached the next headline: *Purchase of Starline Media Group complete*. "Everyone is going to be looking for me."

"Everyone already was looking for you." Donovan took the phone and scanned through the article before handing the phone back to Troy. "Did we ever get word from the embassy about whether your father RSVP'd?"

"No." Cas shook her head. "We've gone to all this trouble so I can see him, and he's so focused on finding me, he's making it harder on all of us."

Cas's cell phone rang.

"Who is it?" Donovan asked.

"Bridger." Cas pressed Talk. "Don't tell me you're planning to claim the reward."

"Thought about it, but I'm calling for something else," Cole said. "We picked up some chatter about a member of Alnaazir in Paris. We think he could be meeting with the leadership of the coalition."

"That's huge. We've been trying to connect the coalition to their foreign sponsors for years." Cas repeated the information for Donovan and Troy. "I wonder if the information came from your source in Sudan."

"Probably," Donovan said.

"I'm afraid I have other news you may not be as excited about," Cole said.

"What's that?" Cas asked.

"In the intel we received, there was a mention of your father's company. From what we picked up, it appears someone high up is involved with the coalition."

Roshaun. "Do you know who?"

"No. The message we intercepted mentioned that they would be using Edge Broadcasting to get their party started."

Cas's stomach clenched. "Any idea what party they're talking about?"

"Could be another bombing," Cole said. "Could be another fake news story."

"Any idea of when this is happening?"

"Soon. That's all I know so far."

"Thanks, Cole. I'll be in touch." Cas hung up the phone.

"What was that all about?" Troy asked.

"One of our CIA contacts said they picked up chatter that the coalition leadership may be meeting here in Paris with someone from Alnaazir," Cas said. "They also mentioned that they would be using my father's news outlets as part of their plan."

Troy settled into the chair across from her. "Sounds like we need to get the word to your father about shoring up his cyber security protocols."

"And getting Germain's access removed," Cas added.

"Even if we do that, if Roshaun is involved, there's no way we can be sure getting Germain out of the picture will be enough," Donovan said.

Troy leaned forward and rested his elbows on his knees. "I could go in undercover at the embassy dinner."

Cas studied Troy, with his light hair and fair skin. "I hate to say it, but he'd be more open to talking to Donovan."

"Why?" Troy asked.

"I'm afraid you're a little too pale for Roshaun's taste."

Troy's eyebrows lifted. "He's prejudiced against white people?"

"I don't think he would ever put his opinions in quite those words, but he had a few run-ins with the law growing up, all of which had nothing to do with what he had done and everything to do with the color of his skin," Cas said. "Or so he believes."

Troy shook his head. "No wonder he got caught up with the coalition."

"I can talk to him tonight," Donovan said, "but first we need to know for sure he's going to be there. According to the state department's system, your family still hasn't RSVP'd."

"Cas, you obviously know your father well. What can we do to make sure he attends?" Troy asked.

"I have an idea." Cas picked up her phone and dialed Cole.

"That was fast," Cole said. "Do you already have something for me?"

"No, but how would you like to go to an embassy dinner tonight?" Cas asked. "You can help Ghost question my family firsthand."

"I'm already in Paris. Just tell me what time."

"The dinner will start at seven, but first, I need you to do something for me."

"What's that?"

"You need to contact my father. It looks like you may be collecting that reward after all."

* * *

Donovan shook his head as Cas laid out her plan. "I don't like it. It's one thing to have Cole talk to your dad, but having them meet at the embassy? You're risking the coalition knowing you will be there."

"So we keep Cas here at the apartment," Troy suggested. "We can set up a video call with her father."

"That was our original plan, but if my father is expecting to hand over a million dollars, we can't be sure he will believe it's really me if I'm not there in person," Cas said. "He's spent half his career identifying fake videos and verifying sources."

"I'm sorry, Cas, but we can't risk it," Donovan insisted.

Cas lowered her eyes, but not quickly enough to hide the disappointment that flashed there.

"Donovan's right," Troy said. "If Roshaun is still working with the coalition, you might not even make it into the embassy alive."

Cas let out a sigh. "Troy, what kind of toys did you bring with you?"

"I have a couple microcameras, but they won't do us any good in the embassy. Everything will be swept for bugs when we get there, and we'll have to go through security on our way in."

"Any chance you have an intel ID on you?" Donovan asked Troy.

"No. It was too risky to bring something like that in my carry-on."

"I had the same problem." Donovan pondered for a moment. They needed a way for Cas to be able to communicate with them while they were at the embassy. She would know better than anyone what questions to ask or if anyone was lying.

"What about Cole?" Cas asked. "He's CIA. He probably has some kind of credentials to get into the embassy."

"And he would have access to the local CIA office," Donovan said.

"I'll call him." Cas stood and walked into the kitchen.

"Do you trust this guy?" Troy asked.

Cas nodded. "Yeah, I do."

Donovan sensed Troy's hesitation. "Cole Bridger isn't just another agency man. He practically grew up in intelligence."

"And he's worked with me several times before," Cas added. "He has a pretty good understanding of what the guardian program is all about."

"You've had your share of time working with Alnaazir," Troy said to Donovan. "Do you really think the two organizations could be connected?"

"I don't know." Donovan rolled the latest information over in his mind. "Alnaazir's primary objective has been to undermine Western society. Terrorism is the only thing they think we understand."

"The coalition doesn't share the same methodology, but they do have a similar view on disrupting our current democracy to make things different, even if it doesn't make them better," Troy said. "If nothing significant changes,

Jim Whitmore has an excellent chance of becoming president. Neither one of these groups would be thrilled if that happens."

"Of course not. Whitmore represents stability and moderate change to help improve our country. His opponent is a radical, feeding hate and social divisions to stir up votes."

"I never have been a fan of Matthews." Troy dropped onto the couch. "Be glad you've been out of the country for all the campaigning."

"Even in Africa, I hear plenty."

Cas walked back into the living room. "Cole is going to pick up some surveillance equipment for us so you can both wear cameras."

"What do you mean 'both'?" Troy asked. "I thought I was monitoring from outside."

"You are. Cole will be the other inside man."

"It'll be good to have another set of eyes and ears in there," Donovan said. "Sorry it won't be you, Cas."

"Yeah, me too."

"Where are we meeting up with your CIA buddy?" Troy asked.

"He'll be here in an hour."

"You're bringing him here?" Troy asked.

"Yeah. You aren't going to want me leaving the apartment, and I'll need to get set up to receive the feed from the hidden cameras before you two leave."

"This apartment is getting overcrowded fast," Troy said.

"It's about to get worse before it gets better," Cas said. "Cole is staying here tonight."

Troy sent her a pleading look. "You aren't serious."

"I'm afraid so. It didn't make sense to have the two of you using public transportation, and it'll be easier for everyone if he can stay here and debrief with us in the morning."

"Better tell him to bring his own sleeping bag," Troy grumbled.

"I already did."

CHAPTER 32

Cas stood up to answer the knock at the door, but Donovan grabbed her arm before she could move forward. "I'll get it."

She couldn't even answer the door by herself. After fighting to stay invisible for the past few years, she should be used to the protocols and precautions, but the last two weeks were wearing on her. Knowing her parents could learn the truth, or at least the part of the truth that confirmed she was still alive, added another layer to her bubbling emotions.

Donovan opened the door and let Cole inside. Troy emerged from the kitchen.

"Cole, this is Ghost," Donovan said.

"Another one?" Cole shook his head. "Don't you think we're taking this whole hidden identity thing a bit too far?"

"It's what keeps us alive," Troy said.

"Can I at least call you by whatever aliases you're using tonight?" Cole asked.

Donovan glanced at Troy, who shrugged.

"I guess we can give you that much," Troy said. "Tonight, I'm Tony Hansen."

"And I'll be going by Daniel Smith," Donovan said.

"Smith? That's original."

"Hey, we use what works."

Cole jutted his chin toward Cas. "What about our she-ghost over there?"

Donovan took a protective stance beside her. "She's still Ghost to you."

"Even though I know her real name?" Cole asked.

"He knows who I am." Cas put her hand on Donovan's arm. "It's more dangerous to have him slip and refer to me as Ghost in front of my family. Besides, he has to use my name if he's going to claim the money."

"With the publicity campaign Josiah Edgemont has been blasting all over the world, I doubt there's anyone who doesn't know Cassidy right now anyway," Troy said.

"I guess you're right." Donovan motioned to Cole's backpack. "Did you bring the equipment we need?"

"Yeah." He set his bag down and unzipped it. "I went with cameras disguised in tie clips and lapel pins." Cole laid out two of each and added earpieces for the men to communicate with Cas and each other.

"While you three decide who wants which one, I'm going to set up my surveillance area." Cas picked up her laptop. "Tony and Daniel, can I use yours too? It'll give me more views at the same time."

"Sure," Donovan said.

Cas collected the three guardian laptops and set them up on the kitchen counter. After she calibrated the various microcams into her surveillance program, she adjusted the two laptops on the end so she could easily see them. An image of her sitting on the kitchen stool appeared on her screen, and Cas turned.

Donovan approached, now dressed in a black pinstriped suit.

"You look handsome," she said.

"Thanks." He fiddled with his lapel pin. "How's the picture quality?"

"Good." Cas motioned to the laptop on her right. "The security cameras at the embassy haven't shown any activity except for the caterers arriving, and the microcams Cole brought are all up and running."

"I'm sorry you can't come with us."

"I know." Cas pushed the worst of the disappointment aside. "Maybe with me not there, you'll be able to get information out of Roshaun. I doubt he'd say much if he knew for sure that I was alive."

"Trust me. Talking to Roshaun is my top priority for tonight."

Cas tried to visualize her ex-boyfriend chatting with her current boyfriend. Her cheeks heated at the term *boyfriend* being applied to Donovan. A couple of private moments didn't necessarily mean a relationship would follow.

"You okay?" Donovan asked.

"Yes. Just worried about tonight."

"Everything will be fine. Cole arranged to meet with your father right after dinner."

"I thought he was going in with you to help run interference."

"No. He thinks that if he meets with your father too early, all the focus of the evening's conversation will be about you," Donovan said. "By waiting until after dinner, that gives Troy and me a chance to talk to your family and assess how Roshaun fits into the current dynamics."

"Troy's going to the dinner with you?" Cas asked.

"He was going to run support from outside, but since Cole can do that for the first hour or so, it makes sense to bring Troy in to dig for information."

"What cover is he using?"

"He is now the owner of a private airline charter company."

"Since you're going in as a businessman, that will make it easy for you to vouch for him."

"That was my thought." His gaze met hers. "We'll set up the meeting with your father as soon as we can make sure it's safe."

Myriad emotions streaked through her, and Cas pressed her lips together. Not trusting herself to speak, she nodded.

Donovan ran his hand along her arm. "I know this isn't easy. Just hold on a little longer."

Troy walked in, and he looked from Donovan to Cas and back again. "We're ready when you are."

"Give me a minute?" Donovan asked.

"Yeah. We'll meet you at the car." Troy disappeared back into the living room. "Come on, Cole."

The door opened and closed. Donovan reached out and put both hands on Cas's shoulders before he leaned down and kissed her.

Like a match to kindling, the spark between them ignited, and the kiss warmed and soothed. Donovan drew her closer, and a shiver worked through her. Her hands slipped around his waist, and the muscles in his back tensed beneath her touch. In that moment, she let herself draw from his strength, her thoughts swirling into the dangerous land of what if. What if they lived in the same place? What if they could forge a future together?

The questions rattled her, and she drew back before she let her unspoken dreams consume her.

Donovan held her close and touched his forehead to hers. "I'm sorry I'm meeting your family for the first time without you."

The normalcy of his comment struck her, and for a moment, she let herself believe she could have a normal life again. Reality slapped her back. She couldn't have normal. Not with Donovan. "You say that like you'll get to see them again."

"Maybe I will. I care about you. If you're able to make them part of your life again, that will make them part of mine."

Cas shook her head. "It could never work. The paparazzi are constantly following them. Even if the coalition is shut down and the threats against me finally end, you're still a ghost. You would never be able to live outside the shadows."

Donovan stepped back, and his eyes darkened. In his quest to protect her, had he forgotten the threats against him? Or did he not understand the extent of the media's presence in her family's life?

Not able to add another log to her emotional fire, she leaned forward and kissed him once more. "Be careful tonight."

"I will." Donovan gave her shoulder a squeeze and turned away. She followed him to the door, but when he slipped outside, he didn't turn back. The door clicked shut between them, and Cas forced herself to move forward. She flipped the lock closed.

Her mind whirling, she walked back into the kitchen. Was it possible for the coalition to be stopped? And if so, would she be able to go back to her old life? Would she even want to?

The family she had missed for years or the man who was slowly capturing her heart? No matter who she chose, another heartbreak lay in her future. Of that much, she was certain.

* * *

The local news sounded through the speaker beside him, and Donovan tried to stretch his legs into the passenger side of the back seat. He supposed sitting in the back of Cole's tiny hatchback was a small price to pay for his private goodbye, but Cas's words wouldn't stop ricocheting through his mind. Troy's relationship with Jocelyn, a civilian who now worked in a limited capacity as a photographer for the guardians, had made it seem possible to have a relationship with Cas, even if she were to come out of hiding. But the picture Cas painted tonight indicated that hope was not only unlikely to be fulfilled, but it was also unobtainable.

The female newscaster repeated the latest information about the million-dollar reward to find Cas. That was followed with the breaking story that Josiah Edgemont had received a tip and was expected to make an announcement later tonight.

"Uh-oh," Donovan said.

"What?" Troy glanced at him in the rearview mirror.

"On the news."

"Translate for me. French isn't one of my languages," Troy said.

"Someone tipped the press that Cole is meeting with Josiah."

"Great. With our luck, the press will be all over this." Troy shook his head. "You would think that someone who owned a multibillion-dollar company would have the sense to keep this quiet."

"Let's hope we can get into the embassy without any trouble," Donovan muttered.

The newscaster's voice increased in volume and speed when she launched into her next story. "This just in: The city water supply in Paris has been poisoned. We are still gathering information, but we can confirm that fourteen residents in the first arrondissement and another twenty-three in the eighth have already been hospitalized. All residents are urged to treat all open-source water supplies as impotable. Authorities are encouraging everyone to drink only bottled water until they identify the source of the contamination. The water authority is currently taking samples from all sections of the city."

"We have another problem." Donovan grabbed his phone and called Cas.

"Why are you calling me?" Cas asked. "I can hear everything you're saying."

"Did you hear what was on the news just now?"

"No. Is it more about the reward?"

"That too, but there's a report that the water in Paris has been contaminated."

"Has it been verified?" Cas asked.

"I don't know. The report said there are a couple dozen people already hospitalized in the first and eighth arrondissements."

"I'll check into it."

"And while you check, don't drink the water."

"I won't," Cas said. "Make sure the embassy knows of the threat too."

"I will." They turned the corner, and the American flag came into view. The four-story building in pale yellow sat back from the street, the wrought-iron fence stretching between concrete pillars.

"We're almost to the embassy. I'll talk to you soon." Donovan hung up and pocketed his phone.

"Poisoned water?" Troy asked. "You've got to be kidding."

"That's what's on the news. Cas . . ." He hesitated briefly before he corrected himself for Cole's benefit. "Cassidy is going to try to verify the story."

"You can call her Cas in front of me," Cole said. "I already know her nickname."

"Everyone have their IDs?" Troy asked.

"Yeah." Donovan pulled out the ID consistent with his current alias. As soon as Cole pulled up to the main gate, a Marine guard approached and verified their identities. A second guard emerged from the guard shack, holding a dog on a leash. The black lab sniffed the car as they encircled them. As soon as the dog handler finished his sweep, he nodded his approval and stepped back, taking the dog with him.

"You are good to go, sir." The first guard handed back their IDs and gave them instructions on where to park.

"Thanks." Cole took all of their IDs and handed everyone's back to them. "Also, not sure if you heard the news, but there's a possibility that the city's water supply has been compromised."

The guard's eyebrows rose. "Are you serious?"

"Yeah. Better stick with bottled water for the next while," Cole said.

"Thank you. I'll notify the embassy staff as well."

"Great. We appreciate it." Cole drove forward and parked the car.

"What are you going to do while we're inside?" Donovan asked Cole.

"After I go in and give you both your sidearms and comm sets, I'll keep an eye out for anyone we didn't see on the guest list," Cole said.

The three men made their way into the embassy. As soon as they cleared security, they headed toward the dining room.

When they were almost there, Cole led them into a small alcove near the restrooms. He handed over their surveillance devices and weapons. "As soon as Roshaun gets here, I'll search his car to see if there's anything worth finding inside."

"He may come with the Edgemonts."

"Then I'll search their car." Cole shrugged. "It'll give me something to do."

"Don't get caught," Troy warned.

"I won't."

As soon as Donovan and Troy walked into the dining room, the ambassador approached with his wife. After the introductions, the ambassador said, "I'm afraid dinner will be served later than planned. We were notified about a problem with the water a few minutes ago, and our caterers had to make some substitutions to ensure everything is safe."

"I'm sure everyone will be more than happy to wait if that means we can avoid getting sick," Troy said.

Voices carried to them, and new arrivals appeared in the doorway. Donovan turned and got his first look at Cas's family and the man she had once loved.

CHAPTER 33

Though Cas knew she should verify the story on the poisoned water supply, when her family walked into the embassy dining room, she couldn't tear her eyes away from the screen.

She braced against the onslaught of regret and longing when Donovan shook hands with her dad. Had her father not gained so much fame through his success, this could have been a meeting between the two most important men in her life, but in truth, no matter what happened with the coalition, one of them would no longer be allowed in her world. Would it be her family she was forced to abandon again, or would it be her budding relationship with Donovan that was sacrificed?

Donovan greeted her mother and sister before shaking hands with Roshaun. The small talk started, and Cas forced herself to access the hospital's emergency room database to check on the latest sensational news story. When she didn't find any admissions related to suspected poisonings, she picked up her phone and called Kade.

"What do you want now?" Kade asked.

"I need you to help me verify a news story," Cas said. "The news just broke on the radio that the water supply in Paris has been contaminated."

"That's going to cause a run on bottled water."

"Yeah, but I need updates on what sections of the city are really affected, and if the rumors of people being hospitalized are true."

"You think this is fake news?" Kade asked.

"With what we've been finding over the past couple weeks, I want to rule it out."

"That makes sense, but why can't you do it?"

"Because Donovan and Troy are at the embassy with my family right now, and I can't feed them questions for Roshaun if I'm researching at the same time."

"Fine. Give me what you know."

Cas passed on the basic details Donovan had related to her.

"I'll call you as soon as I find anything."

"Thanks, Kade."

"You still owe me chocolate. It's time to pay up."

Cas laughed despite the weight of the situation. "I'll see what I can do."

She ended the call and scanned the images on the computer screens. One revealed the interior of a car, clearly Cole searching the vehicle her family had arrived in. She had no idea how Cole had managed to slip past her father's driver, who would most certainly be guarding the car, but when it came to Cole, sometimes it was best to not ask questions.

From the camera in Troy's tie clip, the ambassador and his wife were visible, chatting with Cas's parents in the background. Makayla stood in front of Troy, the two of them engaged in conversation. From the animation on her face, Makayla had to be talking about some of her favorite charities. Troy had clearly taken Cas's advice to engage her on that topic.

Cas turned to the feed from Donovan's lapel pin, where Roshaun's face filled her screen. She turned up the audio on Donovan's microphone.

"Are you working while you're here in Paris?" Donovan asked.

"I've done a few newscasts related to the bombing, but this is supposed to be a family vacation," Roshaun said.

"I saw the ring on Makayla's finger. Congratulations."

"Thanks."

"When's the big day?"

What was he doing? Donovan was supposed to be questioning Roshaun about her and the coalition, not about Roshaun's happiness with her little sister.

"October ninth. It can't come soon enough."

"I bet." Donovan must have taken a step away from Troy and Makayla, because the view changed. "I understand you used to date Makayla's sister."

That was better. "Yeah." Roshaun's eyes darted to the floor for a moment. "It was really rough on both of us when Cassidy died."

"I'm sure it was, but I have to say, I was surprised to hear you dated one sister and are now engaged to the other."

"It sounds bad when you say it like that, but I didn't start dating anyone for a couple years after Cassidy died." Roshaun turned his head, and the love and contentment in his eyes couldn't be missed.

"How long have you and Makayla been together?"

"About a year." Roshaun looked at Donovan again, and the corners of his lips curved up. "I ran into Makayla at a charity event, and she roped me into helping her with a silent auction. It didn't take long for things to go from friendship to what we have now."

"I hate to ask, but what's going to happen if you find out Cassidy is still alive?"

Roshaun's eyes darkened in the way they always did when his guard went up. "I know Josiah wants to believe it's true. We all do, but I don't know that it's possible. I don't know how anyone could have survived an accident like hers. Even if she did, she would never let all of us believe she was dead if she wasn't."

"Maybe she ended up in the witness protection program. Rumor has it that someone in the coalition wanted her dead."

"I've heard that rumor too, but the police never found any evidence."

"Just because there isn't evidence doesn't mean it isn't true."

"Maybe not." Roshaun shrugged. "I joined the coalition years ago. I thought it would be great to do a story on them and their rising membership, but I stepped away from it after Cassidy died."

"You were doing a story?"

"Yeah. I convinced Cassidy to join the coalition with me so it wouldn't look like I was a reporter digging for information," Roshaun said.

Cas gripped the side of the counter. Everything that happened—the accident, her ultimate involvement with the guardians, her years in hiding, the recent attempts on her life—everything was because of a story? How could Roshaun not have told her that he was investigating?

"Did you ever find anything worth reporting?"

"I was close, but a few weeks after we joined the coalition, Cassidy died. I packed my notes away and never went back. End of story."

* * *

Doug tried for more than a half hour to communicate with the airport authority in Paris only to learn two things: his rudimentary French was even worse than he'd thought, and the man on the other end didn't like Americans.

Though he couldn't confirm Germain's arrival in Paris, Doug proceeded with his search. When the hotel registrations in Paris didn't turn up anything, he started tracking the location of Germain's family and known associates. He only had to go as far as the man's father. After making a call to a hotel in Paris, Doug picked up his new cell phone and called Ghost.

"What do you have?" Ghost asked.

"I haven't been able to confirm it, but we think Germain Peters flew into Paris yesterday."

"Sorry, I was about to call you and give you the latest. We found him in Paris. He arrived yesterday morning, but we don't know where he's staying."

"He's at the Four Seasons," Doug said.

"Are you sure?"

"Yes. The desk clerk confirmed that he was signed in as a guest in his father's suite yesterday."

The anxiety in Ghost's voice rose. "We have intel that his father is staying there with the Edgemont family."

A sense of urgency streaked through Doug. "As in Cassidy Edgemont's family?"

"The very same."

"If Cassidy really is alive, he could be following the family to find her." Doug doubted the woman could have survived the accident, but that didn't negate that her family could now be in danger.

"I'll contact the local authorities and ask for them to pick him up," Ghost said.

"What about the other passenger with him?" Doug asked. "Any idea who he is?"

More clicking on a keyboard. "This is odd. He's a chemist who works for a government contractor."

"Doing what?"

"I don't like this," Ghost said. "He works in a lab that specializes in developing defenses against chemical warfare. Any evidence that he had any toxins with him on the plane?"

"According to the manifest, all they had was personal luggage and ten cases of water bottles."

"Water bottles?" Ghost asked. "Oh no."

"What?"

"The water supply in Paris wasn't tainted until after they arrived. If they brought water bottles with them . . ."

"They knew they were going to need their own supply."

"It would make sense." Urgency filled Ghost's voice. "I need you to track down the lab Nathaniel Norton was working at. See if they are missing any toxins, specifically ones that could be administered in a liquid form."

"You think Germain and this chemist are behind the poisoned water in Paris."

"It's a possibility we need to explore."

"I'll make the call." Doug hung up and immediately looked up the number for the lab. Two transfers, an ID verification, and five minutes later, the managing director came on the line.

"Sir, I understand you are asking about possible missing inventory," she said.

"That's right. We have reason to believe one of your employees could be involved in poisoning the water in Paris."

"That is highly unlikely. The amount of inventory we're missing isn't enough to pollute a water source of that size."

"What are you missing? And how much?"

"It's an experimental water-soluble toxin called HK4," the director said. "Our inventory check yesterday identified a shortage of two vials."

"How much damage can a vial do?"

"Depending on how it's distributed, one vial would be enough to kill thirty to fifty people, more if it's given in individual doses."

Doug's blood chilled. "What if it was added to water bottles?"

"That would significantly increase the kill ratio. Two vials would be enough to dose between two hundred and two hundred and fifty standard-sized water bottles."

"Is there an antidote for this HK4 poison?"

"No. That's what we've been working on."

"Thank you." Doug hung up and dialed Ghost.

"Any luck?"

"Yes, and I'm afraid we have a different problem than we thought."

CHAPTER 34

Guilt rose within Cas as Donovan chatted with Makayla and Roshaun. She couldn't imagine the suffering she would endure if her sister died, and yet she had deliberately inflicted that pain on her family and friends. Thankfully, Donovan steered the conversation away from her and onto Roshaun and Makayla's activities during their time in Paris.

Cas checked the video from Cole. He had taken position near the caterer's van, a steady stream of workers carrying trays and disposable aluminum pans into the embassy kitchen.

Troy had worked his way around the room and now chatted with her parents and the ambassador. Her parents appeared at ease, but Cas didn't miss the telltale signs of their stress. The way her mother's smile didn't reach her eyes and the way her father's hand kept finding his pocket and fisting there. She couldn't fathom the turmoil they both must be experiencing while they waited to find out if she really was alive.

Her phone rang, breaking her out of her thoughts. She turned down the audio on the three men's microphones and answered.

"We have a problem," Kade said without preamble. "Germain and the man traveling with him are responsible for the story about the water contamination."

"They contaminated Paris's water supply?"

"I don't think so. I've had Renee checking hospital records. We can't find any cases that appear to be related to what is on the news."

"So it's some kind of scare tactic."

"We think so, but it's possible that Germain and his partner are using it as a means to kill people through poisoned water bottles."

"Any idea who?"

"No, but I have to think it will be today. It shouldn't be too much longer for the city officials to test the water and come out with a statement."

"Do we know anything about where they're staying or where they are now?"

"Germain is signed in as a guest in his father's suite at the Four Seasons, but neither of them have cell phones we can track."

"He's staying at the same place as my parents?"

"We think so, but there hasn't been any sign of him on the surveillance feed."

"What about the plane? Who does it belong to?" Cas asked.

"It's owned by some company based out of London. Starline Media Group."

"Starline? They were just in the news today."

"For what?"

"The company was just sold." Cas opened a search on her laptop. "Here it is. It was purchased by Frontview Enterprises."

"Never heard of it."

"Neither have I, and I grew up in the industry." Uneasy, Cas did a search for the new owner. "This looks like a shell company." She did a second search and then a third before a familiar name popped onto the screen. "This is unexpected."

"What?"

"Frontview is hidden beneath a couple of shell companies, but the owner is Steven Powell. He's the son of the man who sold my father his television network. That business deal was a huge step along my father's journey to success."

"Is there a reason he would want to hide the purchase of Starline?"

"Not that I can think of, but it's hard to imagine him being into something illegal either. The man is a billionaire."

"Maybe he's involved with the coalition."

"If he is, it would have to be on a worldwide scale. He wouldn't be involved with the group in the US."

"Why not?"

"He's racist. No way would he work with a group that, on the surface, is fighting for equal rights."

"On the world stage, though, the coalition sponsors all sorts of ideologies, especially if they disrupt society."

"The coalition makes news." A chill ran through her. "Everything it does feeds his business."

"It helps your father's too," Kade pointed out.

"You're right, but I don't think for a second my father would ever be involved with the coalition or any group that sponsored terrorism."

"Whoever is behind this, we have to find Germain before it's too late."

Movement on the exterior surveillance feed at the embassy caught Cas's attention. A white delivery van pulled up to the guard shack. She switched views so the camera that showed the driver would be visible.

Though the man's hat obscured part of his face, Cas recognized him instantly. She tensed. "I found him. He's making a delivery to the embassy."

Cas unmuted her microphone. "Cole, stop—"

That's as far as she got before all of the surveillance views turned to snow, and the audio distorted into an unrecognizable hum.

"Cole, Ghost. Can anyone hear me?"

"What's happening?" Kade demanded.

"I've lost both visual and audio."

"Hold on. I'll have Renee call Troy."

Cas pushed away from the counter and crossed to the door. "Anything?"

"He's not answering. Neither is Donovan."

"The coalition used a dampening field when they came after me at my apartment. They must have one in their van."

"I'll contact the local authorities and get the police over there."

Cas grabbed her purse and yanked open the door. She was halfway down the stairs when Kade said, "Stay where you are. You can't afford to be seen."

"I can't sit by and hope no one drinks the water." Cas reached the ground floor. "I'll call you later."

She hung up the phone, broke into a run, and prayed she wasn't too late.

* * *

Donovan hated this. Making small talk was bad enough with people he didn't care about, but trying to chat with his girlfriend's family was brutal. They had no idea how important Cas was to him . . . or that she was still alive. It would have been so much easier if Cas could have come tonight.

Despite the oddity of the circumstances, Donovan couldn't help but like the Edgemonts. Josiah had a sharp mind and a quick wit. Both Shantelle and Makayla wore the latest fashions, yet their conversation centered on what should be done to help the recent bombing victims and their families.

Their appearance might exude wealth and privilege, but they were far from the divas the paparazzi often made them out to be.

"I don't think covering funeral costs is enough," Makayla said. "These people lost a member of their family. They need time to take a step back and grieve."

"I couldn't agree more," Shantelle said. "We know a thing or two about that."

Donovan glanced across the room where Roshaun was chatting with the ambassador. Troy hovered nearby but wasn't included in the conversation.

"I'm sure there are more pleasant topics we can discuss," Josiah said. "Mr. Smith doesn't want to hear about losing family."

"It's okay." Donovan waited a second for Cas to guide him in the conversation. When he only received silence, he forged forward into uncharted territory. "I couldn't help seeing you on the news this week. Have there been any developments on your daughter?"

"Hundreds of people have called with tips, but so far, we've only had a few worth pursuing."

"May I ask what changed? It's been several years since Cassidy's accident. What makes you think now that she's still alive?"

"She left an electronic footprint that's uniquely her own."

Makayla tucked her arm through the crook in her father's elbow and squeezed. "Papa, we all want to believe she's still here with us, but it must have been someone who found her login information."

"I'm afraid I agree with Makayla," Shantelle said. "Cassidy wouldn't let you believe she was dead if she wasn't."

"I hope you're able to find the answers you're seeking very soon," Donovan said.

"Thank you."

Troy moved away from Roshaun and the ambassador and tilted his head toward the far side of the room. Reading his signal, Donovan said, "Will you excuse me for a moment?"

He moved to where Troy now stood. Donovan turned toward the window. "I haven't heard anything that points at Roshaun being involved. How about you?"

"No. He seems like a nice guy." Troy lowered his voice and whispered, "Sorry, Cas."

No response.

"Cas?" Donovan said quietly. "Can you hear me?"

Nothing.

"When was the last time you heard from her?" Troy asked.

"I don't know. Maybe five or ten minutes."

"It's been at least that long for me too."

A dozen scenarios flashed through Donovan's mind. Had someone found her? Had she followed them here? His concerns multiplied when Cole walked through the door.

Donovan skirted around the dining room table and met him halfway to the door. "What's going on?"

"I don't know. Our friend at the apartment started to say something, but then the comm cut out."

"What did she say?"

"'Cole, stop.'"

"Stop what?"

"I don't know. I didn't hear the rest."

Donovan put a hand on both of the other men's shoulders and guided them into the hall. "When the coalition came after Cas at her apartment, they used a dampening field."

Troy pulled his phone out and dialed. "Nothing."

Cole held his cell up. "Me neither."

"Something's going on." Donovan's gaze swept the room. The ambassador and his wife, Roshaun, the Edgemonts, three other prominent American couples, a dignitary from France with his wife. Any of them could be the target of an attack, or none of them.

A server walked into the room holding a tray of bottled water. He opened one at a time and filled the water glasses on the table.

Should they alert embassy security and let the dinner continue as planned? Or was more extreme action warranted?

"I say we don't take any chances," Troy said. "We need to secure everyone here."

"He's right." Cole crossed to the ambassador and flashed his credentials. "Sir, I'm sorry, but there's a situation. We need everyone to move to the safe room."

"What's going on?"

"I'll explain on the way." Cole turned and spoke to the room at large. "Everyone, I'm sorry to interrupt, but we need you all to follow the ambassador down the hall."

"I need to check with security," the ambassador said.

"Comm is down. That's why we need to secure everyone now until we can determine what is happening."

That tidbit prompted the ambassador into action. "Please follow me, everyone."

Though confused, the attendees headed for the door. As Makayla passed by the table, she picked up a water glass and lifted it.

"Miss, please put that back," Troy said.

"I just want a drink."

"I'm sorry." Donovan moved forward and took the glass from her. "We have a possible security threat. You need to get to the safe room as quickly as possible."

Makayla blew out a frustrated breath and gave Donovan a firsthand look at the expression the paparazzi liked to capture for the tabloids.

"This way." Donovan nudged her forward.

As soon as the other guests had filtered into the hall, Donovan said, "I'm going outside to assess the situation."

"I'll go find the security command center and see if they have any video of what the problem is," Cole said.

"And I'll try to reestablish comm before Cas shows up," Troy said.

Donovan's heartbeat quickened, and fear streaked through him. "You don't think she would risk coming here, do you?"

"If she really identified a threat, she's already on her way," Troy said with certainty. "Her family is here. And so are you."

CHAPTER 35

Every lesson about staying invisible vanished as Cas raced down the sidewalk. She weaved her way past pedestrians and street peddlers. She skirted around the tables at a street café. Her lungs burned as she made the final turn and the embassy came into view. Despite her fear for her family and Donovan, her training finally kicked in and she slowed long enough to assess her surroundings. The stately yellow building, the stars and stripes of the American flag fluttering in the breeze, the Marine guards standing at their post at the entrance.

Where were the police? She'd thought they would have been here by now. Had the threat already been neutralized, or were people being poisoned inside while the guards remained unaware?

She slowed her approach long enough to retrieve the US passport for one of her aliases. She flashed her ID, and a guard unlocked the gate to let her in.

Though she struggled to catch her breath, she asked, "Is your comm working?"

The guard, who couldn't be more than twenty, furrowed his brow. "What?"

"Can you communicate with the other guards?" Cas asked, impatience squeezing at her. "I need you to check."

"What's this about?" the second guard asked.

"I think someone has a dampening field set up here."

The second guard pressed the button on his radio. "Comm check. Jacobs, can you hear me?" He shook his head and motioned to the other guard. "Try yours."

"Comm check." He shook his head. "I'm only getting static."

"I need to get to the loading area. The water delivery that just came in may be poisoned."

The second guard motioned to the first. "You stay here. I'll check in with Zanoni at the garage entrance." He took a step forward. "Ma'am, you should wait here."

"No. I'm intel, and I'm coming with you." Cas turned down the walk that led to the vehicle entrance for the embassy.

The guard followed behind her and grabbed her arm. "Ma'am, I must insist you wait here."

"We don't have time to argue." Her sense of urgency increased, and Cas tried to jerk her arm away, but it was firmly caught. "Look, I care about the people in there. Every second we waste out here, the more likely it is that someone isn't going to see tomorrow. You can either help me or get out of my way." She jerked her arm again, and this time, the guard's grip faltered and she broke free. She pushed forward, her fear for her loved ones and coworkers strangling all concern for her own safety.

"Ma'am!" The guard's footsteps sounded behind her.

Cas reached the corner of the building. Two guards stood at the guard shack by the street. In the loading area, two men loitered at the back of a white cargo van, the rear doors obscuring them from view.

"Hey! You there!" Cas called out.

The objects of her attention froze for a brief moment. Footsteps pounded closer. The delivery man closest to her peeked out from behind one of the back doors. Recognition dawned on his face at the same time Cas identified Germain. His jaw dropped. Then his eyes narrowed.

His hand disappeared beneath his jacket, and Cas made a move for her weapon. Her finger had barely grazed the handle when the guard grabbed her from behind.

"Gun!" Cas shouted and tried to point, but it was too late.

* * *

Donovan was nearly to the exit when a gunshot rang out and his steps faltered. His gut clenched, and a jagged pain cut through him. Cas! Was she here? Had she been shot? He reached for his weapon, and his fingers wrapped around the grip.

Troy passed him, yanked the door open, and peered outside. Donovan fought against the impulse to blindly rush outside, and he took position opposite Troy. A wash of light illuminated the front of the embassy, and a glow of security lights cast a haze from the far side of the building.

"I don't see anything," Troy said.

Shouts echoed, followed by another gunshot and then another. "The shots are coming from the driveway." Donovan led the way outside, his eyes scanning.

The driveway gate was locked down, and the guard shack was empty. He rounded the corner of the building, and his heart stuttered. Cas lay on the ground beside a Marine guard. Another shot fired, and Cas rolled onto her knees and hooked her hands under the guard's armpits. She dragged him behind a nearby tree as another shot fired.

Relief swept through Donovan, and he took in the rest of the scene. Another guard lay on the pavement a short distance from the guard shack. A third had taken cover behind the caterer's van.

"Freeze!" The guard by the van turned his gun toward Donovan.

"No!" Cas shouted. "They're with me!"

"Where's the shooter?" Troy shouted.

"There are two of them. One is behind the delivery van. I'm not sure about the second one. He was near the front of the van a minute ago."

Cas, the uninjured guard, the two shooters, and Donovan made up the four corners of a square. Unfortunately, where Donovan and Troy stood, they had no visual of the men who had apparently already shot two guards.

Footsteps approached at a rapid pace, and Donovan turned to face another guard with a weapon pointed at them.

Donovan kept his gun aimed at the ground. "Don't shoot. We're on your side."

The guard stopped a few yards away, his assault rifle pointed at Donovan. "I heard gunshots."

"A shooter has injured two of your guards. Comm is down," Troy said.

"We need to get the shooters out of there." Donovan scanned the area again. "Suggestions?"

"One of us needs to work around the far side of the van," Troy said.

"I'll go," the guard offered.

A quick look at the man's pale skin and Troy's white shirt was all Donovan needed to make a decision. "Better let me." He nodded at the guard's weapon. "Besides, if I flush them out, your rifle will have better accuracy at this range."

"If you use the trees and the barriers, you won't be exposed until you have to cross to the caterer's van," Troy said.

Donovan plotted his path out in his mind. The tree to his left. Then the row of concrete barriers. From there, he would be able to reach Cas and the downed guard. That was as far as he got before he was prompted into action. "Cover me."

Troy raised his weapon and fired the moment Donovan made his dash behind the nearest tree. Donovan lowered to the ground and crept forward, the shadows from the barriers hiding him from view.

When he reached Cas's side, he knelt beside her. "Are you okay?"

"Germain is one of the shooters. We think he was bringing poisoned water bottles into the embassy." Her gaze lifted to his, and tears swam in her eyes. "My family?"

The image of Makayla lifting a water glass popped into his mind, and the gravity of how close the Edgemonts had come to losing another daughter crashed through him. "We sent everyone to the safe room. They went up before anyone drank the water."

A relieved sigh whooshed out of her.

"How is he?" Donovan asked.

"Not good. He stepped into the line of fire when Germain aimed at me."

"I'm going to circle around to the other side of him."

"Signal me if you need me to draw him out."

"We don't have comm. Besides, I don't want you to become a target."

"It may be the only way to get him out from behind that van." Cas gripped his arm. "Fire a single shot, and I'll create a distraction."

"Only if I can't neutralize the threat on my own."

"Be careful."

"I will."

CHAPTER 36

CAS PRESSED HER GLOVED HAND against the guard's wound, her gaze on Donovan as he disappeared into the shadows. He was barely out of sight when she sensed another presence.

Cas turned as Troy materialized beside her.

"We need an ambulance," Cas said, stating the obvious. "And you need to go back into the embassy and make sure no one drinks the bottled water that was delivered tonight."

"Bottled water?"

"We think the water is poisoned."

"Oh man." Troy shook his head. "That was close."

"What?"

"Never mind." Troy glanced behind him. "Any idea who these guys are?"

"One of them is Germain." Cas tried to keep her voice steady but failed. "I think he was trying to murder my family."

"He didn't succeed. Your family is safe," Troy said. "What about the other guy?"

"If I'm right, he's a scientist who stole the toxin from one of our government labs."

Troy glanced toward the van. "You should be the one to go inside. The rest of us are only a threat to them if we get too close, but you're someone they want to see dead."

Troy was right. As much as she wanted to stay and help, protecting the people inside was equally important. How many people had gone to the safe room? How many remained in the danger zone? With no ability to communicate except in person, she had no way of knowing.

"Fine, I'll go." Her gaze darted to where Donovan had been a moment ago.

"Wait until Donovan makes his move for the caterer's truck. That will help create a distraction."

The thought of Donovan out in the open, exposed to gunfire, sent a new surge of terror crashing over her.

"Don't worry," Troy said. "I'll cover him."

Cas nodded. She took off her scarf and folded it into a bandage and pressed it against the guard's bullet wound. "I'll be back as soon as I can."

"Stay out of the line of fire," Troy said.

"I will."

Cas pushed to her feet but stayed in a crouch.

"Now," Troy whispered. Using the three-foot-high concrete pillars as shields, Cas crept toward the embassy.

Troy fired a shot and then another.

Cas made it to the third barrier before another gunshot fired. Concrete dust and debris exploded into the air. She dropped down and used both hands to cover her head as bits of debris rained down on her. Rock impacted her shoulder and sent pain shooting through her arm.

When more shots rang out, it took only a second to discern that her colleagues were laying down cover fire. Taking advantage of their efforts, she sprinted forward, her body low, her hands still protecting her head.

She made it to the second-to-last barrier before she stumbled and rolled to the ground. Silence ensued.

Despite the pain throbbing in her shoulder, she crawled the rest of the way to the sidewalk, then tried to get a glimpse of the cargo van, but it was no longer visible. Now safe from the bullets flying in her direction, she used her hands to push to a stand.

A hint of movement crossed into her view, and a rifle lifted. Cas froze. She forced her gaze to look beyond the weapon to the young man aiming it. "I'm on your side."

"Who are you?"

Cas swallowed, tempted to speak the truth long buried. Even though her name might sway the guard, she couldn't share it with a complete stranger. "I'm working with intelligence." The rifle didn't lower, and a flicker of doubt lit the guard's face. Cas pressed on. "The men shooting out there delivered water bottles to the embassy. They're poisoned."

"Are you sure?"

"Sure enough to risk getting shot to make sure no one drinks it."

Troy must have seen Cas's dilemma because he called out, "She's with us. Let her go."

The gun lowered slightly.

"All I want to do is make sure no one drinks any of it." Cas nodded toward the main entrance. "Or you can go."

He debated a brief moment. "No, you go. I'm not leaving while there is a threat out there."

"Fine, but do me a favor."

"What's that?"

"Don't shoot me when I come back."

The man nodded and lowered his weapon to let her pass.

Free of her latest obstacle, Cas broke into a run, each step sending new pain jolting through her. She reached the gate, where a single guard remained, the same one she had spoken to when she'd first arrived.

Breathless, she gripped the cold metal of the gate. "You need . . ." She took a breath and started again. "You need to tell everyone not to drink the water. I think the water bottles delivered tonight have already been taken inside."

"The ones you said are poisoned?" The guard opened the gate and clicked on the walkie-talkie attached to his shoulder.

"Comm is still down." Cas stepped inside. "Where is the kitchen?"

He pointed. "That way, but you should notify the ambassador."

"The ambassador is already in the safe room with his guests. It's the staff I'm worried about now."

"Alert the guards inside. Straight inside and then to the left."

Cas rushed inside to where two guards stood at a security booth.

"Can I help you?" the dark-haired guard asked.

"Comm is down, there's a shooting outside, two of your men are injured," Cas said, shooting off facts in rapid-fire succession. "The water bottles delivered tonight are poisoned. I need to find the kitchen and warn them."

Her words were met with surprise and doubt. Cas slammed her diplomatic passport on the counter between them. "This isn't a drill. Where's the kitchen?"

The guard with light hair checked her ID and sprang into motion. "Show her the kitchen. I'll check outside."

"The shooters have taken shelter behind a van by the loading dock. Two men, both midthirties, one Black, one Caucasian."

"We can come at them from behind," the other guard said.

"Go," Cas urged. "Just point me in the right direction, and I'll warn everyone about the water." When the men hesitated, Cas snatched her diplomatic passport back and forced a tone of authority into her voice. "You already have two men down out there. You'll need backup."

"She's right." One of the guards gave her directions to the kitchen. Then they both hurried toward the far staircase. Cas raced through the main lobby and turned down the hall. Her heart pounding and her shoulder throbbing, she pressed forward and prayed she wasn't too late.

* * *

Donovan reached the guard by the caterer's truck. "How many shooters?"

"Two. A woman shouted at them, and they opened fire on us." He held his position, his eyes on the van and the open back doors that shielded their targets from view. "I called for backup, but comm must be down."

"We think there's a dampening field in that van." Donovan jutted his chin toward the front of the embassy. "The guards at the entrance should have heard the shots."

"They won't leave their post. To be drawn away during a possible breach would break protocol."

"Okay, then, we'll have to take these guys out ourselves."

"How? We don't have a clear line of sight for a shot, and we don't have the numbers to flush them out."

"I'll do the flushing. You be ready to shoot." Donovan identified where their backup was currently positioned. He didn't know if Troy or Cas had moved back to the side of the embassy, but either way, he wasn't going to risk anyone being a victim of friendly fire.

Donovan assessed the open space between him and his objective. If he rushed straight forward, he would be an easy target, but the longer he waited, the more likely it was that someone inside would get thirsty and possibly drink the water that could lead to their death.

Opting for another solution, he opened the door to the truck and leaned in. His hope to find keys dangling from the ignition vanished. It would have been too easy.

Relying on the skills learned years ago with the CIA, he removed the panel covering the wires that would allow him to bypass the ignition. "Come here. I need you to drive for me," he said to the guard.

"Drive where? I can't leave the wounded."

"I'm going to hotwire the truck, and you're going to crash it into the van."

"You want me to *what*?" The guard stepped back and focused on him fully.

"You heard me. If you crash into the van, hopefully it will break this stalemate." Donovan sensed the other man's hesitation. "It's our best chance of getting your men medical attention."

The guard shouldered his weapon and moved to the driver's-side door. Donovan moved to the passenger side of the truck to make room. The guard climbed behind the wheel.

"As soon as I start this up, hit the gas. I'm going to run beside the truck and take out anyone who tries to get out of the way."

He buckled his seat belt in place. "This is crazy."

Donovan didn't dispute his claim. He exposed the wires needed to start the car. "Ready?"

He nodded. Donovan started the truck and pushed open the passenger door. The moment he was clear, the guard hit the gas. The width of the parking area didn't give the truck enough space to gain much speed, but the front of the truck crunched into the van with enough impact to knock it back into the concrete barrier in front of the loading dock. Someone cried out in pain.

Donovan raced around the side of the truck, his gun aimed at the back of the van. Proceeding with caution, he crouched beside the vehicle and approached the back door that now hung drunkenly from only its lower hinge.

He peeked through the open space. A man was pinned between the back of the van and one of the concrete barriers that lined the loading dock, both of his hands empty. Donovan took a quick look at the man's face. Not Germain.

The door to the caterer's truck opened, and footsteps pounded along the other side of the van. The guard came into view, leading with his rifle.

"Cover me." Donovan climbed onto the loading dock and peeked at the closed door leading into the embassy, but no one was visible. He stepped farther so he could see into the back of the van.

The gunman's weapon lay in the back, likely knocked there when the truck had impacted the van and made it ram into him. A case of water bottles occupied one side of the van, and a device that could only be the cause of the dampening field took up the other side.

Donovan used the height of the loading dock to scan the surrounding area. "Did you see the other shooter?"

"No. If he isn't here, he must have gone through that door."

"Clear!" Donovan called out.

The guard who had come outside with them rushed forward, as did Troy.

“Where’s Cas?” Donovan asked.

“She went inside to make sure no one drinks the water.”

Donovan’s heart rate doubled. “Germain is in there.”

Troy climbed onto the loading dock and spoke to the guards. “Disable the dampening field and call for backup.”

Leaving the guards to deal with the wounded and the prisoner, Donovan sprinted from the loading dock into the embassy. Sirens wailed in the distance. Donovan pushed through the door with Troy racing behind him.

CHAPTER 37

Cas burst into the kitchen, where a mixture of French and English was being spoken. The scent of french onion soup, roasted chicken, and melted cheese hung in the air. One kitchen worker plated salads while another ladled soup into bowls and sprinkled croutons and cheese on top. Yet another stood at the stove, stirring something.

"Take these salads up," a chef called out in French. He caught sight of Cas and waved dismissively toward the door. "You aren't authorized to be down here."

Sidestepping a serving cart, Cas scanned the room. Her gaze landed on two servers, one of whom held a water bottle. He lifted it to his lips. "No! Don't drink that!" Cas rushed forward and knocked the bottle from his hand.

Shock was quickly replaced by anger. "What are you doing?" the man yelled in French.

"The water is poisoned."

"The city water was contaminated, not the bottled water."

"These are not safe." Cas turned to the chef. "Don't let anyone eat or drink anything here. Not until the authorities can check it out."

The man's face paled. "The ambassador. We sent water bottles up to serve them ten minutes ago."

"They're okay. Everyone is in the safe room. You need to take your staff up there now," Cas said. "And tell anyone you see along the way not to drink the water."

"Who are you?"

"I'm here to keep people safe."

Though doubt shone in the older man's eyes, he nodded. He called out orders to his staff, first in English and then in French. After he turned off the ovens and stove, he ushered the others out of the room and toward the closest stairs.

Cas conducted a quick search of the kitchen until she located an open case of water bottles on the floor of the pantry. Only a dozen water bottles remained, and Cas prayed the others hadn't been distributed to the guards or other staff who hadn't been at the dinner. Uneasy about leaving the potentially hazardous water unsecured, Cas stepped out of the pantry, flipped the lock on the inside of the door, and pulled the door shut.

Satisfied that she'd done everything she could for now, she started back through the kitchen. When someone appeared in the doorway, she pointed toward the stairs. "You need to get—"

Cas focused on the man's face as his hand lifted, an automatic pistol gripped there. Germain! A shot rang out at the same time Cas dove for the floor. The bullet whizzed by her, missing her by mere centimeters.

She scrambled behind a metal serving cart. Another shot fired. Metal clanged. Her heartbeat racing, she crawled the two meters to take cover behind the prep counter.

"I knew you were alive, but I didn't expect to find you here," Germain said.

Cas drew her weapon, and her fingers flexed on the grip. A footstep squeaked against the floor, but she couldn't determine which direction Germain was moving. "How did you know?"

"Logging into the Edge database was a big mistake." Another footstep. "I might have bought into someone finding your login and password written down somewhere, but then my men brought me the cookies from the house in Bruges."

Those stupid cookies. She should have known better. She toed off her shoes, placing them on the floor in front of her. "Why are you doing this?"

"You wouldn't understand."

"Maybe I would. Try me." She rolled onto her hands and knees, her gun still gripped in her right hand.

"You tried to go to the FBI. You have no clue how the world really works."

"That was years ago. I know more now." Moving silently, Cas crept forward. Germain's lack of response sent a red flag flying.

Keeping her body low, she squatted and prepared to shoot. Another footstep squeaked on the floor, and Cas jumped up and took aim. She squeezed off a shot, but the bullet went wide. Germain returned fire, and Cas ducked back behind the prep counter. "You'll never make it out of here," Cas said with forced confidence.

"I was about to say the same thing to you." Evil vibrated through his voice when he added, "No one can help you this time. Not your parents, not my father, and not your friends at the FBI."

Germain might be right, but she had new friends now. She only hoped they could help her find the miracle that would spare her life again.

* * *

Gun in hand, Donovan ran down the hall that he hoped would lead to Germain, or at least to the guards who could help him conduct a search. This building was huge, and Cas was somewhere inside with no idea that the danger she had been running from for years was within these walls. Germain couldn't have made it far.

Donovan and Troy reached a line of doors that appeared to lead to offices.

"I'll start searching rooms." Troy slowed as he reached the first door. "You find Cas."

Footsteps pounded toward them, and two guards came into view. Both men drew their sidearms and aimed.

"Freeze! Drop your weapons!" one of them shouted.

Donovan held his hands out to the side to indicate he wasn't a threat, but he didn't release his gun. "We're intelligence operatives. We need your help to find a suspect. Black male, midthirties."

"Nice try." The light-haired guard kept his gun trained on Donovan. "You two are being detained for questioning."

"We're the good guys," Troy protested.

"You fit the description of our suspected attackers. Two men, one white, one Black, both midthirties."

"I'm only twenty-nine." Troy glanced at Donovan. "Do I look like I'm in my thirties to you?"

"No." Though normally Donovan would have welcomed the use of humor to defuse the situation, or at least would have taken the time to contemplate how he had aged five years in the past few minutes, his sense of urgency over-shadowed all else. Cas could be in danger.

"One of our partners came inside a few minutes ago," Donovan said, hoping the truth would push these men onto their side. "She needs backup."

"Drop your weapons," the guard repeated. The guards' radios crackled to life.

"They must have disabled the dampening field," Donovan said. "Check in with your colleagues. They'll tell you they already have one suspect in custody."

Before they could comply, a voice came over the radio. "Security breach at loading dock. Black male, midthirties, wearing gray overalls."

"We have two men in custody. Black male and white male, but they're both wearing tuxes." The guard didn't get any further before a response interrupted him.

"Those are friendlies. Assist them in the search."

"Are we good?" Troy asked.

The guards both lowered their weapons as the voice on the radio issued a warning about the bottled water.

"You two help him search," Donovan said. "I need to find our partner."

"Who's your partner?" one of the guards asked.

"She's midtwenties, attractive, dark skin."

"I was working the gate when she came in a minute ago," he said. "She went to the kitchen. Take the stairs on your left and then turn right at the bottom."

"Thanks." Donovan rushed past them and headed down the open staircase. A gunshot rang out. His gut clenched. "Cas!"

He sprinted the rest of the way, a blur of movement approaching when he reached the landing. He took aim at the man racing toward him.

"Don't shoot," Cole shouted. "It's me."

"I heard shots fired." Donovan's gun lowered.

"Germain has Cas pinned down in the kitchen."

More footsteps approached, but this time, it wasn't backup. It was Josiah Edgemont. Cas's father.

"Where is she?" Josiah asked.

Donovan jutted his chin toward Josiah. "Get him out of here."

Josiah didn't slow. "That's my daughter in there."

"And if you want her to live, you'll let us do our jobs."

"Sir, come with me." Cole grabbed Josiah's arm and yanked him away from the kitchen door.

"But Cassidy . . ." Josiah tried to jerk free.

Cole's hand still gripped the older man as he stepped in front of him and met his gaze. "You walk in there and you'll end up dead before we have a chance to free her."

Josiah swallowed hard, but he stopped fighting.

Though he wasn't entirely certain Cas's father was under control, Donovan lifted his weapon and grabbed the doorknob. Time to neutralize Germain and eliminate the threat against the most important woman in his life.

CHAPTER 38

Cas peeked over the counter long enough to send another bullet flying toward Germain. He had taken cover on the far side of the industrial ovens. The doorknob rattled against the lock that kept the door bolted shut.

"Cas!"

Donovan?

The rustle of clothes against metal accompanied Germain's movement. Cas popped up as Germain took aim at the door.

"Watch out!" Cas yelled. Even though Germain was still protected by the oven, she fired again. Her shot merged with another, Germain's bullet tearing through the wooden door.

Concern for Donovan's safety merged with fear. The possibility of not making it out of the embassy alive was one thing, but she couldn't stand the idea of Donovan not surviving. Fury welled within her along with a ripple of impatience. This standoff needed to end, and so did Germain's reign of terror.

Cas scooted back to where she had left her shoes. She needed a way to flush Germain out of his hiding place, and the serving cart might give her just the distraction she needed.

The door handle rattled again, but this time Germain held his fire. Cas reached the metal cart and gripped the bottom. Gathering all her strength, she shoved it toward the ovens. A metal clanging rang out in the same moment another thud sounded at the door. The wood of the door frame splintered. A chain rattled. Fear for Donovan prompted Cas to send a preemptive strike. She fired another shot. The door splintered open, and Donovan led with his weapon.

Cas rose and aimed at the spot where Germain had disappeared behind the ovens. "Over there."

Donovan rushed forward but lowered his weapon an instant later. "He's gone."

"What?" Cas reached Donovan's side and scanned the empty space where Germain had been a moment ago. A faint mechanical hum sounded, and her gaze landed on a built-in cabinet and the elevator buttons beside it. "He must have escaped through the dumbwaiter." Cas hit the button to retrieve it to the kitchen level.

Donovan stepped beside her. "Can you tell where he went?"

"No."

"We need to get you and your father to the safe room."

"My father? I thought he was already there."

"He was, but he must have seen you on the security monitors up there because he followed Cole down here."

Cas pulled her phone from her pocket, relieved to see she had a signal. She dialed Cole.

"Are you okay?" Cole asked.

"Yes, but where is my dad? Germain is on the loose."

"We're in the hall outside the kitchen."

"Can you get him back to the safe room?" Cas asked.

"I'm not sure I'll be able to get him to cooperate until he sees for himself that you're okay," Cole said.

Donovan put his hand on her arm. "I don't think your dad is going anywhere without you."

"Cole just said the same thing."

"Let us chase down Germain." Donovan leaned forward and pressed his lips to hers. "I want you safe."

Cas wavered. The opportunity to see her father was something she had dreamed about for years, but she couldn't shake the overwhelming unease of knowing Germain was still on the loose.

She didn't have the chance to debate options before the kitchen door opened and Cole rushed in. "Where did Peters go?"

Cas motioned to the unexpected escape route. "He went up the dumbwaiter."

"I'll alert security." Cole pulled his phone out and dialed. "In the meantime, there's someone who needs to see you."

Cas turned toward the door as her father walked in.

Disbelief and hope radiated from him. "Cassidy?"

Emotions rose within her and rendered her speechless for a moment. Then her instincts took over. "Papa." Cas rushed into her father's arms, the regrets and doubts giving way to comfort and joy she hadn't experienced in longer than she could remember.

"It's you." Her father pulled back to look at her, his own eyes moist. "It's really you."

"It's me." She breathed in the familiar scent of his aftershave. "Papa, I'm so sorry."

"You're back now."

Donovan stepped forward. "I hate to break this up, but you need to go to the safe room until Germain is in custody."

"What if you need my help?" Cas asked.

"We have an embassy full of guards," Donovan said. "The best thing you can do for everyone right now is get to safety. You can be our eyes on the security footage while you're at it."

"Okay, but please be careful."

"You too."

* * *

Donovan made it only three steps before he turned around. He should join the search for Germain but not until he was sure Cas and her father were safely tucked away. "I'll escort you up there."

"The guards said to bring Mr. Edgemont to the security office," Cole said. "It's closer. Cas can work as our liaison with embassy security from there."

"Which way?" Donovan asked.

"Follow me." Cole walked out the door.

Donovan peeked into the hall before he waved Cas and her father forward. He then fell in behind them, his weapon still in hand. Josiah put a protective hand on Cas's back. The endearing gesture pounded two things home in Donovan's mind: Josiah Edgemont had no idea that his daughter was fully capable of not only taking care of herself but also protecting others, and Cas no longer belonged exclusively to the guardians.

Uncertainty pricked his heart. Would her reunion with her family remove Cas from his life? Doubts rose within him, but he pushed them aside. For now, they needed to find Germain and take another step toward giving Cas the freedom to choose her future.

Cole stopped beside a door. A sign mounted to the wall read Security Office. Cole pulled out his phone and made a call. "We're outside."

The door opened, and a Hispanic guard motioned Cas and Josiah inside and pointed at a row of chairs along the far wall. "You two can sit over there."

Sit over there where they wouldn't be able to see anything on the monitors. Donovan opened his mouth to protest, but Cole beat him to it.

"She's one of us. She knows all the players and needs to coordinate with our men."

"Fine." The guard motioned Cas and her father inside. Before Donovan could offer any words, the door shut and the locks clicked into place.

"Where do we start?" Cole asked.

"Germain took the dumbwaiter upstairs. Let's start there."

"The closest stairs are over here." Cole broke into a jog.

Donovan followed, modes of possible escape flooding his mind. What would he do? Germain was outnumbered and outgunned. Would he try to hide in the embassy and evade the search? Or would he attempt to slip past everyone despite the numerous guards and police officers outside?

He only had to think back to the incident at Cas's apartment two weeks ago to answer his own question.

Donovan spoke out. "Cas, can you hear me?"

"Yes. Did you find him?"

"No, but have the guards check IDs for any emergency personnel leaving the compound."

"You think Germain will try to sneak out of here."

"It worked for you at your apartment building."

"You're right." Cas relayed the instructions to the guards in the office. Ahead of him, Cole came to a quick stop and put his hands up. Donovan lifted his weapon but held his fire when two guards stepped into view.

"Drop your weapons," one guard ordered.

"Here we go again," Donovan muttered.

"What's wrong?" Cas asked.

"Can you have the guards with you tell their buddies that we're part of the search team and that we're on their side?" Donovan asked.

"I'll take care of it," Cas said.

"Who are you talking to?" the other guard demanded.

"The security office," Donovan said. "Like we said, we're on your side."

CHAPTER 39

As much as she wanted to talk with her father, Cas tried to pretend he wasn't sitting across the room so she could focus on the job at hand. She located the screen that held the image of two guards holding Cole and Donovan at gunpoint. "Tell these guards to stand down," she said.

The guard, Garcia, spoke into his walkie-talkie. "Private Murray, stand down. Your two suspects are part of the search team." He offered the security code to verify the order was authentic, and the two guards lowered their weapons.

Donovan's voice came through Cas's earpiece. "Any suspicious movement?"

"Nothing yet." Cas turned her attention back to Garcia. "Is there any place where our suspect could get ahold of a guard uniform here in the embassy?"

"We have a locker room area here." He pointed at a screen.

"Have your men search that area. We think our suspect might try to sneak out of here in disguise."

Garcia dispatched two men to carry out Cas's suggestion.

"Did you catch sight of him on camera near the dumbwaiter?" she asked.

"There was a delivery guy on the second floor a few minutes ago."

"We need to track him." Cas debated for a moment. "Set me up with access. I'll try to track where he went while you monitor the live feed."

Garcia logged into a workstation and stepped back. "Here you go."

"Thanks." Cas sat down but sensed movement behind her. She glanced over her shoulder to see her father now beside her.

"Let me help. No one has more experience scanning video feed than I do."

"Sir, I'm sorry, but—"

"He's right." Cas cut the guard off. "Let him help."

Garcia hesitated only a brief moment before he shoved an extra office chair toward him. Her father sat beside her. "What are we looking for?"

"We're looking for Germain Peters."

"Germain? As in Antoine's son?"

"Yes. He was the one shooting at me in the kitchen. He escaped through the dumbwaiter," Cas said. "We think he might try to slip past the guards while everything is crazy out there."

"Germain? You're sure?" Josiah asked.

"Yes. I'll explain later, but for now, see if you can find him anywhere on this screen." Cas set up one monitor to show six different views. She then adjusted her monitor to display the exterior video feed. "He'll likely be alone."

"You got it."

Trusting her father to figure out the display features on his own, Cas hit the rewind button and sent the images backward to the approximate time when Germain had escaped into the dumbwaiter.

She scanned the exterior views showing the two ambulances in the driveway, paramedics tending to the wounded, four police cars parked just outside the entrance, the crumpled delivery van and the caterer's truck that had crashed into it. Three guards examined the van while two others stood at the exit, coordinating with the local authorities.

Cas did a quick look at the other views of the exterior—the dumpster in the back corner, the guards at the back and side entrances. She did a quick count of the people present before she fast-forwarded the feed, taking one view at a time to make sure she didn't miss anything.

She checked the cameras showing the fire escapes first. Nothing. The exits didn't reveal any new personnel arriving, and the only movement was from the guards scanning the area. She moved to the view with the dumpster. The opening image didn't reveal anyone in sight. As she fast-forwarded, an unexpected rush of movement appeared at the bottom as something or someone fell into the dumpster.

"I've got something," she said in the same instant that her father straightened and said, "I found him."

Garcia turned toward them. "What did you find?"

"Something came out of the trash chute. It may have been a person." Cas backed up the image to play it at normal speed.

"What about you, sir?" Garcia asked.

Her father focused on the screen. "This looks like Germain to me."

Cas leaned closer. Though Germain's ball cap hid his face from the cameras, the hat and the clothes were the same as when she had seen him in the kitchen. "That's him."

"Roll the feed forward," Garcia said. "Where did he go?"

Her father hit the Play button. A moment after Germain appeared on the screen, he disappeared. "I didn't see him after that spot."

"How close was he to the trash chute?" Cas asked.

"There's an opening to it in this hall," Garcia said.

"That must have been him in the dumpster." Cas replayed her sequence, but this time, she slowed it down and froze the image when the blur of motion appeared. She zoomed in. Shoes, pants, hands, ball cap. "That's him."

Garcia picked up his walkie-talkie and gave the latest location to the other guards.

At the same time, Cas spoke into her comm earpiece. "We have a visual. Germain came down the trash chute. Rear corner behind the loading dock." Static buzzed in her ear. "My men aren't responding. Did they answer you?"

Garcia shook his head. "Something must be interfering with our communication systems again."

Cas tried her cell phone but didn't have a signal.

"Great." She switched to the camera view of the loading dock and scrolled through the images. She stopped when a paramedic appeared behind the van to treat the wounded scientist. "The dampening field originated from the van. That paramedic must be Germain."

"How could he have gotten a uniform?" her father asked.

"I don't know, but you two can search to find out." Cas pushed out of her chair. "I need to stop Germain before he gets away."

"No." Her dad grabbed her arm to stop her. "Let the guards handle it."

"Garcia can't leave his post. I can." Cas leaned down and kissed her father's cheek. "Stay here. I'll be back." Cas took a step toward the door. "And whatever you do, don't drink anything while I'm gone."

* * *

Pistol in hand, Donovan stopped beside the side entrance. "Say again. You're breaking up." When Cas didn't respond, he asked Cole, "Did you catch what Cas said?"

"No. Just something about they had a visual."

"If comm is down, my bet is Germain is outside."

"You don't really think he would go out there and turn the jammer back on, do you? He would be walking right into the middle of a bunch of guards."

"He's former FBI. He knows how to look the part. Besides, we're the only people who know what he looks like beyond his clothes."

"If he changed his clothes, he's invisible."

"I'm afraid so." Donovan headed for the door. "Come on."

"Better let me go first. We don't want to get detained again." Cole led the way outside to where two guards were stationed at the rear of the building. He flashed his ID. "Have you seen any sign of anyone back here?"

"Only a paramedic checking on someone by the dumpster." One guard pointed.

"Thanks." Donovan sprinted toward the dumpster and drew his weapon. He slowed as he approached and peeked around the edge. The delivery van was a short distance away, along with the caterer's truck, still positioned where it had crashed into the van. A third ambulance had arrived, and emergency lights flashed.

Donovan peeked into the dumpster, several of the plastic bags split open as though something heavy had landed on them. "Looks like he came down the trash chute."

"I don't know if he could have gotten out of here without being noticed though." Cole started to circle the dumpster, but he stopped abruptly. "Daniel, we've got a man down here."

Donovan closed the distance between them. He reached the back side of the dumpster where a man lay, his only clothing a pair of boxers, an undershirt, and his socks.

"Is he alive?"

"Yeah, but it looks like he took a blow to the back of the head."

"Check the jammer," Donovan said. "I'll get one of the guards and see if someone can ID him."

Cole holstered his weapon and rushed toward the van. Donovan followed his lead and tucked his gun into his waistband before he hurried to the nearest guard, a Marine sergeant. "We have a man down over here. We need a medic, and I need you to ID him."

"Medic!" the guard shouted. A paramedic by one of the ambulances started toward them. "Where is he?" the sergeant asked.

"Behind the dumpster." Donovan pointed. "He's missing his uniform. Our suspect must have taken it."

The guard shouted at a nearby Marine, "Hundred percent ID check for everyone leaving."

"Yes, sergeant."

Donovan led the sergeant to the unconscious man.

"I don't recognize him," the sergeant said.

The paramedic reached them and immediately started speaking in rapid French. "I know him. He's a medic." He began an initial assessment of the man's condition. "What happened? Who did this?"

"What's he saying?" the sergeant asked Donovan.

"He said this man is a medic. Our suspect is wearing his uniform."

CHAPTER 40

Cas rushed past the guard who had originally been outside with her when the shoot-out had begun. She took in the scene. The guard she had helped treat initially now had an IV in his arm, and he had been moved onto a stretcher. Two other ambulance attendants knelt beside the other wounded guard, and yet another paramedic was visible at the front of the van.

Cas moved forward and took a moment to check the patient being treated near the van. Nathaniel Norton. If they could capture Germain and track down all the tainted water bottles, this ordeal would finally be over. She skirted the side of the delivery van and moved toward the back. The jamming equipment had to be inside.

She sensed movement behind the vehicle, but the door blocked her view. She gripped her pistol. Could Germain still be hiding so close to all these guards? Or was it someone else back there?

She lifted her weapon. A few more steps. That was all she needed to answer her questions.

Her earpiece crackled with static and then cleared.

"Anyone read me?" Cas asked.

"Loud and clear," Troy said.

"Cas, check the exterior images," Donovan said. "Germain is disguised as a paramedic."

Before Cas could correct Donovan's assumption that she was inside, Troy responded, "Heading your way."

Cole stepped out from behind the van, and Cas's grip on her pistol relaxed.

"What are you doing out here?" he asked.

"The comm went down. We had no way of telling you that Germain came down the trash chute."

"We figured that out." Cole stepped beside her and scanned the area. "He's got to be out here somewhere."

"We need to start checking IDs."

"The guards already are."

Donovan came into view from the back corner of the embassy. His eyes searched the area as he approached the ambulance closest to him. When he saw Cas, he hesitated.

"Cas, you should get back inside. Germain is out here somewhere," he said, his voice filled with urgency.

She debated his suggestion for a fraction of a second but rejected it. "I'm already out here. I can help with the search."

"Germain wants you dead."

A paramedic appeared at the front of the ambulance nearest Donovan and limped forward. The sense of familiarity was enough to push Cas into motion. She lifted her weapon, but Donovan was in her line of fire.

"Behind you!" Cas shouted at Donovan.

Donovan started to turned, but before he could complete the motion, the man behind him lunged forward. He knocked Donovan's weapon from his hand and grabbed Donovan around the neck, the barrel of his gun pressed against Donovan's temple.

Cole took a step to the left, his gun also raised and aimed at the two men. "Drop it. You don't have any way out of here."

"Come any closer, and he dies," Germain said.

"I'm already dead," Donovan said.

Donovan's even tone sent a chill through Cas. He might be dead on paper, but he was alive in every way that mattered.

"Let him go," she said.

"And let you shoot me?" Derision filled Germain's voice. "Not a chance."

"Give yourself up, and you'll get a fair trial."

"We all know what happens when former feds end up in prison." Germain shook his head. "You might as well kill me now."

"That can be arranged," Donovan said.

How could he be so calm? Didn't he know that if he didn't survive the night, her life would never be the same?

Troy's voice came over Cas's earpiece. "I'm working my way behind the ambulance. I need you to get our boy's attention aimed toward the street so I can slip by without being seen."

Cas took a step to the side, her aim still on the part of Germain's head that was visible behind Donovan. "Let him go."

Three guards rushed forward, their guns raised. "Stay back!" Germain shouted, turning his body back to the position he had held a moment ago.

"You heard him," Cas called out. "We've got this. Secure the perimeter and back down."

The guards didn't move.

Cole spoke in a firm voice. "You heard her. Back off, and let us handle the situation."

The guards pulled back a few steps, but their weapons didn't lower.

Cas took another step to the side in the hope Germain would readjust his stance.

"Don't move," Germain demanded. "Not another step."

Cas froze, and her stomach plummeted. The guards who had tried to rush to the rescue might very well have cost Donovan his life.

* * *

Donovan's arm flexed, but he held his position. A well-aimed elbow would free him under normal circumstances, but with a trained federal agent, he couldn't be sure the man wouldn't get trigger-happy. He had no intention of dying today, and he wasn't about to let a stray bullet go flying into the crowd of emergency personnel, especially when Cas stood among them.

"I can't get an angle," Troy said through Donovan's earpiece.

"What now?" Donovan asked, his words intended for both his colleagues and his captor.

Germain jerked Donovan back a step and then several more until the ambulance was right beside them. "Open the door."

Donovan reached for the handle.

The gun barrel pressed more firmly into his temple. "Slowly."

Donovan pulled the handle and opened the door a few inches. Keeping Donovan in place as a shield, Germain pushed him forward a step, nudged the door open, and leaned into the driver's side.

"Someone get me the keys, or I start shooting."

"Who has the keys to this ambulance?" Cas asked.

A paramedic working on one of the injured guards stood and reached into his pocket. He held up the keys.

"Cover me," Cas said to Cole. She crossed to the paramedic, slowing as she passed one of the guards. A whispered comment buzzed through Donovan's comm set, but he couldn't make out the words.

A moment later, Cas returned with the keys to the ambulance. "I've got them. Now let him go."

"Toss them over. And make sure your throw is accurate," Germain said. "I'd hate for you to have to try a second time."

Cas tossed them the thirty yards that spanned between them, the keys landing with a jingle at Donovan's feet.

"Pick them up." Germain squatted, pulling Donovan with him. Donovan took his time hooking the key ring with his finger in the hope that someone would get a clear shot, but silence reigned.

Dozens of hostage scenarios flooded Donovan's mind, but each option for freedom carried the risk of a stray bullet flying. He couldn't chance it. If his colleagues didn't get a clear shot, he would deal with Germain after they left the embassy grounds, when Cas was no longer a potential victim.

Germain's grip tightened around Donovan's neck, and he pulled him backward until they were again standing at the open driver's-side door.

"Get in." Germain climbed in first, releasing his grip just enough to slide into the driver's seat. He pulled Donovan backward, leaving Donovan no choice but to climb into the ambulance or be strangled.

Donovan pushed himself into the ambulance, and his hand fisted. The moment Germain's grip loosened and the metal of his weapon pulled away from his head, Donovan struck out. He swung his right arm up full force, and his fist impacted Germain's nose.

The man cried out and pushed farther into the passenger side to gain a good enough position to bring his weapon up again. Donovan twisted and punched with his left hand. The impact knocked Germain back, but he swung his pistol toward Donovan.

Donovan grabbed Germain's wrist to keep the barrel pointed away from him. He tried to reach for the weapon with his free hand, but Germain blocked his efforts.

With the gun still giving Germain an advantage, Donovan thrust Germain's gun hand into the dashboard. Germain grunted, and the gun clattered onto the floor.

Germain brought his knee up to create distance between him and Donovan, and he leaned down to scoop up the pistol. Donovan stretched his arm out to prevent his efforts, but he was too late. Germain kicked out, successfully pushing Donovan back.

Germain's gun came up in the same instant a shot fired.

CHAPTER 41

Cas's heart stopped when the gunshot sounded. Her gun gripped in her hand, she sprinted forward, heedless of the threat Germain might pose to her. She had to see if Donovan was okay, if he was still whole, if her life had lost meaning.

"Cas! No!" Cole called out as his footsteps pounded behind her.

Cas skidded to a stop when she reached the open driver's-side door. She drew a deep breath, fought back tears, and led with her gun. In a fraction of a second, she took in the unlikely scene. Blood splattered on Donovan's shirt, Germain motionless beside him, a single bullet hole through the windshield.

Donovan grabbed Germain's weapon from his hand and straightened.

"Are you okay?" Cas leaned closer so she could check for injuries.

"I'm fine." He nodded toward where Troy had taken position a moment ago. "Someone shot Germain before Germain managed to shoot me."

Cas wrapped her arms around him and breathed him in.

Donovan lifted his hand to her head. "Hey, it's okay."

Cole appeared on the other side of the ambulance and checked Germain for a pulse. "He's dead."

"It's over," Donovan said.

Was it over? Was Cas free? She focused on the more immediate problem and shook her head. "It's not over until all the tainted water is found and disposed of."

"Embassy security can take care of that," Donovan said. "For now, we need to get out of here before anyone wants to question us."

Go with Donovan, or stay with her family? Her father already knew she was alive. The choice was hers.

"I need to talk to my family first," she said. "They deserve an explanation."

"You can talk to them later," Donovan insisted. "I want you away from here. I want you safe."

Cas could imagine herself saying the same words if the roles were reversed, but the need to set things right burned inside her. "I appreciate that, but I'm not one of your clients. I need to do this."

Donovan tensed. "I don't like it."

"You don't have to like it. You have to trust me."

Donovan climbed out of the ambulance. The muscles in his jaw clenched as his eyes met hers, his expression unreadable. "I do trust you." He leaned forward and touched his lips to hers as though offering an unspoken goodbye.

Troy appeared beside them. "We have to get out of here."

Donovan released her and stepped back. "Cas is staying with her family."

Surprise lit Troy's face. "You sure?"

"I want to make sure they get back to their hotel okay," Cas said. "I'll meet up with you as soon as I can."

"We'll understand if you want to stay with them," Donovan said.

"I'll call you. I promise."

Two ambulance attendants loaded one of the wounded guards in the back of another ambulance. Donovan and Troy followed behind them. Cole spoke with one of the guards before he approached her. "It'll be a little while before we get this scene cleaned up. Do you want to go inside with your family? The guards can give you a private office for you to talk to them."

"I think it's better if I meet them back at their hotel. I don't want to get cornered by people asking questions I can't answer."

"I'll tell the guards," Cole said. "Then I'll drive you out of here."

"Thanks, Cole."

"Consider this payback for liberating me from that warehouse."

"After tonight, that debt has been paid a dozen times over."

"Good. I like the idea of having a guardian owing me a favor." Cole lowered his voice. "Assuming you'll still be a guardian after tonight."

"I don't know. I still have a lot of questions that haven't been answered."

"That may be, but we made some pretty good strides forward tonight toward neutralizing the coalition's influence."

"I hope you're right."

* * *

Doug fast-forwarded through security images at the Four Seasons lobby, but as of yet, he hadn't seen any indication of Germain arriving. Hector straightened in his desk. "This might be him. I've got a man wheeling four cases of water into the hotel through the service entrance."

"When?"

"Last night."

Doug crossed to him and stepped behind Hector so he could see the screen. A ball cap on the man's head shielded his face from view, and he kept his head tilted toward the floor. "He's the right build, but that's about all we can tell with this image. See if any of the other cameras caught a better view."

"I already did, but none of them caught his face."

"Can you tell where he dropped the water bottles?"

"They went into a storage room on the fourth floor in the south tower."

"What about the rest of the water bottles? Did he make a second trip?"

"I didn't see one, but I'll keep looking."

The cell phone Ghost had given Doug rang. He snatched it off his desk. "I was about to call you. I think we found where the tainted water bottles are being stored."

Ghost's voice came over the line. "I've already got people on site. The embassy is locked down, and security is searching for any remaining water bottles."

"The embassy?" Doug asked. "The water bottle delivery we found is at the Four Seasons."

"What? How sure are you?"

"We couldn't see the delivery man's face, but he was the right height and build. He was wearing a black ball cap, and he deliberately avoided looking at the cameras."

"Send me photos of your guy and of the water bottles."

"You got it," Doug said.

"One more thing. Do you know where the water bottles are now?"

"The storage closet on the fourth floor in the south tower."

"Contact the hotel and warn them about the water bottles."

"I will," Doug said.

"Also, work forward from when they were stored there and see if any were given out. If those are part of the supply that was tainted, we need to track them down before anyone drinks them."

"I'll have my partner take care of that. I'm going to keep looking for Germain."

"No need. Germain is dead, and Nathaniel Norton has been taken into custody."

"What happened?"

"He messed with the wrong guardians," Ghost said. "Call me as soon as you track down those water bottles."

* * *

The pain wasn't new to Donovan, but when he'd abandoned his daughter to join the guardians, he hadn't ever expected to feel this way again. Cas said she'd call, but that didn't change the inevitable. She was no longer in imminent danger, which meant he was no longer needed.

Walking down the street beside him, Troy asked, "Now that Cas is safe, how soon are you going to head back?"

"I'm not sure. What about you?"

"Jocelyn has a neighbor taking care of the dog for us, so we'll probably be able to stay for a couple weeks before we have to get back home."

"A house and a dog. Your life sounds so normal."

Troy glanced around the quiet street. "Not many people have a helicopter in their backyard, but yeah, it's been a nice change of pace," Troy said. "It's going to be an adjustment when I move back to Europe."

"Have you decided when you're going to propose?"

Troy slowed his steps, and a grin spread across his face. "If all goes well, she'll be my fiancée by the time we leave Helsinki."

A streak of envy shot through Donovan, but he pushed it aside. "I'm happy for you. Congratulations."

"Don't congratulate me yet. She hasn't said yes." Troy started forward again.

"If she's lasted with you this long, I think the odds are in your favor."

"It's only been seven months, but I can't imagine my life without her."

An image of Cas formed in his mind. "I know what you mean."

"That's right. You were married before."

"My ex-wife isn't who I was thinking about."

"Cas?" When Donovan didn't respond, Troy continued. "I'd have to be blind to miss the way she looks at you."

"She won't be looking at me again anytime soon. Her life is here." Or was it? "And that's assuming she doesn't leave the guardians. If Germain was heading up the US branch of the coalition, she could be safe now."

"We both know better than that." Troy headed toward the metro station. "Germain may have been high up with the coalition, but someone else had to be pulling the strings, someone with enough power and money to keep the pressure on."

Troy was right. Despite taking down a number of coalition members over the past two weeks, the threat against Cas wasn't over.

"Come on." Troy entered the station and purchased two tickets.

"Where are we going?" Donovan asked.

"To the Four Seasons. Neither of us is going to rest easy until we get Cas hidden out of sight again."

Donovan followed Troy through the turnstile and down the steps onto the platform. A moment after they arrived, their train pulled in.

Donovan's phone rang, and he answered as he stepped through the doors.

"Donovan, I need you to get over to the Four Seasons," Kade said, his words clipped. "We think some of the poisoned water bottles were delivered there."

"We're heading there now." Panic clawed up his throat. Would Cas know not to drink from a water bottle once she was away from the embassy?

The doors whooshed closed, and the train started forward. "Have you already called the hotel to warn them?"

"I tried, but the phones are down."

Donovan pressed the tiny button on his earpiece to turn on his microphone. "Cas, can you hear me?"

"What's wrong?" Troy asked.

"Some of the water bottles were delivered to the hotel, and their phones are down," Donovan said. "We need to find out where they were delivered."

The phone went dead. Donovan tried to call Kade back, but the call failed. "I lost my signal."

"We'll call when we get to our stop," Troy said.

"Assuming our phones will work," Donovan countered.

"You think there's another signal jammer at the hotel?"

"It would make sense, but that also means we're missing someone."

"Who was on your suspect list who wasn't at the embassy dinner?"

"Cas's ex topped the list, but he's still at the embassy. I didn't see Tyrell there, but I assume he was their driver tonight," Donovan said. "That only leaves the cook, Germain's father."

Troy glanced at the display at the front of the train. "That gives us a place to start."

CHAPTER 42

CAS GRIPPED HER HANDS TOGETHER as Cole drove to the front of the hotel. She had expected him to drop her off, but he pulled into a parking spot across the street.

"You ready for this?" he asked.

"Are you coming with me?" Cas narrowed her eyes. "You aren't planning on collecting that reward, are you?"

"No, but after what happened tonight, I thought you'd want some backup while we clear your parents' hotel suite."

"Good point." Cas looked around the well-lit hotel entrance before she climbed out of the car. "Maybe we should go in through the back."

"The hotel desk is more likely to give you a key if you come in the front door."

Under normal circumstances, Cas would have used one of her tools to override the hotel lock, but in her haste to get to the embassy, she hadn't grabbed anything beyond her sidearm. "Let's hope they believe I'm my sister."

"You two look enough alike, I think you can pull it off."

"Unless the clerk already knows her."

"Only one way to find out," Cole said. "You go in first. I'll follow and meet you by the elevators."

Cas ran a hand over her hair to smooth it into place. Her jeans and blouse were a far cry from the evening gown her sister had been wearing at dinner tonight, but hopefully the staff had changed over since they'd left.

Attitude. It was all about attitude.

Cas lifted her chin and walked with purpose through the hotel entrance. She approached the nearest clerk. "I left my purse in my father's car. Can you make me another key?"

"Name?"

"Makayla Edgemont."

"Oh, of course, Miss Edgemont." The clerk typed in her sister's name. "Can you tell me which room you are in?"

"We're in the presidential suite." Her family always stayed in the presidential suite.

"Yes. Here you are." The hotel clerk picked up a blank key, ran it through the reader, and set it on the counter. "Will there be anything else?"

"If you see my father, can you let him know his daughter is waiting for him upstairs?"

"Of course."d

"Thank you." Cas took a step back before a new thought struck. "One more thing. Can you tell me what room Antoine Peters is in?"

"I'm sorry. I can't share that information."

"Can you call and ask him if it's okay for you to give me his room number?" Cas asked.

"Of course." She dialed the phone, and Cas watched the clerk's fingers dial the room number. Four oh nine. "I'm sorry. The call isn't going through."

"Thanks anyway." Cas moved to the south tower elevator. As she approached, Cole hit the Up button and waited as though he had never seen Cas before.

As soon as the doors slid open, he stepped aside and waited for her to enter before he followed. Cas hit the Close Door button to ensure they would remain alone, then pressed her key to the control panel and hit the button for the fourth floor.

"I thought your family was staying on the top floor."

"They are, but we need to make a stop before we go up there." Cas glanced at Cole. "Germain's father works as my family's chef. I want to ask him a few questions."

"Do we need to play some good cop/bad cop on him?"

"I don't know. We'll find out soon enough." The elevator reached the correct floor, and Cas led the way out. When they reached Antoine's room, she knocked on the door and then stepped to the side so she wasn't visible through the peephole. Her first attempt was met with silence, so she knocked a second time.

"Do you want me to try to override the lock?" Cole asked.

A thump sounded from inside followed by unsteady footsteps. "Sounds like he's coming." The words were barely out of Cas's mouth when the doorknob turned and the door cracked open. It started to shut again, but Cole stuck his foot against the door to keep it from latching.

"Mr. Peters?"

A heavy thud vibrated across the floor.

Cole pushed the door open until it met resistance. Cas peeked inside, where Antoine lay on the floor, his face pale, his breathing unsteady. Concerned for his safety, Cas slipped inside and squatted beside him.

Cole followed and closed the door. "Is that him?"

"Yes."

"I'll clear the apartment." Cole continued past the bedroom area to the door across the room.

Cas pressed her finger against Antoine's neck. His pulse rabbited beneath her touch. "Call an ambulance." She focused on Antoine. "Antoine, can you hear me? What happened?"

"Cassidy." He croaked out her name. "You're alive."

"Yes. I'm alive." As much as it pained her to press, Cas asked, "Do you know who wanted me dead?" Awareness and regret lit his eyes. "You know, don't you?" Cas pressed.

"Cassidy, the phone's dead," Cole said. "My cell too."

The implication crashed over her. Their communication was out here, the same as her apartment and the embassy. Could the coalition be attacking here too? And if so, why?

"I didn't know he'd try to hurt you." Antoine gasped for air.

Cole approached with a water bottle in his hand. "I think I found the problem."

Cas focused on the label, the same label she had seen when she had secured the poisoned water bottles in the kitchen at the embassy. "Oh no."

Antoine gripped Cas's arm. "Powell. Don't . . ."

"Powell?" Cas's eyes narrowed. "You mean Steven Powell? He's the one who wanted me dead?"

Antoine opened his mouth, but instead of speaking, he gasped as though he couldn't get enough air. A white foam appeared at the edge of his mouth, and his body convulsed.

"Antoine." Cas watched helplessly as the tremor faded and her former chef's body went limp. She checked for his pulse but, this time, didn't find one.

"Sorry, Cassidy." Cole put his hand on her shoulder.

"If Antoine had a water bottle here in his room, there may be others in the hotel." Cas pushed to her feet.

"Who knows how many people may have already drunk some." Cole moved toward the door. "We should pull the fire alarm and clear everyone out of here."

"No. We can't be sure people wouldn't take the water bottles with them." Cas stood. "We have to warn people of the danger, not scatter it farther into the city."

"Then, let's start knocking on doors. We can start with the top floor and work our way down."

"I'll check my parents' suite," Cas said. "I need you to go to the lobby and tell the staff what's going on. We need to get more people knocking on doors before we have more casualties."

"Got it." Cole headed for the door. He cast a glance over his shoulder. "Be careful."

"I will."

* * *

Donovan rushed into the hotel lobby. Two patrons stood at the service counter, and three others waited in line. Donovan pressed past them and spoke to the nearest clerk in French. "Where do you keep your bottled water?"

"Sir, I'm sorry, but you'll need to wait your turn."

"Someone delivered poisoned bottled water here today. Where do you keep it?"

The clerk was still processing the absurdity of Donovan's statement when Cole sprinted toward him.

"What's wrong?" Donovan asked Cole.

"Some of the water was delivered here. We already have one casualty."

Fear snaked through him. Not Cas. Please, not Cas. "Who was it?"

"Antoine Peters."

Donovan let out the breath he hadn't realized he'd been holding and turned back to the clerk, who now held the phone to her ear.

She pressed several buttons before hanging it back up. "The phone isn't working." She motioned to her coworker beside her. "Go get the manager. Now."

Donovan repeated Cole's report in French in case the clerk didn't speak English. He turned to the wide-eyed, middle-aged man who stood at the counter beside him. "You. Do you have a car out front?"

He shook his head.

Donovan turned to the handful of people still in line. He spoke in French first. "Does anyone here have a car out front?"

"*Oui.*" A woman in her thirties raised her hand. "I do."

"I need you to drive away from the hotel and call the police," Donovan said. "Tell them we have an emergency at the Four Seasons and the phones are down."

The woman fished her keys out of her purse.

Satisfied, Donovan turned back to the clerk. "We need help knocking on doors to tell people not to drink the bottled water."

"Yes, sir," she said, now speaking in heavily accented English. "The bottled water is stored in the kitchen storage room on this level and on the fourth floor for the south tower executive suites."

"Our casualty was on the upper level," Cole said. "We should start there."

Donovan nodded to Troy and Cole. "You two start knocking on doors on the upper levels in the south tower. Where's Cas?"

"She's making sure there isn't any bottled water in the presidential suite. Then she was going to help warn the hotel guests."

"We don't have time to knock on every door," Troy said. "It'll be easier to pull the fire alarm."

"We were going to, but Cas was worried people might grab their water bottles on their way out since they still think the city water is unsafe," Cole said. "We can't risk the poison getting distributed even farther."

Donovan debated their options. He turned to the desk clerk. "Can you get staff onto all of the floors in the south tower? We'll need someone at every stairwell and at the elevators."

"I believe so."

"Good. We'll hold everyone on their floors and inform them of the problem," Donovan said. "That'll let us also search any rooms where we might already have casualties."

"What about the north tower?" the clerk asked. "We don't have enough staff to man every stairwell on every floor."

"If you put staff on the exits here on the main level, you can direct everyone to the restaurant or your ballroom and hold them there." Donovan waved at the guests in the lobby who were still watching in stunned silence. "Use your guests here to help you."

"Good idea," Troy said. "When the police get here, let them know someone has set up a jamming signal here at the hotel that's interfering with phones."

"I'll take care of it," the first clerk said.

The other clerk returned with a man in his late fifties rushing behind him.

"What is happening?" the older man said.

"You tell him." Donovan motioned to the clerk. "One more thing. We need master keys in case guests don't answer or have already drunk the water."

"I'll send staff members up with keys right away, sir." She swiped a key through her reader. "This will allow you to access the upper floors."

Though Donovan had hoped she would give them the master keys, he could understand her hesitation, and he didn't have time to argue. "Come on."

"This way." Cole sprinted to the elevator, and Donovan and Troy followed.

Donovan swiped the key against the access panel and hit the button for the floor below where Cas was currently searching. "Let's hope the hotel staff gets up here quickly. Otherwise, we may be opening doors to a bunch of dead bodies."

"I'm praying that doesn't happen," Cole said.

"We all are."

CHAPTER 43

Doug was tired of sitting by helplessly. The phones at the hotel had gone unanswered for the past several minutes, and his attempt to alert the police about the problem had been met with an insurmountable level of red tape. He'd finally kicked the communication problems up to his boss. Hopefully word would get to the right people soon.

"Oh, this isn't good." Hector looked up, a panicked expression on his face. "I fast-forwarded past where the water bottles were stored in the storage closet."

"And?" Doug asked.

"A couple staff members came in and took them all. It looks like they distributed them to the different rooms."

"Can you tell which rooms?"

"It'll take some time, but I'll do what I can to track them all."

"Start by narrowing down which floors are affected."

"I know one of the cases was taken up to the top floor," Hector said. "We have to get the local authorities involved."

"We're already trying." Doug let out a frustrated sigh. If he couldn't solve the problem, he would have to kick it back to Ghost. He picked up his cell phone and dialed the elusive guardian.

"Did you get the water bottles secured?" Ghost asked.

"No. They have been distributed to some of the rooms, but the phones aren't working at the hotel. My boss is trying to work with the police right now."

"I'll call and make sure the authorities get the information. Text me any details you have on the location of the water bottles."

"We know they've been taken to the top floor. We'll track down the rest."

"One more thing."

"What's that?" Doug asked.

"Get your passport in order. I want you on a plane to Paris tonight."

"Me? Why? We have agents overseas."

"I know, but I need someone to question Nathaniel Norton, and you need to be the one to do it. You have the insight into the coalition to make sure we don't have any other threats heading our way."

"Okay. I'll talk to my boss about getting a travel order cut. I'm not sure I'll be able to convince him though."

"It's already done. You fly out of Dulles at seven forty tonight," Ghost said. "The travel orders and airline reservations will be emailed to you in a few minutes."

"I guess I'd better call my wife, then, and let her know."

"You can do that after you find the rest of the water bottles."

A new resolve coursed through him. "We'll find them."

* * *

Cas passed through her family's hotel suite, a surge of nostalgia rushing over her. The elegant living room and the adjoining formal dining area—how many times had she sat in one of those chairs, playing hearts or Uno with her parents and sister? The possibility of making new memories with her family brought a sense of hope and uncertainty. No matter what her future held, she could never go back to the world of innocence she had once lived in before becoming a guardian.

Cas struggled to push aside her unsettled emotions so she could focus on the task at hand. She stepped into the first bedroom. Shopping bags littered the floor beside the closet, and a water bottle sat on the dresser. Cas grabbed one of the bags and dumped the contents onto the bed. She then put the water bottle inside. She moved to the next bedroom, where her parents always slept.

Sure enough, her mother's slippers lay beside the bed. Cas collected two more water bottles from the table in the sitting area by the window. The common areas came next. Four more water bottles in the refrigerator in the kitchenette. She added them to the bag.

Not thrilled with the prospect of carrying the water bottles with her, but with no way to dispose of them, she grabbed the kitchen's metal trash can and dragged it with her out the door. Setting it a few feet away from the suite entrance, she dumped the water bottles inside.

Gathering her courage, she walked into her old bedroom. The moment she stepped inside, she breathed in the scent of men's cologne. Polo. Roshaun's favorite. She crossed to the dresser and retrieved the unopened water bottle that lay beside a pair of cuff links and a pad of paper. She read the note written in Roshaun's handwriting. A checklist: invitations, caterer, tux. A wedding checklist.

Cas turned away from the life Roshaun and her family had experienced without her and exited her family's suite. She headed for the nearest suite, dragging the trash can behind her.

She knocked on three doors before someone answered. The woman wearing a thick robe over her pajamas glared at her and spoke in English. "You have the wrong room."

"I need all of your water bottles. They're poisoned." Cas pointed toward the elevator. "One person has already died."

"What?" She let go of the door and shouted, "Joseph!"

Leaving the woman, Cas hurried to the next door. Again, no answer.

The stairwell door opened down the hall. Cas's senses heightened. Why would someone use the stairwell on the fifth floor? Only two reasons came to mind. Either someone was just navigating between a couple of the upper floors, or they were avoiding the cameras in the elevators.

A dark-skinned man stepped out, and Cas's eyes narrowed. Tyrell Fenmore, the man who had been working security for her father for nearly two decades.

Cas ducked into the alcove by the elevator. Was he coming upstairs to check on her family, or was he involved with Germain?

Cas's mind reeled, images from tonight tumbling over one another until she isolated two. The security feed of her family arriving at the embassy, Tyrell behind the wheel, and the view of Cole searching her parents' car. If Tyrell had driven her family tonight, why wasn't he still with them? And why hadn't he remained with the car as he always had before?

The dots slowly connected. If Tyrell knew her family was going to die, he wouldn't want to be anywhere near the embassy. But then, why poison the water in their suite if they would be murdered at the embassy?

The questions were still swirling when Tyrell started down the hall, likely to her family's suite. Another door opened, and the American woman's voice carried to her. "She was right here. She said they're poisoned."

Cas pressed herself into the corner of the alcove so Tyrell wouldn't see her unless he looked behind him as he passed.

"Ma'am, is everything okay?" Tyrell asked as he walked by.

"The woman. She was just here. She said our water bottles were poisoned."

"She must have been mistaken. It was the city water that wasn't fit to drink."

Cas pulled her gun and held it at her side, where she could keep it out of sight. "Don't listen to him. It's the water bottles that are poisoned."

The woman looked from Tyrell to Cas as Tyrell turned.

Cas met his surprised gaze but directed her comment at the woman. "It isn't worth risking your life. Now I need you to go back into your room until the authorities get here."

"Cassidy Edgemont." Tyrell spoke in an eerily calm voice. "Your dad was right." He glanced at the woman.

"Ma'am, please go inside," Cas said.

"First I want—" The woman's words cut off when Tyrell grabbed her arm and yanked her in front of him. His pistol came up in the same instant Cas raised her weapon.

The hostage squeaked in alarm, and the gun lifted toward Cas. She jumped back into the elevator alcove as a shot rang out. She pressed herself to the wall closest to Tyrell. Rather than peek into the hall, she relied on sound to visualize the scene she'd left behind. Footsteps shuffled away from her.

"There's no need to hurt her." Cas hit the Down button on the elevator with her elbow. "She didn't do anything to you."

"If you hadn't interfered, she'd be dead by morning anyway."

Keep him talking. "Why are you here? Did you come back to see how many people you killed?"

"I had a loose end to tie up. Now that I know you're alive, I have another."

The hum of the elevator grew louder.

"Let her go."

"I don't think so." More erratic footsteps. The doors of the elevator farthest from her slid open. Still pointing her gun at the hall, she hurried backward. Tyrell appeared around the corner, the woman still in front of him as a shield. A shot fired as Cas rushed into the elevator. She hit the Close Door button several times.

The doors started to close. More footsteps, another gunshot.

The bullet clanged off the door, and the door started to open again. Cas hit the button to close it and fired at the floor in front of her.

She breathed a sigh of relief when the elevator doors slid into place. Now she had to find a way to get back upstairs, free Tyrell's hostage, and warn the other guests before the death count rose.

CHAPTER 44

GUNSHOTS? HERE? CONCERN FOR CAS drove Donovan to the stairwell. He was halfway there when the elevator chimed. He drew his weapon and whirled toward the sound.

Cas darted into the hall.

Relief poured through him, and his confusion spilled out. "Were those gunshots I just heard?"

Surprise flickered in her eyes, but she nodded. "Tyrell Fenmore is up there. He has a hostage."

"So he was involved."

"Yeah. We need a plan." She looked both directions down the hall. "He's not expecting you. You go up one stairwell. I'll go up the other. One of us should be able to get a clean shot."

"From the sound of things, he wants you dead." Donovan shook his head. "Troy's only one floor below us. You can go downstairs and trade places with him."

"There's no time." Cas ran toward the stairwell closest to her. "I'll see you up there."

Donovan swore under his breath. With no choice but to support her, he sprinted in the opposite direction. He darted up the stairs and opened the door slowly.

Only six doors were visible, two on one side of the hall and four on the other. Tyrell stood at one of the doors, his arm hooked around a woman's neck. She tried to fight free but only succeeded in tipping over the trash can in the hall beside her.

"Knock it off, or I'll put a bullet through your head." She quieted. The man pushed her up against the wall, face-first. "Hold still." He pressed his gun against the side of her head and released his hold on her long enough to dig a hotel key out of his pocket.

The woman's body still shielded Tyrell from Donovan, and if Donovan stepped into the hall, he would be an easy target. Donovan focused on the stairwell door on the far side of the hall. It creaked open at the same time the elevator chimed.

Tyrell swiped his keycard and shoved the room door open with his free hand. If he made it inside, there was no telling how many casualties they would have trying to get him out of there.

Donovan hoped Tyrell would abandon the hostage, but he grabbed her and yanked her in with him.

"Hold it!" Cas shouted.

Donovan aimed at the gunman, but without a clear shot, he fired at the next best thing: the trash can.

The bullet clanged against metal; the woman screamed. Three hotel employees emerged from the elevator.

"Get back!" Cas yelled.

Tyrell whirled toward her. Cas dove to the floor as he fired his weapon.

Donovan's heart stuttered. Had she been hit?

The hostage stumbled, and Donovan focused on eliminating the threat against her. He fired again. His shot grazed Tyrell's arm, but the injury seemed to only increase his determination.

He yanked his hostage back to her full height and aimed at Cas again.

The fire alarm sounded, and the woman startled. The unexpected motion sent Tyrell back a step, giving Donovan a clear view of him.

Donovan squeezed the trigger, and this time, the bullet hit its mark.

The hostage screamed, her wails competing with the shrill fire alarm.

The residents of a suite near where Cas lay rushed into the hall. Cas pushed to her feet and held up a hand to stop them. She was okay, and finally, if they were lucky, she was safe.

* * *

Cas sent a hotel employee to the lobby to ensure the staff was keeping the hotel guests from scattering into all areas of the city. She then instructed the other two to contain everyone in the area by the elevators and explain the situation. After they assisted their guests in removing all water bottles from their suites, they allowed them to return to their rooms. The terrified woman who had been held hostage had returned to her room with her equally terrified husband, the hotel's assistant manager keeping them company.

Cole emerged from the stairwell near where Donovan currently leaned over Tyrell's body, undoubtedly searching for weapons and ID. After a brief word with Donovan, Cole continued to where Cas stood by the elevator.

"What's the status downstairs?" she asked, raising her voice to be heard over the constant buzzing of the alarm.

"Three dead from apparent poisoning. Another is on her way to the hospital."

Cas's stomach churned uncomfortably. "Does the death count include Antoine?"

"Yeah. What's the status up here?"

"We were lucky. Only three of the suites were occupied, and obviously, my family isn't here."

"Actually, they are now. They arrived a few minutes ago."

Butterflies took flight in her stomach. "They let them in even though the fire alarm was going off?"

"They got here right before the manager activated it."

"Where are they now?"

"The hotel manager has them down in one of the unoccupied rooms on the second floor. He didn't want them to come up here until we cleared their floor. They're in room 205."

Cas glanced at Tyrell's body crumpled on the floor. "I don't want them to see this."

"I'll let the police know we have a crime scene up here." Cole pressed his fingers against his ears for a second as though trying to gain temporary relief from the overly loud buzzing of the alarm.

"Better give Ghost some warning so he can clear out of here."

"Already did," Cole said. "I can let you know when the coroner is done up here if you want to go talk to your family."

Cas couldn't deny that the instincts honed during her years with the guardians demanded she leave the hotel now while she could do so anonymously, but she needed to talk to her family first. She owed them that much.

The alarm cut off.

"Thank goodness." Cas breathed out a relieved sigh.

"Yeah, I was about to lose my hearing."

Donovan approached, a manila envelope in hand. "Cas, I think you'd better take a look at this. Tyrell had it in his pocket."

Cas took the open envelope and pulled out the contents. "My father's will?" She flipped to the last page, but the document ended without a signature page. "Why would he have an unsigned copy of my dad's will?"

"The pages all have your father's initials on them."

She turned back to the front sheet. Sure enough, her father's initials were scribbled in the lower right-hand corner. She looked closer.

"Is that his handwriting?"

"I don't know. It could be." She slipped the document back into the envelope. "Cole said my dad's downstairs. I'll ask him about it."

"Do you mind if I come too?" Donovan asked. "I need to get out of here anyway."

Cole shooed them toward the elevators. "You two, go. I'll deal with the police."

"Thanks." Cas led the way to the elevator and hit the Down button. Jittery nerves took flight. How many times had she dreamed of hugging her mom again, of hearing her sister's laugh, of debating politics with her father, of confronting Roshaun and demanding answers? The last thought replayed in her mind.

Donovan put his hand on her waist. "You okay?"

She shrugged. How could she possibly articulate the myriad emotions swirling inside her? The elevator doors opened, and she stepped inside. Donovan followed. He put both hands on her arms and turned her to face him as the doors closed, ensuring their privacy. "Hey, talk to me."

Cas looked up at him. Unable to find words, she slipped her arms around his waist. Donovan drew her close, giving her the comfort she so desperately needed.

"You don't have to do this," he said. "You can wait until the authorities have this mess sorted out and after the FBI questions Roshaun."

"Assuming the FBI questions him." Cas pulled back and lifted her gaze. "Is there even a way to know for sure if he was involved?"

"Maybe I should have another chat with him."

"What good will that do?" Cas asked. "If he's been lying all this time, he's not going to suddenly confess tonight."

"You're right, but I'd still like the chance to get a better read on him," Donovan said. "Interrogation is one of the skills I used a lot back in my CIA days."

"You've used that skill a lot since you've been a guardian too."

"True, so what can it hurt?"

What could it hurt? The only two men she had ever cared about enough to dream of a future with would be in the same room, but this time, she wouldn't be able to hear the words being spoken.

"I'm not sure about this," she said.

"Trust me." Donovan hit the button for the second floor and leaned in for a kiss.

"I do trust you. It's Roshaun I'm not so sure about."

CHAPTER 45

Donovan couldn't explain the protectiveness that surged through him, but he didn't try to fight it. When the elevator doors opened on the second floor, he put his hand on Cas's arm to hold her in place.

"Hold on a minute." He pressed the button for the ground floor. "I don't want to question Roshaun with your family there, and I'd prefer he not see you."

"What do you suggest?" Cas asked.

Donovan didn't answer her question but rather led her into the lobby when they reached the ground floor. He escorted her through the crowd of people waiting by the elevators.

"I guess they're letting everyone go back to their rooms." He approached the front desk and spoke to the clerk. "I need a place to question a couple people who may have been involved tonight. Is there an office or empty hotel room I can use?"

"The police are using the manager's office, but I have rooms available on the second and third floors."

"Let me have one on the second, preferably close to room 205. I'll only need it for an hour or so." The clerk nodded, and a moment later, she laid a key card on the counter. "Thanks. I'll bring this back as soon as I'm done," Donovan said.

"Of course."

Donovan took a step back. That was as far as he got before the clerk spoke again.

"And, sir? Thank you for your help. I don't know what would have happened—"

"Thank you." Donovan cut her off. He laid his hand on the counter and met her gaze. "You helped save lives tonight."

The woman blinked back tears and nodded.

Donovan moved beside Cas.

As soon as they were out of earshot of the front desk clerk, Cas said, "I gather you know her?"

"She helped pave the path to get the manager on board and set our plan in motion to limit the damage tonight." He opened the door to the stairwell and waited for Cas to go first. When they reached the second floor, they passed an open dining area where long tables stretched along the far wall. "Maybe you should wait here until I get Roshaun out of your family's room. I'll come get you as soon as I get him into the other room."

Cas stepped into the dining area and positioned herself out of sight of anyone who might come by.

Donovan continued to room 205 and knocked on the door. An instant later, Josiah Edgemont yanked it open.

"I'm sorry to bother you, sir, but I need to ask Mr. Davis a few questions," Donovan said. "Is he here?"

"Yes, but first, may I speak with you a moment?" Josiah glanced behind him. "Privately?"

"Of course." Donovan stepped back. A few guests approached from the stairwell. Donovan motioned to the room across the hall. "This way."

He opened the door and escorted Cas's father inside. As soon as the door closed, Josiah turned to face him. "You work with Cassidy."

Though training demanded that he deny his association with Cas, tonight's events overrode that protocol. "Yes."

"Is she okay?"

"She is. She's down the hall right now."

"Here? At the hotel?"

"Yes." Taking the opportunity to prepare for his interrogation of Roshaun, he asked, "Who knows that your daughter is still alive?"

"Everyone in the world knows I'm looking for her."

"I'm aware of that, but who have you told since seeing her at the embassy?"

"No one." Josiah paced farther into the room before turning back to face him. "I need to talk to Cassidy first."

"I can bring her to you, but I need to speak with Roshaun privately before he sees her."

"Why do you want to talk to him?"

Donovan debated how much to say. "I have some questions for him regarding your daughter's accident four years ago."

Josiah's eyebrows shot up. "You can't think Roshaun had anything to do with that."

"His previous interaction with the coalition does raise concerns."

"When he joined them, he thought they were a group promoting free speech and the freedom of the press. He hasn't had anything to do with that group since Cassidy . . . since her accident."

"Your daughter needs to be here for this conversation." Donovan reached for the doorknob. "I'll be back in a minute."

Josiah nodded. "I'll be waiting."

* * *

Cas walked beside Donovan, her nerves battling in her stomach. Part of her was grateful for the opportunity to speak with her father privately, to explain what she could about her involvement in the situation at the embassy, but part of her wanted to see her mother and sister and explain everything to all of them at the same time.

Donovan stopped outside the hotel room. He gave her hand a squeeze before he released her and unlocked the door. She walked inside, and her nerves eased when her father approached, his arms outstretched. She stepped into his embrace. For a moment, she didn't say anything, just held on to the man who had been the cornerstone of everything good in her life for as long as she could remember.

Finally, her father pulled back and studied her face. "I'm so glad you're safe. I saw what happened outside, what Germain tried to do."

"I'm fine." Cas glanced at Donovan. "We're fine."

"What have you been doing all this time? Where have you been?"

"I've been in a kind of witness protection program." Cas lifted her eyes to meet his. "The people I work with have been keeping me safe, and by pretending to be dead, I was trying to keep you safe."

"Maybe we should sit down," Donovan suggested.

Cas and Donovan sat on the edge of one of two full-sized beds, and her father sat across from them.

"Daniel said you think Roshaun had something to do with your accident." Her father looked at Donovan. "It is Daniel, right?"

"Yes, sir."

"Roshaun was the only person who knew I was going to the FBI," Cas said.

"That's not entirely true. He came to me the morning of the accident and told me he was worried about you."

"He told you I was filing a report with the FBI?"

"Yes. I called Tyrell to have him escort you to the FBI's field office, but by the time he found you, it was too late."

Cas turned to Donovan. "So it could have been Tyrell who ran me off the road instead of Germain."

"Tyrell? He's been working for me since I bought Powell Broadcasting."

Antoine's final words replayed in her head.

Donovan put his hand on hers. "Maybe you should show him the will."

"Will?" Josiah asked. "What will?"

Cas held out the envelope Donovan had given her. "Take a look at this. Is this yours?"

Her dad scanned the document. "This is an excellent forgery, but it isn't mine." He held it up. "Where did you get this?"

"Tyrell," Donovan said. "He was attempting to enter your hotel suite when I intercepted it."

"By any chance, do you have a copy of your original will here in Paris?" Cas asked.

"Yes." His eyebrows drew together. "I needed to update it, so my attorney offered to bring it to me at the airport. I signed it on the plane, and he gave me my copy to take with me."

"Tyrell knew about this?" Cas said.

"Yes." Josiah held up the forged document. "Does this have anything to do with what happened tonight?"

"Possibly." Cas moved to sit beside her father. "Look through this. Tell me what is different from what your original will said."

He flipped through the first several pages. Then he sucked in a breath. "This isn't the same."

Cas scanned the page. "Oh wow."

"What does it say?" Donovan asked.

"This will leaves $50 million each to Tyrell and Antoine." Cas looked up at Donovan. "Or if Antoine doesn't outlive my dad, his share would go to his son."

Donovan shook his head in disgust. "Germain murdered his own father."

"What? Antoine is dead?" Josiah asked.

"Yes. Poisoned." Cas placed a comforting hand on her father's arm. "I'm sorry, but can you keep looking? Is there anything else in here that doesn't look the same?"

He read the next few pages before he pointed at a clause in the center of the page. "I certainly didn't authorize this. It says here that if none of my heirs outlive me, Edgemont Broadcasting and all of its holdings will go to Steven Powell."

"That's who Antoine was warning me about."

"I don't get it," Donovan said. "If the coalition was after you, why would some rich guy be trying to kill off your family?"

"He's right," Josiah said. "If there is anyone out there who doesn't believe in racial equality, it's Steven Powell."

"That may be, but racial equality is simply the face of the organization, a way to encourage donations," Cas said. "The reason I went to the FBI was because of the political corruption going on inside the organization."

"And what better way for Powell to hide his involvement than to create a front that no one would associate him with." Her father held up the fake will. "And if you hadn't stopped Germain tonight, Powell would have ended up with the broadcasting empire I built along with what was left of his father's."

"Yes." The pieces of the puzzle snapped into place and created a whole. "The Paris bombing, the reports about the police ignoring the bomb threat, the tainted water supply." Cas shook her head. "It wasn't the coalition trying to create chaos. Powell was using the coalition as a way to hide my family's murders."

"He nearly got away with it."

Donovan pulled out his phone. "I'll get a message to the FBI to make sure they take Powell into custody."

"Thanks." Cas waited for Donovan to place his call, likely to Troy, before she asked, "Is there anyone else in that will who shouldn't be?"

Her dad read through the rest of it and shook his head. "No. Those were the only changes."

"Is Roshaun in there anywhere?" Cas asked.

"No."

Donovan hung up the phone and asked, "Did he ever work for the Powell family?"

"No."

The facts of Cas's fictional death splintered and rebuilt themselves into a new reality. "He really wasn't involved."

"It doesn't look like it." Donovan stood. "Are you ready to see the rest of your family?"

Cas drew a deep breath and let it out slowly. "Yes."

"Is it safe for your mom and sister to know the truth?" her dad asked. "If telling them you're alive is going to put any of you in danger, I can pretend I never saw you."

"After what happened tonight, I doubt Cassidy is in any more danger than the rest of your family," Donovan said.

"He's right. You, Mom, and Makayla were the intended victims tonight. Not me."

"That's a terrifying thought."

"Yes, it is."

CHAPTER 46

DONOVAN'S PHONE RANG AS HE followed Cas and her father into the hall. Cas stopped and waited for him to answer.

Troy's voice came over the line. "We found the jamming device. It was in a car in the garage."

"That's good news," Donovan said. "What's the update on the casualties?"

"Four dead from the poison, one more at the hospital. She didn't drink much, so they think she's going to make it," Troy said. "You already know about Tyrell?"

"Yeah."

"Also, the testing on the city's water supply came back. It's safe to drink."

"Then it was fake news."

"It was," Troy said. "The police have taken over the collection of the water bottles here in the hotel, so I'm pretty much done here. Do you want me to wait for you and Cas before I head back to the apartment?"

"No. You might want to see if Cole's done though. If he is, he can give you a ride. I can catch the metro."

"What about Cas?"

"I'm not sure yet." Donovan didn't dare say more. He didn't want to think about a future without her in it, but she had choices about her future now, choices he didn't share. "I'll see you later."

"Okay. Good luck."

As soon as he hung up, Cas asked, "Is everything okay?"

"Yeah. The city water is fine. It was fake news to create a reason to make sure the bottled water was used while your family was here."

"I wonder why they tried to get my family at both the hotel and the embassy," Cas said.

"Maybe Powell was making sure he didn't miss anyone," Josiah said. "Until today, we hadn't decided for sure to go to the embassy dinner."

"I'm sure the death of an ambassador would have generated a lot of income for the broadcasting companies too," Cas added. "It's also possible that it was a way to gain support from Alnaazir. The ambassador is their kind of target."

"That's true," Donovan said.

Josiah reached the door to his temporary room. "Are you ready?"

Cas clasped her hands together. "Yes."

Her father opened the door and led the way inside. The moment Cas walked in, her mother's eyes watered.

"Oh, it's you." Shantelle Edgemont rushed the short distance to envelop her oldest daughter in a hug. "It's really you."

"Mom." Cas breathed out the single word as she clung to her mother.

Donovan's heart squeezed in his chest as his own regrets tangled with his dreams. What he wouldn't give to hold his daughter the way Cas's mother now held her.

Makayla leapt up and hugged her sister in turn. "I can't believe you're here. We all thought . . ."

"I know." Cas sniffled her own tears back. "I had to pretend to be dead to protect myself and to protect all of you."

Donovan's gaze swept the room and landed on Roshaun. The man's normally polished demeanor had fallen away, and he looked like he was staring at a ghost. Little did he know that he was.

* * *

Cas felt Roshaun's gaze at the same time her sister withdrew from her embrace. Makayla glanced at her fiancé, and apology lit her eyes.

"We thought you were dead." Makayla took a step back, aligning herself with Roshaun. "Why didn't you tell us? How could you let us think . . . ?"

"I told you, it was to protect all of us."

"To protect us from what?"

"Someone close to us tried to kill me."

"Why would someone want to kill you?" her sister asked.

"It's a long story, but the bottom line is we didn't know for sure until tonight who it was."

Roshaun's gaze darkened. "You thought it was me."

Cas didn't deny it. "Yes. You were the only person who knew where I was that day."

"I know it wasn't Roshaun." Makayla slipped her hand into his. The absolute loyalty was admirable, and it was more than Cas had been able to give him.

Donovan put his hand on Cas's waist, a silent signal of his support.

"Who was it?" Roshaun asked.

"Tyrell and Germain were both involved," Cas said. "I'm not sure who ran me off the road, but it doesn't matter now. They can't hurt any of us anymore."

"How did you survive?" Roshaun asked. "I saw the wreckage."

Cas gave the basic details of how she had been thrown from the car. When she finished, her mother said, "But it's all over now. You're safe."

"I'm not sure." Was she safe? Cas had been asking herself that question since leaving the embassy. Did she dare step back into her real life, or would doing so invite disaster? "I know it's a lot to ask, but for now, can we keep all of this private? I need to talk to the people I work with before I can even consider admitting that my death wasn't real."

"You want us to pretend you don't exist?" her mom asked.

"At least for now." Cas took her mom's hands. "I'm sorry for all I put you through, and I know this isn't easy, but keeping my secret could be the difference of me living or dying for real."

Her father stepped forward. "Who do you work for? Who are these people who have been hiding you all of this time?"

As much as Cas wanted to tell them everything, she couldn't. "I'm sorry, but it's classified."

"We've been through a lot," her mom said, cutting off her father before his inherent curiosity could take over. "It's late. Why don't we get some sleep."

Cas wavered. Did she go with her parents to their hotel suite and crash in Makayla's room, or should she go back to her apartment and risk trying to meet up with her family later?

"You should stay here," Donovan said. "It will be easier to keep out of sight, and it will give you more time to decide what you want to do next."

"You should both stay," her dad said. "I'll arrange with the desk to reserve another suite."

Donovan looked down at her and appeared to waver.

"You should stay here tonight," Cas said. "Like my dad said, it's late. Besides, our friends will probably appreciate having the bed and couch to sleep on tonight."

"If you're okay with that, I would feel better if I can make sure you're safe."

"There were some empty suites beside my dad's." Cas turned to her father. "If we stay on the same floor, it will simplify things."

"I'll call the front desk." Her dad moved to the hotel phone.

"One thing though," Cas said. "Please don't give any names for who is staying there."

He nodded. "I'll put it under my name."

"Thank you."

* * *

Donovan escorted Cas and her family to the top floor, where a hotel staff member stood waiting. "Sir, here are the keys to the additional suite."

"Thank you." Josiah took the keys and discreetly slipped a tip into the man's hand.

"I assume you want Cassidy to sleep in her old room," Roshaun said. "I can stay in the other suite with Daniel."

Cas shook her head. "No. I'd rather stay in the other suite."

"With Daniel?" Her mother's eyebrows rose.

"I'm sure the suite has two bedrooms," Cas said. "Besides, I'll feel safer with him close by."

Josiah handed the keys to Cas. "You should have everything you need in there, but you can call the front desk if there's anything you're missing."

"Thanks, Papa." Cas kissed his cheek.

Josiah gathered her in his arms and hugged her for a long moment. "It's so good to have you back."

"It's good to be back." She hugged her mother before nodding to her sister and Roshaun. "Good night."

Everyone filed into their respective rooms. Donovan took only two steps inside before he stopped and stared. "This is bigger than the apartment."

"Welcome to luxury living." Cas continued to a seating area and collapsed on the couch. "I can't believe I finally know what happened. Four years, and now I know the truth."

"It's been a big day for you." Donovan followed and sat beside her.

"Thank you." She slipped her hand into his.

"You don't need to thank me." Donovan ran his thumb over the back of her hand. "You did as much as anyone else to get through the challenges tonight."

"I wasn't sure I was going to get out of the kitchen at the embassy alive though. I might not have had you not gotten there when you did."

"It's all over now." Donovan said the words and cringed. Was everything over now? Once Steve Powell was arrested, it was possible Cas would truly be safe. Conflicting emotions of relief and regret filled him, the thought of moving forward without Cas in his life leaving him hollow. “Do you have any idea what’s next for you?”

“I don’t know.” She leaned against him, and Donovan stretched his arm around her shoulders, nestling her to his side.

“It’s hard to imagine not having my parents in my life now that I’ve seen them again,” Cas said, “but I also can’t picture not working with the guardians. It’s like my two pasts aren’t compatible, but neither of them is giving me a path forward.”

“You’re the first guardian to ever be in this situation.” Donovan traced his finger along the smooth skin of her neck. “What do you want most?”

“I can’t even think straight right now,” Cas said.

“You’ve got to be exhausted.” Donovan stood. “Come on. You should get some sleep.”

Cas reached out both hands, and he pulled her to a stand. He kept her hands in his and leaned down to kiss her good night. Their lips met, and the day’s events began to fade. He didn’t want this to end, and for the moment, he pushed the past and the future from his thoughts. Her hands gripped his, and the kiss lingered.

Donovan’s phone rang, interrupting the moment. He pulled it from his pocket, and his heart sank.

“Who is it?” Cas asked.

“Kade.” Donovan answered.

“Hey, I hate to break it to you, but Alnaazir is on the move again,” Kade said. “Ace wants you back in Cairo.”

“How soon?”

“Tomorrow. Your flight leaves at sixteen hundred.”

“Thanks.” Donovan hung up.

“You have to go back?” Cas asked.

He nodded. “Tomorrow afternoon.”

“I’ll miss you.” Cas pushed onto her toes and pressed her lips to his again, but this time, the kiss tasted of goodbye.

CHAPTER 47

Cas draped her arm over her eyes to block out the sunlight streaming through the window. Dreams of the past threaded through her mind and joined memories of yesterday. She jolted awake and shot up in bed.

Her hand ran over the soft sheets and then down the sleeve of the silk pajamas the hotel staff had left on her bed. Last night was real. Germain and Tyrell were both dead. Nathaniel Norton had been taken into custody. Her parents were across the hall, and Donovan was in the next room.

Cas checked the time. Nine thirty. She must have been more exhausted than she'd thought.

Her fingers curled around the phone, and an unsettled feeling came over her. Her family knew she was alive. Technically, she could come out of hiding. She was free. But what should she do with that freedom? And would Steven Powell come after her and her family again? His arrest would give them some sense of security, but it wouldn't be until after his conviction that they would truly be able to put these latest obstacles behind them.

As the questions circled through her mind, she pushed out of bed and grabbed the robe hanging in the bathroom. After she slipped it on, she walked into the empty living room and glanced at Donovan's open bedroom door.

"Donovan?" When he didn't answer, she knocked on his open door and peeked inside. "Donovan?"

Still no response. She flipped on the light and took in the room. The bed appeared to have been slept in, and the pajamas the hotel staff had provided lay across the foot of the bed.

Retreating back to the living area, she walked past the couch and into the dining room. A single sheet of hotel stationery lay in the center of the table. She picked it up and read it.

I'll miss you. D.

He left?

Cas turned and rushed back into her room, grabbed her phone, and dialed his number. It went straight to voice mail.

Had something happened to cause him to leave earlier than planned? Or had he wanted to leave because he didn't want to face a goodbye?

If she'd had her guardian laptop, she would have been able to check the message board, but without that capability, she went to the next best thing. She dialed Troy. No answer.

Determined, she dialed again. The phone rang three times before a groggy Kade answered. "I just got to sleep two hours ago. This had better be good."

"Sorry, but I don't have access to the message board right now. What's the latest?"

"Really? Couldn't you have Troy or Donovan give you an update?"

"I could if either of them was answering their phones."

"Why aren't they answering?"

"Excellent question. Maybe you can look on the message board and tell me."

"They'd better have a good reason," Kade grumbled.

Despite her concern about Donovan, Cas couldn't keep a smile from forming. Renee's voice sounded in the background, and Kade's tone changed. "I've got it. Go back to sleep."

The simple kindness brought with it a wistfulness in Cas. She wanted that, the connection with someone who loved her, the caring that went beyond herself.

An image of Donovan filled her mind, and her heart swelled. As incompatible as their lives were, Cas wanted Donovan in her life.

"Okay, here's what I've got," Kade said, his voice gruff once more. "The local authorities gathered all the water bottles and are testing them."

"What about Troy and Donovan?" Cas asked.

"Looks like they're both still in the air. Troy is on his way to Helsinki, and Donovan caught an early flight to Sudan. The situation there escalated during the night. We have an operative who went missing."

"Any idea if Cole Bridger is still at the Paris safe house?"

"Says here he is driving back to Vienna today. Troy will be back tonight to help you close the Paris safe house down before we relocate you." Kade hesitated. "It looks like the people trying to kill you are all dead, but Ace won't want you staying in Paris."

"Almost all of them are dead," Cas said.

"I'm sending Doug Valdez to Paris to question Nathaniel Norton," Kade said. "I don't want you anywhere near him, but we need to make sure all the loose ends are tied up."

"I appreciate that, but from what we found last night, it looks like Steven Powell was behind the murder attempt on my family. It's possible he's the missing link in the coalition."

"Wow. That's something."

"Yeah," Cas said. "Donovan asked the FBI to put out an arrest warrant last night. Can you see if he's in custody yet?"

"Hold on." Silence filled the line for a moment. "Sorry. It looks like he left the country on his private jet over a week ago."

"Where is he?"

"The FBI is still trying to track him down. His itinerary had him going to Canada, Spain, and the Maldives."

"I hope it's not the Maldives. We don't have an extradition treaty with that country."

"Yeah, but if he's there, he's surrounded by water and has nowhere to go."

"True."

Kade fell silent for a moment before he asked, "You are sticking with the guardians, aren't you?"

"I don't know. It's hard to think about walking away from my family now that they know I'm alive." Did she have options? Could she find a balance between both worlds?

"I'm afraid you have to choose," Kade said as though reading her mind. "Your life is too high profile for you to work with the guardians if the public knows you're alive. We can't have the paparazzi following you."

Her heart sank. Her new life or her old one. Which one could she live without? "I need to think about what to do next."

"Troy will be back in Paris around nineteen hundred. Stay out of sight until then."

"I will."

"Oh, and, Cas?"

"Yeah?"

"Do me a favor. Next time, call me during *my* daylight hours."

"I'll do what I can." She hung up and headed for her room. She had just finished dressing when a knock sounded at her door. Expecting to see one of her parents on the other side of the door, she peeked through the peephole. To her surprise, Roshaun stood in the hall alone.

Emotions tied her insides into a complicated knot. She pressed her hand to her stomach and blew out a breath, then, pasting on her most calm expression, she opened the door.

Roshaun's eyes met hers, and he shifted his weight from one foot to the other. "Can I talk to you for a minute?"

Cas had to remind herself that all evidence pointed toward Roshaun's innocence. "Yeah. Come on in."

He passed through the door and crossed to the sitting area. He waited for her to sit before he claimed one of the two plush armchairs. "I don't know how much you have kept track of your family while you've been hiding away, but you need to know that I've been dating Makayla for almost a year now."

Cas pressed her lips together, not sure how to respond.

"I've asked her to marry me." Roshaun swallowed hard. "She said yes."

"You're a lucky man."

"Yes, I am." Roshaun shifted in his seat as though struggling to contain his nervous energy. "You have to know I never meant for this to happen. I've always cared for you."

Though it would have been easy to let Roshaun suffer, Cas had seen the connection between him and Makayla last night. "But you love Makayla."

"More than anything." He rested his elbows on his knees and clasped his fingers together. "She couldn't be happier to know that you're still alive, but she spent half the night worrying about how you will feel about her being with me."

"Makayla always has worried more about everyone else's feelings than she does her own."

"Yes, that's true."

Though Cas suspected it would take time to fully move past her shock of her sister marrying her former boyfriend, she took a tentative step toward bridging the gap between them. "It'll take me some time to get used to how things are now, but I want both of you to be happy."

His posture eased as though a flood of relief had crashed over him. "Thank you. I want the same for you."

"Does Makayla know you're here?"

"Yes. She was going to come with me, but I thought it would be better if we talked first," Roshaun said. "She's been pretty emotional about everything."

"I can't imagine it's been easy on anyone learning that I've been alive this whole time," Cas said. "I half expected my family to be angry that I hid the truth all these years."

"They love you. Besides, from what I understand, none of us would be alive right now if it hadn't been for you and your friend." Roshaun looked around. "Where is Daniel?"

"He had to leave town. Business."

"That's too bad. He looked like he mattered to you."

"Yeah, he does."

CHAPTER 48

Donovan crossed the tile floor of his Cairo apartment and looked out into the city lights shimmering in the darkness. For nearly two weeks, he had buried himself in work, first liberating an intelligence operative after the man had been mistaken for a member of a rival tribe and then providing surveillance support for a raid on Alnaazir's base camp in Sudan.

Last night, he had slept on his own couch for the first time in over a month, and he had spent the day catching up on the activities of his fellow guardians, specifically looking for posts from Cas. Unfortunately, her only activity had been a post confirming she had closed down the Paris apartment and that it was once again ready to be used as a safe house. Where she was now or if she had left the guardians entirely, he didn't know.

His search for her on the internet didn't reveal any new useful insights either. One article mentioned that the Edgemonts had been present during the incident at the Paris embassy and had gone into seclusion. No mention of where they were or when they were expected to return to their normal lives.

An indictment against Steven Powell for conspiracy to commit murder had been issued in the United States, and though the man had yet to be taken into custody, his personal assets in the US had been frozen. The likelihood of his gaining access to the Edgemonts had been greatly reduced, but Donovan wouldn't rest easy until the threat was removed entirely. Cas and her family deserved some peace.

In the distance, a plane crossed into view as it descended toward the airport. Too bad Cas couldn't be on that plane. He would so enjoy sharing his love of this city with her, to help her discover the many wonders here the way she had shared her knowledge of Paris with him.

Disappointment and hurt swelled inside him. As much as he wanted to deny it, his feelings for her weren't going away. Whether this was love or something that could grow into it, he wasn't sure, but every moment away from Cas added to the ache that had settled deep inside him.

A knock sounded at his door, and his hand whipped beneath his shirt, emerging with his pistol firmly in his grasp. No one ever came to this apartment. And why hadn't the proximity alarm in the hall gone off?

Silently, he moved to the kitchen counter where his laptop lay and clicked on the program that would reveal the security feed for the hall. A dark-skinned woman with long straight hair and a slender build was standing in front of his door. Cas?

He set his gun down.

His visitor turned her face toward the camera as though staring right at him. Cas!

Donovan rushed to the door and yanked it open. "What are you doing here?"

A slow smile bloomed on her face. "It wasn't that long ago that you were standing on my doorstep and I was asking you the same thing." She stepped past him and held up a pair of pajamas, the same ones he had worn at the hotel in Paris. "You forgot these."

He shut the door and gaped at her. "You came to Egypt to bring me pajamas?"

"That, and I wanted to see you."

"I was looking through the message board, but I didn't see any entries by you since the day I left Paris," Donovan said. "I thought maybe you left the guardian program."

"I considered it." Cas wandered farther into the apartment and glanced at the window. "Great view."

Not about to be distracted, Donovan asked, "Are you still a guardian?"

"I am."

"What about your family?" he asked.

"For now, we'll let the world believe the story that I was killed four years ago," Cas said. "They'll let everything that happened this month fade until it's all yesterday's news and then try to get back to their normal lives."

"They're okay with that?"

"My father is buying a villa in the south of France where we'll meet as a family when we want to be together."

"He's buying a villa?"

"Yeah. It's actually a pretty great place. You'll have to come see it."

"Is that where you're going to live?" Donovan asked.

"Sometimes, but I talked to Ace about setting up shop somewhere else for now."

"Where?"

"Spain."

"Why there? I thought you weren't comfortable with staying in western Europe."

"I wasn't when my dad had a reward out there for information about me, but he'll be making a statement in the next few days announcing that they've received proof that I did die in the accident four years ago."

"That won't be easy on him."

"I know, but he insisted. He wants me to be safe."

"If western Europe is a possibility again, why did you decide on Spain?"

"Because it's closer to the guardian apartment in Morocco." Uncertainty flashed in her eyes. "I hoped you might make that your home base so we could see each other more often."

"As in date?"

"That is what people in a relationship do."

Joy took flight. "You're absolutely right." Donovan settled his hands on her waist, and he lowered his lips to hers. The moment he kissed her, his stomach somersaulted and the loneliness of the past two weeks melted away. He drew her closer, reveling in the faint scent of coconut from her shampoo and the silkiness of her skin. An unexpected future danced through his mind, and his heart tumbled at her feet. He accepted the sensation for what it was. Love. Pure and sweet love.

He drew back and struggled for composure. "Do you have any plans for the next few days?"

"What did you have in mind?"

"First, I want to show you around Cairo."

"And then?"

"Then you need to help me do some shopping in Morocco," Donovan said. "If we're going to spend any time there, you'll need cooking supplies."

"Wait, you're volunteering to go to the store?"

"For you, I'll do anything."

"Wow. You must really love my cooking."

Donovan grinned. "I love that too."

ABOUT THE AUTHOR

Traci Hunter Abramson was born in Arizona, where she lived until moving to Venezuela for a study abroad program. After graduating from Brigham Young University, she worked for the Central Intelligence Agency, eventually resigning in order to raise her family. She credits the CIA with giving her a wealth of ideas as well as the skills needed to survive her children's teenage years. She loves to travel and enjoys coaching her local high school swim team. She has written more than thirty best-selling novels and is a seven-time Whitney Award winner, including 2017 and 2019 Best Novel of the Year.

She also loves hearing from her readers. If you would like to contact her, she can be reached through the following:

www.traciabramson.com
Facebook group: Traci's Friends
bookbub.com/authors/traci-hunter-abramson
twitter@traciabramson
facebook.com/tracihabramson
instagram.com/traciabramson.com